Lost Lad

A Mystery set in Derbyshire 1960

by

Narvel S Annable

British Library Cataloguing in Publication Data.
A catalogue record for this book is available
from the British Library

ISBN 0 9530419 6 4

Published by
Narvel S. Annable
44 Dovedale Crescent
Belper
Derbyshire DE56 1HJ

narvel@narvelannable.co.uk
www.narvelannable.co.uk
Tel: 01 773 82 44 83

To

Stephen Johnson

For inspiration

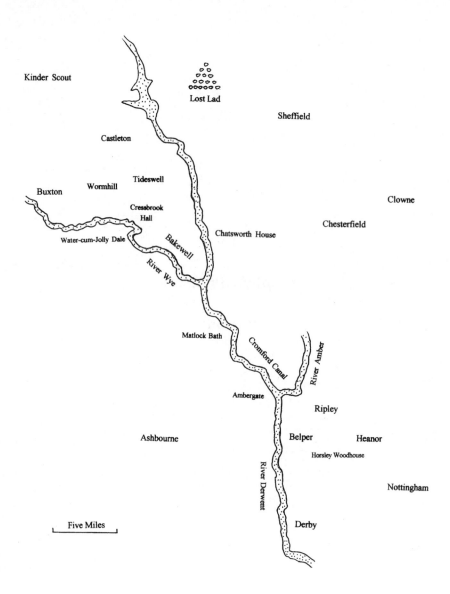

Kinder Scout

Lost Lad

Sheffield

Castleton

Tideswell

Wormhill

Buxton

Clowne

Cressbrook
Hall

Chesterfield

Water-cum-Jolly Dale

Bakewell

Chatsworth House

River Wye

Matlock Bath

Cromford Canal

River Amber

Ambergate

Ripley

Ashbourne

Belper

Heanor

Horsley Woodhouse

River Derwent

Nottingham

Five Miles

Derby

FOREWORD

by

John Holmes
of
BBC Radio Nottingham

Narvel has a penchant for subjects 'close to home', but until now he's always written about the lives of others in relation to his own. There was the social history focusing on his "Heanor Schooldays" which inspired the entertaining and intriguing novel which follows. Such was the influence of his first teacher, not only has he written an affectionate reminiscence of "Miss Calder's Children", but he's also woven a fictional murder mystery, "Death on the Derwent", around the formidable schoolmistress! His major biographical work centred on his former teacher His Honour Judge Keith Matthewman QC.

"Lost Lad", in contrast, places Narvel centre stage, along with five other pals on a cycling holiday in Derbyshire. As the journey unfolds, one member of the gang goes missing and it takes nearly a half century before Narvel finally reveals to us the secret of his devilishly clever conjuring trick. Here is an interesting tale in which the line between truth and fiction is blurred. How much is true? Even I'm not sure and I'm part of it when Narvel visits me at BBC Radio Derby requesting help from our listeners.

I've never featured in a mystery thriller before, and I must say that I've enjoyed every minute of it. And stand by: there could be a sequel!

Pronunciation

In the speaking voice of some of the characters, I have attempted to show the Derbyshire accent. A principle feature is the closed 'U', which is sounded 'oo' as in 'took', **not** the sound as in 'boot'. The native Derbyshire tongue makes no distinction between the past tense of take - 'took' and 'tuck' - something to eat. To the Derbyshire ear, the open 'U' or standard pronunciation of 'tuck' sounds rather like 'tack', a short nail. Accordingly when local Derbyshire folk say 'duck' (which they often say), I have indicated it as 'dook'.

Relatives are often referred to as 'our' pronounced 'arr', such as 'Arr Fred'.

In an attempt to maintain the flavour and accuracy of the 1960's, I have referred to African-Americans as Negroes.

CONTENTS

Introduction

My first novel published in 1999 was called "Death on the Derwent" - A Murder Mystery set in Belper 1949, ISBN 0 9530419 2 1, which features the formidable Miss Florence Calder and her cantankerous sister Miss Madge, as they go on the trail of a clever criminal in a leafy, smaller Belper, half a century ago. Miss Florence Calder was a real person, the subject of my first book - "Miss Calder's Children" - A Social History of Belper, Biography and Critique on Modern Education, published in 1997.

For this second novel it seemed fitting that I draw on the setting and atmosphere of my second book, an autobiographic work published in 1998 - "Heanor Schooldays" - A Social History, ISBN 0 9530419 1 3, which majors on the period 1955 to 1960. It tells the story of two schools. The hard forbidding Dickensian Mundy Street Boys School was claustrophobic, hateful and cruel, but in the September of 1958 I went down the hill to William Howitt Secondary Modern School which was open, sunny and leafy - a culture of kindness.

For this fantasy of my imagination I have subsumed part of "Heanor Schooldays". The pupils in this novel are fictitious, but are a composite of the types of boys I have known, those good people who changed my life for the better in that wonderful period of 1958 to 1960.

It is the passage of four decades and these considerations which are the inspiration of this book. It is an attempt to re-visit the 'lost' world of a happy adolescence which once existed in a place we all knew as William Howitt Secondary Modern School.

Apart from a few agreed cameo roles, all the characters in this book are pure fiction.

Cast of Characters

Big Boy Born in 1945. A leading bully at Mundy Street Boys School when he was a well developed twelve year old in 1957, Simeon Hogg's darkest year. Enjoying delegated authority from a sadistic schoolmaster, Big Boy inflicted pain and took his pleasure at will.

Adolphus Coggan known as **Dolly** Born in 1930, 30 in 1960, 73 in 2003. Gardener to Mr Hardman. Softly spoken with a silver tongue of beautiful rounded vowels. Dolly, deep, dark and mysterious, is an amusing and smooth scented rotundity who has lived at the lodge to Cressbrook Hall since childhood.

Tom Day known as **Titch** Born in 1945, 15 in 1960. The class clown and smallest of 'the six' pupils of William Howitt Secondary Modern School who take a cycle ride up into the Peak District in 1960.

Duck and Mrs Duck Plump and cosy residents in an end of terrace house known as 'The Duckery' at Bog Hole in Horsley Woodhouse. Soft, cushy, downy and ductile, they spend their days twittering over the trifling and the trivia of everyday life.

Brian Forrester Born in 1945, 15 in 1960. One of the non-identical twins of 'the six' who shares the same qualities as his brother Danny, but also with a keen sense of humour and a slight tendency to mischief and teasing.

Danny Forrester Born in 1945, 15 in 1960, 58 in 2003. Easy-going, open, honest, good natured lad who is ever cheerful, generous and trusting.

Kelly Grocock Born in 1988, 15 in 2003. The 'village bicycle' of Horsley Woodhouse. A teenager of easy virtue who shocked respectable opinion by boasting of being a 'loose bitch' - but, also, a 'hard bitch'.

Guzzly Granddad Ugly, unpleasant, smelly old man of uncertain age who resides in a squalid terraced house in the back streets of Derby entertaining a harem of teenage boys. Toothless, slimy and slavering, his frequently seen glistening tongue advertised his wanton speciality. Addressed as 'Granddad' but his real name, according to letters, is Mr T. Piggs. Rumour has it that 'T' stands for Toby.

Algernon Hardman Born in 1912, 48 in 1960, died at age 71 in 1983. Haughty, cold, aloof, academic acetous owner of Cressbrook Hall from 1944 to his death.

Charles Hardman Born in 1948, twelve in 1960, 55 in 2003 still residing at Cressbrook Hall. Son of Algernon Hardman. As an adult he is an acclaimed author of Derbyshire folklore. A charming and popular gentleman with impeccable manners. He has mixed feelings and no small amount of fear about re-opening the investigation which appears to throw suspicion on his late father.

Helen Hardman Born in 1951, 52 in 2003. Upright proud 'county' lady of 'good breeding' who married Charles Hardman in 1976. They have two daughters and five grandchildren by 2003. Helen is determined to protect her husband from the *'irresponsible amateur detectives'* who have travelled 4000 miles to threaten the peace and contentment of her family.

Isaiah Hardman 1858 to 1944. Cotton mill owner who bought Cressbrook Hall in 1888. Father of Algernon.

Marjorie Hardman Born in 1914. Married Algernon Hardman in 1945, mother of Charles. Killed in Albania in 1960.

Gertie Hogg Born in 1922, 81 in 2003. Sharp tongued matriarch of the Hogg family. This highly entertaining harridan is Simeon's favourite Aunt living with her husband Fred (the same age) at number two Bog Hole.

Joyce Hogg Born in 1925, 78 in 2003. Maiden aunt of Simeon and everything Gary Mackenzie hates! She is old fashioned, bovine, slow, pleasant and inoffensive. A shy rustic provincial spinster, very nervous of men, who spends her days chatting to the budgie on the kitchen table in her terraced, life long home at number four Bog Hole, a scruffy but quaint back street corner of Horsley Woodhouse.

Simeon Hogg (Dobba) Born in 1945, 15 in 1960, 58 in 2003. One of 'the six' who is haunted for 43 years by the memory of the inexplicable disappearance of a good friend back in 1960. In April 2003 he retires from a teaching career in the USA and returns to Derbyshire to find the 'Lost Lad'.

Wilfred Hogg Born in 1919, 84 in 2003. Grumpy old fashioned uncle of Simeon. Insular and narrow minded, retired coal-miner with a horror of travel and all things foreign. Lives with his crumpled and ruckled wife Nelly at number three Bog Hole, Horsley Woodhouse.

Rex Lloyd Born in 1945, 15 in 1960. Compact, well proportioned, powerful, muscular member of 'the six'. A strapping popular vibrant personality, confident and raucous, second only to Scott North.

Gary Mackenzie Born in 1948, 55 in 2003. Long standing American friend and foil for Simeon Hogg. Cosmopolitan, well-travelled and intolerant of the parochial introspective world of Heanor and Horsley Woodhouse. Over sexed, energetic, fast moving, highly strung, hyper-active with a short fuse.

Scott North Born 1945, 15 in 1960, 58 in 2003. Athletic blond lad with stunning good looks and leader of the original 'six'.

Aggie Oaks Born in 1924 aged 79 in 2003. Long time enemy of Gertie Hogg, Aggie has owned and served in the corner shop at Bog Hole for as long as anyone can remember.

Detective Inspector Derek Russell Born in 1915, 45 in 1960 when he headed the search for the 'lost lad' and is still a lively, fit 88 in 2003. An officer with natural, easy charm: cordial, polite and patient.

Barry and Yvonne Peirson Born in 1932 & 1934, 28 and 26 in 1960. Owners of Wellhead Farm guest house in Wormhill where 'the six' have an enjoyable and interesting holiday with three dogs, six cats, four chickens, a goat and a sheep.

Simon Tonks Born in 1926, 34 in 1960 and still a very young looking 77 in 2003. Butler, cook, cleaner & general man-servant to the Hardman family since 1952. Likeable, laughable, slightly built clairvoyant with a notorious and hilarious history of erotic 'incidents' which usually take place in public lavatories. This very funny and common little queen is probably the real star of the book.

Detective Sergeant John Winter Born in 1922, 38 in 1960, a rather tubby 81 in 2003. Solid 'run of the mill' copper who for many years was an assistant to Detective Inspector Derek Russell.

Jasper Wormall Born in 1875, 85 in 1960. Small, hideous and effeminate with deep set leering eyes. Looking positively Jurassic, 'The Goblin' as he was known in Belper, lived in a primitive isolated cottage up Shire Oaks practising his legendary talents of body massage and very keen to offer the 'extras'.

Chapter 1

Fantasy of Death

Simeon Hogg was thinking of death.

His 12th grade history students, silently sitting before him in their correct places, in neat rows, scratching away on their exercise books were quite oblivious to his utter despair. To them he looked much the same as ever, old, stern, hard and unfeeling, staring at them with a familiar forbidding countenance which held complete control. Of late he seldom smiled, had become even more strict than ever: no talking would be tolerated, no turning round, no fidgeting and no rocking on chairs.

Simeon Hogg was thinking of death. He was sitting very still in this chamber of silence, looking at his class when, suddenly - he was visited by a grotesque fantasy. An intriguing thought which was possibly born out of the depths of his misery.

What if he suddenly died? Here and now in front of these thirty young people. He would not fall over. As ever, as an example to others (especially other staff) he was sitting bolt upright, perfectly balanced on his chair. The authoritarian eyes, if now unseeing, would continue to remain open and, as ever, continue to maintain discipline in that classroom. The occasional face would, now and then, look up to test the rigorous regime and, quickly, return to work.

Suddenly the bell would shatter the oppressive silence, ringing out to announce the end of the school-day. In most other classrooms it would trigger an immediate uprising of excited youthful humanity - all rushing and crushing to the door, a joyful evacuation and escape from the Dwight D Eisenhower High School located on the south side of Lincoln Gardens, near Detroit, Michigan in the USA. In most other classrooms the sole adult voice would be raised to out-shout the din caused by the stampede in a futile attempt to, perhaps announce homework, or at least try to end the day in a civilised manner with a few words of conclusion.

But this was not most other classrooms. This was the dreaded Room 76, the room of Mr Hogg who had thirty-four and one half years of

13

experience in dealing with youngsters who (possibly from other more lax members of staff) might have formed the extraordinary idea that the bell is a higher authority than that of the schoolmaster. Mr Hogg's students had long learned the lesson that he, and he alone, at his pleasure and convenience, dismissed a class in his own time - and that time was usually at some point following the sounding of the school bell. After his short valedictory address, they would hear the command 'stand' followed by 'lead on' when each row in turn would file out of the door.

Tracing through this day-dream of sudden death, the master imagined his cadaver, still motionless in that academic chair, throughout the shrill ringing of the bell, a corpse continuing to command absolute obedience through the sightless eyes set in a frozen pale face. Perhaps after a few minutes a brave boy would venture -

"Bell's gone, Mr Hogg."

After two seconds of meeting the hard unflinching stare, the student would fear an imminent sharp reprimand, lose courage and return to his task. A second student would make a similar attempt and interpret the same ominous silence in the same way - and again, continue to apply himself to composing acceptable answers to the test before him.

At some point shortly later, a student might rise to her feet, approach the master's desk and ask a question. Mr Hogg would appear not to see her. He does not move his head. He still stares to the mid-distance of his class. He ignores her question. She is fearful of his stony silence. The 'Horrible Hogg' is today even more grumpy than ever, but her feminine temper is aroused by his refusal to, at least look at her! Rank bad manners! And now, six minutes into her free time, she is becoming angry and about to summon up the courage to think the unthinkable, to openly complain to the unapproachable Mr Hogg when ....

Something odd ... something different ... he is too quiet, too still ... She has an instinct to reach out and touch ... Mr Hogg falls to the ground - dead. She screams.

Enough of this nonsense - he could not get so lucky. Simeon wearily looked at his watch to find that the bell was indeed imminent. After all, this was a good class and they had worked well during this last

14

hour. They deserved to be dismissed on time. A few words were followed by the usual orderly exodus which left this miserable master alone, but now, in a different kind of silence. As with many times in the last few months, he considered his position - and he considered his position to be grave. How long could he carry on?

In total despair, but with new resolve, he marched to the office of the Principal, fully prepared to put his job on the line.

Unfortunately the Principal had gone home. It was Wednesday, April 16th 2003.

Chapter 2

The Dreaded Confrontation

Simeon Hogg and Principal Betty Lou Vanderburgh had tolerated an uneasy professional relationship over the previous eight years since her appointment after the Easter of 1995. Always pleasant, friendly and caring, she was a difficult woman to disagree with. When she imposed a 'comments only' form of student assessment and outlawed all traditional grades in 1996, Mr Hogg was outraged, but could only summon up the courage to politely express -

" ..... *serious concerns!"*

" *Oh, how unfortunate you see it that way, Simeon! I do hope you don't mind me calling you 'Simeon'? Please call me Betty. After a semester or two, I'm sure you'll notice how much happier our students have become when they're free from the pernicious doctrine of segregation by outcome. We must move forward, release their self expression and unchain their spirits. Let them fly!"*

They flew all right! Many to more traditional schools. And many **were** 'much happier', especially the bone idle who no longer had to worry about returning home with a grade 'D' - or worse. The new 'Records of Achievement' had replaced the report cards and were largely written by the students themselves - with minimum input from the staff. All remarks were required to be couched in positive terms. It was the opinion of Mr Hogg, one of a minority from the 'old guard' plus a majority of parents, that the end of semester report had now descended into a nebulous and worthless evaluation of euphemistic verbiage.

Every graduate of Eisenhower was now a winner! There were no losers and therefore no distinction between the hard working conscientious and the lazy disruptive contemptible. Indeed, if you attended classes at least half the time you were guaranteed to graduate. In desperation, at a second meeting, Mr Hogg raised this very point with Principal Vanderburgh. But once again, he was thrown off balance with her firm hand in the iron glove of clever diplomacy -

*"But, Simeon, you surprise me! A well respected educator such as yourself is **much** better off. Think of all the extra time you now have to invest in your lessons. Time which was once wasted on preparing*

tests and exams which only serve to distress and disadvantage our young charges."

Once again he emerged in a daze of confusion. Had it really happened? Had accountability gone for ever? Worse was to follow in the following months. Students were addressing teachers by their first names. It had become school policy, but Mr Hogg had adopted his own policy of being deaf to the word 'Simeon' and only hearing 'Mr Hogg' from the lips of any student.

Unbeknown to Mr Hogg, during that very Wednesday afternoon of his imagined demise, a fourteen year old girl had decided to drop into the office of her 'new friend' Betty Lou, and complain about the 'old fashioned' practices still being perpetrated in Room 76. The next morning Mr Hogg found an affable note in his pigeon hole -

Hi Simeon. Would you be kind enough to pop into my office sometime today? Thanks, Betty Lou.

He looked at this missive for some moments. In spite of the friendly casual tone, he felt sick to the very pit of his stomach.

He decided to counter attack and confront her with a list of all the recent philosophical changes which had damaged the school, a school which had once been the pride of Lincoln Gardens. He would draw attention to the sloppy dress of some teachers turning up to classes in jeans, track-suits and tasteless body piercing rings and studs. He would complain about the pressure from his newly appointed young and trendy Head of History, who was implementing fundamental changes to the teaching and very understanding of the subject. Indeed there were structural changes afoot regarding the total abolition of history as a separate and discrete subject. He would object to that particular rankling occasion when he walked into his room to find that all the desks had been moved into a group arrangement, where the students would face each other - instead of the teacher. He would protest about the new 'discussion document' which spoke of getting away from traditional 'content led and factual history' and into a 'more meaningful skills-based approach'.

The ever increasing gobbledegook was driving him crazy. The stress was mounting, not least that he could no longer exclude difficult adolescents who disrupted his classroom -

*"These disturbed people **need** us, Simeon. We mustn't keep sending them to the counsellor. Try not to see it as bad behaviour, try to see it as **challenging** behaviour. You've taught in that same room for the last 34 years, Simeon. We're all so very proud of you and we're all trying to help you. You're experienced. You can do it, I **know** you can!"*

This from the diminutive and politically correct Principal, who was little more than half his age and looked even younger, rather like a little girl with her long, straight, shoulder length hair. Despite the up-beat words, her fresh pleasant face regarded him sadly. It was unspoken, but they both knew that Mr Hogg had nowhere to go. No other school, no matter how traditional, would appoint him (nine years from retirement) over younger applicants in their twenties and thirties. After a lifetime of specialisation in British History, his command of the subject was absolute and he delivered lessons which were exciting and dramatic. They held their audience in complete silence. The Principal and other progressive colleagues respected, but could not agree with his strict classroom management which was inconsistent with the new relaxed approach.

Furthermore, there was something nasty and insidious about this charming, friendly, smiling little girl. She had power. She was imposing an alien and flawed philosophy upon the frightened man before her. It was like science fiction films where invading creatures from another planet get into, and take over human minds. Many had already been 'converted', but Mr Hogg was the only one who was still able to see real education. He could imagine her persuasive, soothing and sinister voice with an eerie echo saying -

"Don't resist us, Simeon, we're too strong. Join us. Give in. Yield. Come with us over to the left. Sleep. You'll feel so much better when you wake up and then ... and then, Simeon ... you'll be one of us."

He was swimming against a tide of left-wing liberalism and losing the battle. Indeed Simeon Hogg was suffering from battle fatigue after eight years of prolonged and useless struggle. He was becoming the butt of jokes from the new appointments who seemed to be getting

19

younger, more trendy and more progressive. Every day he was getting more depressed, and the job to which he had given his life, and once so much enjoyed - was becoming meaningless.

The assorted, casual, chattering historians in the third floor staff-room seemed to Mr Hogg to get more and more cheerful every day. A cheerfulness which increasingly irritated him. Standing by the kettle waiting for it to boil, he tried to avoid social contact by staring out of the window. He dreaded their teasing comments. A miserable countenance said it all.

"Cheer up, Simeon! Think of all those exam scripts you'll never have to mark again!"

The window looked out on to private gardens. A scene Mr Hogg had contemplated for over 30 years, but now it appeared to have a new meaning. He saw not just shrubs, trees and lawn: he saw freedom. A cat was idly cleaning itself. Happy cat, contented cat, lucky cat!

They had all recently entered into a new millennium. This would be his fifty-eight year, and he had reached the time of life when most other people were younger than himself. It had not seemed five minutes since the reverse was the case. For the first time he started to think about death. How much longer did he have left? He had recently read that the average life expectancy for a white man in the Detroit area was seventy-three.

"Seventy-three! Only fifteen years left! My God!"

To get the scale and size of fifteen years he considered the scope of the previous fifteen years. 1988! It was nothing - yesterday! It was hardly worth calling it 'the past'. 1988 was still very modern. In that year kids were already walking around with personal stereos and wearing digital watches on their wrists. Satellite TV's, video recorders, computers and electronic games were in nearly every home.

Fifteen years! It was like a death sentence .... and he was wasting the little time which was left: the few precious remaining years!

Ten minutes later he was in the rest room washing his hands and, suddenly, noticed his pained old face in the mirror.

"Too right! I am the picture of gloom."

But it was **his** face, only older. Inside he was the same. He could go back much further than a brief fifteen years. He could go back a length of time which made a big difference. He could go back half a century to the 'stone age' when he wrote on a slate, using a slate pencil, under the stern authority of a Victorian schoolmarm. He could go back 40 years to the time when .....

Suddenly he looked at the reflected image and tried mentally to delete the many lines and other sad, sagging acquisitions of age. He particularly studied the eyes. Basically they had to be more or less the same eyes which had looked back at him in 1960 - a year he often thought about. He imagined the constant cheerful expression of those eyes, as they once were. Smiling, dancing eyes, lit up with joy...

He leaned forward to the mirror -

"Are you there, Dobba? Are you still there ... somewhere?"

At the end of that day he stood outside the 'Office of the Principal', but the old sign, with the old name 'W.M. Forbes Ph.D.', had long been removed and now with egalitarian simplicity it said - 'Betty Lou Vanderburgh'.

With the crumpled note, which had requested this interview, stuffed in his grey suit pocket, together with his contentious list of grievances, he was fearful, but, notwithstanding, now prepared to engage in a full scale confrontation. He gave the door two firm knocks.

It was opened at once by the child within causing a waft which sent several papers flying to the floor. The great desk of Dr Forbes had been moved up to the wall, away from its previous intimidating 'position of power' which was directly in front of the summoned, subordinate member of staff.

There were now two comfortable chairs in the centre of this room facing each other giving the impression of parity and democracy. Simeon was not fooled. For all her skill conveying the sympathetic and empathetic approach, Betty Lou was the same powerful dictator which Dr Forbes had once been. The window dressing was different, but the reality was the same: what Betty Lou wanted, Betty Lou got!

Instinctively he wanted to get stuck in. Unilaterally he would resume making his students once more accountable. He would return to writing grades on scripts. He would give regular tests and end of semester examinations. He would ignore the new computer generated reports and issue his own, which proclaimed grades, percentages and class positions together with real honest comments. He would re-introduce and publicly display his league table of the ten best achievers of each class. He would go it alone .... and he intended to tell her so!

He wanted to get it over with. She could not actually fire him, but if open hostilities came to the surface, she, and her progressive Mafia of recently appointed disciples, could make life even more intolerable for Mr Hogg. He steeled himself for the appalling scene to follow and its aftermath.

However, it was she who had called the meeting, and it was she who would have to launch the reprimand - **then** he would respond.

It seemed to take an eternity as she stooped to pick up the papers. He helped.

"*Oh thank you, Simeon, so kind. If only my office could be as neat and organised as your pristine room. They tell me you actually clean it yourself?*"

"*Well ... just a few minutes at the end of the day ... I ..*"

"*If only all my troops were as conscientious as you are! Do take a seat.*"

She beamed a wide smile. This initial benign banter was interpreted by Mr Hogg as a softening up process to prepare the way for the censure and possible ultimatum to follow. She reached for a file and sat facing him. Apprehensively he noticed it was a file inscribed with his own name. His throat went a little dry. She looked up and smiled again.

"*Do you know, Simeon, that you're the longest serving teacher here? Really! You're not quite as old as Tim Bucheye, but out of 178 teaching staff, you ... Here it is ... September 1968. 'Magna cum laude'. What an achievement!*"

On the face of it the tone was sincere, but he could not help thinking that possibly she despised his long dull career spanning three decades in the same old subject, in the same old school, without any effort to seek promotion and move around the country. To Simeon it was simple. He loved history and had only ever wanted to be a classroom teacher. Management had never interested him.

22

She leaned back and smiled at him again. The smile faded slightly to an expression of concern with a gentle hint of puzzlement as she put the next question -

"Have you given much thought to retirement, Simeon?"

So that was it! That is how she would solve her problem. But how? The earliest possible date was 2005 when he was 60. He had every intention of breaking out of the 'Socialist Republic of Eisenhower High School', even at a reduced pension at this first chance. Colleagues would tease him -

"Are you going at 60, Simeon?"

"Is the Pope Catholic?" was his standard response. He would sell up and return to England, to the 'sceptred isle' he had left so long ago and so loved. Mr Hogg responded to the Principal's question.

"I certainly intend to apply for the early option of 60 if it can be achieved."

"That's what I wanted to talk to you about, Simeon. It's a hard fact of fiscal life that a valuable teacher like yourself is much more expensive than an inexperienced probationer, and as you know, I have to balance the budget. At risk of sounding like 'The Godfather', I'm going to make you an offer you can't refuse." She took a breath.

"As you know the Board of Regents had their meeting on Friday and, Ed Dyer, the Chairman who has just negotiated our new state Constitution with the State Senate ... Well you know all about that. The long and short of it is this, Simeon. Strings have been pulled. If you want to cut loose, you can go this year on the same terms as if you were 60 years of age!

In fact ... if you wish Simeon .. as it's the last day of Semester, tomorrow being Good Friday ... you can go this very day! What d'ya say?"

Mr Simeon Hogg could not contemplate a better Friday. He wanted to leap up into the air and say - *'Whoopee!!'* But in fact, he said in his quiet dignified British tone -

"Thank you, Miss Vanderburgh - I'll go today."

Chapter 3

The Agony, the Erotic and the Ecstasy

Simeon floated out of the Principal's office and into the familiar, comfortable retreat and blessed silence of the rest-room. Once more he took an interest in the image in the mirror. This time it beamed back at him two generations younger. He reached out to touch the hand of the boy in the reflection. He had reached out over, and through a time-span of 43 years. He had made contact with Dobba.

Out in the hall, a few students were walking towards him. He recognised one young man who had been very difficult during this winter semester. Right now it all seemed so trivial. The rejuvenated teacher was bubbling with mischievous excitement and had a sudden urge to lunge towards the youth, give him a kiss and big hug. The wild urge was wisely suppressed and, as expected, Mr Hogg walked past the group with his usual quiet dignity.

"Mustn't lose my pension before I get it!" he thought.

He became thoughtful. Was it something to do with this process of escape? For some reason his mind travelled back forty six years and four thousand miles to a hill-top mining town called Heanor in Derbyshire. It was the end of a lunch-time when, once again, he was 'unwillingly creeping' back to his hated destination, Mundy Street Boys School, a place of endless Monday mornings inflicted by a sadistic master with the willing assistance of his cruel disciples. This day was going to be different, on this day an extraordinary event occurred.

Hangdog and dawdling up the right side of Market Street - he stopped dead in his tracks and stared at the sight before him. It was beautiful. It was stunning and magnificent. A visual orgasm symbolising all the promise and hope of a future, in stark contrast to an unbearable present. It was everything to love and he loved every part of it as he slowly walked around this long, low, wonderful orgy of dazzling chrome. His eyes caressed the knife blade fins, with their rocket launcher taillights and were delighted by the aggressive bullet bumpers. It oozed power and seduction, occupied a wide swath of the road, but common-sense and practicality was put on hold when this dream machine was conceived. Motionless it was, yet one knew that in motion it would glide in silence and complete superiority. Simeon gazed through the tinted huge wraparound glass windshield onto the bright array and multiplicity of controls. Automatic transmission, air conditioning, power steering, photoelectric beam adjuster and of course - cruise control.

Do not forget, reader, this was 1957! In 1957 very few people in Heanor were fortunate enough to own a car. If they did have a car, almost always little, boxy and black, a **heater** was considered a luxury extra! This bright gleaming vision could have been an alien craft from another world. In fact it **was** from another world, a world with advanced technology called the United States of America, a promised land which Simeon Hogg would one day visit. But on that day, in Heanor, on Market Street, he found all the other cars small, sad, ugly, dull and contemptible.

Perhaps it was that brief shaft of light, that defining and electrifying moment nearly half a century back which gave birth to his present pride and joy. His 1959 Cadillac Eldorado was patiently waiting for him in an individual locking garage. A few long standing members of staff had this facility, a valuable and important privilege for Simeon Hogg. The original owner would have purchased this luxury model for under ten thousand dollars. It was now under-insured for $100,000, and had cost its present doting owner a small fortune to lovingly keep it in mint condition over the last 28 years. A magnificent monster from a past age, this eighteen foot, two ton dream on wheels was the most American part of the stern British schoolmaster who had never lost his English accent.

But once behind the huge wraparound windshield and space-ship style dashboard with every conceivable gadget at his fingertips, Simeon would bring the massive engine to life and slowly, the long, low, orgy of dazzling chrome would silently glide past curious pedestrians. Young people admired, people who would not have been born for another three decades after the original conception of this beautiful sculpture of mobile grandeur. They saw it every day, but every day they stopped and they looked. They looked with varying responses. Some were critics and condemned the automobile as gaudy arrogance, an affront to the ecology and common-sense. Others shared the adoration of its proud owner and savoured the vision, delighting in the knife blade fins, with their rocket launcher taillights and gleaming, aggressive, front bullet bumpers.

He sat back comfortably on the hand-stitched leather seat, and with one finger on the immense power-assisted wheel, guided the stately and lovely expanse of poetic metal out of the campus.

A sadness descended. He pondered the practicality of taking his alluring automobile back home with him to narrow country lanes in the wilds of Derbyshire where he intended to live. There was the high cost of trans-Atlantic transportation, not to mention expensive specialised maintenance and the bankrupting thirst of a V8 seven litre engine to consider.

"I'd love to have you over there, if only just to look at you, you gorgeous hunk! You're the best part of the United States, the one part I'd dearly like to take with me. Sorry, darling. You're too big and too ravishing! It just won't work. At long last it's time to say goodbye."

His ambition was to live in a remote part of the Peak District in modern comfort but tolerating no neighbours and no modern noise. It would be a considerable expense to achieve this ambition, making a big hole in the totality of his wealth. This consisted of the retirement lump sum, the proceeds of his house sale and life savings. He would need a new car in the United Kingdom and there would be very little money to spare. The vintage Cadillac had been an investment. Even back in 1975 they were becoming increasingly rare and soaring in value. This was an excellent specimen with all original gadgetry in working order. Even the Autronic Eye (automatic head-lamp dipper) was fully operational.

A wave of grief swept over him as he imagined a stranger owning and touching his cherished choice. Yet again he went through the mental calculations and considered the feasibility of taking the car back to England. Once again the rational answer came back; a clear no.

Homeward bound, he was now driving due north out of the city limits of Lincoln Gardens and into the city of Allen Park. But there was no change, everything looked just the same. Indeed the table-top, perfectly flat, urban environment of the vast Detroit conurbation was all one to Simeon Hogg who had never come to terms with the American landscape. The vista before him was an endless, ugly, untidy clutter of utility poles supporting a mesh of phone wires and power cables. The edge of the sun dazzling, rough white road, gave way to soft mud into which no flowers were ever set and no weed would grow in the hostile salty and gritty mix. Beyond this bleak margin were numerous dull parking lots, used car lots under the tasteless, garish, ever clattering, cheap plastic buntings. Hideous gas stations were scattered among cheap and flashy hamburger joints - all with their myriad gaudy signs screaming out low low prices in an endless blitz of unrestrained and unplanned commercialism. It sounded nice on the map - Lincoln Gardens and Allen Park, but parks and gardens they were certainly not.

The great car floated on bravely soaking up jolts from deep pot holes in the ill-repaired, cracked concrete pavement. Almost every road was a straight line running exactly north-south or east-west, forming a grid of depressing metropolitan sameness within a fifteen mile radius of Downtown Detroit.

It was a cruel functional world which the foreign driver had suffered since he first disembarked from the old Queen Elizabeth in 1963, the day before John F Kennedy was assassinated. The death of the President also signalled the death of Simeon's 'American Dream'. Within days he was pining for his homeland, but in all these 40 years Simeon had never found the courage to make the big return. In those far off days in the previous century, emigration was massively expensive, a one-way trip: it was forever. Family, friends and the American people in general told him daily that he was very fortunate to be in 'The Land of the Free'.

"What's ya beef, Mack? Most young guys like you, back in ol' decayin' yorup; why, they'd give their right arm to be able to come to the United States! Quit ya whingin'."

As time passed, connections were formed, friendships forged and new roots put down in terms of employment and eventually college. Earnings were high and material living standards were good. In 1969 he heard about the scandal of English teachers eking out a living on a net starting salary of twelve pounds a week. Starting American teachers in south Michigan were paid nearly seven times that amount. Home-sick he may have been, but the ex-patriot was able to accumulate capital, and at the same time, visit Britain every long summer vacation to see it at a level of comfort, and luxury, denied to Englishmen of average means.

But he had not seen bluebells since the spring of 1963. He had not seen the mellow mists of October in the Derbyshire Dales, or the romantic fog of November, or the glistening white brilliant frosts of January since being a teenager. Every part of the British year, save for July to early September, had been denied to him for over a third of a century - and now he was entering the autumn of his years. That special meeting of just a half hour before had changed everything. He was going home. He was going back to England - forever.

The car was safely garaged and the driver now indoors. He could not settle. He was churned up with an excitement which Simeon had not known for some time. He reached for the 50,000 scale Ordnance Survey map of Derbyshire -

"Where shall I look? How shall I look? By car? Cycle would be better. Where to stay? Hotel in Buxton?"

He looked at the complex geography of sharp peaks, twisting dales and tangled ravines which could not have contrasted more with the monotonous, horizontal expanse beyond his window. This was a pointless exercise without knowing what properties were available, but it mattered not. At this moment he needed the nostalgia. He needed to soak up Derbyshire. Home. Memories. His eye drifted to the south east corner, looking for Heanor, a hill-top coal mining town which was just three miles off the map.

Heanor. Many is the time on the annual vacations he would cycle to this begrimed and rather seedy little community which never failed to fascinate. This was the place where he had known agony, eroticism and ultimately - ecstasy: the place where he had been hated, loved, used and abused. He would dismount and walk his cycle over to the cruel Dickensian Mundy Street Boys School and look on, savouring an inexplicable kind of ghoulish compulsion. It was rather like watching a horror film, but knowing you were perfectly safe, because now, Mr Hogg, the respected schoolmaster, was nearly half a century and an ocean away from that nightmarish regime.

Simeon Hogg often looked into his old playground, a dismal hard flat area bereft of any comforting foliage. He noted the very places where he had been taunted, shamed and brought low with pig grunts. In the 'rough and tumble' of the Heanor code of ethics, a boy who would not fight was regarded with contempt and soon fell to the bottom of the pecking order. Simeon was soft: Simeon was 'fair game'. He looked at the high classroom window and re-played several excruciating incidents of public ridicule which were frequently engineered by a sadistic teacher. Incidents such as the time when this master read out one of his compositions and encouraged uproarious laughter and shouting catcalls. Inside that hard, unfeeling building, he had been phlegmed on and remembered feeling sick and broken in the struggle to clean off the disgusting thick mucus. He remembered being made to smell a ruler which had been drawn over the anus of a bully. The same bully, in front of other boys, forced him to acknowledge sexual slurs about his mother.

Simeon's timid and gentle disposition was such that physical force was rarely needed to bring him to heel in that hell-hole. Encouraged by the all-powerful classroom teacher, other boys found him a convenient target. Sanctioned by that same authority which was supposed to protect him, other boys felt perfectly justified in giving the screw one turn after another - and then - perhaps - just another turn. It was easy to find a tender spot, to touch just the right nerve ... A favourite nerve was the Promised Land. Young Simeon had a great passion for the USA. One day he would go there. One day he would be happy.

Friday, December 6th 1957 was a particularly bad day for Simeon and millions of Americans. Headline news reported that the United States had made a failed attempt to launch its first artificial earth satellite. Newsreel footage showed a Vanguard Rocket crumpling back to the ground amid an inferno of exploding flames at Cape Canaveral after achieving barely ten foot. The tiny 14 kilogram sphere in the top cone was still pathetically sending out its radio 'bleeps' when the smoking stricken vessel lay prostrate.

The teacher made comment on this exciting news. He reminded his class that only two months before, the Soviet Union had astonished the world. For the first time ever, they put into orbit an artificial 'moon', six times heavier than the sad little American satellite. He added further weight to the Russian cause by drawing attention to the ground-breaking event of November 3rd. The Communists had launched a device thirty times heavier containing a doomed dog called Laika sent to test conditions for the first manned space flight.

The thrust of this lesson was to show that the Americans were well behind the space race and the other boys took full advantage as they loudly leered, jeered, hooted and mock machine-gunned one miserable little boy in their midst, who, although suffering internal agonies, was still trying to put on a brave face. This conduct was tolerated and the ordeal ran its full course. A popular record sung by Perry Como ran -

"Catch a falling star and put it in your pocket, save it for a rainy day." A revised version was sung at Simeon in the playground -

"Catch a falling satellite and put it in a matchbox, send it to the USA."

Having brought their victim to a very low point of esteem and easy malleability, it was now possible for one particular boy (with the reputation of being a *'dotty sod'*) to put his slave to good use in this all boys school, this culture of cruelty which was also a culture of homoeroticism. With groping commonplace and 'ticker-on-balls' a favourite game in the school-yard, it was only a matter of time before Simeon, now broken in spirit, pliable and obedient to his masters, was ordered into the boys lavatory.

Simeon never forgot the appalling stench of that filthy place whose depressing Victorian brick walls were decorated with stinking lines drawn by crayons of excreta. As far as possible, to avoid a visit, he ignored the call of nature and, as a result, suffered constipation for the rest of his life. Looking back over the years (with an honest smile) he admitted that these coerced erotic activities became more and more agreeable, albeit in such a malodorous venue.

"Didn't need to be threatened the next day!" laughed Simeon to a friend years later. *"Make no mistake, in front of the others he was often very nasty to me ... but, well, in the dark and silence of that reeking WC, I suppose he was as near to a friend as I was ever likely to get."*

"You couldn't have been very old. What was it like?"

"What was it like ... it was a form of ... sensual sanctuary. It was exciting. I was very excited! So was he. Nothing elaborate, quite simple, two lads satisfying mutual curiosity. Gentle examination with little touches, strokes, caresses, pats and pets." Simeon stared out into the infinite distance. *"Could have been yesterday. It's odd, but ... I can still recall his body scent ... I can smell it now ... "*

"Cute?"

"Oh yes! Boy was he ever cute! Not much room, we were very close in there. Turned up nose, sweet little nose. Light sandy hair. Freckles ... Yes, very close, face to face - but it never got more friendly

31

than that. The action was down below, down in the hairless, milky white, nether regions."
    "Did ya cum?"
    "At the age of eleven! Younger perhaps. No, not for a long time, but ... well, it did happen - eventually - to me. We were both quite shocked - and him none too pleased. Got a bit messy then."

Simeon never spoke to anybody about that other boy, the bigger dark boy who, in the end, nearly pushed him over the edge. The Big Boy was not so bad at first - a simple command was easily complied with -
    "Aye, coom 'ere."
    "What?"
    "There's a pencil in me pocket. Put ya 'and in."

Rather more one-sided than his usual partner, this was a different task but just as interesting. Raggy britches [breeches], often handed down from older brothers, seldom had sound pockets. But at Mundy Street Boys School power had nothing to do with smart dress. Power was established by force of personality and, more important, force of the bravery and skill of bare knuckle fist fights in the play-ground. This high ranking pupil was a particular favourite of the schoolmaster and, just as long as his disciple was receiving pleasure, Simeon was useful and relatively safe. It happened at Big Boy's bidding - in the toilets, in the playground, even in the classroom - often in the classroom. In the few minutes duration, it had a beginning, a middle and a wet sticky conclusion when the worker was usually thanked with - *"Get lost."*
    The beginning looked innocent - just two boys sitting side by side apparently absorbed with work, writing in an exercise book. The middle would see the larger boy's penmanship get slower, become less accurate, less steady. Having achieved so little in his short miserable life, Simeon noted these subtle changes to his desk-mate and became intrigued with the practical, pleasing results of his own delicate handiwork. Subtle changes to Big Boy's breathing were noted: unsteady, slightly deeper and more intense. Occasionally the servant would steal a glance at the face of his close master who was attempting to maintain an air of detached industriousness - but, affected by ever mounting ecstasy, was gradually failing. Just for these precious moments, Simeon, working skilfully with his soft, sensitive, naughty little hand - it was **he** who now had the power: the power to speed up or slow down: the power to fumble, fondle and seek out those special little

places, special little favourite places - the nooks and crannies of bliss. Eventually the subject had ceased all pretence to write. His eyes were half closed, legs slowly widening, lifting, plus small changes in posture to improve ease of accessibility. At this familiar point Simeon would look upon that face: a face handsome rather than cute: a face darkened by sporting hours under the 1957 sunshine: a face in seventh heaven but too ashamed to look upon the face of his adept and conscientious servicer: a face more and more transported with sexual euphoria ...

The end was near. The end had to be near. That deft little hand, wet and gooey with excited dribble, was too clever, too cunning in technique. Simeon was accustomed to the signs, the opening mouth and a low, slow, barely audible moan ... Sometimes a gruff *'finish it'* was uttered in a shaking whispered voice. Sometimes it was an urgent breathy order. Sometimes that weak adolescent croak was almost pleading. Sometimes it could not be articulated.

The climax subsided and so did the protection. A thin shabby little boy wiped his hand on a drab post-war pullover, slunk away back to his usual desk, hoping, once again, not to be noticed by any opportunistic tormentors. But, for a few boys at Mundy Street, the fun went on and on - as on that terrible grey cold morning when Simeon, possibly for the first time ever - combed his hair.

Simeon was alone, always alone. As usual, for security, he made himself as small as possible, his back pressed hard up against the school wall. Warily he watched Big Boy and his small Mafia of thugs stroll by. Even in fear, he was unable to keep his eyes off the well proportioned Big Boy who so nicely filled out those raggy britches of which he was so very familiar. But this was an unkind hour. Having noticed the neat hair, three lads detached themselves from the group and confronted him. Just for a moment Big Boy looked over and, just for a moment, Simeon hoped that he might intercede to prevent the coming atrocity. But nothing was done to stop that vicious and total humiliation of ruffled hair, pokes, pushes, pig grunts, jeers and sadistic twisted leers from that cruel gathering congregation of amused faces.

A whistle stopped the show. Blown by a schoolmaster, this was the command for all boys to freeze and be silent. A second blow was the command for all boys to *'walk, not run'* to their class lines. A whistle stopped the entertainment - but not the intense shame and pain which would last all day and all night for one slow walker who had been brought very low.

Five minutes later all the boys in the school were marched into the Hall for morning assembly where they faced the stage, strictly standing to attention in straight lines, hands by sides in stillness and silence. No talking, no whispering, no shuffling - just waiting respectfully to receive the headmaster. On dark winter mornings, in those few quiet seconds before the appearance of his Dread Lord, Simeon could hear the gentle hissing of gas lamps. Boys at his side, boys to the front and rear, clean boys and dirty boys all created an unpleasant Dickensian crush of musty odour and stifling lack of ventilation. He looked up at the high open window hoping that some fresh air might enter, and, less likely, that he might fly out to freedom and away from the pain of school, home and Heanor.

All eyes focused on the strict headmaster, a stern theocrat, distant and detached, who reigned with absolute power over this culture of cruelty. His baton, seen daily as an instrument of oppression, would be raised -

"To whom the lips of children
Made sweet hosannas ring."

One of the head's frequent favourites, but this dismal, doleful dirge will always be associated with humiliation, pain and suffering. In later years it came as a surprise to Simeon that some people actually liked hymns! He assumed that they were deliberately composed to be depressing and dreary to enable the suffering singer to atone for his sins.

After a sleepless night came a morning when his spirit was broken beyond repair. He was afraid of the consequences of failure to attend school, but, could not find the courage to walk up that hill from his home at Red Lion Square, a first floor flat above a tobacconist. Simeon was totally alone. He had no friends to advise him. There were no adults he could approach. He was disliked by his parents. They took the view that boys must learn to fight their own battles, consistent with a long held working class ethos. Sink or swim, he sank. A boy who could not mend a puncture, a boy who had no aptitude for football (in a macho culture where football was important) was a great disappointment.

For the first time ever, Simeon feigned illness and stayed at home. He was unable to think beyond the next 24 hours, but with both parents out at work, he was savouring a period of calm and respite until... He heard ominous footsteps along the dark narrow entry.

34

Silence. He waited. He had half expected that this would happen, that the insidious tentacles of Mundy Street Boys School would reach out into the safety of his own home. The door reverberated and filled the building with several loud bangs. Cautiously and quietly he crept down the stairs and peered through a peep hole to see an alarmingly familiar face. Big Boy was excited. He was bobbing around, impatient and keen for an answer. He had been sent by the schoolmaster to investigate. He had been given a mission to bring Simeon Hogg back to school. Such was the power of a classroom teacher back in 1957.

Stealthily the truant withdrew, ascended the stairs and hoped that the unwelcome visitor would give up and return to the evil hell from whence he came. But no: utter horror: the door handle moved: the unlocked door opened and the intruder entered. Like a pursued animal in fear, Simeon, barefoot and still in his pyjamas, silently sprinted up two flights to conceal himself in a small box room on the second floor.

Big Boy had no fear at all. Why should he? He was the 'chosen one' who was expected to do a good job. He was acting in the name of the schoolmaster who authorised this errand. Had he encountered Mr or Mrs Hogg, he would have asserted his delegated authority and claimed it included permission to enter and search. This was no trespass, 'the Hogg' had to be, if necessary, dragged back, had to be taught a lesson. Mr X knew how to deal with 'the Hogg'. If Big Boy succeeded, they would all be in for a good show that morning.

From faint sounds heard inside the box room, the intruder appeared to be taking his sweet time to investigate the main front living room. Family photographs would be studied providing information which could be useful in the playground at a later date. The kitchen and bathroom were next. Simeon, remaining very still, held on to the hope that the explorer would get bored and go away. Matters could hardly get worse, but they did. He heard Big Boy creaking up to the second floor coming to rest in front of the box room door - which was not quite closed. Curiously, the snooper gave it a little push. Clutter caused resistance and, just for a moment, a partial view of miscellaneous junk was now possible in poor light. Just for a moment, but for the pathetic cringing child, deep in shadows only inches away, that moment was an eternity. The man often looked back on this excruciating moment and angrily asked -

"Why? How? How did I let that happen?"

But he knew the answer to that question. He knew that three years later, a re-invented Simeon, christened Dobba, the new confident confidant of Scott North would have challenged the rude brazen trespasser, would never have allowed that appalling situation to arise.

A systematically bullied child, bereft of wise counsel from any adult, is imprisoned in his own private hell. This child had been groomed as a victim and was, as usual, obediently behaving as a victim rather like the unfortunate captives who were brainwashed in Korea just a few years before. Indeed, this child had already reached an advanced stage of humility and obedience to his class guards, to Big Boy and to the teacher whose sarcastic tongue he dreaded daily. Simeon's usual body language in and around the area of Mundy Street Boys School said it all - head bowed and eyes downcast. After the style of the concentration camp, Mundy Street Boys School, if not tattooed on his arm, was, and would be for the rest of his life - tattooed in his mind.

Big Boy did not notice Simeon in the box room. He passed on. He prowled on to the principal front bedroom, neat and therefore not very interesting save for the long view from the north western facing window: an uninterrupted third of a mile, way down High Street to the very bottom of the hill. Back on the landing, once again passing the box room, he found the back bedroom - his coup-de-grace. On the door a child-like crayoned sign was incorrectly spelled 'PRIVET'. Mortified, Simeon heard the click of entry into his own inner sanctum. Leisurely, the prowler set out to examine all parts of the interior which included the contents of drawers, diagrams and pictures on the walls, clothes, books, comics, toys and all manner of personal effects. All this took quite a span of time for one miserable shrinking child now cold and huddled nearby. The agony of these minutes was not born of the fear of burglarious activity: the agony was born of the sadistic objective - the intent, to bring low one who has already suffered much.

Descending steps announced the end of the ordeal. The measured unhurried creaks seemed to enhance the cruel satisfaction of the exercise and the smug hint of a smile playing around Big Boy's lips could be imaged. The door closed - he had gone.

Arriving at school the next day confirmed Simeon Hogg's worst fears. Hesitantly with stony expression, he approached the entrance and halted before a large group - gloating, smirking, sensing blood. A raucous chorus quickly surrounded him to shout, stab and wound him with the news of the previous morning. The schoolmaster had invited Big Boy to deliver his report publicly before the oversized class of 46 pupils and that class was allowed to break into a rapture of noisy merriment. Included in the entertainment was a reference to the 'Privet' sign, drawings of space rockets on the wall, a painting of an American car, comics considered too young and any amount of embarrassing material which could be retained and used at will for future tortures. Simeon's private world was laid bare. Uproarious laughter, catcalls and continuing ridicule followed him throughout that terrible day, one of many bad days in the year of 1957.

It had been going on and on, day after day, week after week, month after month. Like the wording of a medieval torture -
'... as much as you can bear, and greater.'

On that day after school it was too great. A great relief came over him when he contemplated a drastic solution. It was under a bleak mid-winter miserable sky, darkened by drizzle when Simeon opened the sash window and assessed the length of drop from that second floor bedroom onto the glistening pavement below. It seemed like a high fall, but would it be enough? Would it be quick? It needed to be quick. These contemplations were a relief for the unhappy little boy. Despair had produced its own balm. The resolution itself made things better, because, now, there was a way out. The intolerable had now become just a fraction more tolerable.

During these cogitations he leaned out further and noted the views. In the far distance, the hills of Derbyshire were shrouded with low grey cloud. He noted industrial scars of mining and, in the near distance, the foot of that long straight road. At the end of that road, just to the left there was another school - a better school.

Simeon the man has often looked back at that moment. He often stood on Red Lion Square and looked up to his old home which still had the date marked out in carved bricks - 1888. And above the date, there was that depressing, now slowly rotting top window, the window of despair. He was thankful that Simeon the boy did not jump, because Simeon the boy was only months away from attending that better school down the hill.

Enough of this unhealthy brooding. Heanor had better things to offer. The following autumn would see a bigger lad flying down that same hill to another regime and a much kinder campus. A left turn took the cyclist into a cul-de-sac called Allandale Road where the sun was always shining. This was the leafy glade of William Howitt Secondary Modern School. At this nostalgic east gate, years later, an American tourist often stood where a boy had once stood. Once again he admired the mottled effect cast by the same mighty lime tree and the equally splendid copper beech. This was the site of that one magical brief moment in his life when he enjoyed being part of the realm of Queen Mary McLening as she ruled over her Camelot, a culture of kindness. This school too had its rough powerful lads who were feared and respected, but to his delight, Simeon discovered that **these** guys where dressed differently - they wore the **white** hats. These tough lads gave him back not only his self-respect and dignity - they gave him a more precious gift yet - they gave him friendship.

Today on Thursday April 17th 2003 in his home near Detroit, he was thinking of this friendship now. He wondered what had become of those good people after all these years. Often he wondered about the friend who had simply disappeared one day: an event which had haunted him all his life.

In all the years of annual trips over the Atlantic, he had never once tried to reunite with his old school pals. Why? Was it fear? Fear that the memory and idealised image was so precious, so fragile it could so easily be shattered?

He had worshipped Scott North, the successful athlete who ruled the school and had generously bestowed a small portion of his prestige and kudos upon Simeon. Rather like being knighted by a king. It transformed his life. Scott North was the distinctive dazzling blond hunk of popular memory who confidently swaggered his well proportioned body across the playground, flashing his good looks to admiring girls, some of whom had tried to pretend a lack of interest. It was this same Scott who had reinvented and re-moulded the image of Simeon Hogg.

Simeon? It was not entirely a suitable name for a member of Scott's inner circle .....

Chapter 4

Looks Good, Feels Good, Tastes Good

Just before 9.00am on the Monday of September 1st, 1958, a scruffy, introverted, nervous and academically weak new pupil with no self confidence was, as usual, standing with his back hard up against the school wall, as usual, trying to make himself small and inconspicuous. Auspiciously it was a warm sunny day. Auspiciously he saw a sea, a swirl of unfamiliar faces because his enemies - were gone! They were safely removed to a different secondary modern school, thankfully a good mile away, on the other side of the hill at another place called Aldercar. This was the west side of town, this was William Howitt Secondary Modern School.

After the chronic misery, the hardness of the military macho regime up the hill, he found his new teacher, Mrs Cook, cordial, benign and encouraging. All was propitious right from the very start. The classroom, preponderant with glass, constructed of wood was cheerful, light and airy. Just outside the window, healthy light green shrubbery and beyond, shaded grassy areas under handsome mature trees. A complete contrast to the darker, hard, viewless, deadly interior of his previous Victorian classroom, built in the days when windows were deliberately placed high to deter distraction.

Simeon proceeded with great caution taking stock of those around him. With an apprehensive spirit, his confidence and self esteem were very low. For the first time since infant classroom days he was now in mixed company. A potentially hard masculine regime of an all male school had been softened by the presence of sensible girls. The gentle sex were civilising, had a mature calming effect, shaming and reducing the yob element.

But there was something else, something beyond a change of circumstances, a magical change had come upon him during that summer of his thirteenth year. It had crept up almost without notice. A stealthy metamorphosis consistent with the song of an airy spirit called Ariel -

"Nothing of him that doth fade,
But doth suffer a sea-change,
Into something rich and strange."

39

The newcomer arrived at this leafy campus with the gifts of a deeper voice, taller stature and a macho if somewhat brooding disposition. Together with anonymity, Simeon Hogg, once boy now pupated into a young man, had the golden advantage of a new and fresh start.

Mrs Doris Cook was a dramatic contrast to the previous sadistic master up the hill. This cosy, kind, motherly teacher, presided over an odd collection of quirky characters - often the case in a group of slow learners. This was a secondary modern school where the emphasis was on practical subjects. The 'eleven plus' examination, a tool of selection, had already creamed off the more able into the Heanor Grammar School which had a more academic curriculum. Those fortunate few were destined for the professions or white collar jobs in offices. The rest of them were expected to be shop assistants at best, 'clock on' in factories or get labouring jobs such as 'going down the pit'.

The William Howitt Secondary Modern School, one of the best of its type, was divided into same age ability groups. There was the top ability 'A' class and a lower ability 'B' class. It soon became apparent that Mrs Cook's motley brood of cheerful chicks was the very bottom class, below 'B' and therefore fell into a category which could be described as - 'the lowest of the low'!

"So what!" were the thoughts of young Hogg. To hell with academic status! For the first time in his life since being a small child he was really happy. For the first time ever, he was in a position to shine against a background of limited competition.

There were just two television channels: the BBC and the commercial ITV. On the latter, a brand of parakeet seed was making "Budgies bounce with health." In his new classroom, an ongoing circus of boisterous conviviality, Simeon was bouncing with joy. Heanor folk were poor, but in late 1958 they all had 'the Telly' and all enjoyed the commercials. Several times every night, a roughly spoken, dowdy, low class woman responded to questions about a new soap powder. Simeon became an amusing mimic, delighting in affecting her accent and manner.

"Since av bin usin t' Omo, thes noow neeed fa me - ta use bleach!"

These popular mini performances, often ending up in class uproar, were not always relevant to the lesson in hand. Neither were they conducive to class discipline. Accordingly, the ever laughing impersonator was told in no uncertain terms to restrict his performances to break time in the playground. This he did with relish, because now he had access to the caretaker's yard brush which became a crutch to do his impression of Tony Hancock, impersonating Robert Newton's interpretation of Robert Louis Stevenson's colourful character - Long John Silver, from his 1881 book - 'Treasure Island'.

"Aarr Jim lad!" and the occasional *"Avast there!"*

This nautical romp consisted of hopping around the playground with a limp neck and an imaginary squawking parrot on ye shoulder screeching *'Pieces of Eight!'*. It took off, and soon there were several 'Silvers' capering around the school. Simeon savoured his new found influence but had to find new material when the novelty waned.

A half crazed, boggle eyed hermit, complete with stout wooden staff, screaming imprecations after the style of -

"REPENT!! Ye lusting sinners! Hear me! Ye are DOOMED!!" had little impact, miserably falling short of the desired effect, especially when Rex Lloyd said -

"Shut it!"

"Nay, Brethren, give heed, I have seen the light."

"Y'll see my fist in a minute."

Miss Brentnall added -

"Don't be so silly, Simeon. Do be more quiet."

Undaunted, an insane exaggerated Ben Gunn, with a piercing effeminate falsetto cackle - *"Sez you - sez me."* had more success.

For all his efforts, Simeon was not the class clown. That honour went to little Tom Day who was often in trouble for his 'one liners' which would cause the class to crack up into fits of laughter. This would be followed by *"COME OUT!"* and a short slow walk to the front. There he would stand, wearing a half grin/half ashamed expression, shuffling around in his short trousers next to the much annoyed mistress. To her dismay, the effect of this absurd situation was more amusing than ever to the audience who were trying very hard not to crack up. When Mrs Cook moved, he had the habit of jerking his head back in the expectation of a slap - evidence of previous experience.

On one occasion, Tom, known as Titch, was discovered with pictures of naked women. Necks were desperately craned and eyes strained to get a glimpse of the grubby little booklet in Titch's naughty little fingers. Beyond a quick flash of boobs, nothing could be discerned as the outraged schoolmarm ceremoniously tore up the obscene images into small pieces. Eleven pairs of lascivious eyes sadly watched their slow descent to the classroom floor.

Titch may have been small in stature, but he did have some standing and in no way allowed himself to be pushed around. A pecking order was certainly established in this class and the school in general, but Simeon never saw it put to the test. No one was ever tormented and no one was ever challenged in what appeared to be a tolerant atmosphere of acceptance and good will.

Simeon Hogg laughed his way through the shortening dark winter days of 1958, up to Christmas, when his parents moved out of Heanor, four and a half miles south to a straggling mining village called Stanley Common. Travelling to school now meant a one mile walk from his tiny terraced house, westwards to the bus stop at the Rose and Crown on the Derby - Heanor road. There he stood and shivered until an elderly bus trundled along to collect a frozen Howittian determined to get to the warm cosy nest of Mother Cook.

His fourteenth spring was the first to be noticed and completely embraced in the intoxication of delirious happiness. Adolescence is often associated with the discovery of sex. In this Simeon was no exception, but it should be remembered that all senses come of age, in that everything new and exciting looks good, feels good, tastes good and smells good. Each cycle ride to and from school was an adventure and slightly different as the season advanced. The excellent sunny summer of 1959 started early with a lime green April and was still clinging to life in the late, warm October, amid a blaze of colour.

He savoured every moment of every day, watched the buds develop into bright green leaves, discerned flowers come and go, perceived the magnificent views to Crich Stand and the Derbyshire hills beyond.

The morning ride out of the old mining village became more interesting as the distant westerly green patch work panorama opened out. To his left, the fragrant nodding bluebells, a sea of colour from a fragment of the larger Morleyhays Wood. Turning north up to Smalley Green between thick thorny barriers of hawthorn, and occasional tangles of white flowered bramble. Singing his little heart out at the same spot each day, a spirited soaring skylark seemed to share the boy's zest for life. Glimpses of glossy yellow celandine and patches of wood anemone flashed by as he came to the leafy inviting Bell Lane which appeared on the right. He pushed and pedalled through the pretty village of Smalley, and then onwards, into Heanor.

A warm April turned into a hot May and he began the after school habit of cycling the seven mile journey to the old mill town of Belper, to swim and cool down in the Herbert Strutt Baths. Never actually having had a friend before, it was quite a compliment when, one day, Titch suggested in his Horsley Woodhouse vernacular that he might like to come along - *"Al goow we ya!"*

At the point of leaving, two brothers from another class, Brian and Danny Forrester also came along to add to the fun. Having been crushed by the dark years before, it is difficult to put into words Simeon's ecstasy resulting from the mix of that adolescent scruffy quartet, joyfully pedalling up High Street, issuing shrieks of delight under the warm afternoon sunshine. Such a good time was had, the next day, they decided to do it all over again. This time, the four became five when Rex announced he would join them.

Rex means 'king', and Rex Lloyd was certainly the king of Mrs Cook's class and one of the 'kingpins' of the school. A strong tough youth enjoying the respect and fear which usually went with these attributes. The vibrant up-beat personality was as big as the muscles. Always cheerful, everybody liked Rex who never abused his power and was ever popular treating his subjects kindly.

On that day, Simeon was standing on pedals, pushing his bicycle up the steep High Street with all his might in a significant effort to remain just behind the beefy newcomer - and just behind the mesmerising and intoxicating motion of his firm, full and well rounded buttocks. An endless high pressure area created a persistent endless blue sky. Rex had stuffed his shirt into a battered old saddlebag and the sun illuminated glistening sweat beads on his bare, sinewy, powerful back. Passing the Milk Bar, they heard the slow beat of 'Lonely Boy' by Paul Anka which seemed to accord with the rhythm of their slow progress. Rex, raucously sang out and yielded to the temptation of the local current rearrangement of the words from the correct -

"...lonely and blue, I'm all alone with nothing to do..." to the naughty substitution of *"...nobody to do."*

In that glorious happy July of 1959, Simeon had climbed to achieve the status and heights of friendship with Rex Lloyd and was now a long long way from being a lonely boy.

Some 45 minutes later five excited pals dismounted at the entrance of the Belper Baths. Eagerly they shoved their dirty scruffy bikes into a crush of other dirty scruffy bikes forming a rough cycle park outside the entrance. After stampeding up to the pay box, a grumpy and shapeless old attendant relieved them of the four-pence admission charge and warned them to *"Be'ave ya sens"*. Inside they were hit by a blast of warm air, chlorine and a multitude of shrieks and shouts of echoing delight. As usual it was very busy, as usual all the cubicles were taken, making it necessary to undress in a large back room of stacked metal boxes. Most of them were occupied by the clothes of other bathers. Scanning for a vacant box, following Rex, they rushed round, turned several corners through the metal maze ending up in a dead-end corridor when Rex shouted - *"Over 'ere, 'eres some!"* After a quick strip, clothes slung into a box and tatty suits donned, they were splashing away with many dozens of others.

Simeon was keen to show his friends that he could swim, swim fast and swim well. He boasted to Rex that he could swim underwater and was thrilled when ordered to prove it. He boasted about holding his breath underwater for more than a minute and again, with the Forresters counting, he scored more points of kudos and bathed in the glory of sweet success. After a while they were admiring the athletic feats of Rex skilfully bouncing off the high board, gracefully flying through space before spearing the water with a million bubbles. He did it over and over, standing proud on that board, massive confident grin, laughing, yelling for clearance, enjoying all the attention, pleased as punch sticking out firm, well formed shining wet pectorals over a rock solid abdomen. The twins were amused, Titch dismissed him as a 'show off' but Simeon - Simeon just watched and watched and watched ...

Ahead of his friends, Simeon decided to dry off and get dressed. He set out to navigate the box puzzle which was peaceful after the ongoing screaming row back in the main hall. He turned the corners, left and right and then left again, made one mistake but, eventually he recognised the cul-de-sac at the far end where they had left their clothes.

The sight which met Simeon's eyes was truly arresting. For a moment he stood frozen to take in and make sense of the scene before him. A big strapping well tanned youth was standing, naked, firm and confident, feet apart, hands on hips, strong and powerful, a la Henry VIII - but the kingdom of this stripling was of another time and another place. This was Big Boy - no less.

Big Boy was smiling with condescension at his one time servant. In two years of fast adolescent growth, the tyrant had filled out in all the right places and was magnificent. The mind-blowing scene was not just the vision of this Adonis, but the stunning eroticism due to his collection of conscientious acolytes. Possibly about seven puerile admiring attendants were busy, touching, tending and ministering. One appeared to be stroking the inside of his leg and one at the back was caressing his bottom. An urchin was doing something else back there in a dark recess and another in front was examining a nipple. His scrotum was being fondled by a fair haired youth and two lads nearer to his own stature were, in turn, giving their best efforts to the one place where it counts. Things had moved on since 1957, and Simeon, mesmerised, was unable to take his eyes off it. The acolytes, some with protruding tongues, some open mouthed, were uttering tiny sounds and sighs of wonderment and scrutiny along the lewd paths of their sensuous journey - but, as to be expected, the big sounds came at the end.

Several squeals of surprise came with a powerful ejection which passed over the heads of two workers. The only indication of this finality was a softening of Big Boy's arrogant smile. It dissolved into a countenance controlled by the ecstasy of that special one moment which had so often been fashioned by Simeon's own hand at Mundy Street Boys School.

Most impressive about this bizarre show to the voyeur was the total lack of fear or embarrassment. Simeon's arrival on the scene had not fazed any of them - why? Was it due to the cast iron protection which would be afforded by Big Boy himself? Had he ever been afraid of anything, this youth, who simply took his pleasure at will?

An unsettling event! It had exited and stirred Simeon beyond measure. Painful memories and instinct warned him to carry on and show no reaction. He fumbled with his shirt, tried to dress, tried to hide the

45

embarrassing effect of the previous minutes - but could hardly concentrate. The others were quicker and filed out in front of their hulky master who was still wearing his superior handsome half smile. Languidly he strolled towards his former slave - and then stopped! One hand cupped the balls and the other closed round the hard secreting shaft. Simeon stood perfectly still and looked up into that dark face. It was a pleading look. Again, just as in the old dark days, he was entirely at Big Boy's mercy. Again he caught the familiar distinctive body scent of physical closeness. He was vulnerable. At that moment that big strapping youth had the power to inflict pain or pleasure - fortunately the grip, although locked and firm, did not, as feared, tighten.

Simeon Hogg would remember those seconds all his life. A myriad kaleidoscope of mixed emotions. He hated Big Boy. He loved Big Boy. Smouldering eyes, unwilling to forgive a mountain of past humiliations defiantly met the cruel attractive dark eyes just inches away and he lusted a lust which would never be equalled. The warm hands very slightly relaxed. They become more mobile, more kind, and, during those precious seconds - gave intense pleasure. In retrospect it could be described as a passing grope, a leisurely grope, but a short lived grope which was soon ended - much too soon - devastatingly too soon. Big Boy moved on. Big Boy was gone.

Simeon Hogg was a bit better off than most of the other pupils of William Howitt Secondary Modern School. Mum and Dad had always been generous and two incomes made it possible for Simeon to be given five shillings a day for food and bus fare. Cycling to school released extra funds to dine out for lunch. Having an independent spirit, he preferred to leave the campus at midday, walk the half mile up the hill and enjoy the delights of the comfortable Market Cafe. Mr Hogg the young schoolmaster was coerced to stay, suffer the daily cacophony of clink and clatter and force down poor quality school dinners during a daily penance which was called 'supervision duty'. Simeon Hogg the boy, (having an aversion to slugs) was appalled to hear accounts of unwashed lettuce and the occasional appearance of a slimy mollusc creeping across a plate.

Miss McLening the headmistress once lined up the daily chip shop and cafe brigade and put them under pressure to abandon their midday wandering habits and dine in the school canteen. This line included the meaty and muscular Rex Lloyd. She singled out Simeon

46

and directly challenged his judgement: why should he reject such good value, a full meal costing just one shilling?

"I get choice, Miss," was not well received from the impudent acned urchin who stood before her august presence.

"Oh!" replied She, lovely eyes blazing, *"What a pity it is not possible to go and check the canteen menu and walk out if it is not to sir's taste!!"*

Silently standing, sensing being on very firm ground - he stood his ground, savouring the point scored. After a regal dismissal the little group walked back to class, proud smiles quietly cheered the rebel a hero. Mrs Cook heard the full drama from the power house of the form, Rex Lloyd, no less. To have earned **his** good opinion was for Simeon, a big step up the ladder of prestige.

Yet Simeon was sad to have annoyed the enchanting dark handsome lady who had become a goddess. His eyes were always drawn to a beauty mole on the face of that charming and gracious headmistress who reigned over an all too brief magical and happy period of his life. A woman held in great affection by all her subjects, a queen who filled the school with sunshine and love. Love! That was the one word which continued to re-occur. The love from, and to, Mary McLening permeated the very fabric of the building and hallowed the ground of William Howitt Secondary Modern School.

At the Market Cafe, Simeon chose from various items on toast costing 'one and something'. 'Something and chips' went into the two shilling mark, add three pennies for a cup of tea. The cafe had two halves. To the right of the central corridor was the snack bar and to the left a quieter dining room for meals. Above the clatter of pots, cutlery, comings and goings and the continuous hum of conversation, the young diner could hear and enjoy melodic strains which travelled across the two rooms and passageway. The music came from something very un-Heanor, something new and different, something rather like Simeon's dream car: a space aged, push buttoned chrome and gaudily illuminated cabinet called a 'jukebox' which needed to be fed a threepenny bit for one play, a silver sixpence for two plays, or five plays for a silver shilling. Fascinated eyes watched a mechanical arm lift selected popular 7" 45 rpm records and place them precisely on an automatic deck. As the needle fell into the lead groove, an anticipatory delicious electronic 'thud' would precede the ecstatic sounds to follow.

For the teenager in the next room munching through his beans on toast (or whatever) - this was the birth of real music. The charts of 1959 and 1960 were the very epicentre of his musical experience. Simeon Hogg would spend the rest of his life worshipping at that shrine of talented excellence. He will, forever more, listen with nostalgic reverence to the lush orchestrations and sexy boyish voices which sang out through that small window of creativity. Marty Wilde, Bobby Vee and Adam Faith crystallised and defined his fresh green hopes, inspired his dreams and fuelled his fantasies.

One day he was entranced by what seemed like a sweet sounding choir of angels ascending and descending the scale, complemented by a resonant twangy bass guitar. Into this euphonious mix came, exactly at the right time, a deep masculine voice with just a hint of the sexy adolescent croak so typical of this new young genre. He could easily have been mistaken for Elvis but, these dulcet tones were a touch lighter and, for Simeon's taste, with great respect to the King - better. This sensuous singer had composed both the music and lyrics for this beautiful work which lasted barely more than a precious two minutes. After such an orgasmic audible experience, in complete contrast to the hateful pious dirges of just a stone's throw away; this new music now became an important part of his life at William Howitt Secondary Modern School.

During the following weeks, the same record was played every day. Simeon struggled to hang on to those illusive, hypnotic notes, above the ambient din of the busy Market Cafe. A few occasional words were discerned -

" ... and in the evening, by the moonlight ... "

He knew not the name of the singer nor the song title to be able to ask for it in a record shop. A pointless exercise not possessing a record player, let alone the expensive seven shillings needed to purchase. Eventually the time came when, nervously, this scruffy youth entered a shop and held the precious vinyl disc, with its grooved integral encoded magical music, bearing the legend - "Maybe Tomorrow".

Later, in that same store, examining the sleeve of a prized long playing record, he stood very still and looked. He peered long and hard into the stunningly handsome features of his teenage idol - Billy Fury: a typical image of the popular culture of 1959.

48

Chapter 5

The Golden Oarsman

The long hot summer of 1959 slowly and reluctantly cooled into a blazing, bright red and yellow sunny autumn. Cycle rides clung to life until finally, cold, fog, frost and early murky damp nights forced an end. Christmas saw the leaving of pupils who had already turned fifteen. Into the power vacuum, ascended a new crop of those high ranking lads who already held status by virtue of physical size, competence and prowess on the sports field, together with sheer force of personality and popularity. So by January 1960, it came to pass that Scott North, the handsome, flaxen haired, record-breaking athlete from the 'B' class, became the new King of the School.

This new status quo in top management had little relevance in the chatty, cheery classroom of Mrs Cook where Simeon continued to develop and prosper, savouring the agreeable flavour of daily life.

It was gradual, little by little, imperceptibly at first, but Scott North started to notice the dark haired pimply associate of Rex Lloyd who was forever spreading sunshine with his funny voices and infectious laugh. This was the consolidation of a totally new personality and a million miles away from his previous existence of living death in a never ending series of 'Mundy mornings'. A few witty words were occasionally tossed at Simeon's 'John Silver' within the accepted good natured framework of working class youth culture.

"That parrot needs oiling!"

Such comments were an important form of 'lads together' communication. Communication with a complex hidden agenda. Scott was telling Simeon that he enjoyed the show, but more important, was the fact of public approbation. Simeon had been lifted in the eyes of the others, and over the days and weeks which followed, steadily but surely, Simeon Hogg became a friend of the mighty Scott North.

The hard cold winds under the grey skies of early spring had no discouraging effect on the bubbling boy who enthusiastically jumped on his Palm Beach Raleigh bike every morning, eager to get to school.

Among his many physical accomplishments, Scott was a keen cyclist and made frequent excursions up, and into the hills of Derbyshire, sometimes with other lords of the school and sometimes alone. He was fast and it was said that he could keep up with any bus. Simeon reflected that buses made frequent stops, but was wise enough to keep those thoughts private. In the week after the Easter holidays, the weather was looking very promising and Scott caused a flurry of excitement when he turned up one morning on his brand new, gleaming BSA 'Golden Wings' 10 speed racer. In this rather grimy mining community, Heanorians were not well endowed with income or material possessions and it was very unusual to witness this level of opulence. Admirers, including a curious teacher, asked questions and paid genuine compliments. The handsome top calibre machine and its tall well built powerful owner were a good match.

This little moment of respectful appreciation was rudely and loudly interrupted by Carol Bestwick violently agitating her old [probably Victorian] clanging hand bell. She was completely indifferent to this particular gathering of approbation, being one of a minority of girls who were well able to resist the renowned 'pulling power' of Scott North. Big and well built, the mighty Carol was enjoying her few moments of power and importance, enthusiastically proclaiming the start of the school day.

Cycles were simply leaned next to the school wall as the boys and girls drifted to their various classrooms to be registered. They were never chained and never locked. After being formally noted and counted, staff and pupils assembled in the bright, open Main Hall, where happy voices rang out with -
> *"Glad that I live am I, that the sky is blue.*
> *Glad for the country lanes and the fall of dew*
> *After the sun the rain, after the rain the sun ..."*

One of their number was an exuberant adolescent with a raucous voice, over active oil glands and greasy black shining curls, carefully arranged after the style of pop idols to fall over a shiny forehead. For this bad case of acne, the uplifting melody and words struck a chord. The sky **was** blue and indeed Simeon **was** glad to be alive.

True to form, March came in 'like a lion' and had gone out 'like a lamb'. Simeon the cyclist was very 'glad for the country lanes' where, like the previous year, he would soon be enjoying the fragrant nodding bluebells in fragments of woodland under that same spirited soaring skylark.

50

That evening after the final bell, Scott was mounting his new bike and making plans with a few senior strapping disciples about a visit to some sort of a castle. Not knowing of any nearby castles in the area, the eavesdropping Simeon was intrigued and very agreeably surprised when Scott suddenly addressed him directly with a terse -

"Are ya comin' then?"

The youthful quintet raced two miles to the north, through the village of Loscoe and into the next rural community of Codnor. Bikes were then carried over a few styles and they rode across open fields until an ancient ruin came into view. A cool easterly wind tempered what otherwise would have been a warm sunny early April evening. Noisy cawing crows combined with the sweeter song of blackbirds. Despite a dry spring, bright lime green had not failed the grass or healthy hawthorn. Craggy, crumbling, grotesque shapes could be seen in the outline of the southern wall which appeared strangely top heavy. Ancient windows, chimneys and dramatic zigzag cracks due to age or mining subsidence completed the picture.

During the exploration of Codnor Castle, little was said except for the usual jocular comments from Scott, firmly in command, who frequently made reference to somebody or something called a 'dobber'. One of the group pointed out to Simeon that it was in fact a reference to himself and added -

*"Well wot d'ya expect! 'E can't call ya **'Simeon'** can 'e?*

Simeon Hogg understood this at once, but, notwithstanding, was still a little hurt. He had always rather liked his unusual Biblical name, but had to agree that the odd sweetness of sound in several awkward syllables, was unsuitable for a youth who would aspire to an association with the likes of Scott North. The former Mundy Street Boys School inmate was grateful that surnames were never used as a form of address at Howitt Secondary Modern School, either by staff or pupils. Thus he was spared the dreaded derogatory appellations in connection with filthy swine and mucky pigs. On the contrary, it was explained to the new recruit that Scott had honoured and christened him well.

In the Heanor youth culture, a large heavy 'dobber' was the king of marbles used to knock lesser marbles out of a ring drawn on the

51

pavement. A boy was lucky if he owned this cast iron ball which was about an inch and a half in diameter. So the next day at school, the boy who was previously known as Simeon, received further advancement and extra kudos when equals yelled out 'Dobba!' across the playground. One greasy teenager had been remoulded and reinvented.

Many weeks later the long balmy days of June had arrived and on one occasion an old Will Hay comedy was shown in the canteen after school. At the conclusion, Scott North and his pals tumbled out of the pre-fabricated building in an ecstasy of joyous camaraderie giggles and fun. Hearty *'cheerio's'* and *'see ya's'* echoed around the campus as the jolly guys and gals dispersed, some of them heading up the hill to savour the delights of Santa Elliot's large chip shop and cafe, a social centre for teenagers.

Later on this particular celebratory evening, the sun had already set leaving a gorgeous deep red to purple glow over Loscoe, and over the direction of Ilkeston, there emerged a fat smiling orange moon as if to bestow a blessing upon the happy youth of Heanor.

Noting the lateness of the hour, Dobba hurriedly left his friends on the Market Place and raced back down to school. He mounted his bike and was launched onto a fragrant journey of growing darkness. Soon in open country with fields at either side, there were multitudinous scents of meadowsweet, saxifrage, cowbane, cowparsley, hemlock, yarrow, evening primrose and the occasional nostalgic whiff of damp ramson, together with any number of roadside weeds.

Growing coolness gave an exulted increase in energy as he stood rampant on pedals for greater power, acceleration, more and more speed through the balmy aromatic darkness. Such a blissful fleetness, un-measurable, never exceeded since that enchanted ride which was more like flight!

In the idyllic world of early teens with minimal responsibilities, Dobba and his friends had all the time in the world outside of school hours. This was not quite the case for Scott who rose early each day for his paper round and apportioned principal evenings (Friday, Saturday and Sunday) to a seemingly endless supply of willing girlfriends.

Within the world of teenage boys ranging between their fourteenth and fifteenth years there is a great diversity of physical development. In

52

retrospect, most former pupils described Scott North as being nearly six foot tall. The reality was a little less impressive at five foot ten inches. Dobber and the Forester twins were a typical 'five foot seven', but looking **up** into the handsome countenance of the school hero had the effect of exaggerating the memory of those extra three inches. At the age of fourteen, being endowed with extra inches is vitally important for one's social standing. Scott was justly proud of his advanced physique and on one occasion at the baths drew attention to the space between the top of his trunks and his naval. His luxurious pubic hair had extended up into public view proclaiming new manhood. To hammer the point home he commented on those less well blest -

"D ya know, Dobba, Foresters 'aven't an 'air between 'em!"

His erotic fame may well have been exaggerated in Howittian circles. After all, it was common knowledge that Scott never had need to boast about any particular conquest. Indeed, he was never heard to name names, times or places: a fact alone which gave extra fuel to the reputation of this legendary 'jack the lad'. The rumours flew, very often with regard to girls of another school or even older girls who were working, but salacious claims were always attributed to a third party. When these lewd tales were ever repeated within his hearing, Scott North simply responded with a maddening enigmatic smile.

Equally intriguing was the prurient interest in the North's washing line which was visible from a hosiery factory employing rough girls with something of a naughty reputation. It was said that the titillating display of Scott's underwear, pegged out and hanging on the washing line, caused a temporary drop in production as hordes of excited girls rushed over to the windows with leering eyes. On hearing this interesting and intriguing account, Brian, Danny and Dobba sadly reflected on the lesser impact of their own underpants having no power at all to disrupt a factory!

No one had thought to ask about birthdays. It would have come as a surprise to all members of that particular quartet to find that at the start of July of 1960, they were all still fourteen years old, and all of them born within six days of each other. For all his bulges in all the right places and manly maturity, the tall athletic Scott was in fact the youngest of that group and two days younger than the twins who were born on the very day when the first ever atomic bomb was exploded in the New Mexico desert by the Americans. The flash on that day, which was seen 250 miles away, had cast a shadow over all their lives. The threat of nuclear annihilation was ever present with frightening TV images of a furious little fat bald-headed Nikita Khruschev banging the table at the United Nations with his shoe and threatening to 'bury' us! The prospect of dying a virgin was a constant worry to Dobba.

But not a worry to the 1960 version of 'The Fonz', when one lazy Saturday afternoon he raced over to Stanley Common to pick up Dobba to accompany him on a cycle ride to Matlock Bath. Hurtling north along the (then quieter) A6, under the mottled glades of overhanging woods, eventually they reached the picturesque Swiss-like resort with its cheerful parade of gift shops and cafes. The lads took comfort and rest, slowly sipping hot steaming tea from old quaint cups. They sat in an ancient tea shop which had probably not changed in half a century, except for the radio, somewhere playing in the back kitchen. Simeon was savouring his tea, trying to catch fragments of lyrics, intermingled with pizzicato strings which enhanced the silvery tones and adolescent nasal sounds of Adam Faith -
        " ... but I can't, resist, the thought of being kissed by - someone else's baby ... "

A beautiful tune which stayed dancing around his head for the whole of that day.
        They ended up in a rowing boat on the Derwent, deep down inside a heavily wooded green and dank rocky ravine in a soup of delicious air, thick with the scent of ramsons. Girlie giggles from aloft floated down through the sun glinting ferns causing them to look up to see two wenches giving friendly waves. Dobba, embarrassed and awkward was relieved when his companion, panting and struggling with oars, gave an appropriate 'Heanor style' response -
        "Ave got energy fa you dook, but not fa this!"

High summer endured day after day and mid-July saw the same two friends on that same river just north of the Belper River Gardens. In that gentle, civilised, lost world of Kenneth Grahame, after the style of Rat and Mole, they drifted under the willows enjoying the mottled reflected sunshine under the riverside foliage and heard the friendly Derwent rhythmically lapping their little boat.
        Simeon Hogg was fully aware of the total magic and enchantment of that long summer and fully aware that it would not and

54

could not last. It was all held together by Howitt. The friends and friendship and the stage upon which to perform. Like an ugly unknown blackness, leaving day was remorselessly approaching, followed by the chill wind of autumn. Soon Simeon would be unwillingly creeping **away** from school.

Overhead, the occasional flash of white from magpies, and the dank nostalgic scent of tiny starred wild garlic from the bank. The passenger looked affectionately at the happy golden oarsman laughing and splashing and thought - *"It will never get better than this!"*

And it never did.

Chapter 6

Journey to the Far North

The approach to the end of term was tinged with sadness. Very soon the Howitt lads would be going their separate ways, into the big world, to work for a living. Responsibility and a harder discipline was not to their taste.

Having failed to amuse them with yet another 'Silver', Dobba sat down with the twins, Rex and Scott who were somewhat downcast, idly sunning in the playground. It was the last day, Friday, July 22nd. None of them had found jobs and none of them had looked very hard but different possibilities were discussed. Ever teasing and mischievous, Brian said that Dobba would probably go far and achieve high status in a really important post -

> *"Yo 'n be 'ead dustman, Dobba!"*

He went on to sing Lonnie Donegan's 'My Old Man's a Dustman', knowing how it irritated his pal since this inane ditty had quickly reached number one in the Hit Parade - overtaking Dobba's beloved 'Maybe Tomorrow' by Billy Fury - which, to his deep chagrin and disbelief had, at best, struggled to reach number 18!

This banter was part of a mild cycle of teasing which they all enjoyed. Popular records were a principal part of the popular culture. Great loves and hates were formed and regularly disputed in passionate polemics such as when Brian, waving his 'New Musical Express', took malicious pleasure in telling Dobba that his much championed 'This Love I Have For You' by the young Lance Fortune was still languishing down the charts at number 26 - at the same time that the comedian, Ken Dodd, had just reached the dizzy heights of number eight with his (in Howittian terms) mawkish and mushy 'Love Is Like A Violin' - despised all the more by Dobba since hearing his Aunty Joyce sing it whilst pegging out clothes.

Lonnie Donegan, far too old at the unforgivable age of 29 and Ken Dodd, even older at 31 did not fit Dobba's image of gorgeous young pop stars.

When these acrimonious exchanges had subsided, Scott suggested that tomorrow he might have a ride up into the Peak and stay somewhere to

57

be able to explore the area for a few days. Rex, who had once cycled up to Buxton [and back in one day] with Scott, immediately enthused about an expedition to the uncharted Far North. This self-invitation was accepted. Dobba was elated when Scott asked him if he and the twins were interested in coming as well. The mood had now become more hopeful.

That last afternoon, lessons were abandoned and leaving Howittians were allowed to listen to popular records on the old school gramophone played in the canteen. People had little to say to each other. They were reflective and introspective. These last hours were sad with sweet, sensuous melancholia, as staff and pupils heard the nasal strains of Adam Faith singing 'From Now Until Forever' with pizzicato strings - a silver sound for a blue mood. It was played several times, echoing through that large long room: simple words with a simple message of love, hope, companionship and the passing of a lifetime.
    "As the years go rolling by, I'll turn to you and sigh ... "
A portentous song of separation foreshadowing many divergent paths into the unknown.
    And then it came - the final dismissal.

Reluctantly and slowly walking up to the bicycle wall, the four were receiving instructions from their leader regarding the Big Trip. Scott and the twins who lived in Heanor would pick up Rex who lived in Horsley Woodhouse two miles to the west -
    "Dobba ad betta be at Rex's ass [house], *or we'll go we out 'im!"* It made good sense, but, at that moment, a cultured voice chimed in with -
    "Have you given any thought to your accommodation?"

This was the English master, Mr Matthewman who had over-heard bits of this proposed journey and, as an experienced scout and scoutmaster, was a little concerned about the inadequate planning. Five respectful faces turned to hear more. He pointed out that on the steep hills of the Peak, Brian, Danny and Simeon, inexperienced cyclists, would not find the ride as easy as the more beefy Rex and Scott.
    "What about the best route? Can you read a one inch OS map?"

Five minutes later they were in the master's room poring over an old

58

cloth map. During previous excursions into Derbyshire, Scott had always taken main routes by simply reading road directions. He was now intrigued by the alternative suggestions being offered involving canal paths, tiny back roads and footpaths through ravines and dales which eliminated many of the steeper hills. These sensible, quiet, more interesting courses provided an exciting challenge to Scott in his new role as the navigator and avoided the motorcars, lorries and other dangers of the A6.

'Digs' had not been considered. Mr Matthewman suggested a Youth Hostel but they were not members. He was then struck by an idea. Would they like to stay at a friendly farmhouse with dogs, cats, a sheep and a goat in a remote hamlet near Buxton? This welcome proposal was accepted by a spontaneous hearty cheer - tempered by an ominous silence when a ten shilling fee was mentioned -

"Mr and Mrs Peirson are old friends of ours and Wellhead Farm is an excellent and interesting 16th century house. For a five course dinner, comfortable bed and substantial breakfast at half their usual terms, that is very good value indeed - not much more that you'd pay at a Youth Hostel. You couldn't expect them to do it for less. Don't forget that you'll need a little extra cash for drinks and small treats."

This precipitated a short financial conference. The money was not a problem for Scott or Rex who had paper rounds. Simeon had generous parents who both worked. The Forrester twins, much less well off, were more concerned about the affordability of this short holiday on top of the annual August week at Skegness which was already spoken for.

"A can go. I'll gerrit from me granddad!"

This was a voice from outside the room, the voice of little 'Titch' Day standing in the doorway who had just invited himself to make the five - now six. Keith Matthewman was touched by the kind lack of dissent and immediate acceptance from the others -

"You'd better come in here, Tom, if you're going to be one of the team."

After a few very gentle but firm words about the need for good conduct in representing William Howitt Secondary Modern School and reminding Scott in particular of his special responsibilities as the leader, the schoolmaster disappeared to make a brief long distance telephone-call from Miss McLenin's office to book in six 'reliable well behaved' boys for the following night at Wellhead Farm.

Mr Matthewman returned and wrote the name and address of their destination on the edge of the time-worn map which he handed to Scott.
"No need to give it back, it's done good service here. You do understand the route I proposed?"
"A think so, sir."
"Good. Mrs Peirson is expecting you at about six - at the latest. You'll need to wash for dinner. Don't bother taking soap or towels, they provide that sort of thing. You all have saddle bags?"

Six heads nodded. Apart from Scott's new bag, all were serviceable, if battered.
"Good. Take a toothbrush and a change of clothes in case you get wet. The weather's settled, you should be OK. Puncture outfit and basic tools?"

Again common assent which left little else but to dismiss the pupils with 'bon voyage' and good luck. He expected an excited dash out of the room but, once more, Keith Matthewman was pleasurably impressed by the way these kids, albeit in their rather rough way, remembered to thank him as best they could for his interest and help.

Early the next day was bright indeed, sparkling and blue, if a touch cool, when Rex, Dobba and Titch were exhilarated at the sight of Scott and the twins speeding through the village of Horsley Woodhouse. There had been a question mark over the appearance of Brian and Danny, but even in straitened circumstances, money had been eked out to make this treat possible.

After the four nightmarish, friendless years of Mundy Street, Simeon Hogg found the Forrester home simple, spartan, but diffused throughout with an ineffable quality of consideration, comradeship, caring and kindness. A cheerful atmosphere was presided over by the attractive Mrs Forrester looking more than a decade younger than her 36 years. Those good looks had descended to her twin sons who were not identical and further separated by subtle differences of personality.

60

Both had a certain charm which defied analysis, both were buoyant and uplifting, both had fresh faces which were totally unblemished by any unkind or unworthy thoughts - but, the childlike innocence of Danny was not quite so apparent in Brian, whose round baby face and twinkling eyes seemed to mitigate the amiable teasing he so enjoyed. Simeon Hogg the man would often look back over the years and recall these minor pricks to his occasional pomposity. Wind-ups were delivered with Brian's characteristic mischievous grin and the quick sexy sliding out of the tongue - the face which ever haunted, the face which was never to age.

Chapter 7

Adventures Along the Cromford Canal

Initial progress was swift. Six eager cyclists turned right at Four Lane Ends in Horsley Woodhouse, headlonged northwards down the narrow lane to cross Bottle Brook, through Denby Bottles and Smithy Houses into open countryside following the dead straight, old Roman road, Ryknild Street, known locally as Street Lane. Slower progress was made through the more interesting Upper Hartshay and Heage when an old melancholy windmill to the right was intriguing enough to stop them. Suddenly, behind them in creepy tones, a voice said -

"Can ya still 'ear the creak and sweep of the sails?"

This was followed by an un-nerving, if gentle chuckle from the old woman who continued -

"Sometimes we see the ghost of the miller! Yes, ave seen 'im. 'E stands on t' brow o' t' hill watching ghosts of 'orse-drawn wagons, trundling along dusty lanes with sacks of grain to feed into the stone jaws of the 'ungry mill."

Forcing an artificial laugh followed by a curt *'See ya then'*, Scott ordered his men to keep in close formation and expect two right turns in Nether Heage which were going to be tricky.

Hurtling down a very steep hill, they quickly negotiated a knot of old quaint houses in this small nucleated back-water: too quickly for Simeon who was seeing this little gem for the first time. He felt a pang of sadness that such beauty had to be rushed instead of savoured and marvelled at the extraordinary diversity of landscape just a few miles from his home. Indeed, the cycling summers of 1959 and 1960 started his love affair with Derbyshire. It would make such a deep and lasting impression, that Simeon Hogg would attempt to re-visit his youth and repeat that experience by crossing the Atlantic Ocean 70 times to savour 35 English summers for the remaining years of that century.

The peace of a hamlet called Ridgeway, briefly shattered by a short section of the busy Ambergate to Ripley road, was restored after they pedalled under the main Derby to Chesterfield railway line and up to a small community called Bulbridge. A narrow footpath on the left of another bridge over the Cromford Canal led them onto the tow path and into a magnificent wooded valley created by the River Derwent flowing southwards from the distant High Peak.

Entering an attractive quiet nature reserve was a pleasant contrast to sharing a road with motor vehicles. Suddenly they were alone on this industrial through-way which had been disused and gently decaying since they were born. If slightly eerie at first, they soon soaked up the special canal atmosphere of ducks, coots and dabchicks nicely shielded by tall grasses, yellow flag and bulrushes - all illuminated by glittering, mottled sunshine reflected from the water and the deep blue sky.

Titch squealed with excitement when he saw a water vole, Brian tried to persuade Dobba that an enormous dragonfly was, in fact, an ugly fairy but, he was more interested in a small island of assorted small sticks in the canal centre. Several tiny fluffy black faces were peeping out of the safety of soft downy feathers belonging to a mother moorhen sitting on her nest keeping her chicks warm and cosy. It was getting warmer and Rex, who tanned well, stuffed his shirt into the saddlebag.

Suddenly they were transfixed with fascinated horror by an ancient rotting longboat, slowly, year on year, being consumed into deep black mud. It seemed sad and symbolic of a lost age, a vessel with many tales to tell of old Derbyshire - but must remain untold.

The old fashioned dank smell of the canal mixed agreeably with pungent creamy meadowsweet which filled the morning air. It was late July and the ferns and meadowsweet were already higher than the mounted boys. Moving along, the lush foliage alternated between light and dark - mainly clinging dark ivy, sycamore, oak and alder. Still waters littered with leaves were agitated when baby ducks and coots darted and tweeted around in search of morsels.

Minutes later their progress was arrested by an old man with long shoulder-length white hair standing on the tow path. Scott had an urge to say 'Look, Ben Gunn!' but was restrained by a sudden foreboding that they were about to be reprimanded for trespassing on British Waterways property.
    "Nar then! Wot's all this? Where yo gooin'?"

Scott gave a polite and respectful itinerary which seem to pacify the questioner. In his roughly spoken manner, the old gentleman gave them a brief summary of points of interest not to be missed along the way. It was one of those rare moments which made an impression and would always be remembered in the life of Simeon Hogg. With an extraordinary economy of words, this (apparent) local yokel gave an effective, if brief, history lesson, made all the more vivid and intelligible to the wide ability range before him by using clear plain language and simple analogy. In short he was a good, if unlettered, teacher.

Hand dug by labourers with spades 166 years before, this artificial river was created for the purpose of making it easy for heavy goods to be pulled by horses between Cromford and Nottingham at a time when roads were generally much worse than the pathway upon which they were standing. There was a need to keep the waterway as level as possible. They should watch out for a point when the canal plunged straight into the bowels of the earth: a place called Gregory Tunnel.

Further on, 18th century folk were amazed to see a 'river in the sky' when the Wigwell Aqueduct was first built. Effectively a man-made river flying 30 feet over the River Derwent.

"Mind it don't fall down! It did when Mester Jessop finished building it in 1791, but 'e put it all back straight away. A 'spect it's steady now."

They were told to observe a spooky and gothic looking stone building which had a huge chimney with an odd distinctive wide parapet. This was Leawood Pump House, the home of a massive 1849 beam steam engine, still in working order which could suck up water from the river to replenish the canal at the rate of 31 tons every minute.

Further still on the left and high up in the wooded hills, they should note another mighty, even older hissing and spitting steam engine which used an endless rope haulage system to pull heavy materials 1000 feet up a steep incline. The High Peak Railway moved goods from the Cromford Canal all the way across the top of Derbyshire to Manchester.

The old man bid them farewell and told them to be careful of snakes! A warning received by Scott with some scepticism, but, in warm summers, the occasional adder has been spotted.

All those advertised features caused considerable comment and provided great excitement; especially the murky depths of the tunnel with its dark echoing drips, a spooky journey with a tiny window of daylight at the far end. They explored a 'haunted wharfinger's cottage', an old picturesque crumble of masonry and invasive foliage just south of the aqueduct where a short canal branches off to Lea Mills.

The canal came to an end at Cromford Wharf next to the one-time water powered cotton mill, according to the old man, the world's first factory. Across the road, briefly, they noted the pleasing proportions of St Mary's Church and its densely shaded churchyard. Nobody was there to tell them that it was a mausoleum for the Arkwright family who once ruled the area.

It all became different. It became colder with the fast racing river and tall trees on their right, a sheer rock face on their left with more trees, big trees, high up at the very top of the rocks - all creating deep cool shade. Titch found it a little intimidating, Dobba loved it. Feeling the chill, Rex put his shirt on and Scott, keen to be back on course, was looking for a castle over the river which should be, but was not in sight. Having raced on ahead along the rough path, the twins saw it first: dominating the valley, a solid baronial eminence proclaiming the wealth and power of Sir Richard Arkwright who had built Willersley Castle in 1792.

It was a right turn at the end which took them onto the busy A6 which curved between Masson Mill with its unusual convex weir and the mighty Masson Hill on the left which is honeycombed with old lead mines. All six boys had visited the popular Matlock Bath, a happy resort of thermal springs, Victorian nostalgia, old hotels, little cafes and a maze of intriguing rocky nooks and crannies. Obediently they steeled themselves to pedal past the temptation of garish modern amusements following the leader who was determined to reach Wormhill before 6.00pm.

They were keen to identify to each other familiar landmarks. Victoria Tower surmounted the wooded hill of the Heights of Abraham on the left and the impressive sheer cliff face of High Tor loomed on the other side of the river. Titch insisted he could see a face in the rock. Danny suggested it was the face of the old man on the canal watching over them.

It was a relief to turn left and escape the busy traffic at Matlock Bridge, but Dobba and the twins had to dismount in the face an incredibly steep hill: a capitulation which forced the others to do likewise. Scott assured them that it was worth the hard labour and detour through Snitterton to avoid five miles of the main A6. At the summit they were rewarded with magnificent views of Matlock town climbing up the far eastern hill sporting the distinctive Victorian Smedley's Hydro and the mediaeval looking Rockside Hydro. Mr Smedley's one time home, Riber Castle, crowned the adjacent hill to the south.

Descending down the windy narrow lanes through a tiny wooded community called Oker, the group felt that they were the first outsiders to visit that remote hamlet in hundreds of years. A shaded narrow lane came into sunny open fields but was abruptly barred by a very private looking gate which precipitated an urgent conference and studious perusal of the map. All was well, this was the gated road, as foretold by Mr Matthewman. The next mile would require the opening and closing of several gates but had the benefit of being dead flat on the meadows of the Derwent river plain. Now they had a vast amount of room under a big sky. This journey was blessed with extraordinary sharp contrasts of scenery, even by English standards.

Suddenly they stopped! A menacing group of staring cows stood close, too close, to the open road which did not have the usual protection of a kind hedge. Scott tried to re-assure by insisting that the cattle were all cows and everybody knew that cows were perfectly safe. However, the lads were more alarmed still when the usually fearless Rex (sporting his tight bright red jeans) commented on the look of one particular unfriendly, glowering 'cow' of distinctly masculine build which did not seem at all pleased to see them. He added -
   "A canna see any tits on that cow!"

Nobody wanted to use the word 'bull', but all eyes were straining to discern any visible male genitalia. After a few tense moments, the impasse and indecision was broken by the boss who - *"'adn't time ta muck about."* Bravely and with dignity he rode past the beast. His troops followed, immediately overtook him and, with considerable anxiety and maximum effort, accelerated up to the safety of the next gate.

Chapter 8

Water-cum-Jolly Dale

When in Derbyshire, any route from river level is almost certainly to involve very hard work. So it was that the climb up to Stanton Moor was slow and hard going for the cyclists who (never having heard of it anyway) were unaware of being just below the ancient, legendary Nine Ladies Stone Circle. Simeon loved his leafy glades and this beautiful wooded minor road to the east of the moor was a treat. Huge gritstone rocks, perilously piled up on the left caught narrow beams of sunlight giving an occasional sparkle from fragments of quartz. They went down the hill, taking a right fork, avoiding the village of Stanton-in-the-Peak - which would have been another treat had time permitted.

Speeding Down Pilhough Lane, Dobba's shirt flapped furiously in the wind and even more so down the steeper and narrower Stanton Hall Lane until they came to a small, timeworn, mossy bridge crossing the River Lathkill which was about to join the River Wye. Moments such as this were pleasantly consuming the day: leaning over stone parapets looking into crystal waters, spotting fish, making humorous observations, exchanging adolescent comments - all part of the bonding process.

It was midday - they had to move and move quick. Re-joining the mercifully flat, if busy A6, gave them an opportunity to zip along the last two miles to Bakewell in this wide valley created by the River Wye.

Again it was the observant twins who yelled out the discovery of a mighty castle with medieval battlements from fleeting glimpses through heavy foliage on the far side of the river. As all heads turned right, Scott took satisfaction in calming the excitement and airing his superior knowledge by a dispassionate, deep voiced announcement of -

"'Addon 'all".

"Wot's 'e say?" said Titch

"A think 'e said - 'Bugger all'," said Rex.

"No! Ay said - 'Sod all'," shouted Brian.

Bakewell was busy. Bakewell was always busy on Saturday, but from past experience Scott had discovered a quiet, high quality route into the town centre, cutting a mile off the main road. Just opposite Intake Lane, a footpath took them into the Rutland Recreation Ground. Here they could walk by the river side and then straight into a wide choice of cafes and tea shops located in a pleasantly confusing maze of quaint little streets. Dobba's eye was caught by an autumnal woodland oil painting -

"*Nice intit. Forty nine an' eleven!*"

"*If ya look at it 50 times it's less than a shillin' a look,*" said Scott.

"*Look at it 600 times, Dobba, then it's only a penny a look!*" said Titch. The innumerate Dobba was quietly envious of Titch's quick arithmetical ability.

They were all hungry. Many of the eating houses looked a little on the posh side to this little bunch of ragamuffins who were sensitive to their casual appearance and social standing. A cafe, snack bar or even a humble tea shop would be OK, but something which looked like, or proclaimed itself to be a 'Restaurant' was definitely out of the question. They risked being made to feel unwelcome, or worse, told to leave, not to mention the small matter of having enough money. As this was a special treat it had been decided that a cafe was better than squashed sandwiches in the saddle-bag. After a brief reconnaissance, the 'Honey Bun Cafe' seemed about right, providing various items on toast with a cup of tea for under two shillings and a warm welcome from two attractive young women.

It was nearly 2.00pm when they were replete and resting on long comfortable benches in the colourful and well stocked Bath Gardens. Looking up the hill, rising out of the trees, dreamily, Simeon unconsciously noted an interesting gothic profile of an elegant spire surmounting an octagonal tower, battlemented walls and finials. All Saints Church gave him pleasure together with the good company of his, now more sedate, companions. Simeon Hogg was very happy.

The day was blessed with high pressure and blue skies but the temperature only modest in the mid to high sixties. A damp, well shaded main road going north was decidedly cool. Hard work pressing against a gradient helped to warm them up. The thin and slightly undersized Forresters gave triumphant bell rings as they overtook Rex and Scott who usually occupied the second and first positions.

Ashford-in-the-Water gave another opportunity to be pleasantly sedated, viewing big fish in clear swift cold waters. Moving on, some chance comment sparked a heated debate over a football celebrity, which ended with the humorous diversion of a noisy farmyard on their left, which, in turn, sparked Rex to do his brooding hen impression. All followed suit. All the way up to Monsal Head, they indulged in a performance which often irritated Mrs Cook, their former teacher. Six large 'hens' were clucking with varying degrees of emotion, starting with a relaxed, puffed out, slow contented cluck-cluck, up to an alarmed, feather scattering, panicked, squawk - as fowl after fowl pressed the pedals ever harder, each trying to get ahead of the other.

This jolly madness was respectfully stilled when they reached the impressive view-point at the summit of Monsal Head: a panorama which was all the more breath-taking with such good visibility. Eyes travelled several miles, taking in the lush beauty along the Wye Valley to the north-west, and then, to the south-west, along Monsal Dale.

Dobba became excited and voluble seeing a hand made faded sign over a cottage door offering pint mugs of tea. Scott consulted his map and watch before assenting to this much welcomed refreshment, eagerly enjoyed by the parched chickens as they admired the 1861 Monsal Dale Viaduct. A fragment of conversation between two fellow onlookers was overheard -

"John Ruskin hated it! He said it destroyed the valley and ... 'now every fool in Buxton can be in Bakewell in half an hour and every fool in Bakewell can be in Buxton in half an hour.'"

Scott North was the only boy to have had experience of the dangerous and precipitous drop from the heights of Monsal Head down into the depths of Upperdale. Mindful that his was the only bicycle in optimum condition in contrast to the others, particularly the rickety Forrester machines; he realised this posed an extra risk in addition to the inevitable bravado of kids showing off. A narrow road with a hazardous bend to the left would cascade them, hell for leather, 300ft into the valley in less than a quarter of a mile. In the absence of any adult, this knowledge kindled a heavy responsibility on Scott's leadership and accordingly he warned them to -

" ... keep hold of brakes and go easy on the speed."

Even so, the daring Rex reached nearly 40mph in those pre-safety helmet days and it was only by the Grace of God that all the racers reached river level without serious injury. Speed gradually subsided at a stand of dense conifers. Simeon was fascinated by the effect of sun beams penetrating deep into the gloom of the forest, falling on, and illuminating thick, dark purple beds of needles.

A little past Upperdale they came to an area called Cressbrook Dale where Cressbrook stream meets the River Wye. A large textile mill, which had seen better days, dominated the area on the left and caught their interest. Pleasing Georgian symmetry was surmounted by a cupola and a handsome pediment housed a clock which appeared to have stopped many years before. This once prospering mill was owned by William Newton [1750-1830] the carpenter-poet known as the 'Minstrel of the Peak' who made sure his little apprentices had sufficient rest, good meals and pleasant working conditions in brutal contrast to the appalling conditions at Litton Mill just a mile upstream.

Scott looked for a footpath to the riverside, which, in spite of its apparent invisibility, he knew had to pass between the mill and a very steep, densely wooded hill to the north. Success! A narrow passage took them, as it seemed, into another world. Like entering the 'secret garden', they had been transported into a beautiful secluded deep valley, shut in by rocks and woods, the first of a chain of lovely limestone ravines.

Suddenly, here in Water-cum-Jolly Dale, it was cooler, more tranquil with a totally different atmosphere - save for a rush of water to their left which required investigation. Smooth, clear, polished water, slow at first, and then bending, dipping, just before getting cloudy and agitated as it tumbled over a rocky fall. For a few moments they were entertained by the occasional leaf which would accelerate and get pulverised in the turmoil below.

The waterfall formed a constriction which created a small lake bounded by overhanging, sheer limestone faces: faces which amplified and echoed the evocative euphony of various water birds calling and crying. Nobody spoke, but everybody knew that this was a place to savour, a place to walk rather than cycle. There was a shared feeling of safety in the comfortable seclusion of this 'Shangri-La'. In this deep ravine, a serene, silent world of enchantment, steep rocks painted with lichen

72

and moss gave a protective shield against modern noise.

Rocks and trees everywhere. They looked upwards following interesting craggy forms which became ruined castles - crooked medieval castles. But, unexpectedly, above the natural finials, arose out of the high foliage - an unmistakable man-made gothic structure, fashioned after the style of a fairy tale castle. This fantastic riot of sharp pitched roofs, steep gables, ornate tall chimneys and stone mullioned windows - broke the silence. They had discovered the home of Dracula! As if to confirm the fact, a solitary hawk was hovering high in the distant blue.

As they progressed, the lake became a river and the valley narrowed to become a gorge.

The warmth of the afternoon reacted with the cold of rocks, water and shade to created sudden gusts which stirred up willows. Zephyrs flashed the underside silver of leaves making a stark, bright effect, which travelled along the riverside, waving in waves and swathes, rippling, swaying, bowing and beckoning - before subsiding and returning the foliage back to green.

Ubiquitous ferns with their distinctive smell covered the banks, sometimes marestails pushed out of the mud and sometimes a delightful patch of forget-me-nots turned the riverside blue.

The water had mood changes. When it was slow it showed shimmering reflections of ash and sycamore. When it was deep they saw long, gently waving green weeds stretched out in the direction of the flow. Inches above, cute little black balls of fluff were going 'tweet tweet' and 'squeak squeak' racing along to keep up with mum. Just occasionally, the sun struck through this gorge of contrasts and shadow to glisten, sparkle and twinkle off the river surface - a surface often broken by the quick leap of a fish catching a hapless fly.

The valley seemed to get even deeper like a journey to the centre of the earth. The limestone had a multitude of tints from a flash of white to grey and occasional black. Above and beyond, right at the top, smooth, bright, green fields closely cropped by grazing sheep, were occasionally scarred by eruptions of ancient weather worn rocks.

Down below the boys were entering Miller's Dale and being entertained by sinister grotesque shapes of long dead trees, still

73

majestic in death as in life: living ivy feeding on the rotting wood. Here they scared each other with ugly goblins, old hags and monsters. Dense foliage formed mysterious tunnels and caves, darkened and obliterated with cascading ivy, lots of ivy, harbouring more unknown horrors.

Abruptly, the teasing ceased when they saw an odd looking boy illuminated by a shaft of sunlight.

Chapter 9

Fairies, Goblins and Sacred Groves

The boy spotlighted by sunshine was cutting shoots from a young tree with smooth, grey-brown bark and pale-green feathery leaves. He stopped ... and they stopped. Slightly built, certainly not as tall as Scott nor as well made as Rex, the stranger gave them a warm wide eyed smile. In so doing he appeared stranger than ever - especially at the utterance of a falsetto and comical - *"Allo!"*

Coquettishly, head tilted on one side, just for a moment, his eyes came to rest on each boy in turn - starting with Scott ... and ending with Scott. Processing fresh information at close quarters, it became clear from his confident demeanour that this boy was, in fact, a young looking man - and at 34, not so very young at that. He was something quite outside their usual Heanorian experience, indeed, he was the effeminate and bizarre type which would simply not be tolerated in Heanor. Scott was cautious, Rex was repelled, the twins were amused and Simeon ... well, Simeon was intrigued. Titch was curious and blurted out -

"Wot yer doin'?"

Attention was soon diverted from the appearance of this funny little oddity, to what it was, that he had to say. He launched into an explanation of the magical power of Rowan -

"Witches used it! Ya too late for the sweet smelling white blossom, an too early for the blood red berries ... "

He told stories of Rowan being tied to mine engines to guard against breakdowns. He widened his discourse to an overview of the romantic mysteries, lore and occult associations in the wilds of Derbyshire, giving examples which were not far away from where they stood.

They heard about the elusive fairies of Caldon Low, the cunning goblin called Hob who dwells in a round-barrow near Chatsworth, pagan deities, stone circles, sacred groves, human sacrifices, subterranean dwellings of elementals and flying saucers seen over Kinder Scout. They were told of a mermaid who swims at midnight on the eve of Easter Sunday, the bottomless pit of Eldon Hole, the Eagle Stone near Curbar which is said to turn as the cock crows ... These endless recitations were brought to an abrupt halt by a rude comment from Scott -

"My cock 'ill be crowin' next Satdy nate! We'll av ta get on."

Simeon was a little disappointed, he had enjoyed these curious and uncanny tales. At the same time his back had been comforted by that narrow shaft of warm sunshine striking into the cool gorge. The stranger asked if they had come near Stanton Moor and seized the opportunity to further delay their departure by telling them the erotic legend of nine young girls and just one boy who had angered God by committing an obscene act on the Sabbath day!

The storyteller, now having full attention, warmed to his subject of nine pretty maidens long ago, illicitly stealing off onto the moor with the naughty lad who was also a fiddler -

"Disgusting really! Per'aps you're too young to be ... "

It had the desired effect. Howls of protest urged him to continue with his implied pornographic narrative -

"Oo it were awful! 'E fiddled like mad. An them sluts - no shame! They danced an pranced in a circle, faster and faster, tearing off clothes ... it were rate rude, very rude! It were rude, lewd and nude. I'll tell thee! They went too far ..."

"Yes? What then?" said Rex.

"Oo a can't say. Too embarrassin'."

"No itina! Tell us," said Dobba.

"Go on. What 'appened?" said Danny.

"Well. Ad betta tell ya. It were like this ... ya can see fa ya self wot 'appened if ya go up there on Stanton Moor. They're still there, where they stood, in that circle, all that time ago. An that dirty bugger wit fiddle - im as well. They were petrified."

"A? Oo scared 'em?" said Brian.

"No, a don't mean that. The Lord was furious. 'E turned 'em to stone! An it's a stone circle today - the Nine - Ladies - Stone - Circle.

Not exactly the ending they were hoping for. With curt cheerios and a few see yas, the six departed.

Moving through Miller's Dale they came across another old mill - Litton Mill, which was observed with passing interest and a total lack of knowledge. In less than a decade, a future Mr Hogg, in an alien land, thousands of miles from Derbyshire would be horrifying his

76

students with historical accounts of dirty, unkempt, emaciated boys and girls, trapped, starved and suffering in this grey limestone prison set in such a beautiful ravine.

The pals were blissfully ignorant that more than a century and a half before, sadistic mill owner Ellis Needham took pleasure in seeing his brutal overseers punch, kick, beat and whip these poor wretches. Child-workers, younger than themselves, little better than slaves, started their toil at the demand of an unfeeling, clanging, factory bell in the grim darkness of five o'clock in the morning. In short breaks these ragged little children were fed a meal of rusty, half-putrid, fish-fed bacon and unpared turnips. Needham's pigs were better nourished and more kindly treated because those cruel days did not end for the small sad workers until eight in the evening.

It was six in the evening and miles short of their destination. They were late. Scott could see from his map that the ravine would meander on for more than a mile before they turned two hair-pin bends to scale the last steep, mile long ascent, up to Wormhill - a massive climb of 560ft out of the valley at the end of an already exhausting day. It had been difficult to move this motley group along. It seemed that every few yards some absorbing distraction would waylay one, or more boys bringing the convoy to a stop.

For example - after passing the textile factory, a row of tiny terraced cottages deserved attention and a large black tom cat tempted Dobba to bury his face in an enthusiastic cuddle: all five riders stopped to watch the cuddle. Further on, a sign pointed up a leafy lane to 'Ravenstore', once a large private house, now a Youth Hostel. Opposite, a foot bridge crossed the river - another opportunity to gaze into its crystal depths which, at this point, were brilliantly illuminated by a sunbeam: all six riders leaned over and were mesmerised by the spectacle.

Finally they came to the feet of massive stone legs supporting, far above them, an enormous viaduct which carried the 1861 Derby to Manchester Midland railway line: a relic and symbol of Victorian confidence. Here they turned right and immediately were forced to dismount in the face of a defeating, steep gradient on this last leg, the long and weary climb up to Wormhill where food and rest awaited them at the top.

It would have been a difficult and relatively dull trudge, especially after so much easy and attractive travel at river level, but for a recalled hilarious incident, the month before, which suddenly popped into Danny's head giving him an opportunity to do his 'Mrs Buxcey' - or 'Bookcey' as it was pronounced by the lower orders.

After nearly half a century of service, the small hard faced history mistress had become a legend at William Howitt Secondary Modern School. This squat disciplinarian demanded nothing less than the very best her pupils could deliver. With his carefully honed, gravely Buxcey voice, Danny, standing on pedals, creeping up the hill, re-enacted the event of biting but amusing sarcasm which they had already heard several times, but loved to hear over and over again.

She, of frosty features was watchfully policing a deep silence, save for the faint movement of pens. Suddenly, this industrious peace was broken by the voice of authority - *"Daniel Forrester!"*

All eyes turned to the innocent Danny, open, honest and unsuspecting, beavering away over his book. In anxiety, his youthful fresh face coloured and looked up for further instructions.

"Come out! Bring your book."

After the style of impending execution, up plodded Danny, reverently placing the book before the searching matriarchal square spectacles. What followed next took them all by surprise. Her hard voice softened to a faint shadow of a smile.

"It's nice writing isn't it?"

Instant relief showed on the pleasant round countenance of the unaffected, credulous Forrester, so typical of both twin brothers.

"Yes, it is very nice writing."

The naive lad could not believe his luck and risked a smile.

"You must be proud of this writing!"

Danny Forrester positively beamed and nodded in enthusiastic agreement - until, to his horror, the despotic dame had quickly resumed her more natural, tyrannical glare and gravely curdling threatening voice.

"It's a mess! **Disgraceful!** *Do it again!!"*

A punch line which never failed to cause an explosion of raucous laughter and egged Danny on to entertain them with further excerpts, such as the time in assembly she disrupted 'Onward Christian Soldiers' shrieking *'GET OUT!'* and escorted her victim to Miss McLenin's office.

78

It was the - *"And I am the one who should be annoyed - NOT you."* which would be remembered by Simeon Hogg when he heard himself using the same words 40 years later to reprimand a student and thought - *"Oh no! My God! I'm turning into Mrs Buxcey!"*

At long last the jokes became less funny and the steepness gradually became less steep. A profusion of vegetation, sweet scents and an opulence of colour lined the quiet road as they pressed through a cocktail of insects. A combination of movement and the playful slanting sun began to be entertaining as it moved behind the twigs and foliage making red and orange effects, sparkling diamonds, sparkling like brilliant fire.

Titch said -
"Look at that!"
Miles away, a few specks of beautiful bright golden light glittered and twinkled like jewels. It was the sinking sun smiling back at them, catching, reflecting on far distant isolated cottage windows somewhere on the heights of the north-east. Lowering their sights to the near distance, the Elizabethan stone gables and chimneys of Wormhill Hall could be seen in a valley to the right.

Chapter 10

Wormhill

Wormhill was a little known remote village in an upland hollow with no shops and no pubs. Apart from sighting Wormhill Hall, there was little evidence to indicate that they had actually arrived at their destination. Opposite a leafy lane stood an attractive old farmhouse with a crumpled, long, low roof of uneven stone flags. In a neat garden of sweet peas and climbing roses, a suspended cast-iron sign offered 'Accommodation'.

They were over an hour late. Danny's well polished repertoire of funny stories had got them up the hill in a fit of giggles, but now, at nearly 7.15pm, they were all too aware of fatigue, hunger and a nip in the air. Now there was fear of an unknown adult authority within, an authority not unlike Mrs Buxcey reminding them of their responsibilities: fear of a rollicking to the effect that they were late: fear of a heartless statement to the effect that dinner had come and gone and was now cleared away!

With some trepidation, Scott knocked at the front door ...

Their worst fears were realised. As expected, a sharp reprimand lashed out -

"And about time as well! Where the hell have you lot been?"

However, they took solace in the fact that these hard words came from a round smiling face of decidedly cheerful disposition. The upbeat speaker, a touch on the bonny side, ordered them into a cosy sitting room.

"Shift the cats," said she, and then bade them be seated on an assortment of shapeless but exceedingly comfortable sofas and armchairs. To Simeon's great delight, she insisted that they must be *'dying for a drink of tea'* and bustled out into a commodious kitchen where a kettle had been simmering on a huge Aga for the last hour. After a day's long exertions in the fresh air they were sinking ever deeper into the cuddling upholstery in that quiet cosy room, completely quiet, save for the measured tick of a long-case clock and the soothing crackle of a log fire, bright and cheerful in the darkness. For these boys at this moment - it was pure heaven.

With just a few moments of Yvonne Peirson's forceful, heartfelt and maternal welcome, all six were already under her spell and were very much at home. Yet this home, rustic as it was with bare stone walls, had a level of luxury to which none of these boys were accustomed. After a few minutes catching their breath, and obliging on laps the returning cats, they began to observe this very interesting new environment. The main room had low beams giving way to a staircase going up to roof level. Odd ornaments and unusual decoration made for an entertaining chaos. In half light, a suspended twig was decorated with white Christmas lights and a miscellany of beguiling antique objects - a descending parachute, an ascending balloon, a ladder with a little man climbing up it, an owl, a nest with robins, a warmly dressed bear on a swing and a Victorian new moon with an aquiline profile grinning at them. Near the fire place was an enormous old fashioned green chemist glass holding masses of dried flowers. Two old irons snugly held a row of books on a window ledge which also supported various photographs of pets, past and present, dogs and cats.

Suddenly a creaky door opened and, with the energy of a powerful coiled spring, two large dogs bounded into the room and attacked the resting guests with a massive welcome of enthusiastic friendliness. Several cats flew, but two stood their ground. A third dog of medium size sniffed, snuffled, nuzzled and cuddled all six in turn and all six were utterly delighted with this display of unconditional affection. To return the greeting, once again Simeon buried his face in a mass of jet black fur. Rex caressed a smiling yellow face and the others allowed themselves to be soundly licked in an ecstasy of fuss.

Behind this ebullient scene, by contrast, was Mrs Peirson carefully, very carefully, manoeuvring a heavy tray of steaming tea around the orgy of writhing canine bodies. This was placed on a large low table in the centre of the room -

"Let me introduce you ..." The big black Newfoundland was called Willow, the Golden Retriever was Rupert and the laughing, especially friendly Welsh Border Collie was called Brindley.

After a few minutes of sipping calming tea, tea which tasted of nectar, the dogs subsided onto the carpet and the room returned to something of its original sedate mood. Scott felt the need to apologise for their tardiness but his hostess was gracious -

"Don't worry. Dinner's doing slow and will be all the better

for it ... and, incidentally, it's 'Yvonne', never mind the Mrs. Oh - and this is Barry."

At the sound of the door, again, the dogs were stirred into a commotion and spirited welcome for their master who took a few seconds to huddle and snuggle his furry family - before beaming an equally warm reception to his young guests. There was no hint of speaking down to them whilst pleasantries were exchanged. He addressed them with courtesy and spoke to them as equals - which was unusual; a very pleasant and novel experience for these boys who, from a coal mining culture, were accustomed to a more plain speaking, gritty form of address from an adult.

The cats, all having different personalities, seemed quite indifferent to the introductions. The ginger Whiskey was nervous, the white Amos seemed proud and the black Henry, who had become fond of Rex's lap, appeared to be old and dozy. Tuesday, constantly entertaining Tom was playful and alert. Phoebe the tortoiseshell, who loved to be cuddled was ideally matched with Simeon. Diddle Do the wanderer, was absent, wandering. Amos, sitting bolt upright on the top of the sofa at the back of Brian, was glaring at Brindley. Mischievously, Barry drew attention to this impasse and whispered to the dog -
"Ooo that's a naughty pussy that is ... ooo ... "
Thus encouraged, a menacing Brindley approached a suddenly retreating, leaping Amos to the safety of a high sideboard.

These entertainments were followed by a firm suggestion from Yvonne that young gentlemen would, quite naturally, need to wash before dinner.

The feast which followed in the long dining room (which had its own roaring fire) would be remembered for the rest of their lives. Conveniently, a massive Jacobean table sat eight: two threes facing and one at each end for Barry and Yvonne to keep a close eye on the proceedings. Hot well seasoned soup was followed with a plate, best distinguished by a generous serving of slow, Aga cooked potatoes and parsnips, well baked to a delicious, crackled, crispiness. Congenial minutes passed to the happy sound of clinking knives and forks. Scott, Rex and Tom looked at Simeon and the twins through bunches of thick candles. Tall dancing flames burned brightly in antique pewter holders almost hidden by skilfully arranged fresh cut flowers: an effect enhanced in a room darkened by small windows and, now well after 8.00pm, failing daylight. After the sweet and now in mid-session of the cheese and biscuits, host and hostess encouraged their guests to speak about their long ride.

It seemed that the odd looking stranger who enthusiastically demonstrated expert knowledge about the legend and folklore of Derbyshire had made the biggest impression on them. He was identified at once by Barry -

"Simon Tonks! He's harmless enough. A sort of general man-servant to Dr Hardman at Cressbrook Hall. I'm surprised he didn't give you all a tarot card reading. He takes them everywhere in that old paper bag."

Back in the living-room they enjoyed delicious sweet coffee made with milk. After a full day of adventures, fresh air and exertions, a great tiredness overcame the cyclists. Little Titch fell asleep with his feet nicely comforted by the warm huge bulk of a snoring prostrate Willow. Past 9.00pm, Scott caught a view through the old window which showed a lingering essence of daylight mingled with the growing gloom of oncoming night. Glancing at Titch, he commented that it was a bit early for bed and a short walk might be beneficial after being so -

" .. plumped up with such good tuck".

"Take the dogs to the church. It's just over the road and a few minutes down the lane - do them good," said Barry.

Sensing that exciting plans were afoot, Brindley communicated his sudden enthusiasm to Rupert who, in turn, stirred up Willow who then stirred up Titch. Seconds later, three animals, animated and jumping for joy, emitting ecstatic doggy sounds - were impatient to drag six drowsy boys out of the depths of cosy upholstery.

The cool evening air, thick with scent, kick-started the usual chemistry of roguishness and inter-play between the pals. The twins ran in front and then ran back with faces contorted into sheer terror, screaming warnings that a horrible monster, lurking over the right-hand stone wall, in the field - was about to attack them!

In half light, it did indeed look like a horned dinosaur, a triceratops, glowering at them through the gloaming. This 'creature'

84

was no more harmful than a long, dead, fallen tree on the edge of a small, deep, 'V' shaped valley accommodating a stream which was pleasantly audible, if not visible.

The ubiquitous rough stone walls were overgrown with thick dark moss. Simeon was moved to gently run his hand over the deep lushness and sense its coolness. The wall on the left of the rough lane ran into an odd knot of meeting walls, for no apparent reason, forming small enclosures. An adult might have guessed and explained the function of a pinfold. In curiosity, Simeon pushed his nose over and caught the re-assuring distinctive whiff of rank hedge woundwort. He could also smell dead leaves and red dead-nettles - all part of a bonding process with all things Derbyshire which would follow and comfort him for the rest of his life.

Yonder, through deepening gloom, made gloomier by tall beech trees, they saw the gates of St Margaret's church yard. This launched a chorus of ghostly noises made in fun, but quickly quenched by Scott, who, recalling the words of Mr Matthewman, reminded his friends about due respect for the dead. Suitably censured, a silence descended on the group as they went through the side gate. An owl hooted! It came from a nearby dense copse of sycamore and ash, distinctive for mossy craggy trunks. Danny, a touch nervous, came up close to Simeon's ear -

"A don't know about this, Dobba. Wot d'ya reckon?"

These two boys had very different past experiences and reacted in a totally different way to the present situation. Apart from Simeon Hogg, all, in varying degrees, were slightly uncomfortable in this graveyard at this time in the evening having heard spooky stories and having seen the usual assortment of ghost films. Simeon, an unlettered boy of 15, was not able to give his pal an articulate answer beyond - *"S' OK, nowt ere ta ert ya."* His painful years at the rough, all boys Church of England Junior School, had taught him that it was the living to be feared - not the dead. On the contrary, he loved the profound peace at this quiet moment and hung back whilst the others, at Barry's suggestion, solemnly went inside the church.

Now alone, but for the dogs happily sniffing and exploring, Simeon respectfully negotiated old mossy tombstones, ferns, spent lilac, holly, elm and, with some difficulty, perused inscriptions - *'Augustus Adam*

85

Bradshaw MA. Died in 1883. In thy presence is the fullness of joy.'

At the edge of the graveyard he sat on a cushion of thick moss on a half-broken low wall, looked up and noted the unusual 'helmet steeple', a sort of tapered diamond, nicely finished with matching diamond slates. An odd profile, now framed by a few bright stars heralding the oncoming dark blue night. Barry had told them to look out for the home of a dog fox, a hole in the roots of an ancient yew tree near the door, but this was impossible as the dark brown of bark was now almost as black as the blackest hole.

He went over to a large imposing square tomb surmounted by a pyramid of heavy blocked stone decorated with rock weeds, small flowers, possibly purple - difficult to say. A time-worn legend under a proud coat of arms proclaimed this to be the last resting place of *John Needham of Hargate Hall*. Simeon reflected on the grandeur of this impressive monument and recalled a comment once made by his teacher Mrs Cook. She told them about a grief stricken Indian king who spent a fortune building the Taj Mahal as mausoleum for his wife, but ...

" ... it didn't bring her back."

On coming across another epitaph, his thoughts went to the strange little man who had intrigued them earlier down in the ravine -

'James Roger Ball of Wormhill Hall died in 1862. In memory of a faithful and valued servant.'

This darkening garden of funerary, beautiful, yet slowly decaying year on year, was engrossing its observer. He lingered over sunken graves, overgrown with a common sticky creeper, lots of young ash, enclosures of rusting Victorian ironwork, when -

"Come on, Dobba, we'd betta get back."

Approaching Wellhead Farm they heard a reassuring, and now familiar woman's voice musically calling out into the darkness -

"Diddle Do! Where are you?"

Simple words which had a profound effect upon the adolescent who would spend 40 years and a million miles away from that rustic, idealised English village and the high quality of life he had so briefly experienced and so longed to recapture.

Two bedrooms accommodated the six: three in one and three in the other. For Simeon and the twins, it was the back room which was long, narrow and barely large enough for three single beds. A cosy room with a white, low, sloping roof supported by black beams. Nobody challenged Dobba when he laid claim to the bed by the open window. He liked a warm body and a cold face as near to the outer elements as possible.

In the short space of time for undressing, washing and toilet trips, it was possible to take in the room's individuality. There were several old black and white photographs of jolly Manchester print workers: an original painting of a misty coastal fishing village on a wet mid-winter evening; grey cold of steep glistening cobbles contrasted to the warm yellow windows of snug cottages: a needlepoint Victorian sampler and an occasional plate.

Danny switched off the light and a distant hooting owl attracted no comment: all the teasing had gone out of Brian. He was tired, very tired. They were all very tired and, in the luxury of good firm beds and clean white sheets, they quickly descended into a deep sleep - the sleep of the gods.

Sometime later, much later, Simeon was awakened by bladder pressure. All the tea and milky coffee had finally taken its toll and called to the young man from that distant, cosy, mysterious other world of deep slumber. Unwillingly, slowly, he came to consciousness. He disentangled himself from the comfortable arms of Morpheus and in pitch darkness, fumbled and staggered out in search of the bathroom. Desperately trying to be as silent as that dark night, he navigated along an alarmingly creaky complication of steps up, steps down and acute confusing angles before, very gratefully, reaching his destination. Simeon stood before the bowl and breathed a long, deep sigh of blessed easement. He had never read a word of Shakespeare but at that moment could easily have quoted Francisco the Elsinor soldier -

"For this relief, much thanks."

The old house was still warm from the heat of the day. Unlike Francisco, Simeon, clad only in underpants was not cold. As he turned to retrace his steps - sudden alarm! His exit was blocked by a dark form who had stealthily crept out of the deeper shadows. Any fear which had initially gripped the startled lad was short lived, when, faint starlight silhouetted the familiar profile of a friend. In the few moments of tense silence which followed, eager eyes and mouth-watering lust scanned down an adolescent trunk to take in the exciting

view of an urgent and demanding manhood. Hardened by desire, the unsmiling, unfriendly face gave an unspoken command -
"Deal with it."

He did not know or appreciate it at that time, but Simeon would eventually look back over the years and view those early, delicious and relatively innocent teenage moments as - 'the Real Thing'. The Real Thing was true ecstasy in stark contrast to the more contrived and planned experiences of adulthood. Natural rough lads, rough hewn from a coal mining community were totally masculine, totally one hundred per cent butch - butch as the hard bricks which built Heanor. So very different to the many anonymous touches which would follow in later years. Touches becoming repellent when later identified as ministrations from the old, the soft, the slimy, the artificial, the affected, the effeminate, the sophisticated and the piss elegant.

America, more earthy, less inhibited, would be an improvement and, at its most abandoned, would eventually take Simeon to the heights of excitement with organised marathon maulings in public view but, even this, could not, would not, did not compete with those secret snatched moments of early teens and those forbidden fondles born of a playful grope. Quick opportunities of a stealthy touch arose out of a chance meeting of two boys in the changing room, the toilet or any quiet secluded corner of the school. Any shame was eclipsed by the physical excitement of hot blood and desperate need to reach a climax at the hand of another. Any concern was eclipsed by the unspoken assurance that any such illegal and immoral incident would never be mentioned or even whispered again.

Such moments of pure ecstasy would, like this precious incident, begin and end in silence. In silence the two boys returned to their beds never to speak of it again, and, once more, to sleep.

Some hours later it was a noise, a soft noise out of the silence of the night and very close. Simeon saw two eyes staring at him: eyes deep set into dark fur. To gauge the distance, a small head moved sideways before an athletic, liquid body, leaped from the half-open window onto the bed, skilfully and silently landing with no more impact than a gentle kiss. This was not the return of Diddle Do, this was Phoebe who had come to visit her friend. The drowsy welcome lasted for just a few strokes and a few contented purrs before both cat and boy were fast asleep.

Chapter 11

A Gallery of Light in Tideswell

It was a chorus of raucous competing cockerels which stirred Simeon back to consciousness on the morning of Sunday, July 24th 1960. He felt for the cat, but it had gone. Bracing fresh air drifted through the open window, beyond which, all was the sparkling brilliance of a fresh Derbyshire sunny morning. Dopey eyes gradually focused on a complicated walled back garden of many interesting levels and intriguing sundry items. The main feature was a trellis which supported honeysuckle and several bird-boxes. A collection of wooden seats were sheltered below. Up on the next level there was a pot cat, a pot frog and a pot snail reposing around a stone table in front of an assortment of shrubs, geraniums, wild pink roses and one real cat snoozing on a miniature garden set into an old fashioned stone sink. An iron pump from a past century was fixed on to an old water barrel: an oddity which shared a higher level with a wheelbarrow of summer flowers. Yellow poppies interspersed with several fascinating little fairy tale cottages were in the shade of giant mushrooms fashioned from Derbyshire gritstone. The top level was a small lawn dominated by a handsome 20ft Christmas tree.

Simeon dragged his head closer to the window for a better view beyond the garden. In the distance, dry-stone walls enclosed green fields: the familiar patch-work quilt of the White Peak. Beyond that, at the very limits of vision on this crystal clear morning, he made out tiny diamond sparkles of reflected sunlight from silent traffic, slowly moving, on the far A6 main road.

Many miles nearer, but several fields away, he discerned a solitary retreating figure squeezing through a stile and treading carefully over cow-pats. Even if the face were visible, no identification of sex or age would be possible at such a range - and yet, Simeon Hogg knew at once, the distinctive gait, bearing and carriage of his friend Brian Forrester. This meant that the slow, deep, and measured breathing in the nearby bed belonged to the other twin, Danny.

Challenging the scent of honeysuckle, from within, now came the stronger call and meandering whiff of delicious sizzling bacon, eggs, beans, mushrooms ...

89

An hour later that breakfast had been consumed and the six ran over the road to investigate a *'church for midgets'* discovered by Brian on his early explorations. This curious small gothic structure had a steep 'A' shaped roof, one door and no windows. It was sited on an incline, enclosed by a low capped wall and railings to the front. All was attractively set in front of a little garden of neatly cropped copper beech and junipers. Tongue in cheek, Titch suggested that Wormhill midgets must have dirty feet: a reference to the three water troughs which, inexplicably, barred the only entrance. For a few minutes they were all mesmerised by a ballet performed by long filaments of dark green moss, gently waving and billowing in the icy clear current.

Keen to solve the mystery, Danny went to the other side, found something and shouted -

"Ey oop! It's summat ta do wit dog. Brindley!"

Barry explained to them later that Brindley the dog was named after a famous 18th century canal builder who was born nearby. The man was not named after the dog. Throughout his teaching career, Mr Hogg enjoyed describing his meeting with the 'little church' which was actually a memorial drinking fountain to the illiterate James Brindley and went on to quote a higher authority, the historian Thomas Carlyle -

"He has chained seas together. His ships do visibly float over valleys, and invisibly through the hearts of mountains; the Mersey and the Thames, the Humber and the Severn, have shaken hands."

In spite of the early morning cool sharp wind, Rex decided to don his shorts and all followed his example. They were all standard navy blue shorts borrowed from school and most were ill fitting. Poor Tom, with shorts too long and baggy, ran the gauntlet of expected disparagement: *'room for two'.* Rex being thick and meaty filled his shorts out nicely and was very pleased with the revealing sexy effect. Whether by design or chance, Brian seemed to be wearing the same shorts as when he was eight years old and the outcome was only just decent. The rest were somewhat too large, but for Scott, who had clearly taken time and care with his well proportioned snappy choice.

After poring over the map and having taken Barry's advice, Scott decided that the day would be best served by not being too ambitious with regard to distance. He had to shepherd his small flock back home before dark, because Scott's cycle was the only one with working lights.

90

The eager suggestion by Brian and Rex to visit and explore the bottomless Eldon Hole, only four miles to the north (but four very hard miles) was simply not viable, not to mention dangerous! For a compromise they would visit Tideswell and have the luxury of time to explore and enjoy a leisurely return along the same interesting dales as on the previous day.

At long last the front garden was an excited hum of boys making last minute adjustments to saddle bags, bidding goodbye to fussing dogs and conscientious hosts. Yvonne gave them all a piece of fruit and stressed care and safety for the journey back home. In his Heanorian manner, Scott sincerely thanked his hosts for their generous hospitality -
*"... it's bin marvellous, a real treat ... **antit!**"*
The others took the strong hint, remembered 'their manners' and a cascade of ebullient appreciation gushed from his followers.

   Yvonne and Barry Peirson waved and waved until the cyclists were out of sight.

Many times Simeon had thought back to that beautiful morning and could sincerely say that he had no trace, no omen, no premonition of any imminent evil. On the contrary, there was a delicious joy of freedom. He rode near to the road-side and allowed his bare leg to be gently slapped by the passing cool weeds. He was simply carefree.

   It is so easy to look back and make something out of nothing - like the sudden fright on top of the hill which made him stop. To his left, a violent flapping on a fence! Something black and ugly like an old hag. At first he thought it was a distressed crow, but it was just a piece of flapping black plastic, trapped on a post, ravaged and torn by the bleak high winds of winter.

A few minutes were given for an inspection of Hargatewall, a small interesting community or hamlet, as the name suggests, enclosed by a high wall. At this summit the sky was massive and the world laid before them in an impressive panorama.

   There was a subtle change in the weather. The clear blue sky of the day before was now blighted by distant gigantic cumulus clouds, piled up into the stratosphere above a dark ominous base. These mountains of clouds were noted, but were a very long way off in the east and not perceived as a threat to the cyclists who were still soaking up the warm unbroken sunshine.

A tiny road took them quickly, sharp down, into the rocky gorge of Monk's Dale: worth seeing, but a lot of hard, slow work was required to get them out again. On entering the small town of Tideswell, Simeon's first thought was **not** to rush and experience the beautiful *'Gallery of Light'* in the 'Cathedral of the Peak' as recommended by Barry: Simeon's first thought was to find the nearest tea shop. He had gratefully accepted a second pot at breakfast and would have dared to ask for a third had time permitted.

A neat group of outdoor rustic tables tempted the pals to indulge Dobba's craving for the big steaming tea pot hanging outside of 'John and Val's Tea Stop'. It was too early for lunch but a long way before Bakewell, so a toasted teacake seemed an ideal solution at that little collection of outdoor tables viewing the pinnacles, turrets and slender spires of Tideswell Church. They might well have given the stately edifice a miss, but for Barry's enthusiastic description of -

" ... *lovely windows ... unusual 14th century clerestory ... mellowed charm of lofty arcades ... glorious chancel ...* "

Many of these terms were unfamiliar but, not withstanding, sounded very impressive and, when eventually seen in the peaceful interior, were unconsciously appreciated by a form of adolescent osmosis. To illustrate the grand scale, Barry also told them that if they traced a finger around every nook and cranny along the inside wall, that finger would have travelled exactly one mile! It was the thought of miles ahead which prompted Scott to marshal his men up the steep narrow lane which ascended south-east to the village of Litton, yet another 100ft above the height of Tideswell's already substantial 900ft above sea level.

Once again at the top of the world, Simeon noted the massive cloud formations, now closer, billowing from the east. He thought he heard distant thunder. One cumulus pile took the shape of a giant hideous foetus which had come face to face with an ogre. A minute later the foetus had changed into a toothless old crone and the ogre had begun to smile.

Was that the inscrutable omen which foretold the disaster, now just minutes away?

Chapter 12

Hell for Leather

Puffing and panting, the six eventually reached Litton, a neat, level limestone village made spacious by several pleasant greens. A quick check of the map and they took another narrow, flat, well-metalled road to the south. Scott gave the usual alert of a sudden, dangerous, steep decent which would catapult them, hell for leather, down into Cressbrook Dale -

"Go steady and keep left, it's not a race!"

At high speeds, expecting some separation, he suggested they meet at the waterfall in Water-cum-Jolly Dale. The navigator could see from the map that there were two possible ways to descend the 550 feet drop down to the River Wye. Keeping left into the densely wooded valley of Cressbrook Dale doubled the distance, but lessened the steep incline. Scott warned them to look out for a precarious 'Devil's Elbow' bend which would abruptly change their direction from north to south. The alternative shorter, more precipitous route, would risk hazardous breakneck speeds.

The wide-open world of dazzling white stone-walled fields and singing skylarks changed to the relative twilight of leaf and shade when the road began to fall and accelerate the cyclists. Simeon Hogg was determined to be careful because Tom had confided that he had been very shaken the previous day when coming down from Monsal Head. His brakes were *"dodgy"* and he very nearly *".. came a right cropper!"*

Touched by this small act of trust and friendship, Simeon suggested that they keep an eye on each other and simply enjoy gravity's free ride, at a leisurely pace, at the back.

After a few whoops and guffaws, they heard the distinctive coarse singing voice of Rex, flying down the hill, yelling out an increasingly distant, diminishing, rendering of the popular Italian 'Funiculi - Fanicula' - the obscene version much beloved by Heanorian youth -

"Last night, I 'ad the urge for masturbation - oh wasn't it grand, there in me 'and.

Tonight, I will repeat the operation - oh won't it be good, pullin' me pud. Wankin' wankin' wankin' all the way .... "

They were soon out of sight and far, far away.

Three boys were on the road at the foot of the hill, looking up the hill with anticipation. As ever, Scott looked impressive, bronzed and golden in the illuminating sun. Rex, much darker, was still astride his bike, one foot to the ground and one on the pedal showing well proportioned, thick, powerful legs. By contrast Danny looked thin, pale and was now concerned - *"Where's our Brian?"*

It was at that moment that so much changed. The sun did not go in. In fact it was not until late afternoon when the big clouds finally cast their cool shadows. The change was more connected with a failure, a break-down of a cheery relaxed chemistry between pals - or so it seemed to the adult Simeon Hogg looking back over 43 years.

They waited. They waited five minutes. After ten silent minutes, four anxious faces looked to Scott. He made a decision. They were 99% sure that Brian had not beaten them down to the bottom - even if he had taken the steeper, shorter road. Even so, Danny was told to check the waterfall at Water-cum-Jolly Dale. Titch and Dobba were ordered to stay put - and guard the road in case Brian should come down the hill or stagger out of the woods. Rex and Scott would climb the hill. Scott said he would search the short route where Brian was most likely to be found, possibly fallen and injured. Rex was asked to re-trace the path of his ride and urged to check for any signs of a skid on the road. To diffuse the tension, Scott tried to sound optimistic and joked -
> *"Silly bugga's wrapped 'im sen round a tree a summat."*
> *"'E'll wrap 'im sen round me fist! Mekin me struggle oop this bloody 'ill agen!"* - replied Rex as, slowly, very slowly, they both
started to pump up the gradient.
> Simeon was comforted by this threat. If Brian Forrester could be hit it meant he could be found.

Twenty minutes later, at the top, Rex had completed his fruitless search which had covered nearly a mile. A uneasy looking Scott was already there and acknowledged the arrival of his friend by a depressing slow shake of the head. One possible stone had been left unturned. Half way up the steep shorter road, Scott had noticed a solitary house. Still watchful for any signs of an accident, both lads free-wheeled down to a solid Victorian lodge at the entrance to a prosperous looking driveway

94

guarded by large ornate wrought iron gates and two stone creatures on posts, unrecognisable after more than a century of erosion.

Perhaps it was the complete silence and apparent emptiness of this residence which made them aware, for the first time, that they were the sole players in this current drama. Since Tideswell they had seen nobody at all - not even in Litton which seemed completely deserted. It was half past one, pleasantly warm, a time when the birds stop singing and the countryside takes a nap. Even before Scott (somewhat reluctantly) crashed the heavy iron knocker onto the substantial front door, they were almost certain no answer would come: nor was there a sign of curtain movement through small windows which were almost opaque.

This was a low point. Two boys had assumed a heavy responsibility. Two boys were suddenly growing up very fast.

Rex recalled his scant knowledge of Stainsby Lodge and Smalley Lodge: in each case, a house which guarded a great house further down a grand drive. He reasoned that help (or even Brian) may be at the end of that rather forbidding private road. To the troubled investigators, it seemed a long winding way between yews and junipers but, eventually, they beheld the grey mock-medieval front of Cressbrook Hall. It took a few seconds to realise that these impressive steep pitched roofs, towers, lofty pinnacles and finials, proud ornate chimneys and oriel windows were the very same which had been observed and admired the day before looking up from Water-cum-Jolly Dale.

Certain that there must be life somewhere, this time Rex took the lead. Boldly, he strode forward to the massive door and gave a firm pull at a brass lever to the side which, in turn, tinkled a distant bell from within. Following a short eternity, the heavy door slowly opened.

From the experience of various films they expected an immaculately dressed, aloof, superior and possibly spooky butler to appear before them, carefully enunciating a condescending enquiry in the Queen's English. The reality could not have been more different - but for the word 'queen'.

The sight of the amusing small fellow posing and twisting before them was more consistent with a comedy rather than a horror film. Yet again, Rex was repulsed by the large flirtatious dancing eyes and slender form which had entertained them the day before in the ravine. Here was Simon Tonks, no less, the 'butler' of Cressbrook Hall, surprised, but clearly very pleased to see them. Once again they were treated to an enthusiastic greeting, way up high in the upper register -

"*Allo agen!*"

Under pressure of emergency, Scott was irritated to be a part of this inappropriate fiasco and quickly explained the problem. Simon put a finger to his lips and tilted his cartoon-like head in an effort of thought.

"*Is not 'ere!*"

"*Are ya sure?*" insisted Scott. "*There's no where else 'e can be! Ave ya looked?*"

Following a moment's hesitation he said -

"*Joost a minute,*" and disappeared inside.

That minute, through the open door, enabled them to see a gloomy grand entrance hall, a wealth of rich dark panelling embellished by wooden Ionic pillars and pilasters leading to a splendid wide staircase. A faint whiff of potpourri and furniture polish drifted over as the servant returned, his pleasant face slightly marred by a mixture of sad tidings, concern and uncertainty.

"*Am ever so sorry. Is joost not 'ere. Dr 'Ardman said ta say - an wants ya ta go.*"

For a moment the boys stood their ground feeling that having alerted a responsible adult, more could, indeed should, have been done in these serious circumstances. Answering their thoughts written in pained expressions, Simon said -

"*Ya see, it's like this ... Dr 'Ardman an Mester Charles, well, ya see ... thee oopset, thee 'ad a .. bee-reeve-ment. Am sorry ... *"

At this point Scott and Rex turned away and left.

Chapter 13

The Servant at Cressbrook Hall

Gathering up his remaining men, Scott became decisive and announced
that, to get help, they would go back to Wellhead Farm which was not
too far away via Water-cum-Jolly Dale and Miller's Dale. Nearly two
hours later, Yvonne and Barry had heard the full story and telephoned
Cressbrook Hall in the hope that Brian may yet have turned up. Doctor
Algernon Hardman was known to them slightly by reputation only, but
those few aloof and unhelpful words spoken down the wire confirmed a
man who came over as cold, haughty and detached -
    "Hardman by name and Hardman by nature!" said Barry,
irritated by the inappropriate acetous tone in the face of a crisis.
    "He practically hung up on me!"

Barry had hoped that Simon Tonks would have been dispatched to
check on The Lodge inhabited by a gardener. Barry had hoped that Dr
Hardman would have welcomed the suggestion that he, Yvonne and the
boys, come over at once, and start an immediate detailed search of the
area.
    At the best of times Algernon Hardman, ever restrained and
forbidding, was a very private man who guarded his privacy well - but
this was the worst of times, as the Peirsons learned later that evening
from the police. They were told that Dr Hardman had arrived home,
early, from a motoring holiday in Albania: a holiday tragically cut short
due to a car crash which killed his wife.

Cressbrook Hall, was built on a spectacular hillside location in 1835 by
a wealthy cotton mill owner. In 1888, Isaiah Hardman, another textile
industrialist from Manchester bought the house and a full complement
of servants: scullery-maid, cook, housemaid, parlour-maid, coachman,
four gardeners and a footman - all under the firm authority of a stern
butler. The Victorian Age melted into the Edwardian Age, two world
wars and the economic upheavals of the 20th century took their toll on
the once considerable Hardman fortune. When Isaiah died in 1944 the
house with a reduced income and staff passed to his only son Algernon
who was by disposition an academic, not a businessman. He graduated
from Oxford with a Ph.D. in languages. Under pressure from financial
advisors he sold his shares in the family business in exchange for a

97

relatively modest private income. In 1945 Algernon married and they had a son in 1947, the same year in which the old Mrs Hardman died. From a staff of eleven only ten years before, the three young inhabitants of Cressbrook Hall were now cared for by just two servants: an elderly gardener and an elderly housekeeper. Well into her 70's, Miss Banks the housekeeper, was not so much retired in 1952, it was more that she fell down on the job - literally. This, at a time, when servants were desperately scarce. To meet the needs of the emergency, through a friend in Belper, she happened to know of a good and reliable lad who, having recently lost his place, could immediately step into the breach.

To be fair, Miss Banks warned Dr Algernon Hardman that Simon Tonks had a dubious moral reputation. Notwithstanding, for three years he had served the redoubtable Calder sisters well at Bridge House School in Belper, until the younger Madge died and the elder Florence retired to a small town house. Miss Calder had written Simon an excellent reference - *"To Whom it may concern ..."* It stressed loyalty, honesty and diligence but darkly touched on *"...his quirky wayward nature"* and the need for *"... a firm hand and strong Christian discipline."*

When pressed by Dr Hardman to explain what all that meant, Miss Banks (a very respectable lady) bridled slightly and became distinctly uncomfortable -

"Well, as you know, sir, I'm not one to gossip but it's common knowledge in Belper that Simon has dealings with the dead: seances and all that sort of stuff. An upright gentleman such as your good-self, sir, may be able to stomach those goings on but ... well ... everybody knows about all the times that Mrs Tonks had to drag Simon out of that smelly old cast-iron urinal at Bridgefoot ... How that poor woman could still hold up her head walking in King Street, sir, I'll never know!"

In truth, Dr Hardman had little choice: it was either Simon Tonks or nothing and Dr Hardman decided to risk Simon Tonks.

On the whole it worked very well. The new man proved to be reasonably proficient and was certainly very hard working in all his duties. His greatest value proved to be the laughter and sunshine he brought into an otherwise sombre atmosphere created by the ever studious, dour and introspective Algernon Hardman. Mrs Marjorie Hardman and especially the young toddler Charles, both loved their

98

new funny little servant. In view of this positive gain, the owner of Cressbrook Hall decided to turn a blind eye to most of the unsavoury accounts which occasionally reached his ears - third or fourth hand. Of course the 'Buxton incident' of 1953 could **not** be ignored and a firm reprimand had to be delivered in the erudite, book-lined, Hardman study. It was never entirely satisfactorily explained, but the employer gathered that some sort of territorial dispute was the cause.

A furious old tramp abruptly and violently ejected Simon from a public lavatory! An undignified scene in the middle of that sedate Georgian town saw an embarrassed Simon, hopping around on a busy pavement, trying to pull up his trousers in front of bemused shoppers. At the same time the hapless little man was suffering loud abuse from an irate, dirty old man brandishing his fist.

" *... and dunna come back, ya dotty little bugga. Yol get this down ya gob! Ave sat in there fat last forty year. Find ya own bloody cottage ya slut!* "

A few weeks later, Dr Hardman was roused in the middle of the night by an urgent bell. He opened the front door to see two, serious looking, large, burly police officers standing either side a cringing, shame-faced Simon - wrapped in nothing but a blanket!

"What now?" he said in angry exasperation. The naughty servant had been discovered at three in the morning, naked, trussed up like a chicken and suspended under the hornbeam tree at the Bath Gardens in the middle of Bakewell. A carbon copy of an incident in Belper, some years earlier, when he was found by a horrified, devoutly Anglican Miss Florence Calder. The constable reported that several youths were running from the scene when he arrived to find 'the subject' swinging like a pendulum.

Simon Tonks was well known to the police: indeed, over the years in Derbyshire, Simon Tonks had become a legendary figure. On several occasions he had been removed from various 'public places', detained and cautioned, but never charged due to his ability to entertain, amuse and charm the officers at the station. The Derby Police would fall about laughing, recycling stories of his antics - such as the time he was found with two men crowded into a single WC cubicle.

He claimed to be in the middle of a seance with the object of contacting the ghost of 'Edna', a character from the 1920's who, according to popular belief, haunted the Corporation Hotel and its backyard lavatory which was opposite the Cattle Market. The Duty Sergeant had heard of the necessity to hold **hands** at a seance - but ...

"Arr well, ya see, officer, it's like this, ya need t' proper atmosphere ta com-moon-icate we Edna. She died of 'cottage croup' ya know. Oh yes! In that very bog - on that very spot! She were a persistent bitch. Stood hours an hours in t' freezing cold."

"What did she tell you?" asked the arresting officer.

"Well ya see it's like this, she can't rest, poor owd sod. No, 'er spirit can't rest until she finds 'er teeth. She was always loosing 'er teeth. She'd put em down somewhere in 't bog (well lets face it she was a busy owd cow) an then, after dootys performed, many a time, couldn't remember were she'd put 'er teeth. She told me all about it - groping around in t' dark - 'Where's me teeth?' Poor owd Edna! Ya moant get t' wrong idea a wot we were doin'."

But the Duty Sergeant thought that, in fact, he **did** have the right idea - the right idea - exactly.

The police station at Chesterfield once rocked with laughter when a bedraggled Simon had been removed from a public toilet having been in there for five hours!

"Bad case of diarrhoea?" suggested an officer.

That was the day Simon learned to avoid road-works and observant road workers. The real difficulty occurred when he was asked to explain the contents of his battered old bag. The tarot cards spoke for themselves but what of the chamois leather? His explanation -

"Me chammy's fa me face." failed to convince the sarcastic sergeant who suggested that puddles of water on the floor had an inconvenient tendency to reflect activities within the cubicle. On the same theme, he held up a good sized folded bag, found inside the main bag -

"Going shopping, Simon? A bit dirty inside isn't it? Looks like somebody's been standing in it: perhaps several people!"

Certain innocent items such as several past soggy copies of The Beano and The Dandy passed without comment, but the small mirror and rusty old tin of Vaseline were viewed with great suspicion.

In the end it always came down to the same thing: half smiling, half exasperated police officers shaking their heads in front of a half wide-eyed smiling, half teasing little Simon Tonks: head cocked on one side, then the other - in that maddening, philandering, irritating, teasing manner!

Dr Algernon Hardman patiently bore all these painful revelations with Christian fortitude, but often came close to ejecting Simon from Cressbrook Hall as speedily as he had been ejected from the Buxton public toilet.

However, the fact remained that this employee was well liked by everybody and, most important, positively adored by his constantly entertained wife and little son. The work of Simon Tonks could not be faulted. Cressbrook Hall was always clean and brightly polished. In the winter months, fires were laid and lit early, every morning. Every morning without fail, on time, a tray of tea was served at the bedside of the family members. Breakfast, lunch, afternoon tea and dinner was prepared to a high standard and always served punctually in accordance with the instructions of the watchful and autocratic Dr Algernon Hardman.

From 1952 to the end of the 20th century and beyond, Simon Tonks conscientiously performed all the duties which had been the responsibility of seven servants before the war - and he performed those duties exceedingly well. Roughly spoken, lowly, common, ill educated, foolish and over sexed on his days off - he may have been, but, Dr Hardman took the view that his private time and chosen 'recreations' were always carried out well away from Cressbrook Hall and his family.

Simon Tonks was worth his weight in
gold and Algernon Hardman knew it.

Chapter 14

"He Comes not Still, 'tis Dark no Moon"

After the unhelpful response from Cressbrook Hall, Barry Peirson decided that the situation was now serious enough to telephone a friend in the police force. Detective Inspector Derek Russell patiently listened to the full story and acted immediately. He sent a small team to search the area around Cressbrook Hall and drove to Wormhill to interview the boys. It was just short of 5.00pm when he and Detective Sergeant John Winter sat in the living room of Wellhead Farm facing five sad looking youths. Even the dogs were doleful having absorbed something of the melancholic atmosphere.

Apart from having mislaid a friend, they were worried about the problem of getting home before dark since they had no means to pay for a further night. These considerations weighed most heavily on Simeon Hogg. Mindful that he was 'up' before two senior police officers, it would only be a matter of time before the lights on his bicycle may be checked and found wanting - that is, wanting new batteries. In such circumstances, he was disposed to take 'the bull by the horns' and blurted out their difficulties before the official interrogation began. Derek Russell (a father of two boys himself) soon took the measure of his interviewees, decided they were 'nice lads' and put them at ease.

"Don't worry about lights and money. We know all about that plus the fact that you've not eaten since lunch time at Tideswell. Yvonne is cooking all of us a meal and, when we've had our chat, you lot, bikes and all, will be safely delivered back to your homes well before dark in a police van."

At this point Scott, Simeon and Danny were asked to stay with the Detective Inspector. Tom and Rex were taken into the dining room with the Detective Sergeant.

"Nothing sinister!" said the senior man. *"We just need to get all the facts straight and make sure they agree. That's the way we solve serious problems."*

Every detail was wheedled out. Winter noted that Brian Forrester had 'wandered off' before breakfast. Was he a wanderer by nature? Russell

103

noted that the absentee had expressed a desire to explore Eldon Hole. Would he be there? It must be searched. Brian was given to jokes and teasing which in turn gave hope that he might have gone off somewhere, got lost and would eventually turn up.

Little useful information came to light about the fast descent down the steep hill. Scott and Rex were hurtling ahead through the crashing wind in maximum concentration, hardly aware of each other let alone the others. At the hair-pin bend, Rex recalled going slow enough to catch sight of Danny, behind him, heading *'too fast'* into the corner. It seemed highly probable that Brian had taken the wrong, precipitous and dangerous right fork when he had fallen behind Danny: at great speed, an easy mistake to make. At a more leisurely pace, Tom and Simeon saw only themselves.

Not only a boy but a bicycle had strayed, which, unfortunately, could not be described. Not one of the cyclists could describe the colour or make of Brian Forrester's bicycle. As a test they were asked to describe details of their own bikes safely deposited in the Peirsons' garage. The results were not encouraging. Simeon knew that (under the dirt) his was a red Triumph Palm Beach, three speed Sturmey-Archer. None of them could give a single fact about the machines of any of their pals with the notable exception of Scott's, dropped handlebars, splendid BSA Golden Wings, ten speed derailleur gears. The policemen gathered that half the pupils of William Howitt Secondary Modern School could probably give an enthusiastic account of that gleaming blue and silver racer. With the exception of the BSA, the other cycles were all second, third or fourth hand, dark and very dirty.

It was during dinner when Danny, now more relaxed at the conclusion of the 'official inquiry', thought that Brian's bike was a deep maroon colour. Better still, he spoke of a recent 'transfer' which Brian had recently applied to his cross-bar. A transfer was a design or picture made to be moistened and pressed off onto another surface - very popular with boys in the 1950's.

"It were a mounted knight in armour, we a lance an shield, we a red cross on. Just a little n, but a think it said 'Champion' oonderneath."

"Well done! That's what we need - detail," said Derek, but did not mention his fear that Sir Knight could easily be removed.

Later that evening at the humble Forrester home, alarm was tempered by hope: hope that *'silly bugger'* Brian would soon be bicycling back into Heanor. His parents put on a brave face and hid deep concern. They took comfort from the negative result of the initial police search in the Cressbrook area and reassured themselves that Brian would be, somewhere, mounted and moving.

"Once 'e finds a main road we signs, 'e'll be back wantin' 'is tea. 'E'll turn up, you see," said Mr Forrester optimistically.

Detective Inspector Russell explained that taking a copy of their son's fingerprints from personal objects was *'merely routine'*, as was the loan of the best recent photograph - and a poor best at that. Had Brian been on the school football team, like his more sporty brother; a professional clear image would have been available such as the photograph proudly displayed on the sideboard. The fuzzy, badly focused picture of a skinny little youth sticking his tongue out at Uncle Jack (who took the 'snap' on his Brownie 127) was far from satisfactory. This was a tiny black and white print of the family group on a day trip to Mablethorpe in 1957. Brian, an already young looking 15 year old, was no more than a child in this dated picture.

Twelve hours later at 10.00am on Monday, July 25th, Brian Forrester had still not 'turned up'. Russell and Winter were coasting down the winding drive leading to Cressbrook Hall. The car pulled to a stop at a point which gave on to an overall view of the Hardman mansion through the beech trees.

"I'm not at all happy with the thoroughness of yesterdays operation. Parker said he had only seven men and they were beaten by bad light. He's back this morning with three more to give it the full day. They'll have a good look along Water-cum-Jolly Dale as well as up in the Cressbrook hills," said the senior man. *"Any ideas, John?"*

"I was thinking about that old bloke last year, sir. Do you remember? His wife died and ten minutes later his little granddaughter complained that 'Granddad's been rude'."

"Repressed behaviour triggered by grief? It's possible. Is that the path of your mind - has Algernon Hardman been 'rude' with our missing Brian?"

"Hardman sees Brian staggering past the french windows dazed and injured, offers help, takes advantage and tries it on. Brian's not having any, threatens him with The Law, so, Hardman shuts his

mouth - permanently."

"Very neat, John!" The Detective Inspector thoughtfully added, *"All the same, indecent assault is regarded a black sin - punished savagely. Not only do we send them down for a good few years, but turn a blind eye when certain other prisoners, sadistic thugs, give 'em the works. Hardman is an intelligent man. He's well informed. He knows all about that sort of thing. It might be as you say."*

"We just need a body, sir!"

"Not as bad as that - yet - I hope. Those lads have made it all so water-tight. Our lost lad never reached the bottom of the hill, three good witnesses all say so. Two equally reliable boys say he was in front of them. The only inhabited buildings in between are Cressbrook Hall and The Lodge. There were only three people in between: Hardman, his son and his manservant. The gardener at The Lodge claims he was out in his motorcar."

"Lost Lad," mused Detective Sergeant John Winter. *"It seems familiar! Isn't there a place somewhere up here called Lost Lad?"*

"You're thinking of the legend about the boy who went on to the top of Bleaklow Moor one winter. There was deep snow, but he had to get the sheep down. It must be ... oh, about a dozen miles north of here: a vast moorland. The weather changed and fresh heavy snowfall covered all the familiar landmarks. There was yet more snow which obliterated everything; a blizzard - high winds and drifting."

Derek stared out over the endless expanse of the high hills above the chimneys of Cressbrook Hall. Hilltops which would have been painted white just three months before. He shook his head -

"Poor sod was cold, exhausted and disorientated. He and the dog took shelter underneath a rock near Black Tor. He drifted into a frozen sleep - the big sleep, the long sleep. My old teacher, Miss Calder taught us a heartbreaking poem about his mother waiting anxiously down in the old village of Derwent."

"Is that the drowned village now at the bottom of Ladybower Reservoir?"

"That's right. It went something like -
'He comes not still!' she said, 'tis dark, no moon!
Oh! woe betide me, if he comes not soon.'

106

Can't remember anymore. Three months later, in early spring ... they found his remains. He'd scratched the words 'Lost Lad' on to a rock. In reverence, it's an established tradition that every shepherd who passes that tragic place puts a stone on the site. There's a large cairn there now."

Clearly effected by emotion, Derek Russell, took a deep breath, rolled down the window and sat more upright in his seat. He turned to face his junior officer and forced a smile -

"It's all in John Merrill's book, 'Legends of Derbyshire'."

Chapter 15

Acetous, Aloof, Cold and Haughty

At the conclusion of this conference, an officer approached the car and handed Detective Inspector Derek Russell a typewritten note. After a brief perusal he said -

"Well that seems to be OK. Albanian authorities confirm two fatalities in a head-on collision last Saturday. Nasty. Two 'right-offs'. I expect Hardman and his son are pretty well shook up."

"How did he get back so quick?"

"Chartered a plane," he looked down to study the print.

" .. and came from Manchester by taxi ... which delivered him here yesterday at about noon. The driver seems to be fairly confident about the time."

"It'll be interesting to see if he claims he didn't arrive home until after ... What time did our boy disappear?"

"As near as we can get it - 12.45 - give or take half an hour." He added with an engaging grin -

"Anyway, John, you're in for a big surprise!"

The car completed the short distance down the drive up to the front door. Derek enjoyed his mischievous reward when the front door opened to reveal an odd little fellow, head on one side, wearing an inquisitive enigmatic smile and whose legs somehow appeared to perform a half pirouette during the opening process. Detective Sergeant John Winter had exactly the same experience some eleven years earlier when he met Simon Tonks for the first time. On that occasion he was opening the front door of Bridge House School in Belper.

The two policemen had worked together, and nicely complemented each other for over twelve years. With his good looks and natural easy charm, Detective Inspector Derek Russell approached his work with a degree of gentle sophistication and measured compassion. In contrast Detective Sergeant John Winter, slightly inclined to plumpness, not quite so cordial, polite or patient, was more typical of the officious type of police officer. Since Simon Tonks had attracted considerable comment and no small amount of mirth back in 1949, his sudden re-appearance up here in the High Peak precipitated a shriek of laughter which delighted the servant. For a few moments formalities were put aside to exchange reminiscences of the Calder sisters and general pleasantries which created an agreeable chemistry. Simon had that rare beguiling quality which made him everybody's friend - even a friend to the police engaged on a serious investigation.

They were led through a Tudor arch into a substantial and comfortable oak-panelled morning room which, in fact, was the grand and resplendent study of the Master of Cressbrook Hall -
    "Dr 'ardman 'll be with ya presently," said Simon with a little camp bow before he gave a quick twirl and minced off to attend to his duties.
    Derek gravitated to a large mullioned leaded window framed by Virginia creeper. His eye was gladdened by a profusion, a multiplicity of bright colours which smiled back from interesting, geometric flower beds. These attractive formal gardens extended across neat lawns up to a stone balustrade which overlooked the sudden, steep, densely wooded descent down into the Water-cum-Jolly Dale ravine. To each side he noted mature ornamental trees. Looking above, again, he saw the endless vista of green and white, dappled and darkened with the occasional slow moving cloud. Except for the welcome bird-song there was a profound peaceful silence.
    Derek Russell pondered the rich quality of life available to one who has never had to work for a living and has the means to live in such a beautiful house in such a magnificent location. He was not by inclination envious, yet, here and now, he did envy Algernon Hardman. Being reasonably content with a fulfilling career, enjoying a modest level of status in the community, Derek had never been particularly ambitious, but he did occasionally daydream of what 'might have been' if wealthy parents had made it possible for him to try his hand at risky ventures, such as acting or writing. Algernon Hardman could have done almost anything, but was satisfied to be reclusive, bookish, studying languages, foreign cultures and travelling abroad.
    John Winter was sharing similar thoughts perusing a shelf of antiquarian calf-bound volumes. Oak beams and a 16th century style stone fireplace gave the feeling of a much older house. There was porcelain, a china cabinet, some good paintings and a few family portraits looked down on a massive Victorian desk which dominated the room. John was leaning over this expansive piece of furniture to inspect more closely a large Oriental vase of fresh cut flowers when,

110

suddenly, a dark forbidding figure appeared in the doorway.

It should have been obvious that the Detective Sergeant was admiring either the container or its well arranged contents, but, there was something in the quality of the silence of this sinister newcomer: something about the intensity of his disapproving countenance which made John immediately launch into an unnecessary explanation -

"Oh! Sorry! I was just ... I never could resist the scent of ..."

Derek Russell stepped forward and rescued his subordinate with perfunctory introductions which partially relieved the atmosphere. Algernon Hardman moved towards his desk and, with a slight gesture of his hand, indicated two leather easy chairs. Derek knew of this local lord by his formidable reputation but, until now, had never beheld him in the flesh. His dark leathery face, deeply wrinkled around a cruel mouth, gave him the look of a man who was nearer 60 than approaching 50. Perhaps, thought Derek, the horrendous recent experience on the Continent had contributed to this haggard and reproving glare.

Hardman silently slipped into his desk chair and interlocked his fingers revealing long black hairs on the back of his hands. Up to now their unfriendly host had not spoken one word. The uncomfortable silence forced Derek into speech -

"I'm sorry to be troubling you at this difficult time ... "

Impatiently, Hardman interrupted in a stern and commanding tone -

"It would be hypocritical to pretend that you were welcome, Detective Inspector, in this house. My wife is killed! My son and I are both fortunate to be alive, and yet we barely have time to sit down, before an army of your men trample over my garden; trample through my woods ... since yesterday, as I gather - without result."

"I appreciate the inconvenience but ..."

*"**Truants** usually return when the novelty has worn thin. This 'hue and cry' is somewhat precipitant do you not think? The person concerned has hardly had a chance to become hungry!"*

Derek parried. Employing his diplomatic skills he was determined to re-gain lost ground and complete his sentences -

*"I wish I could share your optimism, Dr Hardman, and sincerely hope you're correct. We'd all like to go home ... **however** ..."*

111

He forestalled an imminent interruption. *"However, the circumstances of this particular disappearance strongly suggest that Brian Forrester is somewhere on, or indeed in, your property. We will need ... "*

"Oh please do! Don't waste time getting a search warrant. Bring in your troops, bring them all and explore the cellar. I doubt you'll find any recently dug graves. Don't forget to search the trunks in the attic and when you've finally finished - depart and leave us in peace."

Derek, who already had a search warrant in his pocket, ignored the sarcasm, made a civil remark appreciating co-operation and turned the subject around to the servants. The response was a touch more conciliatory -

"I can understand your line of thought regarding Simon. Quite simply, if I had any doubts whatsoever on that matter, he would not be allowed anywhere near my own family. Whatever his predilections and weaknesses beyond Cressbrook Hall, his record here, has been exemplary." At this point his features and voice softened a little more as he looked down at a pre-war photograph of a young woman. *"Marjorie would wish me to say that. He has been invaluable. Charles needs him ... especially now."* Suddenly, he looked up sharply and resumed his cold hostility. *"To suggest that Simon is capable of, or even able to plan and effect an abduction is utter lunacy. As I believe you already know, he is guilty of many sins, but child molestation is, I can assure you gentlemen, not one of them."*

While that subject was hanging in the air, Derek asked to interview Mr Hardman's son Charles on the grounds that a child can observe things most of us miss. The request was granted, only just and very reluctantly. He rose and pulled the bell for Simon.

"The boy is traumatised: we are all traumatised. Please remember that when you are questioning Simon. He doesn't show it, but he's really very upset indeed. He thought the world of Marjorie."

Simon was given instructions and re-appeared minutes later with a nervous, shy, mousy boy who was thin and looked to be about twelve years of age. He had a pale, pleasant, if vacant face of soft rounded features. Derek greeted him cheerfully and seriously suggested that he might be in a special position to help the police.

"When I was your age, Charles, I had lots of secret hiding places were you could spy and gather all sorts of useful intelligence. Brian could be hiding somewhere in this big house, he could be anywhere. We need to find him because he may be hurt. His parents are very worried and unhappy ... very upset. Have you seen Brian?" This was answered by an almost inaudible *"No"*.

"If you do ever see a boy you don't know, or find a bicycle anywhere, will you please promise to tell an adult - immediately?" Again, a barely audible *"Yes"*.

After Charles was dismissed, a few more general questions established that father and son had arrived home at *"about lunch time"* and that Simon was at his post to receive them and, in fact, had been in Cressbrook Hall all that day.

Detective Inspector Derek Russell decided to ask questions about the gardener.

Chapter 16

A Seductive Suggestive Silver Tongue

The Lodge was built at the same time as Cressbrook Hall back in 1835. The detectives learned that the Coggan family of gardeners were already installed when old Isaiah Hardman took over in 1888. Algernon Hardman referred to 'Old Coggan' (the last of four brothers) in deferential terms due to his great horticultural knowledge, long service and reliability. His wife died young in 1940 leaving him with just one son who was christened Adolph in 1930, just before it became unfashionable and, indeed, undesirable to call any English boy Adolph - hence the family nickname of 'Dolly'.

"Naturally my father refused to address any boy as 'Dolly'! When Old Coggan died about ... let me see ... eight years ago now I think, it was easier to refer to Adolphus simply as 'Coggan', but I must admit, (here he almost smiled) *'Dolly' is entirely apt for such a small comical rotundity."*

"Dolly tub!" suggested Detective Sergeant John Winter when he directly addressed Dr Hardman for the first time. For a frosty moment a steely eye was turned on the junior man -

"Quite so. Good staff is hard to come by in these modern days of ever increasing equality ... I suppose we should be grateful to be clinging on to, at least, the last two servants - however bizarre they are!"

Feeling a little more confident, John put his first question to the Master of the House.

"Is Mr Coggan entirely satisfactory?"

*"If you mean as a gardener ... I suppose 'only just' would be the correct answer. Coggan has never been disposed to hard physical work and puts in a minimum effort in the minimum amount of time which, notwithstanding, I must admit, manages to produce a reasonable show. The grounds are nowhere near the high standard they were before Old Coggan became too ill to work. I can't exactly complain - it will do, well ... it **has** to do.*

"Your gardener can afford to run a car!" said Derek.

"A new motorcar at that!" replied the employer with some disapproval considering that a lowly gardener should also be a private motorist. *"Well it **was** brand new just a few years ago. It would be ...*

115

1956. Yes, that's it ... the first of that type to have a one piece windscreen. I recall that Coggan was very proud. Earlier models had the two panel split screen ..."

"*A Morris Minor 1000cc!*" interjected John.

"*I know nothing of cars, Detective Sergeant, but I do believe that was the model Charles mentioned. He was fascinated by the strange illuminated little arms which sprang out of the sides when it turned a corner.*"

"*Trafficators,*" said John, very sure of his ground in this modern subject of automobiles and fully aware that Hardman was asserting his status by claiming ignorance of anything so common as mechanics.

"*You don't drive yourself then?*"

"*I find the local taxi service adequate for my needs.*"

"*Coggan?*"

"*Coggan is the gardener! And we see very little of him doing that. I would never ask for a ride unless it was an emergency and that has yet to happen.*"

During this exchange, Derek had been consulting his notes on Adolphus Coggan. The upholstery and interior of his car had been carefully examined. There were no signs to show that a bicycle (or indeed a boy) had been squeezed inside recently. The recorded mileage was almost 80,000 well above the annual average of about 7,000 miles for a private motorcar in 1960. It was an economical car of a modest size which would have cost its owner several hundred pounds to purchase. These facts were not reconcilable with a modest income. Derek put his concerns to Algernon Hardman who responded with some animation.

"*That car has always puzzled **me**, Detective Inspector. Coggan enjoys a handsome house with four bedrooms, all to himself (assuming he is not concealing your missing person) absolutely rent free and is paid a generous £35 per month for his rare appearances in my garden.*"

"*Mr Coggan said .. *" continued Russell " *.. he was out driving yesterday from before lunch-time to past 11.00pm. That fits in with our witnesses who didn't notice a car ... *"

"*We never know if Coggan is at home or not at home. The car is simply not visible. It's parked up at the back of The Lodge in rhododendron bushes. It **could** have been there yesterday.*"

116

"Dr Hardman, you know your employee better than we do! May we please have some co-operation here. Are you suggesting that Mr Coggan is lying?"

"Coggan is mysterious and devious. He may have been at home at that time. I don't know. I suppose he would have answered the door ... "

At this point he became thoughtful. Algernon Hardman, a respected upright citizen of the community for some years had been slightly uneasy about the private life of Adolphus Coggan. From time to time there had been an occasional painful rumpus over the conduct of Simon Tonks, but in his case, at least the Doctor knew the worst of it. Dolly was a cryptic character. Infrequently, on a sunny day, employer would come across employee leaning on a hoe and a few pleasantries would be exchanged. Hardman found him suitably deferential with 'nice manners'. Hardly the quintessential rustic of popular imagination, Dolly was, above all, smooth, very smooth, well spoken using beautiful vowels in rounded articulation with an attractive, almost seductive, deep purring voice which often trailed away to a suggestive whisper.

*"Oh yes, Dr Hardman, don't worry about that at all. They'll be in next week. Not much risk of frost now. Oh I **quite** agree, Dr Hardman, pansies are **so** pretty, an excellent choice. They'll certainly be planted in the fullness of time - at the appropriate juncture. The ivy? Personally I considered it quite attractive: the wild look you know. Yes, as you wish, sir, I'll remove it in due course."*

Conscious of his social standing, Hardman was fearful of 'opening a can of worms' if he gave information to the police which was too full and too frank. On the other hand he honestly had no solid evidence to support his dark suspicions regarding the silver-tongued, ever mobile, part-time gardener.

*"You will have to ask Coggan yourself, Inspector Russell. If he claims he was out, he probably **was** out - he usually is. Does he not have (oh dear, it sounds so dramatic) 'an alibi'? Simon used to tell Marjorie that 'Dolly is always in demand': a reference, I gather, to a collection of widely dispersed friends on a long visiting list."*

"An entertaining fellow?"

"Oh very. I suspect some of his stock lines come from those awful shows staged at certain 'low life' public houses: men dressed up as women; that kind of thing. Once I over-heard him tell Simon,

117

'You've got to circulate to be noticed' followed by 'I'm very busy with a tight curriculum.' Double-entendres are common in his regular patter. Marjorie was once admiring his new pullover and suggested that it was probably expensive. He said - 'I bought this for a ridiculous figure' and promptly lifted it up to reveal his fat belly!"

At long last Algernon Hardman was now actually smiling and so enjoying the effect on his uninvited guests that he permitted himself one more 'Dolly quote'.

"Normally I don't approve of eavesdropping on servants' gossip, but I was amused during the time Simon was hobbling about complaining to Coggan about his 'bad foot'. The response came back 'You're lucky to have a foot!'"

At that point the phone rang and was answered by the Master -

"It's for you, Detective Inspector."

"Yes? Oh good! Great! We could use ... Say that again. Are you sure?" He replaced the receiver, looked puzzled, stroked his chin and said very softly to himself -

"Extraordinary! Belper. Jasper Wormall."

Chapter 17

Cracker Biscuits in the Cottage

Momentarily, the name of Jasper Wormall produced a slightly nostalgic effect upon the two police officers. After Simon Tonks, here was a second connection with the baffling 1949 Burgess Case of Belper. Both men conjured up a grotesque image of a small, gnarled, craggy character known locally as 'the goblin'. At that time he was in his seventies but with a large hawk nose, far forward of deep set grizzled, leering eyes, this hideous hunchback looked positively Jurassic.

Derek looked at John and John looked back at Derek.
"He's still alive!" said Derek.
"Must be over a hundred!" said John.
"Not far short of ninety. Perhaps, after all, there is something to be said for using earth closet toilets."
"Perhaps," replied John, warming to his theory, *"Perhaps after years of emptying large buckets of 'jollop' as he called it, Jasper is now totally immune to all known germs!"*

These were references to the long past Wormall family business of nightsoil men. Back in the 1880's Jasper was assisting the 'honey dumpers' (his father and brothers) as the 'limey-lad'. This was a boy with a naked flame torch who would walk after the cart and spread lime over any spillages of excrement to *'get shut at stink'.*

"Detective Inspector ... I think you ought to see this," spoke the hesitant voice of Algernon Hardman, reminding them that he was still there, still sitting behind his massive desk, still giving them his valuable time. His countenance had recovered something of its more usual, acetous severity.
*"I can't imagine **what** Mr Wormall has to do with this mystery but ... well, possibly this may help you."* He passed Derek a letter.
*"Thank you, Doctor. I **two** would like to know what an old man 30 miles away knows about this business. Ten minutes ago he was found trying to hide Brian Forrester's bicycle with the other bicycles parked outside the Herbert Strutt Swimming Baths.*
"My God!" said Winter.
"Positively identified by the 'St George' transfer. A lucky break
119

at last. The attendant saw him, became suspicious and telephoned the police station. Now we can get somewhere. Let's have a look at this letter."

From a neatly addressed envelope, Derek removed a small sheet of note-paper which was filled with tiny, slowly written, painstaking 'copper-plate' handwriting from a past century. The style showed individuality, yet seemed to suggest a crabbed, small minded, narrow and isolated personality. Clearly he was from a school which taught never to waste paper.

Dear Doctor Hardman,

I am very sorry, Sir, to cause trouble to you, but the time has come when I must report to you that your butler, Simon Tonks, has been circulating lies about me. I am sorry to inform you that he has brought shame and dishonour on your good house by frequenting a public house of dubious reputation in Nottingham called The Flying Horse. I would not concern you, Sir, with these sordid matters but he has been making people laugh by telling them that I have been sitting in a public lavatory all day long eating food. Two different friends have told me. I would never take food into a lavatory. It is not true. It is not hygienic. I think you should tell him off or give him the sack. Simon thinks he is very funny but he should not say nasty things about people. I am very sorry, Sir, to bring you such painful tidings but I am thanking you most kindly for your valuable time in reading this letter.

Yours very respectfully,

Mr J. Wormall.

"What's all that about?" asked Derek handing the letter to his assistant.
"I fear another case of Simon being Simon!" replied Hardman.
"You spoke to him?"
"Oh, I certainly spoke to him - at length, and, as they say in the army, I gave him 'suitable advice'! Of course, he was profusely apologetic: he always is. I demanded explanations and gathered that this unfortunate and somewhat ancient Wormall character has a history of being the butt of Belper lavatory jokes. In his defence, enthusiastically, Simon gave me several examples - such as the time when Jasper (as a boy) was ordered to retrieve his father's false teeth

from the bottom of a tank of human excrement!"
   "What did he have to say about the 'food' incident?"
   "Apparently Simon was recycling an anecdote told to him by Coggan who was supposed to have observed Mr Wormall through a hole in a public convenience somewhere. You should, of course, ask Simon about all this nonsense, but Coggan said he 'recognised the spread'!
   "Pardon?"
   "Some sort of picnic of cracker biscuits, butter and cheese - I think."
   "He was, I take it, established in that WC for some time?"
   "So it would seem," replied an uncomfortable Dr Hardman, tersely, with some unspoken sardonic significance hovering in the air.

At that moment there was an unusual and unexpected occurrence. Both police officers burst into a loud and prolonged belly laugh which effected Detective Sergeant John Winter to the point where he was struggling for breath. Algernon Hardman watched this curious phenomenon for a few moments before his expression softened slightly to half smile. Having composed himself, Derek was about to put another question to the Doctor when, once again, he lost control and broke down, into further sobs of laughter.

   Having once taken tea with this cordial, if goblinesque man, they both shared a hilarious picture of his repulsive profile, sitting on a public lavatory bowl, carefully arranging with little camp movements of his wrinkled hands, cheese and biscuits on a napkin supported by his knees.

   The laughter continued until their (hereinbefore) hostile host, in a slightly whimsical, judicial style, interrupted with -
   "Perhaps, gentlemen, this might be a good time to adjourn for lunch?"

Being at the centre of a kidnap investigation, and having been interrogated for nearly an hour, Algernon Hardman would not wish to admit that the whole experience had been - somehow strangely therapeutic! An hour before he had been distressed and depressed. He was, in fact, on the edge of a nervous breakdown. He had dearly loved Marjorie and, for all his intelligence and erudition, he could not see a clear way forward - a way of coming to terms, to deal with this particular light which had now gone out of his life - forever. Algernon

Hardman was not a man who could share his feelings. Apart from Marjorie and his son, he had no best friend to speak to. Algernon Hardman had no friends at all. Marjorie and Charles had been his only real friends.

Just for the moment, with the prospect of these two men, who were good company, joining him for lunch, he was greatly relieved - just for the moment.

Once again the telephone rang. Detective Inspector Russell was informed that his team were ready to search Cressbrook Hall. As resources were finite, he gave orders that the available specialists were to be split into two parties, one to deal with Cressbrook and one to be immediately dispatched to examine the crude isolated cottage and garden of Jasper Wormall. Although not formally arrested, the little man had been asked to remain in the Belper Police Station at The Triangle, until he could 'help' the Detective Inspector 'with his enquiries'. By this time, Daniel Forrester, stoic in brave Heanorian tradition holding back a strong emotion, had positively identified his brother's bicycle.

Derek visualised himself and John, a decade before, trudging up that steep, lonely, narrow, rough road on Shire Oaks Hill, which led to a primordial simple stone dwelling where old Jasper was born in 1875. He recalled the tall trees and the raucous rookery, black crows circling around and around which seemed to accentuate a sense of evil. He recalled the ugly hunched old man, skipping around, looking sinister, piling his garden rubbish on a crackling bonfire and remembered a history lesson - 'bonfire = a fire of bones.'

And yet, on that occasion, nothing was proved against Mr Wormall. Indeed he had a good reputation in the old mill town, a reputation for quaint company and 'olde worlde' hospitality. John and Derek had been welcomed and enjoyed freshly 'mashed' tea from well water and delicious home made cakes from a medieval oven, perhaps even - cracker biscuits!

Graciously, Detective Inspector Derek Russell accepted Dr Hardman's kind invitation to lunch which, by necessity, had to be quick. They needed to get to Belper, it was imperative to find out as much as possible about Jasper Wormall: it was also imperative to interview Simon Tonks.

122

The 34 year old Simon Tonks was easier to deal with than his former self, eleven years before. Both men admired his ability to have staved off the cruel effects of time which appeared to have no power over him. Physically, he had hardly changed, but for a small advancement - improved social skills. The ever irritating enigmatic smile of the well remembered 'Simple Simon' of past years soon faded into an expression, more in keeping with the seriousness of the current situation. He seemed keen to help. He seemed genuinely concerned for the stricken Mr and Mrs Forrester. He was, as Hardman had said, distressed at the tragic loss of his late mistress. Over the previous eight years, Simon (faults and all) had become (almost) one of the family. As the interview progressed with carefully couched questions, the odd little servant became mindful of the burden of suspicion which fell upon his Master and colleague at The Lodge - not least himself. Showing loyalty, he fielded the questions put to him with an air of honest candour. Detective Sergeant John Winter was inclined to believe him but his boss, was a little more cautious, recalling the words of his former teacher Miss Florence Calder who once said -

"Simon may look a fool, play the fool and is often foolish but, make no mistake, Derek, do not be deceived - Simon is no fool!"

The big surprise came from the responses to the questions about Jasper Wormall. Simon had absolutely no idea of how, or why Mr Wormall would have the bicycle of Brian Forrester in his possession. The news came as a shock.

"A didn't think 'e were interested in little lads!"

"Was he interested in big lads?" returned Detective Sergeant John Winter bluntly. Both detectives were now leaning several inches further forward.

"Well ... "

"Well what?" persisted John.

"Well 'e does massage - dunt 'e."

"Does he! **Massage?** *.... "*

The next ten minutes were very revealing indeed. It came to light that the strange and reclusive Belper Goblin had, in the autumn of his life, late autumn at that, discovered latent talents of body massage. So keen was he to deliver a full service to as many as possible that he advertised his skills on hand written postcards distributed to local post offices far and wide.

"Ashbourne."

"Ashbourne!"

"Dolly saw it. It said 'Satisfaction guar-an-teed'. A saw one in Bakewell ... err ... Matlock as well. Thee all over! 'E told me 'e wants ta share 'is precious gift we all a mankind."

"You mean any kind of man will do?" said John facetiously.

This last provoked a sharp look from Derek who was fearful that another collapse into a fit of giggles in front of a comedian like Simon Tonks would precipitate a total farce, but, Simon responded seriously -

"No - 'e's sel-ec-tive. 'E likes rugby players an footballers - an gets 'em! 'E does well."

"How much does he charge for his professional services?" asked Derek.

"A don't know. Nowt a think. Dolly said Jasper pays them!"

John Winter was astounded and horrified that any self-respecting body, at any price, could bear to be touched by those hideous little gnarled fingers. Derek Russell, affected differently, was struggling to suppress an avalanche of guffaws. He visualised a tiny, rough, candle lit bedroom, a drooling slash of toothless mouth, with gloating goggle eyes leering over a recumbent torso - about to be anointed with baby oil. A falsetto effeminate squeak -

"Dat all right? Shall ya 'ave any extras? Does dat want a massage?"

The next few questions sought to establish how well Wormall, Coggan and Tonks knew each other. Clearly any friendship between Wormall and Tonks ended with the letter of complaint sent to his employer -

"No. It ended before that."

"When ... and why?"

"Well it were in t' Flyin' 'Orse. Dolly calls it 'Airborne Dobbin'. Ya know in Nottingham?"

"We've been hearing about it. Did Jasper go there?"

"Oh no. Too old. Jasper goes ta places for 'is postcards an ... some other visits ta different lavatories in different towns ya know. 'E sits in 'em fa hours an hours! 'E does Derby, Matlock, Ripley, 'Eanor, Ilkeston ... "

"All right, Simon, just get on with it," said Winter impatiently.

"Well ya know me, a like ta 'ave a laugh and did me 'Jasper'

124

imitation we 'is little 'ammer an chisel ... "

At this point Simon became hunched, one eye closed and the other wide and leering at some invisible object inches from his face. He mimed the action of a small imaginary hammer and chisel with quick little knocks, as he explained, creating a hole between one WC cubicle and another and ended with - *"Meh! Gettin' bigger."* an impression of the old man's cackley voice.

"And I suppose he was outraged when your impromptu performance was reported back to Mr Wormall?" said Russell.

"Well! 'E as so many visitors these days an 'e can't tek a joke."

It was learned that Coggan occasionally offered Tonks a lift into Derby, Nottingham or Manchester for 'social activities', beyond that, they went their separate ways being colleagues more than friends and certainly not close friends. They were certainly disposed to be a couple of jokers sharing a sense of the ridiculous and very much enjoyed retailing comic anecdotes, most of which were at Mr Wormall's expense. Simon said that Dolly was a regular visitor to the Shire Oakes cottage until, one fateful day when, suddenly, he yielded to a great temptation. He picked up Jasper's false teeth which were reposing on his crude kitchen table -

"Well 'e used em as castanets, chattin' em together an danced a fandango singin' 'Lady of Spain'! Well ... "

"Well?" replied John who, at this point, could barely articulate being on the very edge of convulsed laughter.

"Well, Jasper weren't am-oo-sed. 'E were rate mad! 'E kicked Dolly out. 'Bugga off ya ignorant little fat queen' 'e said, 'An dunna ya come back!' Ooo 'e were furious."

A clearer picture was emerging and all very entertaining, but this petty tittle-tattle fell somewhat short of solving the mystery of the lost lad. The pressing priority was to interview Jasper Wormall, as soon as possible, before he could fabricate a plausible explanation for trying to hide Brian Forrester's bicycle.

The search of the little rough cottage up Shire Oakes had been thorough but yielded nothing. All nooks and crannies and any likely secret repositories for pornography had been checked. There was nothing but a cupboard full of local papers, mostly the Belper News and The Derby Evening Telegraph some of them dating back to the previous century. Russell had given orders that his men should check the adjacent thicket of trees for any freshly dug earth. The garden, bonfire and out buildings which included the earth lavatory and wood shed were also carefully examined.

The dwelling itself, without the benefit of running water, gas or electricity was pre-Victorian. This was the same small home which had housed the Wormall family when the brothers of Jasper's grandfather had been footmen, coachmen, grooms and gardeners to the then Lord of Belper, George Benson Strutt in 1825. This one time 'bucket banger', as nightsoil men were sometimes referred to, was the very last of a large family. In his present precarious situation, Jasper was feeling very much alone.

After such a careful combing of the property there seemed to be no good reason to further detain the agitated Mr Wormall at the police station. Already riled, he scornfully refused the offer of a ride up Ashbourne Road and back home in a police motor-car. Indeed, the fit wiry Jasper Wormall, who had spent a lifetime tramping up and down the hills of Belper, was probably in better physical condition than most people half his age.

It was an angry and resentful goblin who opened the old creaking door to Russell and Winter when they finally arrived at the crumbling cottage in the late afternoon. As expected, after eleven years the hideous effect was just the same. Again, Derek was looking directly into the unforgettable leering eyes of the old crone who offered Snow White a poisoned apple -
"Can we have a chat Mr Wormall?" No response but, to let them enter, the old man shuffled backwards into the dingy room with its smell of oil lamps. *"This has not been easy for you, and we sincerely regret the necessity to rifle through your home: not a pleasant experience for anybody, but you must admit the circumstances left us with very little choice."*

The ancient rustic fell into his armchair by the fireplace and slowly shook his head with an air of hopeless desperation. There was a strong contrast between the feelings of the junior and senior officers. The latter was prepared to entertain the theory that, for some unknown reason, someone had planted Brian Forrester's bicycle next to Jasper's

126

woodshed. Derek felt sorry for the shabby crumpled old fellow before him and felt a little guilty that his privacy had been violated. Such an odd repulsive character must have had a difficult life: a long life suppressing and repressing unacceptable and illegal urges which would have isolated him from general society, which in turn caused him to be even more quirky in his manner.

After petulant protests that he had already given a detailed explanation of his conduct, the suspect was politely persuaded to re-tell his story. He had found the mysterious bicycle leaning at the back of his woodshed at about 7.30 that morning. He heard nothing during the night. The sudden appearance of a boy's bike frightened him. Kids had played tricks on him in the past. The suggestion of reporting the matter to the police horrified him, getting mixed up with 'the law' was the last thing he wanted - let the Swimming Bath Attendant report a bicycle which had been abandoned. Let **him** sit inside the police station and let **him** have his words written down by a copper and be summoned to a court of law to give evidence. Such was the attitude of Jasper Wormall, who claimed to be ignorant of the massive police search for a teenager which, to be fair, had yet to be reported in the media.

On the subject of massage, the old man stiffened with fear. Derek took the view that diplomacy and gentle probing would release more information and put his witness at ease. Cheerfully he said -
"We all have our little side-lines, Mr Wormall. Detective Sergeant Winter here has a few chickens and sells the eggs now and again. I'm sure the Tax Man won't fuss about the odd shilling or two you get from relieving aches and pains."

This last, masterfully succeeded in putting the masseur in the relatively comfortable position where his activities might be considered of more interest to the Internal Revenue Service, rather than the vice department of the CID. Seizing the advantage, Derek subtly and tactfully suggested that some of Mr Wormall's 'clients' might just have a taste for teenage boys and might be in a position to know the location of Brian Forrester since, after all, his bicycle had been found on the premises.

To John the defensive, rambling and evasive answer was annoying but, to Derek - it had the ring of truth. Jasper knew very little of his visitors, some of whom arrived in cars and all cars looked the same to Jasper. A few walked up and a few cycled up. They never stayed very long [it did not take long] and they rarely disclosed any personal information. Most gave Christian names only and he judged that most of those were false.

"*Thee seem ta be a lot o' Johns! Meh.*"

Winter bridled slightly hearing his own name. The old man, now in full flow, went on to say that he suspected most of the men were married. The host was disposed to be chatty but his clients were reluctant to do more than exchange a few brief commonplace pleasantries. His 'patients' were only too keen to get to the nitty-gritty, to have the little man minister to their physical needs, to delve, to seek and tweak those delicious naughty little spots during an anonymous, dimly lit, window of secret stolen time.

When questions were put about his association with Coggan and Tonks he became even more defensive and very alarmed -

"*What 'av thee bin sayin'?*"

Derek made it clear that the purpose of his visit was to hear what Mr Wormall had to say - and he had plenty to say. A series of crabbed and querulous recriminations enthusiastically flowed forth to thoroughly blacken the character of his former friends.

"*... an then there were that stick a rock from Skegness ... that were nasty 'cus ...*"

"*A gift from the seaside! How can that be nasty?*"

"*It were what Dolly said when 'e give it me!*"

"*What did he say?*"

At this point Jasper subsided, slowed down and became reluctant, clearly too embarrassed to continue.

"*Well ... a don't like ta say ...*"

"*Come on, Mr Wormall. We haven't got all day. Spit it out.*"

"*Well. Well it were sort o' nasty ... a didn't like it. 'E said - 'Get ya lips round this for a change'! An 'e bought that rock - just - so - 'e could - say - that. Meh!!*"

In general, Detective Sergeant John Winter took a less charitable view of his interviewee. Personal peculiarities were being noted with some small irritation, such as the repetitive and squeaky '*Meh!*', a contemptuous motif occurring after the delivery of a smug, self-satisfied line. The real Jasper, with his high, effeminate, 'old witch'

128

type voice was actually very similar to the entertaining impression they had heard from Simon Tonks that morning. Simon had also perfected the nod of the head at each syllable which occasionally emphasised an important point - *'just - so - 'e could - say - that!'* Against his will, John was fixated by the bouncing prominent Adam's apple, up and down, the scraggy neck.

He did not like Mr Wormall. He concluded that the petulant unpleasant heap of rags before him, in all probability, had something to do with the disappearance of Brian Forrester. The quaint simplicity which charmed his boss had no effect on John, whose overall impression was of an introspective, small minded man, approaching ninety who had the mentality of a nine year old. It was Derek who finally stemmed the peevish, seemingly endless flow of trite and childish invectives, nineteen to the dozen -

*" ... an am **not** always in that toilet as some as a could mention not fat proper purpose an 'e 'ad no right ta push that bib underneath an saucer fa me teeth an a didn't like that plant pot an comment about 'takin' root' cus ..."*

*"Thank you, Mr Wormall that will be **quite** enough! We have all the information we need on that subject. Our main interest at this time is to find a young man who should be home with his parents. Here is my last question ... for the present. Please try to be brief. Can you think of anybody, anybody at all, friend of foe, who you suspect may have an interest in entertaining young teenage boys?"*

At this the hideous old crone eagerly leaned forward and leered at Derek who, instinctively, leaned back to maintain a decent safe distance. A goblinesque face twisted into gloating triumph -

"'Ave ya bin ta see Dolly's friend yet, 'im at Derby? A don't know 'is real name. Thee call 'im 'Guzzly Granddad' - lives at end a Ebenezer Street. 'E's a dotty owd bugga we 'is slaverin', drivelin' an droolin'. 'E likes em young! Meh!"

Back in the car, a conference took place. Detective Inspector Derek Russell breathed out a sigh of relief -

"It's like finding yourself in one of Grimm's fairy stories." Pitching his voice two octaves higher and nodding on each syllable, he attempted a Jasper impersonation - *"'Come into my cottage little boy. Meh!' And that Simon and Dolly - what a shower!"*

"Perverted, pea-brained peasant!" spat out his colleague. *"I've*

129

a good mind to waylay and interrogate one of those blokes and ... "

"Fighting words, John, but not so much 'pea-brain'. Don't underestimate our little goblin. Taking the bike to the baths - that was rather clever and might well have come off - sheer bad luck that the attendant came out at the wrong moment. Let's address ourselves to the crucial question - is our man a child molester? Is he a murderer to boot? And if so - where is the body?"

"Well it's not here. I've every faith in Raymond's team. The hate between that old fossil and the other two! God! You could cut it with a knife. It rules out the conspiracy theory."

"Does it? You know, John, I was thinking about the classic Agatha Christie plot of the 'forced card'. Misdirection - that sort of stuff. Two back-biting parties apparently daggers drawn in an endless quarrel - and on the last page they turn out to be 'acting the part' and in reality, working together in murderous co-operation. That old man went to a lot of trouble to emphasise his distaste of Coggan and Tonks ... well, you never know do you."

"Bit far fetched that, sir! Our Simon doesn't seem to be overburdened by intelligence - and we've not even spoken to Coggan yet."

"Yes ... Coggan," said Derek thoughtfully. *"Sounds like a smooth one. I'd still like to know how he can drive a brand new car 400 miles a week on an income of eight pounds a week."*

"Anyway ..." said John starting the engine and engaging a more optimistic chirpy note. *"Never despair, let's keep looking for Brian. He **could** still be alive. He **could** be having tea with Guzzly Granddad!"*

Gingerly, avoiding the largest stones and numerous pot holes, they drove down the rough track from Shire Oakes leaving ominous crows still circling around the tall trees under a blanket grey sky.

Chapter 18

Guzzly Granddad

At the Derby Police Station Detective Inspector Derek Russell was able to study the report from Cressbrook Hall. It appeared to be a house of few visitors. The conscientious cleaning of Simon Tonks was not helpful to the forensic team, but, as expected, the re-occurring fingerprints available were from the principal occupants - Algernon Hardman, his late wife Marjorie, young Charles and plenty of prints from the tiny camp fingers of Tonks the servant. No other suspicious impressions were found and no trace, not even a dab from the hand of Brian Forrester. It came as no surprise to Derek that even Brian's bicycle had no trace of his own prints - only the fingerprints of Jasper Wormall -

"That, of course, could indicate naiveté - or clever cunning. If anything at all went wrong (which in the event it did) Mr Wormall would need to explain why he was wearing gloves in July, or why he was discovered cleaning a bike which was not his."

Attached to the report was a message from Tonks offering the police his professional services as a clairvoyant.

"Listen to this, John. Simon thinks that if he could just touch the bicycle he may be able to locate its owner."

"We're not going through all that nonsense again are we, sir, like that spooky charade with Sarah's ring?"

"Might be useful," said Derek slowly. *"If he knows anything at all, he'll reveal it in one of his 'performances'. He plans ahead. He notes, saves and stores up bits of information. He has skills of manipulation. Psychology, my dear, John! Let him be where he wants to be, the centre of attention.*

Anyway, it'll be more interesting now that he's branched out into the mysteries and secrets of Derbyshire. I'm told he's something of an expert on sacred groves, fairy rings, stone circles and all that sort of stuff. Simon Tonks is one of nature's original conjurers. In the past he would have been a druid priest or one of those cryptic Greek maidens who would interpret the spilt entrails of a freshly killed sacrificial goat at an oracle, or ... "

"OK, boss. No more gore. I get the picture."

It was getting into the early evening. Detective Sergeant John Winter hoped that the boss would call it a day, but Derek felt the urgency to leave no stone unturned. Information on 'Guzzly Granddad' was scant and mainly hearsay. Some knowledge came from a local officer who spoke of 'a bit of bother' when a neighbour complained that a bunch of noisy youths were drinking in Granddad's front room -

"*Does this man have a proper name?*" asked Derek.

"*Piggs, sir, a Mr T Piggs,*" replied PC Harris. "*I think the T stands for Toby.*"

"*Toby Jug!*" laughed Sergeant Winter. "*Put him with Jasper, Simon and Dolly and they'll think the circus has come to town!*"

"*I wouldn't exactly call him a freak,*" said Harris, choosing his words with care in an effort of remembrance. He became amused as the recollection became clearer.

"*Certainly a bit on the smelly side, he was piggling his toes when I questioned him. The neighbour said he spent a lot of time sitting in the Arboretum, would get chatting to lads and sometimes invited them back for fags and beer.*"

"*Did you interview any of these boys?*" asked John.

"*I considered it, but the old bloke didn't know any of their names or where they lived.*"

After making a small purchase at a rather dingy, seedy little shop on Ebenezer Street, John Winter engaged the shop-keeper in casual conversation -

"*This part of town doesn't change much does it? I used to pass this shop on the way to work. Is that old man still around ... funny name, now what was it?*"

"*Oh 'im. Dirty sod. Kids call 'im Guzzly Granddad. 'E's still at end. E'll never shift.*"

"*Better off than me anyway, he can run a car.*"

"*Nay lad, 'e's no car.*"

"*Oh. I thought that Morris 1000 was his.*"

"*No, that's one of 'is visitors. 'E's often there, little dumpy chap. Strong smell o' scent but very pleasant, nice manners an nicely spoken.*"

Minutes later this information was communicated to Detective Inspector Derek Russell who was just outside the shop. Both men walked down that rather quiet drab street of terraced houses where doors opened directly on to the pavement. They stopped in front of the

132

last house. About to wield the usual official knock, John was silently restrained by his senior who deliberately gave the door a more gentle, furtive knock. From within they heard -

"Ya 'an come in kent ya?"

Entering, they were enveloped by a musty smell, something between sweaty socks, ash-trays and damp beer-stained carpet. Dark pre-war tatty wallpaper was the backdrop to a mangy old sofa, pressed down by a pile of human blubber, which comprised the ample, odious, unclean person of Toby Piggs. Simultaneously, both visitors saw how he came to be called Guzzly Granddad. Attention was drawn, at once, to a slimy, toothless orifice surrounded by grey stubble. Oozing slobber, this repulsive, glistening cavity was loosely contained by uncouth crooked lips. The sight of the two hunky men touched off a Pavlovian conditioned reflex. A salacious tongue stealthily, very stealthily crept up from the blackness of the thick throat and, slowly, lasciviously, moved side to side making the lower lip viscous in an unspoken, lewd invitation.

It was the one word 'police' which immediately shut down all these wanton succulent secretions and closed the old man's mouth into an expression of alarm and dismay. His voice was coarse, deep and guttural -

"Huh! Ave not done oat [anything], *av a?"*

The total impression was of a mess. Unshaven, he reposed in a once white, collarless, soup-stained shirt. His braces were hauling up, at near nipple level, ancient baggy grubby trousers. At his feet, a growing pile of orange peel and nut shells, by his side, the remains of supper - greasy chip papers. Partly under the sofa, John noticed the edge of a dinner plate with even older food.

It was explained to Mr Piggs that a teenage boy was missing and they had reason to believe that he may be able to assist their enquiries.

"It's that ugly owd 'ag at Belper in tit? Aye's sent ya ant 'e? Huh."

Once more Derek and John were entertained by a string of bitter and biting recriminations concerning Jasper Wormall. Petty jealousies, rivalries and spiteful comments about the abuse of public toilets were delivered, this time, slower and in a lower register. Defensive denials flowed a-plenty, on the incorrect assumption that Wormall had made numerous allegations and the tone gave the impression of one time colleagues rather than one time friends.

"Ays allus in t' bogs, ay stinks like a bog, ay used ta empty bogs when 'e were a lad."

Further questions followed. Yes, like most folk in Derby he often visited the Arboretum. No, he was not interested in boys and never spoke to them. Unnecessarily, he added that he was not in the habit of sitting in a public lavatory all day long nibbling cracker biscuits like a certain -

" ... evil lyin' owd cow in Belper ... 'oo'll be gettin' me fist down 'is bloody throat ..."

"Visitors, Mr Piggs! One in particular: one in a green car."

"That'll be little Dolly. 'E's all right. A decent sort."

He was happy to talk about Dolly who came about three or four times a week. Sometimes he would bring a friend, *"an **adult** friend"* he added significantly. According to Mr Piggs nobody knew Dolly's real name, where he lived or where he worked. John considered this was an attempt to protect a friend, but, put with other information about Coggan, Derek felt it was consistent with the gardener's secretive character.

"Simon Tonks."

"What about 'im?" said Guzzly Granddad.

"Do you know him?"

"Everybody knows Simon, but not everybody wants ta be seen we 'im. 'E won't come 'ere agen."

"Why not?"

"Camp as bloody Christmas! Huh. Ya cana tek 'im anywhere. Ya couldn't walk down t' street we 'im ... "

His flow was abruptly halted by a firm knock at the door. Two more policemen had arrived to make a search to which, reluctantly, Mr Piggs agreed. With such a small property, it did not take long. The hard trodden earth of the tiny back garden had clearly not been disturbed in years. As expected, pornography was discovered, old fashioned and dog-eared. Most of the photographs could have been classified as 'soft core' featuring adult women, but it did cross Derek's mind that such pictures may have been used to intrigue young men.

134

When they were outside on the pavement, a very silly and very amusing thought popped into the mind of Detective Inspector Derek Russell. It was so silly that he would never have shared it with his junior colleague. So impressed with the extraordinary contrasts between the two hideous men they had just interviewed - he imagined them attired as Romeo and Juliet! The lugubrious, lusting, deep throated Guzzly Granddad cast as Romeo looking ridiculous and repulsive in tights -

"But soft! Huh. What light through yonder window breaks? It is the east and Jasper is the sun!" Answered by the high pitched, head nodding co-star, an ugly crone in medieval costume -

"O Guzzly Granddad, Guzzly Granddad, wherefore art thou Guzzly Granddad? O be some other name. Meh!"

This frivolous absurdity was, in truth, a masking device to hide the fact of meeting up with yet another dead end. True, Adolphus Coggan still needed to be interviewed, but Derek had a bad feeling and said as much to his colleague -

"Nay, sir. Surely not! It's not like you to be despondent so soon. We're only into the second day ... what ... 56 hours. Anything could turn up."

"I hope you're right, John. Just can't see these fools as kidnappers. It's beginning to feel wrong. Perhaps this sleazy sexual lead is a red herring ... they don't seem sophisticated enough."

"Hardman is."

"Yes, Hardman ... I wonder ..."

"And then again, sir, our Brian could easily be walking around somewhere with no memory - it's only a matter of time now. We've got lots of publicity in Manchester, Sheffield, Nottingham and Derby ... we'll find him, sir, just you see."

Chapter 19

Dolly, Dolly, Deep, Dark and Devious

At 9.00am the next day, Tuesday, July 26th, under cheerless skies which were still cloudy, Russell and Winter were knocking on the door of Cressbrook Hall Lodge. Adolphus Coggan seemed pleased to see them and, in a soft sighing voice, bade them enter into a comfortable old fashioned living room; a cosy oasis in which there seemed to be all the time in the world. Part of the calming atmosphere came from the slow careful tick of a round clock on the mantelpiece: indeed, the reoccurring theme of that room was roundness. A plump curved settee with matching armchairs and globular pouf set the tone. In a half circle bay window reposed a round heavy Victorian dining table. In the centre of the table, a large bulbous pot was home to an ancient dusty aspidistra plant.

Two police officers sank deep into the soft upholstery of the two seated sofa. The opposite armchair became pregnant when it was filled with the podgy flesh of their host who, at the same time, threw out an odour of expensive cologne into the stagnant air. In an un-hurried measured manner and with exaggerated movements of the lips, fat full lips, he articulated beautifully formed round vowels -

"Now gentlemen, how can I help you today?"

Eyes like saucers set into that soft chubby face intrigued and mesmerised the two visitors. Tilting his spherical head very slightly to the left, Dolly became more than just quizzical, he became slightly patronising and yes, a touch condescending as if he were addressing two little boys.

Derek asked about his movements during the previous Sunday and received the same answers which had been given to his subordinates. The gardener went out driving in his motorcar sometime at about 11.30am and was out until past 11.00pm. Detective Sergeant John Winter jumped in with -

"Where did you go, Mr Coggan?"

With large twinkling orbicular eyes, he replied, slowly, in a thinly veiled sardonic purr -

"Do you know, Detective Sergeant, I'm really not at all sure ..."

"That won't do, Mr Coggan," snapped Derek who was now getting irritated. *"This is a serious matter. I suggest you consider your*

137

position and give us some hard facts. Where did you go and who were you with?"

Unfazed, the fat man started to examine his long finger nails in a casual manner. John had noticed these podgy, delicate, little hands, clean white hands which appeared to have done precious little gardening.

"You see, Detective Inspector," he said with a half smile in deep, rich, silky tones, *"I'm in a rather delicate position."*

"We're in full agreement there, Mr Coggan! Please continue."

"How shall I put it? I was rendering a service to people ... well somewhat unusual people who are very nervous at the mention of the word 'police'."

"Body massage, Mr Coggan?" inquired John somewhat facetiously.

"Oh no!" the other responded persuasively in mock shock with an engaging full smile. *"No no no. Nothing at all like that. You've quite shocked my delicate sensitivities, Detective Sergeant - suggesting that innocent little Dolly here could be so naughty!"*

Having softened his audience to the point where they were now amused with this little comedy, Adolphus Coggan wisely decided to reveal the secret of how a poor gardener (poor in both respects) could comfortably afford to drive a car 20,000 miles a year.

It came to light that some years before, young Adolph had indeed - 'considered his position'. Whilst appreciating the beauties of the countryside, he had accidentally come across the delights and excitement of the city - particularly the City of Manchester. Certain pubs which catered for certain interesting minorities fascinated the little rotundity -

"Have you ever visited The Union? Or, perhaps 'The Rembrandt'?

These establishments, rich in local colour, hosted regional comedians, 'drag shows' and various other bawdy entertainments. In his travels around the Peak District, being a chatty friendly character, Dolly met many shy people who warmed to his tranquil and velvety personality. Some expressed a desire to do these 'pub crawls' and have a chance to rub shoulders with interesting quirky types - but lacked the courage. Bizarre venues were often hidden in the back alleyways, nooks and crannies of sleazy neighbourhoods. Dolly knew where all the 'action' was to be found and occasionally proposed himself as an escort to those of a ... 'timid disposition' who were keen to taste the fruits of the wicked city. As time passed, it was a natural progression from offering the hand of companionship - to holding out a hand for money.

Dolly began to charge. The fee would cover his time and the cost of his entertaining personality, endless jokes - everybody loved Dolly. People were prepared to pay for his specialised knowledge of the metropolis which extended to guided tours of Derby, Nottingham, Birmingham, Sheffield and even London. Like the clients of Jasper, 'the friends of Dolly' came to expect anonymity and total discretion.

"And I have to be very careful."

"What do you mean?" asked John.

"Well, Detective Sergeant," he responded lyrically, tongue firmly in cheek. *"Some types take advantage of a good-looking young innocent like me! Only last week this man, oo such a big man, deliberately put his leg dangerously close to my gear stick. I was appalled! And do you know, Detective Sergeant, that just ten minutes later, parked up, I had to bang on the window with a sponge to attract attention!"*

"Quite so," murmured Derek. *"But I'd like to know more about your special tours."*

"Well now, let me see? 'Victorian Lavatories' is in vogue at the present time."

"Oh yes!" said Detective Sergeant John Winter in a hard firm tone with his arms folded. *"Of some historic interest - no doubt,"* he added cynically. Dolly parried this by stating that people were amused and entertained by anything old and quaint -

"Like my tour of 'Ugly Old Queens'."

"Pardon?" inquired Derek.

"My dear, Detective Inspector, that really is, as your handsome colleague put it - 'of historic interest' and very popular having real living fossils to view in their own habitat. I'm booked up solid for this season. And no surprise, Derbyshire has Britain's best collection of weird and hideous camp old queens ... "

"Such as Jasper Wormall?" interrupted Derek.

"Oh, one the very best! My customers really enjoyed their visit to 'The Crone under the Crows' as I billed him - so deliciously low and common." He sighed and became a little melancholic looking out at the darkening clouds as he recalled the incident of the false teeth.

"'Tis gone, 'tis gone. We pay for our mistakes. But I've still got

*Guzzly Granddad who drools when shown the right one and a **most** nauseating ancient drag act in Ripley. My clients love to be repelled by her 'Gracie Fields' numbers and the 'Old Mother Riley' sketch really is a scream. A mass of wrinkles, dead rough, she trips out in these tiny revolting shorts shouting - 'Ya 'n see t' cheeks o' me arse.' And you should see ... "*

"We'd like to see Brian Forrester, Mr Coggan! Can you help us?

This last ended the comic flow and brought an edge of reality to the interview. Coggan was asked, in turn, to volunteer a personal opinion regarding the probability of Hardman, Wormall, Tonks or Piggs having anything to do with the inexplicable disappearance. He had a great respect for his employer and became (for once) serious when expressing regret about the recent tragedy.

"It'll take years for him to get over it. Poor man, it's knocked the stuffing out of him - changed him you know. Oh yes. Won't let that boy out of his sight. Won't let him go back to school, talking about private tutors now." He shook his head slowly and stared through the aspidistra plant with enormous eyes. The thought of Jasper having any guilty secrets regarding teenage boys amused him -

"Now if you were looking for a missing wrestler, Jasper might be your man ... And when Simon becomes entangled with youngsters he always gets the worst of it. He's either robbed, given a black eye or ends up gagged, tied and suspended under a tree! No, not Simon, definitely not Simon."

With the assessment of Toby Piggs he became thoughtful and chose his words with care -

"It was spiteful of Jasper to send you to Guzzly Granddad, but, ... I'm afraid he was right. I've warned him. He's a fool having kids in that house. Well, they could say anything couldn't they? One thing I do know and everybody knows this - Granddad wouldn't hurt a fly. Anyway you've more evidence against Jasper than Granddad - and I can't see how a cyclist from here could possibly end up at Derby ... unless?"

"Yes, Mr Coggan?"

"Have you considered the sudden onset of - amnesia ?"

"Yes we have," replied Derek. *Any more ideas?"*

"Well, it's a bit far fetched ... but ... " The clock started to chime the hour of ten as Dolly gently patted his thick fleshy lips with

140

four fingers in an effort to organise his thoughts.

"After being separated from his friends in a strange area he may have become disorientated and wandered off into the woods. They do go on for miles you know ... "

"You're beginning to interest me."

"Assuming there was some sort of accident ..." continued Dolly *" ... resulting in some sort of head injury he may have sustained ... Well, he may have just died! I don't know anything about these things, you'll need to talk to a specialist, but I've heard about sudden death occurring after the subject has walked some distance."*

"We've looked. We've combed the woods. He's not there!" said John.

*"You've **not** looked everywhere. It's impossible. It's a massive area. You've not been all the way up Cressbrook Dale Woods: they go on forever. There's swathes of nettles, ferns and weeds taller than me up Hay Dale; if he fell into something like that it'll be years before he's found. What about all those deep mine shafts on Longstone Moor - he could be in any one of them - and you'll never find him ... "*

"We intend to search Eldon Hole," said Derek. *"The lad wanted to go there. But you're quite right, Mr Coggan, we have a marathon task ahead of us but, unfortunately, I don't have an army of ..."* Coggan and Winter looked at him. *"Just a thought, maybe I **do** have an army, the British Army.*

Yes, Mr Coggan, many thanks for your interesting suggestions. We're aware that this part of Derbyshire is honeycombed with limestone caves and traitorous hidden pot holes. We've taken steps to alert all pot-holers and walkers."

"Up to now .." chimed in John Winter looking sternly at Dolly. *"You've not explained how Brian Forrester's bicycle has managed to appeared in the garden of one of your friends: well, OK, former friend. The fact is that the bicycle was not found in a pot hole, it was found with someone who is connected to you and with someone who shares your particular 'lifestyle'."*

Adolphus Coggan sank further into his cosy nest, sighed and gave John a slightly hurt look.

"You disappoint me, Detective Sergeant Winter. I grant you our little roads are quiet, but it is just possible, do you not think, just possible, that somebody came across a bike on the road side and ... simply took it ... stole it ... rode it away ..."

"Thirty miles!" interrupted John. *"Thirty miles south, right to*

someone who (by sheer chance) you happen to know! Surely that is stretching coincidence a bit far! We will start looking into holes when ... "

"All the same, Mr Coggan," said Derek fearing that the atmosphere was in danger of becoming counter-productive *".. you've admitted that you move in interesting circles and I'd be obliged to receive any whispers you may just hear."*

Rising, Derek added - *"Tomorrow morning I'll be giving Mr and Mrs Forrester a progress report, or should I say, a lack of progress report. By this time they'll be in an appalling state of distress; you must realise that. Sergeant John Winter and I are sure that you'll want to do all you can to restore their son back safely to his home in Heanor. If that can be achieved with your good offices, Mr Coggan, I can assure you the police service will not wish to look **too** closely into your 'lifestyle', as Winter put it."*

At this point all three men were on their feet. Adolphus Coggan showed them to the door and said -

"At the start of this interview I told you both that I wanted to help. Rest assured, if I can possibly help, I certainly will."

Back in the car John Winter wanted to discuss the matter immediately, but Derek (not for the first time) warned about the skills of lip reading. The conference took place during a pleasant walk through Water-cum-Jolly Dale. Dark grey clouds had lightened and the threat of rain had abated.

"Well let's hear it, John. Let's have your latest scenario."

"He's a bloody smooth one and he could be exactly what he seems to be - a little fat queer comic who'd run a mile at the sight of a shaking fist ... "

"Did you know, John, that 'Adolph' means wolf?"

"Which brings me to my theory," retorted Winter *"Little Dolly finds a concussed young lad and sees an opportunity for sport. 'I'll take you to Dr Jasper' he says. Bike and boy are put in the car ... "*

"There's no evidence, not the slightest indication of a bicycle being in that Morris. No oil, no grease, no dirt - not to mention the difficulty of getting a bike in that small car."

"Humour me, sir, he may have used a discarded blanket - anything. Boy and bike are taken to Belper. Boy sets eyes on Jasper and runs for his life. Boy is silenced. Body chucked in the River

Derwent. Pure chance it hasn't been spotted, yet - by this time it could be floating northwards in the Trent - approaching the Humber."

Derek rubbed his chin and fell into a brief reverie watching a piece of wood floating down the River Wye. After a few moments, John asked -
  "What's your gut feeling about this one, sir? What do you think?"
  "What do I think? I feel like the character in the Agatha Christie book, the one who says - 'It's all wrong. We're looking at it from the wrong angle.' That's how I feel ... some sort of conjuring trick, some sleight of hand has been played on us ..."

A sudden breeze stirred up the osier trees on the bank and turned the leaves to silver. Derek noticed that John was still looking at him.
  "Gut feeling? I think that Algernon Hardman is an honest respectable man still in shock. There is something .. which I can't quite put my finger on .. no matter. I know Simon of old. Don't forget we went to the same church. He's a likeable fool. He may well try it on if opportunity offers itself but, he's not violent and certainly not homicidal. Our fat friend? Well, I really don't know. Full marks for being enterprising - but where does it stop? What if Mr Client wants a 15 year old boy to play with, does the devious Dolly, for a price, provide such forbidden fruit - possibly using a relatively safe venue in a Derby back street?"
  "Even more safe if the boy has lost his memory!"
  "And would Dolly take the risk of 'planting' the bicycle at the door of an old enemy - for revenge?"
  "If the average bloke found a bike in his garden, he'd report it to the police. Trying to hide it is the action of a guilty man ..."
  "Or a fearful man, John. Gut feeling tells me the Goblin was, as he said so himself, scared. And then of course we have Guzzly Granddad ..."

He became silent, staring into the crystal clear waters. A large dark blue fish was motionless, barely discernible, opening and closing its mouth. After a few moments Detective Inspector Derek Russell produced from his inside pocket a medical briefing which was heavily annotated in his own hand.
  "This is a bit like a weather report during an unsettled period. Our specialist seems to have covered himself for every eventuality, that

143

is, when you can understand it! In brief - if Brian is still alive and if he is suffering from a complete loss of identity ... well it outlines several possible reasons for such loss." He studied the text. *"From what we're told it looks as if we can scrub out 'amnesia following a period of stress', Brian being such a happy chap. Something here about a 'subconscious desire to start again'. That doesn't sound likely. 'Retrograde amnesia'? Not sure about that one. Then we have - 'transient interruption to the blood supply to parts of the brain known as the ... hippocampus or posteromedial thalamus'. In these cases most people make a complete recovery within a few hours. Here it is, this is the one we want - '... after a severe head injury the patient can suffer from post-traumatic amnesia - thought to be the result of damage to the temporal lobe'. Something here about 'residual dementia'."*

"That sounds nasty!" said John.

"I've spoken to this chap about it. There are no hard and fast rules. They simply don't know. Memory can return in weeks - or it can take many months. There may be permanent loss concerning events just before and after the accident."

"So if we ever find him, he may not be able to tell us anything?"

"If we ever find him, John. If we ever do find him."

But they never did find Brian Forrester.

Not in any river, not in any wood, not in any copse, not in any field, nor in any pothole, nor any cave, nor in any mine, nor in any backstreet of any town or city. A few weeks later the Army did lend a hand for several days when the search was widened - without result. The case was reported in the local press together with the rather poor photographic image of Brian's face. Even the Daily Mirror ran the story - all without result. Jasper Wormall suffered a further surprise search as did Toby Piggs - without any result. Within the limited resources available, Adolphus Coggan was watched for a short period. The official report spoke of 'sailing close to the wind' but his 'rather dubious activities' had no known connection with minors and were within the law - just.

Towards the Christmas of that year there was a sudden and explosive fracas in the steam room of the Derby Turkish Bath. The cantankerous attendant ploughed into clouds of vapour to rescue Simon Tonks from

144

outraged recriminations and an imminent violent attack. It transpired he had been 'annoying' two macho construction workers. All three bathers were told to leave and advised not to return. As Simon was being escorted out of the building by the baths manager, one rough looking cleaner leaning on a mop nudged the other and was heard to say

"Yes! 'E stands need ta be a 'clairvoyant'. Ya don't need ta be psychic ta know what that dirty bugger's bin up to." The other cleaner nodded sagely. As ever, these occasional incidents did not effect his good service at Cressbrook Hall.

Simon was not in Derby that day solely to visit the baths. After the style of 'the last throw of the dice', Detective Inspector Derek Russell had invited the little clairvoyant to carry out his own suggestion of touching Brian Forrester's bicycle. This was arranged on the grounds that more information would be obtained from the witness if given the opportunity to 'show off'. Simon was led into a room with five similar machines, all dull and dirty, a form of identity parade of cycles. Russell and Winter looked on closely. It was assumed that if the servant had previous knowledge of the machine, he would seek out the image of the mounted knight on the transfer, the only form of positive identification. The two detectives watched Simon's simple little 'cartoon like' eyes very carefully indeed, as he minced up and down the line, gently touching the handlebars of each bike. He went down and up and then down again - stopping in front of the last bicycle in the line, but one, the very same bicycle which Jasper Wormall had tried to hide outside the Herbert Strutt Belper Baths some five months before. Simon did not appear to notice the transfer, but, with one hand he gripped a handlebar and the battered worn old saddle with the other hand. In front of the two detectives, taking the part of an audience, wearing expressions of supreme scepticism, Simon closed his eyes, began to swoon and began to moan. Finally he spoke in his 'other worldly' voice

"Safe ... well ... 'appy ... leave me alone ... leave me be ... am a long way off ... leave me be ... let me be ..."

Ten minutes later Russell and Winter were sipping tea in the police canteen.

"Well I'll be damned .. " said Winter *" .. if he so much as glanced at that transfer. I watched him like a hawk!"*

*"And he knew you **would** be watching him like a hawk, John. Remember what I told you about the skills of the conjurer. His eyes were sweeping. The smallest fraction of a second is all it takes. He took three trips along that line - of course he saw the mounted knight."*

"Is that it then! If he's seen that bike before he must be implicated. We can lean on him. You shouldn't have let him go."

"Would that it were it as simple as that!" sighed the senior officer. *"No. I've mucked it up. Stupid having five bikes; should've been at least ten. Simon's got a fair chance of getting lucky - he knows that. There are other possibilities. We've never gone public on the transfer business, but a number of our lot know about it. Simon's often in 'the nick', he could have overheard something, or been told something. He's an expert lip reader."*

"What should we make of Brian being a long way off, happy and wanting to be left alone?" asked Winter.

"God knows! Classic Simon Tonks is that. Loves to tease, loves to pose a conundrum. Just like the old mysteries of the oracle. Just like in the Calder days."

Derek Russell became thoughtful and peered into the bottom of his empty mug.

"You know, John, that bit about being content and 'wanting to be left alone' - that puts me in mind of Guzzly Granddad's street boys ... Simon likes to talk, he likes to feel important. If he knows anything at all, eventually he'll talk. Our best friend now is time. Time rolls by and we keep our ears open. We wait, John. That's all we can do - wait."

And the years did roll by and they waited - in vain. Life went on. Charles Hardman, carefully guarded by his possessive father, was educated at Cressbrook Hall by selected private tutors until 1966 when he entered Oxford University to read history. In 1973 he had already acquired a reputation for studious and respected research into the local history, folklore and mysteries of Derbyshire. His first book - 'Cryptic and Curious Corners of Derbyshire', was published the following year. Several similar volumes followed. His writing was distinguished by painstaking accurate documentation and welcomed by sceptics due to a willingness to explore all possible rational explanations for unexplained phenomena.

146

In 1976 he married Helen, an upper class 'county' girl who shared his interest in the occult and encouraged his work. It was a good marriage producing abundant happiness and two charming girls. The family (which included Simon) were devastated by the death of Algernon Hardman in 1983. The 1960 tragedy had brought Charles and his father very close.

And more years went by. The old century made way for the new century. In Cressbrook Hall, little mention was ever made about 'the unsolved mystery of the lost lad'. Indeed, more than four decades on, two new generations had been born who had never heard the tale of the missing cyclist.

Brian Forrester had been completely forgotten by the general public ... until, that is, the end of April in the year 2003 ...

Chapter 20

A Writhing Tangle of Lubricated Bodies

Fast forward to 2003 and we will find Simeon Hogg putting away his Ordnance Survey map of Derbyshire. He walked over to his Derbyshire Life and Countryside calendar which was hanging in the kitchen. Underneath a sparkling spring view of Dovedale, he looked at today, which was Thursday, April 17th which unexpectedly and joyfully had been his last day at school. He looked at the remaining days of April which was just about a week and a half. He made himself a promise. He would get out of the United States before the end of April and he would see the coming of May in Derbyshire. He would, for the very first time, visit the Lea Rhododendron Gardens which were always closed by the time he reached Britain in late July. For the very first time in 43 years he would see the bluebells alongside the Cromford Canal.

For the umpteenth time he cast his mind back over the path of his life and bitterly regretted that, when it came to the crunch, he had always put financial security before quality of life.

Gary! He must tell Gary. Fortunately, having worked the early shift for the taxi company, Gary Mackenzie was home. The excited phone call pouring out excited plans mainly consisted of Gary urging caution and making common-sense objections to what he considered to be precipitate and ill thought out actions.

"To sell your house you really should be here to check it out. Don't just leave it to the real estate guy. What about your car? Furniture? Hold on, don't move - I'm coming over - now!"

The big surprise for Gary Mackenzie was Simeon's sudden release from his hated high school. All of his friends knew that it was an obsession to return home to England, to bury himself in the wilds of the Peak District, to get as far away from Metropolitan Detroit as possible. But suddenly, it had finally happened, the big move was at hand. Thirty minutes later, two old friends sat facing each other.

Old friends. An odd friendship which had survived for 35 years. Simeon Hogg first met Gary Mackenzie at one of Finkle Joe's regular Saturday night parties in 1968. Gary was 20, Simeon, who had just

149

started teaching, was 23. Finkle Joe was so called because he lived on Finkle Street on Detroit's east side. He was choosy. Guests had to be young (teenagers only) and desirable - that is, desirable to Joe. Simeon scraped by on the age qualification as he could just about get away with 19. In truth, if birth certificates had to be produced, very few in Joe's house would turn out to be genuine teenagers. In those days youth was all and mendacity was the name of the game. Thirty was dreaded and 40 was viewed as a form of living death.

Gary was too thin and too tall with a gangling body to pass the beauty qualification. Worse, his less than ideal body suffered the eruptions and past scars of acne, however, an invitation was handed to him in the Woodward Bar one night because Finkle Joe thought that Gary, in the half light, looked rather like Troy Donahue.

The parties, which consisted of between ten to fifteen youngsters, were, in fact, sex orgies. The action was preceded by the assembled guests sitting before a large TV screen watching Star Trek, a new series. A popular theme in the weekly audience was an animated discussion, speculating on how well blessed was the inscrutable Mr Spock. For the rest of his life, Simeon Hogg associated Star Trek as a prelude to sex.

During one slightly boring moment when Dr McCoy was trying to treat an injured alien (of uncertain gender) whose body was made up of living stone (*'It's life, Jim, but not as we know it'*), Simeon's wandering eyes (together with a few other wandering eyes - not least Finkle Joe himself) came to rest upon the striking blond newcomer called Gary. 'Definitely a candidate for the first room', considered Simeon. The 'first room' was the more respectable venue for the orgy which always started at the sound of the familiar closing Star Trek theme. In this dimly lit area, the guests paired off and generally remained 'faithful' - well, for that evening at least. In contrast the second room, pitch black, was a 'free for all', a writhing tangle of bodies well lubricated by much spilt semen, emitting an ongoing murmuring of deep ecstatic moans and groans.

In that predatory world of quick conquests, the delicate flower of lust quickly withers when touched by the frost of familiarity. Two hours later, two new friends, now firmly and forevermore platonic friends, were sitting facing each other inside a small cheap White Tower hamburger joint somewhere in Downtown Detroit. The hard bright fluorescent lighting bounced around the tacky shiny stainless steel

150

surfaces and finally onto the faces of Gary Mackenzie and Simeon Hogg, the only white, extra bright, white faces in the joint. Such cruel light did not improve those faces already ravaged by an evening of over-indulgence and wanton excess. Simeon was biting into his small 12 cent hamburger when Gary asked yet another enthusiastic question about England. This was good because Simeon, who preferred older company anyway, was rather bored with his callow companion. The centre of Detroit, an alien collection of skyscrapers, was the most un-English place in the world. In such a place, competing with raucous incomprehensible Negro chatter, to hold forth on the subject of Georgian buildings in Buxton was, to the chronically homesick young teacher - sheer heaven. With tomato ketchup trickling down his chin, Simeon Hogg, cheering all things British, sneered out at an ugly tangled harsh environment. He waxed polemical, denouncing the brash commercialism and global domination of the United States. He excoriated the abysmal quality of American television, boasting that he did not own a set and heaped praise on the superior standards of the BBC.

The following Saturday evening these strongly felt views were briefly put aside, when that same anglophile, one eye on Lieutenant Uhura, ever fiddling with her numerous knobs and switches *'All hailing frequencies open, Captain'* - and the other eye, sizing up the possible chances of landing a cute little number called Sam.

And so it came to pass that the young and inexperienced Gary (not Sam) started to look up to, and respect, the relatively sophisticated and relatively well travelled Simeon Hogg who came across as cultured and cosmopolitan.

     Gary Mackenzie lived with Mom and Dad and the four ignorant boorish brothers he hated in 'dullsville', commonplace, suburban Allen Park. Quite naturally, there would have been no hate at all had Gary been limited to their conventional 'All American', clean livin', root-beer and hamburger, baseball, cars, cars, cars, girls, girls, girls - lifestyle. But Gary Mackenzie had discovered wider horizons. By sheer chance, five weeks before, in Hudson's Department Store, on the mezzanine ...
well, in certain quarters, Hudson's mezzanine had quite a reputation. On this occasion Gary met two older men who changed his life forever.
     The two introduced him to another two - and so on. A whole

151

new wonderful world opened up. Professionals who went to the opera, to the ballet, to classical concerts spoke to him with respect and treated him as an equal. He was entertained, wined and dined, by well paid executives who lived in beautiful and expensive apartments furnished in antiques. It was all a very long way from 7681 Roosevelt Avenue, Allen Park, Michigan.

During the Mackenzie family dinner, the day before Joe's party, one of the uncouth boys was in baiting mood. Sensitive to Gary's new found values and high aspirations, Chuck Mackenzie engineered an argument about music and said -

"Beethoven's a load a crap!"

The effect, as expected, was verbally explosive. Vicious insults were exchanged over the cheap K-Mart kitchen table. Among a barrage of several other un-manly barbs, Chuck called Gary a *'stuck up ponce'* and Gary hit back with his entire stock of words which described rough young hoods with low taste. A few of these critical terms, those known to Chuck, hit their mark. Unfortunately, Gary's most powerful verbal missile *'parochial lout'* - missed, because Chuck was not sure of the meaning of the word 'parochial'. Finally, when the two combatants rose to their feet, it started to look as if the angry words would turn to blows. This is when Mom Mackenzie also stood up and stopped play.

Such regular 'sport' was only possible due to the volatile nature of Gary Mackenzie's frenetic personality. He was so easy to wind up when you knew which buttons to push - and his brothers knew all the right buttons. After one of his urbane friends had taken him to see a Shakespearean play in Detroit, Gary developed a morbid hatred of the television set, particularly the popular soaps and endless day-time quiz shows which were littered with frequent banal commercials. So it was now possible to irritate Gary by telling him how he looked just like 'Lurch', a tall gangling creepy butler to the 'Adams Family' - and so on.

Meeting Simeon Hogg was yet another stage in Gary's new education. He listened with admiration when told of educational documentaries, the excellent 'Panorama' programme, serious improving plays and rejoiced when Simeon told him that the English had never even heard of 'Lurch'.

As the years passed by, this original boundary between the respectful younger pupil and the older complacent master became blurred. The

152

deference gradually dissolved and gave way to a slowly creeping equality as the friendship gained a firmer and more sound footing.

Gary Mackenzie had an ever increasing appetite to meet and mingle with the avant-garde, to rub shoulders (or whatever) with the international chic, to soak up more and more high culture. He and Simeon spent time together in New York and London, but Gary extended his travelling to Paris, Rome and Vienna. During one long vacation he stayed in France and learned the language. Gary became a francophile whilst Simeon the tenacious anglophile was, and remained, a francophobe and in general terms - a confirmed xenophobe. This entrenched prejudice aggravated the manic and short fused Gary Mackenzie. He was annoyed with his friend for refusing to holiday in France. Simeon's reasons made Gary furious -

"No! Why should I spend my hard earned money only to have outrageously expensive muddy coffee thrown at me by an insolent anglophobe. Anyway, I want tea. I need tea, but they won't serve tea. They take delight in not serving tea. And why, pray, why should I be mugged each time I hail a taxi in Paris? Now Allen's taxis in Belper ..."

"Oh, for God's sake! Give me strength! Who the hell wants a taxi in Belper? I could scream!" He often did. *"You are so narrow minded. Your biased, bigoted world is so pathetically small. When I think of the hours I've wasted waiting for you: you, stooped over a bottomless tea pot, taking endless sips in boring tea shops. And then some stupid old peasant comes shuffling up -*

'Shall ya 'ave a drop more 'ot water, dook?'

Then I have to suffer another 20 minutes watching that cup kissin' that irritating, insular, smug, dozy, dopey face ... "

Such tantrums seemed to accompany a sort of frenzied dance of storming to and fro with flaying long arms. Yet, amazingly, the friendship endured throughout the many years surviving these regular dramas which were precipitated by the vast gulf of temperament between the calm and stolid Hogg and the impatient gesticulating Mackenzie. Gary was all go. He was all energy and highly sexed. Simeon could sleep for eight hours and more. Gary, ever busy hunting, clocking up the tricks, had little time for sleep and accused Simeon of wasting his time in the safe bath houses in which there were -

"... too many creepy old men, and so God awful depressing. Why the hell can't you go to the bars like any normal guy - or live a

little. Get ya ass to Palmer Park ..."

"Oh yes, where Marie was arrested last year!"

"Marie's a slut, she'd been there five hours ... So what! Police raid, once in a while, an occupational hazard."

"You seem to forget that my occupation is that of a teacher, not a taxi driver."

"This is Detroit! This is not Derbyshire. Get your head into Detroit. Three murders a day. The newspapers have more important things to report. Palmer Park. Go there tonight. It's the vice squad's night off - trust me. In bed at 10.30! That's ridiculous. That's pathetic. That is sad! Swing on that bar under the Henry Ford statue - great stuff: or go to the 'meat rack'. Live some. Life is passing you by, Simeon. In three years time you'll be 30. Who'll want to touch you then? Are you listening? Is anybody there? Oh, what's the use!"

Behind these lively exchanges, there was a subtle reason why acrimony never actually boiled over into real resentment. It was so subtle that neither party was really conscious of it. It was this: Simeon was entertained by the tantrums. Simeon enjoyed winding up Gary and watching him whirl around the room with fire coming out of his mouth and steam coming out of his ears. On the other hand, Simeon was a rock of stability in Gary's fast and precarious life. Simeon Hogg was always there for him.

One day the secretary of a proctologist phoned up Mrs Mackenzie complaining about her son's unpaid medical bills. It did not take long for Mom to find out what a 'proctologist' did, and a can of worms was opened at 7681 Roosevelt Ave, a 'Christian house', which resulted in the swift ejection of one 'degenerate son'. Simeon was there to receive the suddenly homeless Gary, but Gary knew that he would not be welcome for very long, especially, after the 'Tom Cruise look-a-like' incident. This was a typical Mackenzie one-night-stand, a gorgeous Canadian hunk who made himself very agreeable and displayed oodles of charm at the dinner table. Unfortunately he took it into his head to leave Gary's bed and Simeon's home in the dead of night, but, alas, did not leave Simeon's wallet. Under extreme duress, Gary quickly found himself a small cheap apartment in north Highland Park which was very handy for frequent visits into Palmer Park.

" ... So quit ya broodin'." ranted Gary in his new home. *"I'll never hear the end of this one. Thank God he didn't take ya precious*

154

Cadillac. That thing's an affront to common-sense and the ecology ... an you rushin' to ya Billy Fury records. What a joke. Who the hell's ever heard of Billy Fury anyway, as if that guy would want one!"

Gary always remained a taxi driver. If he never went to college, it was not for want of intelligence, it was for the want of concentration and staying power. His nocturnal activities always came first. Gary was self educated. He tried to educate Simeon Hogg into an appreciation of fine art. These attempts usually ended in failure and biting recriminations -

" ... and I was horribly embarrassed in front of Hank and Randy when you thought that Nureyev was a Russian car! You were bored out of your skull last Tuesday sittin' through that Fellini movie."

"You didn't understand it either!" snapped Simeon. *"Oh no, don't deny it. That was amply demonstrated at the start when there was no sound. Of course the folks around us thought there was a technical fault and were ever likely to start to grumble. But you didn't have to attack them and call them 'a bunch of ignorant peasants' insisting that it was supposed to be silent. And what happened next?"*

"Well, we can all make mistakes ..."

"It flashed on the screen - 'We apologise for the temporary loss of sound' - my turn to be embarrassed. I thought those teenage girls would never stop giggling. And another thing, I'm through with your high-brow obscure composers. Who was that appalling guy I had to suffer for two hours?"

"Bartok," said Gary, *"Bela Bartok."*

"Oh well, if I must be afflicted by another wretched concert with Hank and Randy, let it be at least a composer I've heard of - Bach or Handel, I can just about cope with Baroque."

"'Pearls cast before swine'! That's you isn't it? Don't think Hank didn't notice you fidgeting, yawning and sighing. So God-awful rude. Baroque! You can't be serious? Martha and the Vandellas is more your speed."

Chapter 21

Butch Numbers and Bitchy Queens

Two old friends sat facing each other: the younger sad, the older elated. Gary Mackenzie was sorry to be losing the companion who had been around for most of his adult life. Over dinner, the talk was about the immediate future in which Simeon Hogg became nostalgic about his English past, boyhood friends and a lost world of green hills, wooded valleys and lush dales. Throughout the years, Gary had occasionally heard about the intriguing mysterious disappearance of Brian Forrester and now, once again, his ever home-sick British friend agonised over the various possibilities. Impulsive as ever, Gary blurted out a suggestion which was aimed at keeping him in the company of his friend for some time longer.

"Why don't we go over there together and look for Brian?"

This proposition was startling in its simplicity, but designed to conform with Simeon's present mood to leave the USA as soon as possible. During the last three decades at the same Detroit taxi company, Gary had proved reliable and built up a strong tenure with his employer who had come to accept the demands for long summer vacations at short notice. Each spring it was understood that Gary would 'quit', but each fall he was always re-hired. Gary was valuable. Regarding the vast expanse of Metropolitan Detroit, he certainly had 'the knowledge' - in more ways than one. He was a good and experienced driver (if somewhat aggressive at times) who could be relied upon to safely convey his passengers near and far: even as far as any major hotel in Chicago or New York. Driving through Manhattan filled Simeon Hogg with horror; it filled Gary with joy.

Gary argued that his imagination, bravery and radical thinking could be useful at this critical moment in his more cautious friend's life. Furthermore, both men were Agatha Christie fans. Here was an opportunity for adventure.

"Why not? We're as good as the next guy! Let's live a little. Let's poke around and see what we can turn up. You've always wanted to show me Derbyshire."

During July and August, typically, Gary would allocate three or four

157

weeks for UK touring with his friend, but this had never included the Peak District. London usually received the lion's share, and most of that in nocturnal adventures on Hampstead Heath which animated and exhilarated the over sexed taxi driver - but left the respectable schoolmaster a nervous wreck! Notwithstanding, the latter honestly admitting being pleasurably drained by a great time, but, at the unacceptable cost of a good night's sleep, dodging the CID and any marauding homophobic yobs.

During the balance of the summer recess, Gary would 'tear up' The Continent and, as usual, Simeon Hogg based himself in 'the sticks' with his Aunty Joyce at Bog Hole in Horsley Woodhouse. This he had done nearly every year since 1965. After the excitement and sophistication of Gary and London, the humble rustic village of Simeon's coal mining heritage was comfortable and safe. Here in this quiet old fashioned backwater of southern Derbyshire, where stress was apparently unknown, he recharged his batteries in order to face the fast moving United States and the students and staff of Dwight D Eisenhower High School in September.

By 1965, Joyce Hogg, a maiden lady, was alone, very much alone having lost her aged parents. Simeon's visits to Grandma and Granddad in the 1950's were a form of sanctuary in the gentle company of a primeval trio. In this cosy, kind, contented narrow habitat he was, for a time, safe: safe from the ongoing cruelties and horrors of Mundy Street Boys School to which, eventually, he would have to return.

Grandma's face under her grizzled hair was deeply etched in leathery wrinkles, rather like the wizened apples she occasionally offered. Granddad was affectionately recalled as a great ancient man, deeply settled in a shapeless comfortable easy chair, amid a haze of blue smoke emitting a nostalgic smell from that old pipe. A well earned rest following a lifetime labouring in the bowels of the earth. After a smile of greeting he had very little to say to his young visitor.

At 78, Joyce Hogg was very old, but then she had always been old. Back in 1955 at the age of 30, she was old. Never seen with make-up, dressed in a dowdy old fashioned style, she absorbed the influences and old thinking of her parents, spoke and moved slowly with a slight stoop. Not actually stupid, but her mind had never been challenged having such limited experiences of people, travel and the wider world. Apart from an annual holiday with her parents to Skegness or Blackpool, perhaps an odd Saturday afternoon in Derby,

Joyce Hogg had hardly been out of Horsley Woodhouse - indeed she had hardly been outside of Bog Hole. Joyce was old, but Joyce was loved by her grateful nephew. He had been generously provided with an annual comfortable summer home for the previous thirty eight years. The back bedroom, once occupied by her beloved parents, was now referred to as *'Arr Simeon's Room'*, and had a pleasant view over to the village of Denby and beyond to the more distant hills of the north.

Bog Hole or Bog 'ole, (as it was called locally) sounded like a slum, but it was not a slum. It was a row of six terraced houses just to the north of the village centre which had always been dominated by the Hogg family. The accommodation was a simple Victorian 'two up, two down' design, purpose built by a coal owner for his colliers.

Gary's desire to take an early vacation with a view to solving a 43 year old enigma appealed to the newly liberated teacher. Simeon was genuinely fond of his energetic, permanently over-wound friend and was touched by this sudden demonstration of affection. However, the staid old schoolmaster was not too naive to recognise within himself, elements of the mischievous schoolboy. Like the evil scientist, he desired to bring together dissimilar substances to enjoy an explosive effect. The outgoing, forward-looking, forward-thinking Gary Mackenzie, eager to grasp the 21st century, could not have been more different from the insular, backward-looking, backward-thinking inhabitants of Bog Hole, eager to cling onto the values of the 19th century. Inwardly, Simeon rubbed his hands with malicious pleasure at the prospect of Gary meeting such types as Aunty Joyce, Uncle Wilf and Aunty Nelly and, best of all ... the Ducks!

This impish streak had long since existed in the relationship between the two. Gary had a horror of outrageous effeminate men which, in turn, tempted Simeon to engineer roguish methods to bring his intolerant companion into the camp of the camp. The Saugatuck incident was a good example. At this well known very active resort, near Chicago on the east side of Lake Michigan, somewhere in the dunes, Simeon fished out, as Gary would term - *" ... one of your freaks."*

This turned out to be a screaming little black queen known as 'Bun Bun' who frequently referred to herself as *'This Lady!'* From Simeon's point of view, shaking with laughter, the introduction was a huge success. There was poor Gary, of stony countenance, sitting on his towel on the main beach, helplessly watching this 'attention grabbing' hullabaloo - a one queen mini circus. Bun Bun danced and pranced around him, wriggling her back side, thrusting out her already prominent begging buttocks, yelling out in a thick Negroid accent -

*"Yea Babe! You is some sweet meat! Ooo oo oo! Hunky honky. Tasty honky. Ooo, This Lady - she hungry - yeah. This Lady is one hot slut! Bun Bun ready for **action**. She want fillin' - yeah! Ooo oo oo!!"*

The outrageous trollop continued to caper and orbited Gary's towel about three more times in her bizarre war-dance-come-love-dance, pre-sex ritual. Diplomacy was the only defence. Bun Bun was thanked for her kind interest but this particular 'hunk' was resting after a busy morning combing the dunes -

"Perhaps some other time?"

The retreating figure of a disappointed little Bun Bun, moving just ahead of her eye-catching, protrusive, rhythmic rump, minced across the sand and disappeared into the deep shadows of a thicket of coarse shrubbery - ever onwards, ever hunting, ever hopeful to find Prince Charming. This is when the volcano erupted.

"How dare you! How dare you bring that vile excrescence near my person." Gary had heard the word 'excrescence' for the first time just an hour before. It was used by a cultured gentleman he had come across during his wanderings around the dunes. The bawling-out continued -

"Look at that butch number over there."

Simeon took note of a very desirable sculpture of deeply tanned muscles, apparently indifferent to their presence, languidly soaking up the sun, looking out over the water, reposing and posing on a nearby towel.

*"Thanks a bunch! You've screwed that up real good! Well done! Ten minutes ago he was looking in **my** direction. I was in with a chance. Having witnessed that grotesque spectacle, he now looks at the lake - no chance, kaput! I hope you're satisfied."*

This underlined the main difference in taste. Gary despised the effeminate, the fat, the ugly, the sick, the old, the poor, the narrow, the parochial, the ignorant, the untravelled, the uncultured, the unsuccessful and the stupid. Only the young, the butch, the beautiful, the intelligent, the rich and the sophisticated need apply. He hated

Simeon's -

" ... *weird and wacky menagerie of creeps. What's wrong with normal people? How could you possibly have become bored with a gorgeous guy like Earl Vandenburg? He looks like Rambo for Christ's sake! And lives at the top of The Jeffersonian Building: a view to die for!"*

But Simeon Hogg had become bored with Earl Vandenburg who held forth at length on an erudite assessment of the merits of Weber. Just to make it even more difficult this obscure composer was pronounced 'Vaber'. The good-looking and trendy 'thirty-something' year old professional, insisted on describing in detail how Carl Maria von Weber skilfully steered German music from the Classical to the Romantic and how he made such an impact on Wagner. As the pedant rambled on and on, the superb view across the Detroit River over to Canada was a pleasant distraction for his dinner guest who would have much preferred to hear about the genius of Phil Spector - a name spelt just as it sounded.

No. Simeon did not wish to hear about Weber. He preferred the company of dear old Hubert, an uncomplicated man of simple taste who enjoyed retailing the latest gossip from the Detroit bars. In Hubert's seedy apartment on the East Side, Simeon laughed until he cried listening to frequent accounts of that -

" ... *bitchy queen Marie. Boy is she ever pure acid! There we are, me and Bill Scruggs, minding our own business, having a quiet drink. She spots us on the far side of the room and the next thing, she screams out for the whole bar to hear -*

'Miss Scruggs! There ya are! Honey am a comin' over. Here comes my body ... '

Then she sails over to us and we nearly died of embarrassment, especially for poor Bill who'd just had a toupee fitted.

'Why, Miss Scruggs - what is that! A rug on ya head arr perceive. Honey - you aint a foolin' nobody - an arr love to pull hair.'

To my horror she gave me a big hug like I was a long lost friend and shouted -

'Ooo so cuddly - that nice big fat belly! Look everybody it's Hubert. Poor Hubert, that evil cretin Danny should not be referrin' to you as 'The Lady of the Vapours'. Not true. You don't go to the Club Baths seven days a week, no, you take Mondays off don't you? But be careful baby, you've had three re-treads on ya tongue this year to date.

161

Yeah, an those teeth 'll need scrapin' again soon. That cum just builds up and up. Well it's true! It is. When I go to the Club Baths they hand me a towel. When you go, Hubert, they hand you knee pads!'"

Gary, who hated such tittle-tattle from the low life of Simeon's quirky collection of friends, had no time at all for any of this nonsense. He viewed old fashioned Hubert as one of the dregs of Detroit, a shabbily dressed overweight beer belly who broke wind too often -
"For God's sake don't suggest another meeting - I can't take the BO. He doesn't like me and I don't like him. Have a good look at him. Hubert is 'The Depression'. He gets his clothes from the Good Will. He belongs to the 1930's. He should have stayed there. And don't - PLEASE don't keep talking about Marie. She may be funny to you but, anybody who is anybody, avoids her like the plague. A vicious mixture of show-off, spite, chiffon and cheap make-up. As for Scruggs, well, he's just a complete waste of space."

Gary Mackenzie was utterly frustrated by the social gay scene. His reasoning was simple. If a man wants to attract another man then -
" ... why in hell's name do they behave like a woman? Why turn themselves into freaks. For God's sake that's just what they are - freaks! I'd like to punch their stupid faces! I really would ... are you listening to me? I'm at my wits end just trying to find one - single - real - macho man!!"

Two old friends sat facing each other. One was thinking about the novel challenge of becoming a detective. The other was relishing his sudden release from educational bondage and now contemplated the naughty pleasures of introducing his avant-garde friend to the reactionary delights of Bog Hole which was already half a continent and an ocean away from Detroit, but culturally, may as well have been on the other side of the moon.

Chapter 22

Babbacombe to Horsley Woodhouse

Having left America and all matters in the hands of his lawyer, Simeon Hogg went to enjoy a few days relaxing in Babbacombe, a very pleasant old fashioned sleepy resort near Torquay. In those same few days, Gary Mackenzie made the most of London and, having had his fill, joined Simeon at the Exmouth View Hotel with the intention of spending another few days. Exmouth was indeed in clear view, over the sea, looking north from Simeon's balcony just before breakfast on that last sunny morning of Sunday, April 27th 2003.

Babbacombe had been necessary. After the stress of the previous months it was important to have had a neutral place of sanctuary to mentally re-group, to collect his thoughts, to lick his emotional wounds. The weather had been very kind. Day after day he had been able to enjoy familiar wooded paths and to discover new ones around that beautiful coast. He drifted around exploring tiny hidden coves. He was mesmerised and soothed by an angry sea delivering giant splashes creating a boil of a million bubbles, flows and runs in all directions. He was fascinated by deep plops and the sun seeking out the shallow bottoms. A dance of sun-lit mottles played across a shallow screen of light grey pebbles and then deeper, across alien foliage of dark green and brown. Rocks galore, some speckled and scarred with barnacles. Rocks everywhere, rocks bare, rocks bald and rocks growing hair of brilliant green sea moss. Leisurely, Simeon investigated headlands and rested frequently, soaking up the warm early springtime sunshine in sheltered nooks and crannies. Getting as close as possible to the swelling clear green water, the crashing waves, tasting the spray, hearing the cry of gulls - were all part of the healing process which he considered reasonably complete on that Sunday morning.

Simeon now felt able to face the gentle fussing of Aunty Joyce who had been informed by letter that he would arrive with a friend 'around about late April'. Painful experience had taught him to be vague with arrival dates. This gave Simeon flexibility and prevented Joyce anxiously waiting at the door and fretting along with the whole neighbourhood.

It should be mentioned that neither Joyce nor anyone else in

Bog Hole possessed a telephone - with the exception of Aggie Oaks at the corner shop. Mrs Oaks had found a telephone useful since its first instalment back in 1969 and considered it her duty to convey important messages to other residents on the row. She was not overly burdened as such messages were rare in that humdrum and uneventful little oasis. This contented and old fashioned state of affairs with regard to primitive communications (notwithstanding the dawn of the 21st century) existed along side teenagers who were walking around using mobile phones. Simeon had noticed them on both sides of the Atlantic, mooching around in little groups, chattering about nothing into tiny telephones. He reflected that when he was their age, only the doctor and the vicar would be 'on the phone'. Indeed, he could not think of a single resident at Bog Hole who could, or would, use a telephone. They all left it to Aggie.

Since pre-war days, very little had changed at Bog Hole. It was a historic, working class community which appeared to be locked into a time-warp. The quaint inhabitants, most of them relatives, all in their seventies, eighties and nineties had, back in his teens, embarrassed Simeon. After a lifetime spent in a brash, commercialised and anonymous urban environment, he now saw this little fragment of Derbyshire as valuable and fragile. These kindly common folk were all old and would soon die. These precious people would leave empty houses: empty houses which (if not demolished) would soon be inhabited by the young, the innovators who would, very likely, destroy the character and charm of Bog Hole forever. Once gone, it would never return. Simeon Hogg the historian was already mourning the inevitable. If possible, he would have the National Trust requisition the old row and slap a preservation order on all the irreplaceable characters to ensure that they would live on forever.

Getting Aunty Joyce (chapel every Sunday) to accept into her home, a strange man, required a carefully composed letter written with the utmost skill and diplomacy. It emphasised that Gary Mackenzie, a long standing friend, was of good character, sober, honest, hard working and, most important - extremely respectable. Utter nonsense of course, but most of the aforementioned, save 'respectable', had a measure of truth.

In truth, Simeon himself would have never been permitted to pass through the portals of Aunty Joyce's very respectable house if she could have seen him (it had to be said many years before) in the centre of the famous circular mattress in the dark and musty bowels of the Ebony Stud Baths in Harlem. The scene giving most offence would be the occasion when a half dozen talented, but exhausted, sweaty, naked Negroes, after long exertions enjoyed the result of their hard work. A further score of fascinated on-lookers in that dim, subterranean chamber, were moved to applaud and cheer when, after receiving great collective efforts and intensive ministrations, the teenage Simeon finally achieved a new record in that murky and much visited (as Gary always called it) den of iniquity - a fifth orgasm. *"Den of iniquity!"* thought the mature man in some surprise, savouring the marathon erotic adventures of the boy he once was. The atmosphere was similar to a noisy evangelical black revivalist meeting or, perhaps more appropriately, blood thirsty Romans at the Colosseum calling for more gore and suffering. But in this instance it was an enthusiastic mob calling for pleasure: a collection of lascivious slavering black men, jumping, gesticulating, hooting, baying and shouting obscene encouragement to the group of workers -

"Yeah man, go to it. Go go go."
"Do it babe, do da white boy. Do it babe - he lovin' it."
"Do it good. Do it. Do it. Do it ... "
"Dat right, hear da man."
"Ooo - move it! Give it gooood."
"Lift it! Lift it! Arrrr yeah, right there, arrr yeah."
"See dat sweet meat. Ooo sooo sweet an milky."
"Hear dat kid. Yeah!
"Oh! Yeah! Moan - moan baby. He so so very close .... "

Such a scene was well outside the scope and compass of Aunty Joyce's experience or, indeed, her understanding. Blissfully ignorant, she was very proud and often boasted to neighbours and other villagers about her favourite nephew, the estimable and dignified schoolmaster who maintained the discipline and high standards of a past age.

On the previous day Gary had been maintaining his usual high standards studying the interesting wild life at Petit Tor Point, which had been especially wild during that afternoon. Simeon was on Oddicombe Beach studying a long letter he had received from a retired police officer - Detective Inspector Derek Russell. This, in response to a request for a full and detailed account of the circumstances and personalities around the disappearance of Brian Forrester in the July of 1960. Simeon telephoned Derek Russell to thank him profusely for such valuable and privileged information and assured him it would be used only with great care and discretion -

"Not at all, Mr Hogg, you have all the advantages of the amateur and I only hope you can succeed where John Winter and I failed. Proceed with caution! Remember murder, if murder it is, is not a game. If somebody has once killed to obtain silence, they may feel threatened enough to kill again. Also bear in mind that there may be no crime here at all. Some people disappear because they want to disappear - keep an open mind. Anyway, let me know the result - if any. Good luck!"

It was about four o' clock on that Sunday afternoon when Simeon's new car came to rest in the car park of the Strensham service area en-route from Babbacombe to Horsley Woodhouse. Of course this extravagance was to alleviate the trauma of having to part with his beloved 1959 Cadillac. A painful separation of which he would never quite come to terms. Even at this stage, it was not too late, he could have it shipped over. Like the house it was unsold, still locked away in the darkness of his garage. Suddenly he was seized by a heart-wrenching pain. His magnificent Eldorado, all alone and abandoned, somehow, might know of his unfaithfulness in this traitorous purchase -

"It's no good. I'll call Larry and tell him to send it ... "

"Oh no, please no, not again ... " replied Gary, rocking on his seat, holding his head. *"**How** many times do we have to go through this? Read my lips - it is not viable. It is too expensive - a fortune to get it over here, a fortune to maintain it. It is old and it will fall apart. It is 43 years old! I've seen you turn down much younger. It is too big. It won't work. For Christ's sake, look at yourself! You have problems parking up **this** car - tiny in comparison."*

Gary looked at the tragic pained face of his old friend and, in sympathy, felt something of his grief. Apart from a few infatuations, Simeon Hogg had never really loved any human as he had dearly loved this car.

"Look ... it's steel, glass and leather. It isn't thinking about you. It can't think. It has no brain."

166

The crisis passed. Simeon consoled himself with a pot of tea. Gary had a cup of coffee which he drank up quickly.

"Well I suppose I've tasted worse." Ruefully, he looked over at the tea pot and estimated a further two cups, perhaps five minutes for each. Elbows on the table, supporting his head, he let out a deep sigh -

"You English never drink water!" Simeon hardly heard this and continued to sip, soothing his throat, mind and body.

"That's it!" added Gary. *"The water is in the tea. You keep drinking tea instead of water. That explains ... "* He was interrupted by a large thick envelope thrust in front of his face -

"You should be reading this. It's the full story from a retired Detective Inspector who was on the case: people, places, times, theories, evidence (mostly lack of) - eleven pages typewritten. Treat it with care. It's highly confidential and for our eyes alone."

Gary received the document and reverently skimmed over the covering letter.

"He's charm itself. Nothing like the cops I've come across."

"It's the way we do things here," responded the Englishman stiffly. This often heard attitude never failed to irritate the American, but annoyance was suppressed by a growing excitement: the excitement of a challenge and a taste for adventure. Some years before, after hearing an outline of the facts, Gary essayed a solution to the puzzle -

"The Lord of the Manor, or the butler, or both, probably tended Brian's wounds. One or both got fresh. One or both were into chicken. Maybe Brian was willing: a new experience. Maybe he wasn't. Keen or not, later he could have got 'a conscience' - it happens to kids. Then it gets real dangerous: dangerous for butler or Lord or both."

"So where is Brian?"

"Probably walled up somewhere in that old heap."

"They looked!"

"They looked! - sure they looked. They did their job and hours later were able to say - 'We've done our job, guys, we've finished, we've looked, we've done for the day'. A team of cops poke around, they mooch around, they go through the motions. It's not difficult to rub dirt or old dust into fresh mortar to make it look old. They didn't tear that place apart. They wouldn't have dared. It's not difficult to carefully remove turf on a lawn, dig a hole, insert a body, take away about a third of the original dirt and carefully put back the turf. Result

167

- no trace at all.

*Oh I could just see it! 'Yes, My Lord, no, My Lord. We'll not trespass on Your Lordship's privacy any longer than necessary. Your Lordship is **too** kind.' I've seen it. I've seen it with you. Like the time we were locked inside Melbourne Hall gardens and Lord Something or other, no less, had to escort us out. So obsequious! You made me sick! Just like that odious Mr Collins in 'Pride and Prejudice', fawning, fussing, bowing ... "*

*"I did **not** bow. I was simply being polite and apologetic to Lord Ralph Kerr for poor time-keeping."*

"Well, you get my point. The respectful kow-towing English police, especially four decades back, would not be eager to upset the lord by looking too hard for a body inside Something Hall."

"Cressbrook Hall. And anyway, Algernon Hardman was a doctor, a PhD, not a lord."

Back to the present. Gary, now armed with a seven page narrative including all the salient points, was confident that he could crack the mystery. This confidence was not only born of conceit but also based on a self-assured enthusiasm in his own street-wise credentials. He felt well qualified to deal with this particular type of crime. Gary had been around. He had attended the 'university of life' and sincerely believed that, given enough data, he could discover the key to unlock this conundrum -

*"You have to remember the limitations of the investigating team. I've not read it yet, but I'll bet ya these guys, no doubt born and bred in the sticks, were pretty innocent when it came down to sexual matters, especially gay sexual matters. Your average 1960 cop, or 1960 anybody, could hardly conceive of any sexual orientation other than the majority heterosexual norm. Back in the 1960's I spoke to older gay guys in London, **London** mind you, who'd never even heard of the term 'gay'. They described themselves as 'queer'! They used the same insulting word which was used by Joe Average.*

"What's your point? How will this find my friend?" asked Simeon.

"My point is this: I can see further than the 1960 Derbyshire Police service. And, I genuinely don't want to offend you, Simeon, but I can see a lot further than you."

"Oh?"

"OK. You've been to university and got all the book learnin',

true, but in many ways you are very narrow and in many ways still in your closet. Don't be hurt. Don't punish me with the sulks. Stick with this - it'll do ya good."

"I'm listening," replied the other, softly, in a controlled manner familiar to Gary which warned him to tread very carefully in the impending mine-field ahead.

"Well, to start with, you have too much faith in your 'wonderful British police'. You'll take this (he held up the envelope) *at face value. I know something about cops. Cops can be bought. I've been there. I'll read this critically and I'll read between the lines. And then there's the problem of your blinkered thinking ... "*

"Blinkered thinking?"

"Nothing wrong with it!" he added hastily. *"It just isn't right for this job. Don't get me wrong. You're intelligent ... but you're not broad. You won't broaden. You refuse. You're too sensitive, too clinical, too stiff and lack imagination. Look at your attitude to drugs."*

"Let's not go over all that again ... "

Simeon was only too familiar with Gary's assessment on his character. Simeon had always taken the view that he would not ingest unknown, untested, unsafe mind altering chemicals for recreation. He had always refused to 'high', and, with the exception of his best friend, refused to associate with those who did. Gary considered this attitude to be insular, parochial, narrow and bigoted. During the 1970's they had many unresolved arguments on the subject. Gary was continually niggled by Simeon's detestation and refusal to touch anything alcoholic. This came to the fore at dinner parties.

"Get out the orange juice, guys, Simeon won't even sniff your expensive wine," was often snapped out with a sharp edge.

Gary's short lecture ended with -

" ... so it can hardly be your fault if you're, by nature, ill fitted to steer through this labyrinth. I often think that the only time I've ever seen you totally comfortable with yourself was in the Harlem Baths.

Anyway, I'm going to be like Poirot. I'm going to despise running around and exerting energy. I'm going to sit down quietly. I'll examine all the facts, arrange them in methodical order and think about it. At the end of a period of reflection, I'll tell you who killed Brian Forrester or, I'll tell you where to look for him or his body. I know I can do it."

"I hope you can," said Simeon quietly.

"But," continued Gary *"before I study this very excellent police report, will you, once again, go through the whole story, as you recall it, from beginning to end? Tell me as much about your five friends as you can remember. Tell me what happened. Tell me what was said, even silly adolescent talk. There could be something small but significant. Go through that journey. Tell me as much as possible of what you heard from the police, your parents, your friends or any comments at all from any adults after Brian went missing - even months or years after.*

*Tell me **everything**, Simeon. I'm listening,"*

Chapter 23

Put Ya 'At on, Joey!

All talked out, Simeon steered his car off the A38 and northwards on to the old A61 which had now been demoted to the B6179. He turned right at Kilburn Toll Bar and followed the friendly A609 to Horsley Woodhouse. This was part of the old Belper to Heanor road; a road which was familiar after umpteen bicycle rides. In the seclusion and remoteness of an automobile, that much loved highway could never have been experienced with such intimacy as with cycling. The annual return home to these kind hills and amicable valleys never failed to thrill a nostalgic part of the man who was once a happy creature called Dobba.

Horsley Woodhouse at the top was broad, straight, open and wide. It became more narrow, more cluttered, more interesting and quaint near its centre. A left turn took them into a curved terraced road and several further turns confused Gary Mackenzie as they negotiated a small knot of dowdy Victorian housing, blackened by decades of open coal fires. Row after row, the sight of these simple dwellings was a pleasant step back in time for Simeon, but a culture shock for Gary. In seconds they emerged into a final short terrace which ended in a pleasant green recreation ground. This was the humble row known locally as Bog Hole. It was quiet and completely deserted. There was a profound sultry peacefulness in that warm lazy sunshine such as if it were a sleepy afternoon in mid-August. Simeon announced -

"My ancestral home! No bay windows, no front gardens, the doors open directly onto the road - but just look at those beautiful white door steps."

Gary felt like an on-looking alien as Simeon explained the Monday morning ritual of 'donkey-stoning', cleaning the front doorstep with a chalky-white brick dipped in water.

"Check-out the windowsills. They've been scrubbed clean too, even the section of pavement (side-walk to you) in front of each house. Rough and common we may be, but it's very important to be clean," added Simeon.

"Do they sit out in the street!" said Gary observing several chairs placed near the doors.

*"Think yourself fortunate they're not actually **on** those seats. A*

little earlier and we'd have been mobbed. Lord how I hate fuss! No, we're safe, they're all inside. It's tea time, that is, 'Sunday tea', a light meal of perhaps a simple salad, sandwiches, bread, followed by tinned fruit and cream, or evaporated milk. Perhaps cakes ... whatever."

"Thank God we're not in the Cadillac," said Gary. "As it is, it feels as though we've landed from space. What will they make of this car?"

"Not a lot. Expect I'll get a lecture from Uncle Wilfred for gross extravagance."

A moment later they stood in front of Aunty Joyce's wide open front door, Number Four, Bog Hole, which, like the other doors had an adjacent chair. The frontage of the row faced south and, unusually for April, it had been a pleasant warm sunny afternoon. To Gary's surprise Simeon just walked in. In a mining community, it was working class tradition: a relative would never be expected to knock. They passed through an old fashioned, hardly used, slightly fusty but highly polished 'best' front room. Simeon called out *'Hello'* as he approached another open door into the equally small and equally deserted rather dingy living-room. Well away from the sun, a black, lifeless fireplace underlined how cold it was. A heavy dark oak 'best table', circa 1930, lived just under the north facing window. High up, much too high, perched on top of a cupboard was an ancient television set showing a very rounded dark orange screen.

Beyond this room was another open door leading to a narrow primitive kitchen. Under the west facing window, Gary noticed a shallow stone sink and a large fluted cast iron hand pump, now disused, which was situated over a well. Opposite, he became aware of the movement of an ample, ponderous form, slowly rising, sluggishly responding to the greeting issued seconds before. The effect was all grey. An old grey head gradually turned towards them. It had grey hair which framed a wrinkled grey face and sunken mouth showing an expression of alarm. Slightly resentful eyes changed to surprise and then pleasure when Aunty Joyce recognised her nephew.

"Well, well, well! A didn't know when ya were coomin'. Ya didn't say but av got a bita tea in for ya if ya'll ave a bit? An ya'll ave a bit a barm bread shant ya?"

Gary could now see that she had been eating at a small kitchen table pushed up hard against the wall to make the best of the meagre space.

On the table he noted a bird cage and a green parakeet firmly imprisoned within: not only within the bird cage, but also within the captive and constant oppressive affection from Aunty Joyce. The green feathers contrasted sharply with the dismal dark green background which appeared to be a pre-war paint job. At a glance, he found something profoundly miserable and pathetic about this sad, rotting old woman, cloistered in such a depressing dank cave-like kitchen with her unfortunate captive, pea-brained companion. Furthermore, he was, at once, irritated by her slow whining voice which seemed to Gary to be full of self-pity.

As aunt and nephew came closer, he was surprised by the lack of physical contact. Gary was not particularly tactile himself and Simeon even less so, but Joyce Hogg had not seen her closest relative in nearly a year and at least a peck on the cheek would seem to be a minimum token of affection required by the occasion: but no, nothing beyond mutual smiles and restrained smiles at that. She fussed and whined a little more before noticing Gary and his outstretched hand. Simeon promptly apologised and made introductions. Joyce became a little flustered, twittered out a few inane comments and quickly wiped her right hand on a dingy apron before allowing it to touch the hallowed hand of this esteemed visitor. Since her guest was an exotic stranger from a distant land and another time, Aunty Joyce felt it necessary to increase the volume of her voice when addressing him -

"Are ya all right then! Shall ya ave a bita tea?"

Gary replied that he was very well and thanked her for her kind offer of accommodation and yes, he was more than ready to eat. These spoken courteous words were at variance with his true inner attitude, but Gary Mackenzie was not a man to spend a dime when a nickel would do. Hotels and guest-houses were expensive and Aunty Joyce's rates were most reasonable, indeed, they were archaic. Over the many years of summer holidays this generous lady was loath to accept any money for 'bed and breakfast', but Simeon had to insist, and even then, she would only accept a modest payment for the use of her back bedroom.

Ponderously, Joyce plodded over to her cupboard, clattered plates, cutlery and set two more places at the tiny table whose surface area was drastically reduced by the bird cage. The bird suddenly became active and sent two feathers drifting down. One landed on a saucer of beetroot and the other on the plate of Aunty Joyce's forlorn unfinished meal. This concerned Gary who also observed fragments of seed on a plate of white buttered bread. Such possible threats to hygiene were soon allayed when he considered, first, that he was hungry and secondly, that more germs would be orally ingested at an all night weekend visit to the Man's Country Baths in Chicago.

After a tin of best red salmon was opened, dished out, and three cups of tea poured out - the 'tea' commenced. Simeon heard a brief account of all the inhabitants of the row and a more sketchy account of the general news in 'Osly Woodas'. There were births and deaths - mainly deaths. With some indignation and barely disguised relish, Aunty Joyce sprung her big story - the teenage, unmarried Kelly Grocock was pregnant! Simeon explained later that Kelly, known as 'the bicycle of the village' had outraged respectable opinion since a scandalous incident which occurred when she only was ten years of age. It was alleged that, on the recreation ground, in frustration and temper, she kicked a boy in the crutch because he had been unable to maintain an erection. Joyce shook her head ruefully -

"We not used to it. Ya wouldn't think she'd do that would ya. Grococks 'av allus bin a roough lot. Common as moock. Owe's no shame. No. Arr Sara shouldn't be gooin we 'er."

Simeon had started to translate Joyce's words to Gary. He found her thick local accent somewhat difficult to understand -

"'Going with' means that naughty Kelly and Sara Hogg are friends. Sara is the granddaughter of Aunty Gertie at number three. 'Allus' means always and 'owe' means she."

After a trio of much tut - tutings and enthusiastic condemnation of the disgraceful conduct of the appalling Kelly, who had brought shame on the village - the subject of scandal was finally exhausted. Simeon took the opportunity to briefly outline their plan to investigate the mysterious disappearance of his school-friend Brian Forrester. The subject of Kelly had produced unanimous agreement but the atmosphere was now more constrained. Aunty Joyce was not at all happy about a Hogg playing detective and stirring up an old unpleasantness -

"A should leave it be if a were you. Ya never know what ya'll rake oop. Ya grandma allus use ta say 'Let sleepin' dogs lie'."

This was not the only reason for constraint, the other was the physical

174

nearness of Gary Mackenzie. Esteemed or not, this tall unknown handsome blond was a man, and Joyce Hogg, the lifelong spinster, had always been very nervous of strange men who came from outside the family and Bog Hole. Each time Gary addressed her directly she immediately averted eye contact, became downcast and examined a filthy old peg rug she had made years ago at school from bits of coloured rag.

The consumption of three minuscule fairy cakes and three further cups of lukewarm stewed tea concluded the tasty, if rather sparse meal. Small talk had run its course. The conversation gradually dried up leaving long and slightly embarrassing pauses causing a small amount of tension. During one silence, Joyce looked up through the window and eased the tension with a slow and easy - " ... *mmmmmmm.* " The bird moved.

> "*Nice parakeet,* " said Gary.
> "*We call it a budgerigar,* " said Simeon.
> "*Mmmmmm,* " said Aunty Joyce.

Suddenly - the bright clean surprise tinkle of a bell! To the rescue came - Joey. All eyes turned upon the little budgie who had cleverly rang his bell and provided a delightful distraction.

> "*Elo, Joey! Are ya showin' off. Joey Joey Joey!*" repeated a delighted Aunty Joyce. She pushed her face up close to the cage and pursed her lips to make a kissing sound which both revolted and annoyed Gary. For the benefit of his hostess, he tried hard to maintain a half smile to suggest his pleasure at such charming behaviour, but was further aggravated when his mischievous friend said -
> "*Joey Joey Joey! Look at Joey, Gary!*"
> "*I can see Joey,* " responded the other, through his teeth.

They were all rewarded by a single chirp, a cocked head on one side and a second peck of the bell. At that moment the show became really interesting when Joey did his party trick. He put his little head under the bell giving the amusing appearance of wearing a hat. Aunty Joyce twittered and chuckled.

> "*Put ya 'at on, Joey. Joey Joey Joey. Look, Simeon, Joey's got 'is 'at on! Joey Joey Joey ...* " and so on.

After a few more minutes of the infuriating trivia, Gary interrupted -

*"You were going to show me that breathtaking view of that ...
what was it ... Christ Stand? The inland light-house?"*
"Crich Stand. It's a war memorial. Come on."

They gave profuse thanks, made apologies and walked out of the
kitchen door into the back yard. Gary was curious about the apparent
kitchen extension and three doors. Simeon smiled before entering into
the vernacular -
*"Coalas, shitas an weshas. But of course we Hoggs never use
words like 'shit'."*

His grin widened as a distant and embarrassing memory drifted through
the years. It was on a similar back yard where Dobba once went to call
on a mate whose uncouth dad, unshaven with braces, was sitting,
sunning on a dustbin just outside the lavatory.
"Ays a-in [having] *a shit! Are ya still in there arr youth?"* he
used his elbow to pound on the door. A deep muffled voice from
within answered with -
"Sod off."
*"Dobba's 'ere. Ays coom fa thee. Wot ya doin'? Are ya
wankin' a summat? Come on out ya dotty bugger!"*
"Sod off."

Simeon decided not to share this memory with Gary and, instead,
translated -
*"Coal-house, lavatory and wash-house. Aunty Joyce never has
to worry about a power cut. Look at this."*

He opened the first door to show the bricked up copper caldron and fire
grate beneath. Simeon's bicycle, ever ready for his annual summer
visits, was leaning up against the wall. Attention was drawn to several
metal pails, the big dolly tub, the ponch and the wooden dolly peg. He
joked that the end part had always reminded him of cow's teats.
"This is simply unbelievable!" said Gary. *"She washes clothes
the medieval way! Can't she afford a washing machine?"*
*"She doesn't want one. Why should she change when she's
perfectly happy doing it the same way her grandmother did it?"*

Although Gary was only three years younger than Simeon, the function
of these items of laundry, including the great cast iron mangle had to be

176

explained. This American could not remember a time when a fully automatic washing machine was not a part of the Mackenzie modern fitted kitchen. One of his early memories as a seven year old in 1955 was the excitement of the delivery of the new colour TV set. The residents of Bog Hole waited a further five years to see their very first black and white television. Only Gary's grandfather could recall an absence of electricity where he lived in a remote part of northern Michigan. Simeon had brutal memories of a gas lit Mundy Street Boys School. Most families in Allen Park had two or more automobiles in 1955, but in that same year, a Heanor youth would be lucky to get a ride in a motorcar at all. Gary had never known a time when he didn't have access to a daily shower. Aunty Gertie and Uncle Fred considered themselves posh to be the only family *'in t' Ole'* to have the modern luxury of an indoor bath. The world of young Gary could not have been more different to the more primitive world of young Simeon and they often had interesting discussions on that subject.

"And I have never, ever, had to go outside of a house to use the toilet! Not even in France," said the honoured guest, slightly revolted at the sight of the Victorian lavatory with its 'pull chain'.

"Shush! She could hear you. She's works very hard to keep this loo clean. Look - it's spotless. Can you smell the Dettol? Like the pavement in front of the house. She's proud of it. Anyway, you won't need to leave the house. There's a perfectly good antique chamber pot in our room. You like antiques. It won't get too full because she empties it together with her own every morning without fail."

Recognising the familiar wind-up, Gary garnered restraint. He met his friend's twinkling eyes, spoke softly and slowly with great control -

"If you think, that I, am going to squat over a smelly orange pot of piss, in that small room, in front of you - then you can start thinking about getting me into an en-suite room in a hotel - hang the expense!"

"She locks us in at 11.00pm. Oh well, I suppose she'll give you a key to use the toilet. There you go," he pointed. *"You'll never see anything like that in Allen Park. Can you see? Right in the distance on the horizon - Crich Stand. It'll start flashing in about two hours."*

"Very phallic," came the slightly testy reply, but Gary acknowledged the north westerly view as impressive. He took a little time and his eyes swept over the patchwork panorama of varying gentle shades of green and grey. He noted the occasional small splash of dark

brown which spoke of far off communities. Further still, a distant misty sea of deeper green could just be discerned, the special green of Derbyshire woodland and fern meeting the sky.

Chapter 24

Clothes of the Dead

It was time to unload the car and check into the room. Gary noted two beds, a double and a single -

"... on the floor! Why do we sleep on the floor?"

"Best way. You recall that awful back trouble I had in the mid 1970's? Aunty Joyce's bed: it cost me a fortune in medical bills. To be more precise, Grandma and Granddad's bed: so old, tired and worn, it was no better than a hammock. No support at all. Just a few nights put me in agony. It's still there, she'll never get rid of it."

Simeon pointed to an untidy heap of ugly Victoriana leaning up against the wall.

"That is disgusting!" said Gary.

"The old bed?"

"No this 'eye'."

Gary had discovered the antique chamber pot which had an open 'eye' looking directly up at the user. He took an armful of clothes to hang in the wardrobe and received a shock.

"What's this! It's full! And there's two of us."

Simeon explained that each year since 1965, Aunty Joyce had always removed about four garments from the wardrobe as a concession to make a few inches of room for his own clothes for the time that he was resident. Gary was close to boiling point.

"A few inches! I need more than a few inches! How can a woman like that need so many clothes? She never goes anywhere. She looks like she hasn't changed her clothes at all since 1965!"

"Calm down, Gary, she may hear you. Look ... they are not her clothes ... "

"Not her clothes?"

"No. They belong to her dead sister, my old Aunty Elizabeth and Grandma. I suppose it's sentiment."

A moment earlier Gary was near to boiling, now he was steaming, struggling for self control and rapidly approaching apoplexy.

"Let me get this straight. For the last 38 years you have been

179

laying your shirts, coats, suits and pants all around this miserable little room because that stupid old woman down there gives priority to the dead. The living need the space but, in her book, the dead come first. Am I correct?"

"Not quite. There is room in the wardrobe for two of my suits. The rest have to lay around. Gary! Think about it. Think of the money I've saved over those 38 years. Some of those years were lean years and I wouldn't have been able to afford an eight to ten week vacation. London is expensive. Derbyshire is central, a good base. Closet space has never been a big issue because I simply accept her rules."

"Do you know what I would like to do to that woman?"

Simeon was silent. He waited for a narration of the forthcoming evil fantasy. These sadistic scenes had been heard many times before. This was, in fact, a good sign. The final stage of the Gary Mackenzie tantrum had now come. Apoplexy had been averted because, now, a dramatised verbal vengeance would be inflicted. All being well, the histrionics would pass and Aunty Joyce would know nothing about it and not be the slightest bit damaged. It also had the added advantage of diminishing the fury of Gary Mackenzie.

"I'd like to tie her up in a chair in front of that fire place and, slowly, one by one, in front of her eyes, burn each item of clothing in that hideous old closet. Oh boy! Wouldn't I just love to gloat watching her struggle to get free and try to scream against the gag."

This monstrous suggestion had the effect of reducing Simeon to roars of laughter which eventually infected his friend who had, by now, reviewed his position with regard to the cost of guest house accommodation.

"Poor Joyce! How could you be so nasty. It would serve you right if she tied you up to a chair in the middle of the Woodward Bar and had Bun Bun dance around you for a couple of hours!"

Minutes later they came down the stairs and heard voices at the front door. Aunty Joyce had received a visitor. Uncle Wilfred from number three had noticed the car and came to enquire. When they came in sight he stared very hard at the two guests. This familiar and rude ogling had never failed to irritate his nephew. Big round rheumy eyes, a pouting lower lip, and an annoying silence seemed to shoot out a reproach from the cantankerous old man who eventually gave voice to

180

his unwarranted grievance -

"Yown com then!"

Simeon translated -

"'You have arrived at last' - I'm being rebuked." He addressed Wilfred Hogg directly, in a sharp manner, to head off a further reprimand. *"Hello, Uncle Wilfred. How are you?"*

"Huh! Our am a? Are think our am a. If a were an os [horse] *they'd av shot me."*

"Sorry to hear that, Uncle Wilfred. You look fit enough to me."

"Know what day it id?"

"It's Sunday." replied Simeon

"Huh. Arr think Soondy. It me bothdy. Am 84 tady."

"Congratulations, Uncle Wilfred. By the way, this is Gary Mackenzie."

"Hi! Happy birthday."

"Huh!"

"Now if you and Aunty Joyce will excuse us, we really must visit all the other Hoggs before it gets too late."

"Thee nedna goo fa may."

Gary looked puzzled. Simeon translated -

"He said 'You need not go for me' or, 'Please don't leave on my account'. It's pit talk from his coal-mining days. I'm not quite sure about 'Huh!' Some sort of recurring expletive, no doubt a censure expressing dissatisfaction ... "

"Yo what?"

"I was just telling Gary we'll have to be going, Uncle Wilfred."

"Huh!"

For a moment the sun went out! It was the shadow of something large and silent drifting overhead. All four were distracted and looked up to see a low flying hot air balloon sailing towards Smalley and Heanor on a gentle westerly breeze.

"Ooo a should loove ta be in that basket," wished Aunty Joyce.

"Huh. Ad sooner cape [keep] *me fate* [feet] *on t' ground!"* demeaned Uncle Wilfred.

Simeon was very fond of Gertie and Fred Hogg. Over the years Aunty Gertie had very kindly pressed him to stay at their house. Over the many years Simeon had thanked her and politely declined on the grounds of Aunty Joyce having much more room and possibly, as a lonely soul, being more in need of the company. Number Two, Bog Hole was rich in company. Gertie Croake was one of a large and fertile family of Croakes who, like the Hoggs, had inhabited Horsley Woodhouse for generations. Gertie, one of fourteen children herself, had personally increased the Bog Hole population by eight: three girls and five boys. As long as Simeon could remember, there had always been little children crawling along Aunty Gertie's spotless floors. In the sixties and seventies these would be the grandchildren, in the eighties and nineties they were great-grandchildren and now Gertie and Fred were fussing, doting and cooing at a collection of great-great-grandchildren. Children were accompanied by parents and sometimes grandparents. The result: Aunty Gertie's living room was often full to overflowing with a humanity of Hoggs. Simeon recalled hanging his coat on one of the clothes pegs: it fell off! Like the room, the pegs, already overburdened, could hold no more. Gertie and Fred were generous to a fault. The kettle was always on the boil supplying an endless supply of tea for the multitude.

"Mash 'em some tea, Arr Fred."

Two mugs arrived and Gary tried to look grateful for the tea he did not want but the home-made fruit-cake looked delicious.

"Get thee chops round that!" ordered Aunty Gertie thrusting a tea plate at her grinning nephew. *"Thas like a bloody Cheshire cat! As bin ta see t' Dooks yet?"*

"Perhaps later."

"Silly owd boggas! Tha'll not see a lot a change. Thee get fatter. Thee dunna walk, thee roll down t' Ole." [Bog Hole Row]

Simeon loved his Aunty Gertie. Her entertaining banter was an annual treat. She sounded and looked like the much loved quintessential, all British battle-axe - Ada Larkin. But the superb actress Peggy Mount was playing a part and Gertie was the real thing. At 81, with robust health she was still going strong, calling, criticising, bossing, dominating and intimidating. This was the first house on the row to get a television but also it was the one house on the row which did not need one. The show went on and on, and it went better when Simeon had an opportunity to direct. As with his friend Gary, Simeon knew which mischievous buttons to press to get Aunty Gertie going. He usually started with Aunty Joyce.

"We've been talking to Joey. He put his hat on for us!"

"Bloody 'ell! An t' bod [bird] on t' middle at table. What must ya friend think?"

"Oh, it was different," said Gary cautiously and slightly intimidated by the crowd in that small room. Aunty Gertie continued her assault on Aunty Joyce -

"Nowt else ta do but talk tat bod all day. Bloody pathetic. Silly owd bogga! Owd fashioned as Methuselah. What must ya think, Gary? An you from America where it's all posh. It must be like goin' in t' bloody Ark. Noah were more bloody modern than owe is. Soft owd bogga 'er!"

At this point Simeon was seated, struggling to drink his tea, convulsed with chuckles, when he felt the familiar heavy hand of Aunty Gertie. It was not unusual to get a smack across the back of his head. He did not mind and it only made him laugh all the more.

"What you bloody laughing at? Daft bogga."

Being a Croake, Aunty Gertie was well disposed and enthusiastic to be critical of the Hoggs because the Hoggs had always been disposed to look down on her family of Croakes who were regarded as a lowly, rough and ignorant tribe. Simeon had always been amused at this ongoing soap opera of the low looking down on the low. Both families were from a mining working class background and both spoke in 'pit talk' but the Hoggs enjoyed a reputation as 'chapel folk' and actual swearing was taboo. In the 21st century, 'strong language' needs to be put in context. It was doubtful if Aunty Gertie knew the origin of her favourite expletive - 'bogga', from 'bugger' meaning a sodomite, but, no known obscenity would ever pass her lips or be tolerated from another. She probably assumed that 'bloody' was a reference to blood, when in fact it is a centuries old contraction of the oath - 'By my Lady', a reference to the Virgin Mary.

Aunty Gertie asked about Wilfred's wife -

"Ave ya bin ta see arr Nelly yet?" Before Simeon could answer, she pressed on. "Rough owd bogga! Owe asna [has not] bin out at t' Ole in twenty year. Owe asna! Owe blames 'im.

Here Gertie did an excellent impression of the ultra common, decayed, tripping, monotonous and toothless voice of Nelly Hogg -

"Owe said - 'A canna gerr 'im ta goo anyweir.' A thought, yo ignorant owd bogga! Fa God's sake don't mention Vivienne. It's arr little Vivienne this and arr little Vivienne that. Am sick a 'earin' about bloody Vivienne."

"I heard all about the much lauded little Vivienne last year - incessantly. Being childless I suppose she tends to dote on her niece," suggested Simeon.

"Great niece. Nowt else ta do that's 'er trouble. Owe were tellin' me what furniture t' owd man Broom'ead [Mr Broomhead] *ad delivered next door ta their Elsie's 'ouse. A sez, arr da yo know? Owe sez - 'A peeped through 'ole in t' fence!' Nosy owd bogga."*

After Simeon felt there was no further mileage to be had from Nelly, he made a mischievous reference to Aunty Gertie's other archenemy -

"I really must pop in and say 'hello' to Annie Oakes."

"Annie bloody Oakes! The owd rob dog 'er. Dunna buy any vinegar, its more bloody water than vinegar, an them bloody eggs, thee more than thee should be." Gertie turned and addressed the gathering. *"Owe'd steal Jesus Christ's shoe-laces!"*

"Owe's bin callin' ya agen, arr Gertie, owe as, owes bin callin' ya black an blue!" This from a prominent big woman, Aunty Dorothy who was Gertie's sister.

"I'll slap 'er bloody chops if 'er sez oat [anything] *about me! Wot yo laughin' at?"* said Aunty Gertie to Simeon as he received his second 'clout'. He quickly recovered to ask after Aunty Dorothy's health. As a child he recalled her massive legs with prominent varicose veins when she did a 'knees up' with Aunty Gertie at the Miners Welfare Club.

"Am all right, me dook," replied Aunty Dorothy and added *"Am in t' ladies darts team nar. Ad never thrown a dart before, but a threw, an it wore 60! An arr Gertie sat there we a face as long as a bloody fiddle!"*

"A never did! Tek na notice of a, Gary. Owe's a soft owd bogga."

Gary took full advantage of this comment to make one of his own. He was listened to with quiet respect by the congregation of mainly women who were curious about him personally and quite fascinated by his accent.

184

"It's really great meeting you all at last. Simeon's told me so much about you."

"Wot's 'e said about me?" asked Aunty Dorothy abruptly.

"Oh, no problem. Simeon speaks kindly of all his relations and tells everybody - 'I'm a friend of Dorothy's'."

To Simeon's relief, no one in the crowd appeared to catch the significance of Gary's hidden agenda regarding his last remark. Forty years before, Aunty Gertie and others in that room would tease Simeon about girlfriends. Thirty years before the questions became more personal and more intrusive. Marriage was mooted. It all became more serious and very uncomfortable for the visiting bachelor who had to field hostile questions and deal with working class homophobic innuendoes which cast doubt on his manliness and virile duty to 'do the right thing', to produce new Hoggs, to carry on the clan. Twenty years before the questions ceased, probably on the instructions of Aunty Gertie who, at long last, had begun to accept, to realise that 'Arr Simeon' was a Hogg of a different colour who had always danced to a different drum.

On this occasion, as well as assorted children on the floor, Aunty Gertie was holding court in front of aunts, uncles, several first and second cousins with a sprinkling of nephews and nieces. Referring to Gary, one woman said -

"'E looks like 'im as were on t' telly last night."

"Ooo arr," said Aunty Gertie. *"Nar oo was it?"*

"John Inman?" suggested Simeon.

"I'll give thee 'John Inman'! It were a proper man not arf a bloody man. Ooo was it, ever so famous, tall and fair?"

Several incorrect names were suggested by the audience. Simeon chimed in with *'Liberaci'* which annoyed both Aunty Gertie and Gary. Following further offerings from the gathering, Simeon made his last and final offer - *'Charlie Drake'*. Aunty Gertie was about to apply a third blow to her nephew's head when, to Gary's delight, Uncle Fred called out -

"Paul Newman!!"

"That's 'im!" cried Aunty Gertie triumphantly, immediately giving her irritating nephew a look of scorn. *"Charlie Drake! Yo silly daft lookin' bogga!"*

185

"A bit early aren't ya? 'Ow long for this time?" said Edna, a somewhat truculent and sharp tongued wife of a cousin who, for reasons best known to herself, always addressed Simeon in a hostile tone. The question gave an opportunity to speak of his recent retirement and the plan to discover the location of Brian Forrester. This information, once imparted and absorbed, changed the humorous tone and left a slightly constrained silence which was interpreted by Gary as privileged local knowledge, possibly dangerous knowledge. The silence was broken by a young woman who was sharing an ottoman with a skinny vacant looking girl.

"Well, it'll be nice ta know after all these years, wunt it, if ya can find oat out. A mean it's nice ta know t' truth in tit, Aunty Gertie?"

But, like Aunty Joyce, Aunty Gertie was not inclined to agree -

"Truth can be too bloody close ta om [home], *then it's not so bloody nice, arr Lilly."*

These proceedings were interrupted by the door opening. In came an attractive blond girl, Sara Hogg the great-granddaughter. Just behind and much bigger, big with child, was the notorious Kelly Grocock. Sara gave Simeon his annual greeting which seldom varied from -

"Ey oop, Yanks are 'ere! Art all rate, arr Simeon?"

Just as Gary had problems with effeminate men, so did his friend have an aversion to working class teenage girls. Especially such an unpolished, uncultured example as the smug, if rather plain freckled slag who now stood before him. Instinctively, Simeon feared unkind comments from an unrestrained acid tongue. Kelly examined him curiously with her typical, over-long feminine leer. He felt vulnerable. This was not his classroom and no threat of punishment was available for protection. However, as usual, all went well.

After cursory introductions and a brief banter of good natured cut and thrust, Aunty Gertie launched into a stinging attack on the state of Sara's new trendy hair style -

"Eee, arr Sara! Bloody 'ell! Just look at thee. Thay looks a bogga abaht t' 'ead!" [about your head]

"Wot ya mean? Ave paid a lot a mooney fa this!"

"Ya could a saved it. It ad looked like that fost thing in t' mornin'! Get shut a thee comb. It 'll save thee plenty a mooney it will!"

186

When the roar of laughter died down, it became clear that Aunty Gertie (a virtuous woman from the 'old school', not renowned for her gentle tact) was receiving Kelly for the first time since the sensational news of her recent, and now all too apparent activities with the tearaway Wayne Pickles. Gertie laid in with a rhetorical -

"*Wot the bloody 'ell 'ave you bin doin' then?*"

"*'E run me round rec.*"

"*We 'n all see that bogga! Chasin' dunt mek ya pregnant?*"

"*Arr - but 'e catched me!*"

This last reduced the two girls to a fit of giggles. Aunty Gertie shook her head and continued with a long reprimand which included harrowing accounts of punishments meted out to hapless girls of her own generation who 'got into trouble'. It was during this censure that Simeon felt a gentle nudge from Gary's knee, the signal that he had had enough of 'the relations'. It was time to give thanks for tea, make civil apologies and move on.

"*NO WAY! I can't take any more. No more visiting. I'm tired. I want to go to bed. Enough relatives for one day.*"

"*Aw come on, Gary! It's not late. Anyway, these two aren't relations. The Ducks are nice people. Just a few minutes to say Hi. They expect it. They'll be very hurt if I leave it until tomorrow. I always visit the Ducks after Aunty Gertie.*"

"*More freaks, if they're called 'the Ducks', they'll be freaks. I know it. I can feel it!*" Gary wheeled angrily around on Simeon and fixed him in the eye. "*I know you of old! You're just trying to annoy me - aren't you? Admit it! Who, for God's sake are the Ducks? Is that their real name?*"

This last gave the mischievous friend something to think about. A simple question - but Simeon had no answer. It had always been Duck and Mrs Duck as long as he could remember. She referred to him as '*Arr Dook*' and he referred to her as '*Arr Mam*'. They referred to everybody else as '*dook*'.

"*Yes, dook, no, dook, shall ya 'ave a coop o' tea, dook?*"

The end of terrace house of number six Bog Hole had always been called 'The Duckery' because the Ducks had always lived there. True, there was a duck pond in the garden but Simeon did not think that was the main reason for their name. How strange, he had never until this moment considered what their real names might be. He explained to his friend that, as a toddler, the Ducks were very kind to him. They took time and trouble to entertain him with cut up cardboard boxes and ... yes, porcelain ducks. Duck was very imaginative with any household materials and paint. He delighted little Simeon with model houses for the pot ducks, all of whom had their own names. The Ducks gave Simeon the most precious gift any lonely child can receive, they gave him time. Aunty Gertie was often busy with her large family but Duck and Mrs Duck talked to Simeon and gave him their full attention. That house was full of love. The Ducks were special. Somewhat unwillingly, Gary listened to this with growing curiosity.

"Was there ever a Mr Duck?"

Again the question took him by surprise! As far back as Simeon could remember there had been just Duck and Mrs Duck, never a Mr Duck ... but ... a glimmer, a distant fragment of a picture came back to him.

"Do you know, Gary, many years ago they used to be visited by a robin! A little robin used to hop on to the window sill. Duck would say -

'Ey oop, Arr Mam, look - it's me dad, it's me dad coom back.'"

"Oh no!" said Gary gloomily, bracing himself for an imminent visit to The Duckery.

No knocking, they just walked in. The Englishman and the American had different impressions. The latter saw two large eggs. The eggs with faces were deeply reposing into a cosy sofa and Gary had formed the impression that they had been sitting there for ever. Each face was wearing an irritating inane grin which Simeon would have described as a smile of welcome. Both fat faces were devoid of a single wrinkle which caused Gary to wonder how old they were, but, there again, his friend could not have given an answer. Duck had never changed. He had always looked the same. He was just ... Duck. The smaller 'Mam' egg cocked up her legs which could not quite reach the floor and spoke first.

"Eee it is nice ta see thee, dook. Are ya all right then, dook?"

The Duck egg appeared to do a quick funny wriggle and with dancing shoulders -

"Bit early aren't ya, dook? Ya don't usually come before t'

188

buddleia."

The strong scented lilac flowered buddleia sprouted all over Bog Hole from mid July onwards. It flourished in gardens, waste ground, any odd corner and shot out of cracks in the pavement. Even Duck's chimney stack sported an excellent specimen and he had always associated the flower with the annual arrival of the child he once entertained.

"Shall ya ave a coop a tea, dook? Will ya friend ave one? Put kettle on, Arr Mam."

"No, Dook. Ave joost sat down. You put kettle on shall ya, Arr Dook."

"All right, Arr Mam, I'll put kettle on."

Inwardly Gary Mackenzie groaned at the thought of more tea but, on completion of introductions, he made a supreme effort to be sociable and communicate with the Ducks. He noted the former toys of his friend, the collection of ornamental ducks and complimented the living room.

"You've made it really nice here. So very cosy and comfortable."

In keeping with the general character of Bog Hole, The Duckery was fixed somewhere inside a time warp, in this case possibly mid 1930's. Cosy and comfortable were apt terms here. Everything was soft and cushy. In contrast to the spiky Aunty Gertie, the conversation in this room was all ductility, well matched to the occupants, mild and downy. It had always been a great place for Simeon Hogg. In this old fashioned feathery room he had always been cushioned from the hard knocks of life. Nothing nasty or hurtful ever came from Duck, friendly podgy Duck, ever mellow and mellifluous. At worst, on the occasions in which he did criticise, he would begin with his characteristic wiggle, dancing shoulders and the one word - 'Meself' Like now, regarding the subject of Annie Oaks and her pricing policy -

"Meself, a think she's a bit dear. Don't ya think so, Arr Mam."

"She is, Arr Duck! Them eggs were five pence cheaper int' village. She teks advantage. She knows a can't walk far."

The conversation continued to touch on similar inanities which included the thoughtless Vivienne whose bouncing ball often annoyed

'Arr Mam', a dripping tap which Fred Hogg had promised to fix last month and an unpleasant character in a popular 'soap' who was -

"Nasty! Is really nasty. No need ta be like that. It's oopset Arr Dook, 'e 'as, ant 'e, Arr Dook?"

As expected these trifles irritated Gary Mackenzie to distraction. Concerns about a person on television who does not exist and an endless stream of minutia caused him to give Simeon an angry glance which said - *'For God's sake rescue me from this!'* Gary was missing the sophisticated stimulation of the dishy BBC producer he had recently met in London -

*"Simeon you **have** to meet him! Incredible background! He was an equity funds lawyer based in the Cayman Islands. He has an apartment in Mayfair to die for, speaks of friends in Hong Kong and owns a motor cruiser on the Thames. Super intelligent conversation!"*

Naughty Simeon knew he was mixing an explosive chemistry by introducing Gary Mackenzie to the trivial and spongy world of The Ducks in which the conversation was somewhat less than 'super intelligent'. Simeon had no wish to meet Gary's new friend. He saw the Ducks differently: they were warm and generous: they were non-contentious and undemanding. He found the quaint chatter balmy and mildly entertaining. He was always happy in The Duckery - but Gary had a face of thunder and now was the time to leave - and leave quickly!

Chapter 25

The Hustler, the Pimp and the Murderer

Dozy tired eyes, unwillingly, gradually, opened early the next morning. Slowly they focused on a clear blue sky: bright blue, happy blue. Simeon's mattress and his head was always situated just under the sash window, always open to the maximum extent when he was resident at Horsley Woodhouse. He was very comfortable, so very cosy tucked up under numerous good quality blankets, some of which dated back nearly 100 years. His body was warm, but a cold face gladly gazed out into that magnificent firmament and watched two black specs, very far away, involved in some sort of aerial ballet. Two large birds, way up high were circling, soaring, tumbling, falling, catching the wind and stabilising - just playing. They were enjoying their freedom, enjoying their life. *"Two for joy!"*

Simeon's heart leapt for joy as he remembered and realised that beautiful and total reality that he, yes, he too was now free. No more yobs to be disciplined. No more slags to be reprimanded. No more scumbags to be tolerated. No more progressive colleagues would ever taunt, needle or control him and no more left-wingers would ever infuriate him with -

"Cheer up, Simeon! You look so miserable. It can't be as bad as that."

The crows were now calling to each other. Their raucous caws blended with other reassuring nostalgic sounds. He was comforted by singing blackbirds, a crowing cockerel and mooing cows from a nearby farm. A distant man called out a greeting to another - *"Ey oop, Jack, art rate!"* It was all as it should be. He was home and safe. He was all right.

Another sound was very close by, the sound of rustling paper from within the room. He struggled his lazy body to peer into the relative gloom and saw Gary, sitting up in bed, studying the long letter written by Detective Inspector Derek Russell.

"Good morning! Sleep well? I've been awake ages and read this several times - interesting, but not very illuminating."

Simeon, still unable to articulate, just grunted. Gary was long accustomed to his friend's initial morning stupor and simply carried on -

"I hate to boast, but, well ... Are you coherent enough to take in my conclusions?"

Simeon grunted for the second time.

"Remember what you told me yesterday, in the car? That long account of your schooldays? The answer is there - not here."

Simeon blinked and grunted a third time.

"Just like a typical detective story. You had the answer all the time!" Gary met his friend's bewildered look and pressed on. *"OK. In short, this document is a red herring. The police are fools."*

Simeon sat up and found his voice.

"So where is Brian?"

"Where I said he was, walled up in Cressbrook Hall. All right, of course I can't be sure of the exact location ... "

"Gary, you're not making sense. Russell's account gives us some very logical suspects. The over sexed Tonks is a strong candidate. Coggan actually provided services to gay men who were prepared to pay. No doubt some of them were chicken hawks ... and that Wormall character, well, he was actually found with Brian's bike."

"Freaks! My friend, they were freaks for God's sake! What do we have: a screaming queen addicted to toilets, a little fat queen ever circulating in an underworld of seedy pubs and an ancient crone running a dingy medieval massage parlour for the desperate. Don't forget, in those days they were all operating well outside the law and outside the approval of society in general. They were scared, Simeon - scared! They lived their sad little lives as best they could. No wonder they were reclusive, reluctant to co-operate. Aware of murder, sure they'd be scared - dead scared."

"But the bicycle ... "

"I've a theory about that. I'll come to it later. Simeon, listen to me." Gary drew up closer. *"You've been around. You must have heard the expression 'hang it on the fags'. You know what I mean - 'let the fags take the heat'? That is precisely what Algernon Hardman did - he let the fags take the heat."*

"But surely ... we're talking about an educated respectable man, a careful man with everything to lose ... if anything should go wrong ..."

*"And it **did** go wrong! But what better place to try his hand*

with two 'known' gay guys conveniently on the spot. *Get real!* He knew the cops would focus on his staff."

"What makes you so sure they're innocent?"

"Who said they were innocent? Far from it. They were both dependent on Algernon Hardman and in it up to their necks. He used them. And he had another accomplice. I'll come to him later. This is a gut feeling based on experience. Freaks they may be, Tonks, Coggan, Wormall and Piggs, but they don't sound the type to be interested in chicken."

Gary Mackenzie leaned back on his pillows, sighed and resumed. He looked at his old friend - a knowing look.

"You've known chicken hawks. I've known lots. What do they look like?"

"What do they look like!"

"You know exactly what I mean. They're not types out of a book of fairy tales like that hideous goblin." He leaned forward. "They look like you!! And they look like me. They look like Algernon Hardman. They blend into the background. They're ordinary, not quirky, not camp, often quite butch. Admit it, Simeon, you've always like 'em young."

"I've liked them old too - sometimes very old - with certain necessary skills - of course. I'm not sure I like where this is going! I've never coerced and never abducted."

"I never called you a chicken hawk. You're too mild, tame, too much of a coward. No. I'd call you a chicken fancier. Back to the point - what do these freaks have in common - apart from their freakishness? They are **all** queens. And you know very well that all queens like 'em big, butch and mature. They'd have no use for a weedy chicken who, if anything, looked even younger than his years."

Simeon considered the wisdom of this statement but suddenly remembered -

"Guzzly Granddad! He doesn't sound very ladylike. He was ready to consume Russell and Winter - well, part of them anyway."

"True. And he liked to have boys around him, older boys according to Russell. But scrub the other three. No point wasting our time. They are probably involved in some way, but I'm certain they wouldn't be interested in Brian Forrester."

"So Algernon Hardman is our man? But, hang on ... you

mentioned an accomplice. Who would ... "

He was interrupted by a gentle knock at the door. As both men were well covered, Simeon called out - *"Come in"*. Ponderously, Aunty Joyce entered manoeuvring a tray supporting a large brown steaming tea pot, milk, an unwanted sugar pot and two large Denby beakers. Averting her eyes, lest they see anything untoward, she placed her burden on an ancient dressing table which was probably a wedding gift to her mother in the early years of the 20th century. Carefully looking out towards Crich Stand and clearly embarrassed, she attempted a little small talk -

"I 'eard ya talkin' an thought yad like a bita tea. Shall ya av a bita breakfast?"

"That is most kind of you, Aunty Joyce. You shouldn't have troubled ... "

"Breakfast sounds real good!" interrupted Gary, who with his lean and energetic metabolism, was always hungry. As Aunty Joyce was heard clomping slowly down the stairs, her nephew, desperate for his morning tea, jumped up, seized the pot, gave the tea a quick stir before completing the ritual so familiar to Gary Mackenzie - who did not want tea anyway.

"An accomplice?" said Simeon resuming, his face partly obscured by a steaming beaker. Gary (making do with the beverage provided as coffee was apparently unknown in Bog Hole) became thoughtful and chose his words carefully. He took a deep breath -

*"Hold tight, old friend. You're not going to like this. Try to take it slow and gentle. I hate to sound like Poirot lecturing Hastings, but ... you really do already have the solution. You know the answer. You gave it to me yesterday in the car. You can't **see** the solution because you're blinded by nostalgia and affection. How much did you **really** know about those kids? Did they see things the same way as you? Did they feel things the same - with the same intensity? OK, let me give you the clues.*

One beautiful, stunning blond hunk desired by all the girls. A gleaming new bicycle which cost a lot of money. A keen intelligence, an independent spirit and athletic frame with lots of energy which enjoyed regular excursions into the Peak District."

Simeon had frozen. The beaker was still up at his face, but the sipping had stopped. He found voice -

194

"What? What ... what is this?

"You know what it is. A gorgeous kid like Scott is going to be approached by somebody sooner or later, probably sooner." He headed off an attempt by Simeon to object. *"Let me finish. I know what you're going to say. Heanor's a small place and 43 years ago it was a different world when that sort of thing was unheard of - but human nature was just the same. Scott was a combination of things. He had beauty, brains and mobility. Just suppose that, one day, out on his tatty old bike, he falls into casual conversation with a smooth type like Coggan ... "*

"Hold it right there! If such a soft scented rotundity ever made a dodgy comment to Scott North - well, he would become very hungry."

"Hungry? I've lost you?"

"You need teeth to eat. That 'Dolly' would have got Scott's fist right in the middle of his fat face. Gary! Hear me good. Scott North was as straight as a die."

"That I don't doubt for a minute," persisted Gary. *" It is not the issue here. Stick with this - somebody, maybe Tonks or even Hardman himself, suggests to Scott that he can have a nice new bike and be the envy of the school. All kids want nice things. I keep hearing how poor the Heanor folk were. Do you seriously expect me to believe that your friend bought his brand new expensive bike with the money from a paper route! Get real! He gets a few shillings a week and then he turns up at school one day with a machine costing more than £20!"*

This last left the two silent for a few moments. A few moments were needed for it all to sink in. Gary continued, slowly, cautiously -

*"He may have hustled a little, many handsome straight kids will, **if** the price is right or, (and this is where it gets a little sinister) he may have been asked if he knows any younger kids who'll do it - again for a price."*

"You're unbelievable!"

"No. Listen to me. Scott may look and act like 18, but really, he's only 15 and he could be persuaded that a 'willing friend' will come to no harm. He may be tempted by good money for just a few minutes work. Hardman was rich. He could afford to part with a nice big bill now and again for his few moments of ecstasy. With sufficient incentive, Scott would overcome his natural disgust ... touching and being touched by a dirty old man can be tolerated - can even get to be pleasant. And Scott would take the view that a 'willing friend' could do

195

the same. I'm guessing of course, but, say .. a fiver for Scott and another fiver for the friend. Tight pants, no underwear, a sexy rough stripling - they get approached - it happens."

"It never happened to me!" spoke Simeon in a slight tone of disappointment.

"You had zits. You said it yourself, a face full of pimples. I can see the pock marks from here. Adults with money can afford to be choosy. Was Brian Forrester desirable? Would he play?"

This sudden off hand reference to his long lost friend made Simeon emotional. His mind went back across the decades to that ever smiling baby face of perfect complexion, that mischievous cheeky grin, the breathy way he said 'Dobba' and that sexy sliding tongue. Gary had said enough. Dobba did not want to answer the question, but it triggered a special secret memory of damp towels, the smell of chlorine, standing on duck boards in a shambling cubicle at the old Langley Baths. Both boys having dried off had donned tatty shirts and nothing else. Both boys were facing each other in a rare moment of guilty silence. One boy had replaced the smile with a downward look of pure wonder. The other, getting highly excited, noted the opening little mouth and a crafty protruding glistening tongue. Inquisitive little fingers of one smooth hand reached out to tickle and tantalise a raging phallus, sticking up, pleading - begging for relief. The other naughty fingers investigated, teased and stroked pleasure regions below. Fiddling fingers, busy fingers, only stopped by a sudden ecstatic spurt of finality: a milky mess hurriedly cleaned up with a dingy raggy towel.

Mindful of this broody silence, Gary softened his tone.

"I'm sorry. This can't be easy for you, but we must consider these things."

Still holding a beaker of barely warm tea, Simeon was recalled back to the current conundrum. In a hoarse whisper he said -

"Is it really possible that a man like Dr Hardman could actually kill an innocent young boy like Brian?"

"I'm afraid it's more than possible - it's probable."

"How?"

"How! Well ... most amateur murders are bludgeons. A crowbar, hammer - whatever. It's quick and effective. He wouldn't be expecting it: wouldn't know what hit him."

196

Simeon had laid back on his bed and now seemed to be in a trance. He was trying to find the two happy crows. Gary got up and started to get dressed. Instinctively, as best policy, he continued to talk.

"You know what the problem is don't you: the problem with us? We're both addicted to Agatha Christie and tend to dismiss the 'most obvious' suspect which is, of course, Algernon Hardman. In real life you stick to the most probable - Algernon Hardman. Don't be fooled by his 'nice family' credentials. Many killers dote on their wives and children. I don't know exactly what happened, but once he had made his move with Brian - well, he may have been horrified by the sudden danger. You said Brian was a chatterbox. Maybe Brian co-operated maybe he didn't. Either way he was a risk. The Master of Cressbrook Hall was facing possible ruin, facing all the horrors of long years inside prison - make no mistake about that. And you know what happens to people who are in jail for that kind of stuff! Faced with that level of risk - yeah, sure ... he'd kill Brian."

"Why didn't he kill Scott?"

"Not the same level of risk! Scott North was like another man. He would have come across as more mature, more sensible, able to be bought off, able to keep his mouth shut. Brian was a child in comparison. Not for one minute am I suggesting that Scott had a hand in the murder. As far as Scott was concerned - Brian just disappeared. He may have suspected murder, but your hero could hardly go to Hardman and remonstrate. He'd just freeze. He was only 15, he was in deep doo doo, really just a kid himself."

"Wait a minute!"

Simeon jumped out of bed, grabbed his underpants and struggled to put them on.

"You've forgotten! The accident in Albania. It couldn't have been planned because Hardman and son returned to England suddenly, unexpectedly ... get out of that!"

Gary Mackenzie smiled a superior smile and put a gentle hand on Simeon's bare shoulder.

"I'm way ahead of you, old pal. Keep your eye on the ball. Algernon Hardman is a rich man, well travelled, familiar with European countries. His wife may have caught wind of rumours, may have already known about his 'extra-curricular activities'. Mrs Hardman may have become a risk - Mrs Hardman has to go! Money

*can buy 'an accident'. Look, I know Europe a lot better than you do. Just after the war, Albania was a mess and stayed a mess for years. It was a miserable little country - bureaucratic incompetence, inefficiency, administrative confusion, language problems, poor records, lost files, people starving, lots of corruption, cops for sale ... get the picture? Think back to what you told me about 'The Journey to the Far North'. **Who** decided to go? Who decided **when** to go? Who decided **where** to go? OK, so a teacher suggested accommodation. That only helped Scott. Hardman expected delivery and received his delivery - on time, as planned.*

Simeon looked dazed. His head was spinning -

"Just can't get my head round all this ... The bike! How the hell did the bike get to Belper?"

"More guess work, but dealing with probabilities ... OK, the police took you all home on .. [he checked the document] that Sunday evening of July 24th. Wormall claims he found the bicycle leaning at the back of his woodshed early the next morning. My theory: take it or leave it. After he arrived home, Scott, no doubt seriously concerned, would need to contact Hardman as soon as possible ..."

A distant image floated up into Simeon's mind, a familiar image of Scott examining a hand full of small change, selecting three large copper pennies to use in a public telephone box. He was the only boy in the school who had the courage to enter and closet himself in that strange forbidding piece of street furniture. Only Scott North had the skill and intelligence to penetrate the mysteries of that high tech, complex and confusing arrangement of 'Press button A' and 'Press button B'. His mates were ordered to stay out on the pavement. It was always assumed he was chatting to girlfriends, making arrangements, planning further conquests.

" ... Algernon Hardman would give his pimp specific instructions. Likely as not, Scott would be assured all was well. Brian Forrester was fine and would 'turn up' the next day. Money was on its way - probably via Coggan at some quiet, regular, meeting place or, it may be simply secreted in a regular hiding place. Hardman, Coggan or Tonks - anyone of them may know somebody with a van, of similar taste, who could transport the bicycle over night. The old freak at Belper may have been suggested by Coggan or Tonks since they were

*both annoyed with him. Remember, he tried to get Tonks fired. Hardman would have approved the choice since Jasper Wormall already had a dubious reputation with his massaging activity - and, of course, in the popular public imagination, a character like 'The Goblin' as he was called, is **exactly** the type who would try and seduce a young boy."*

This triggered a memory. It was in Aunty Gertie's house in 1962. They all heard the familiar plonking of the Steptoe and Son signature tune coming from, their pride and joy, the new TV.

    "Ton that dotty bogga off!" ordered the outraged Matriarch who had just read that the famous, 'dirty old man Steptoe', had been arrested in a public lavatory for 'importuning'. In her opinion he was precisely the sort of ugly, toothless, un-shaven, filthy, stinking shambles who would be haunting a latrine, leering at young men at the smelly urinals.

    Then he remembered her caution when he announced his intention to search for Brian Forrester. She had warned that the truth might not be pleasant, it might be too close to home. Had there been gossip and talk over the years? Did Gertie Hogg know something about Scott North?

Gary Mackenzie was still in full flow -

    *"All this is the most likely scenario. Everything fits. It explains why Algernon Hardman put up with the outrageous behaviour of Simon Tonks. Look at this bit here, it says his butler (or whatever he was) is brought back to Cressbrook Hall by the police in the middle of the night! And look at this - and this! Jesus! It makes **me** look like a monk! Tonks was tolerated because Tonks was useful. Mark my words, if Dr Hardman was so very respectable, that common slut would be out of that house so fast his feet wouldn't even touch the ground!*

    And this 'Dolly'! Boy oh boy! A gardener who gardens - just maybe, once in a while - and only when he feels like it! And has lots of money to spend? That car has the same symbolism as Scott's bicycle."

    "All right - all right! Enough! I've heard quite enough about Scott this morning," concluded Simeon.

They detected the delicious aroma of crackling bacon floating up from the kitchen below. Simeon broke the rather sudden and difficult silence he had just inflicted. He spoke quietly -

*"I don't accept your theory, Gary. But you came here to help and I thank you for that. If it turns out you're correct, (and God knows if we'll ever get any evidence after 43 years) - but, **if** you are right, then Scott North should have received an Oscar for his brilliant acting."*

The response came in a similar quiet measured way -

"When we want something real bad, or when we're in trouble, Simeon, we're all good actors. It goes against your moral sensitivities to find out that Derbyshire isn't really much different to Detroit. We live in a horny world were people take what they can get and look after number one. Algernon Hardman looked after Algernon Hardman. Scott North looked after Scott North.

Devoid of confidence, a sad whining voice drifted up the stairs -
"Shall ya av a bita breakfast?"

Chapter 26

Sluts, Slags and Strumpets

After the pre-breakfast disturbing incursions, Simeon was grateful to press on with his plan of action and was keen to make his appeal for information on BBC Radio Derby. He had written them a long letter from Babbacombe giving details of the 'cause celebre' which gripped the county in late July of 1960. In response John Holmes invited them both to appear on his programme that morning at 10.00am.

Breakfast was good. Aunty Joyce was pleased with the compliments from her two guests and delighted by the diplomatic (if forced) interest shown in her only child Joey, who lived just feathery inches away from the happy industry of carving food. He bounced about his cage and chirped back at Joyce's inane and irritating budgie baby talk. Having knocked back a further beaker of unwanted tea, Gary was keen to escape from Aunty Joyce's claustrophobic world -

"You were going to show me the recreation ground, Simeon. Such a beautiful morning. I could do with a walk after this excellent grill."

But on leaving the house, they were arrested by the sight of a toothless crumpled old woman sitting on a chair in front of number three, right next to Joyce Hogg's number four. She stared up at them, stared hard through crumpled, screwed up piercing bullet eyes. For long seconds, both men were held by this silent leer which was both inquisitive and interrogating. Simeon broke the uncomfortable moment by affecting a cheerful -

"Good morning, Aunty Nelly. And how are you today?" Getting no answer, he exerted himself to more artificial conviviality. *"This is my friend Gary Mackenzie. He lives in America."*

This produced nothing but a sardonic nod accompanied by a contemptuous grimace which seemed to imply - *'Aren't you the posh one then! I expect you'll want a curtsy next.'* Gary, totally repelled by this inward looking wrinkled and ruckled old hag, could not even bring himself to utter his usual civil *'Hi!'* Nelly solved the embarrassing impasse by suddenly shooting out a spray of verbal bullets as if from a machine gun: a cascade of seeming irrelevant speech without benefit of punctuation -

"Our Vivienne were on t' rec an the were a lad oo were goin' t 'it our Vivienne but our Vivienne said 'I've got a stick and I shall 'it YOU!"

As the narrative was brought to an abrupt halt, the two friends took a few seconds to absorb and decode this staccato intelligence. Gary Mackenzie was particularly fascinated by her mouth on the word 'you' which became a perfect circle. It reminded him of the 'oo' sound made by characters recently seen in an animated film called 'Chicken Run'. Simeon mustered a further effort to be pleasant to Aunty Nelly, making a suitable response, polite apologies and a quick exit.

Bog Hole terrace ended with a duck pond in the garden of The Duckery on their right and a rustic stile gave entry into the recreation ground directly ahead of them. It was a large, flat, well tended, close cut field which afforded a good walk across its long diagonal, ending in an other stile which took you into the main village. Apart from two distant girls on the swings, the two strolling men, comfortable with each other, comfortable with a friendly thoughtful silence, had the whole area under a big blue sky - all to themselves.

Near the centre, this little interlude of serenity was impaired when Simeon (ever on his guard with teenage girls) noticed that the two 'swingers' were no other than his relative Sara and the fallen floozy - Kelly Grocock. He had hoped that they would be too engrossed in the whoops and shrieks of their enjoyment, but no, alas, the two interesting aliens from another land were spotted in a loud crescendo of *"You-hoos!"* and frantic waving. Gary was amused. Simeon was alarmed. Notwithstanding, in just over a minute the four were in conversation. Gary was chief spokesperson answering questions about his homeland and fielding a few inappropriate personal questions with admirable skill and tact. He gave nothing away. Kelly was keen to draw attention to her condition -

"What must ya think on me? Ere's me eight months up t' stick!"

In an attempt to be kind, Simeon suggested that some of the inhabitants of Horsley Woodhouse were old fashioned and perhaps rather narrow in their views. He hoped that she had not been subjected to too many hurtful comments. Her response was both shocking and horrifying.

"Nay lad! Am a loose bitch an they all know it. 'Get ya knickers off' - that's wot lads shout at me! The dunna call me Grocock

202

for nowt!" This caused an explosion of yelping giggles and nudges. *"Dunna thee bother thee sen, lad, am 'ard bitch me. Ya know - thick skinned."*

They were all laughing except Mr Hogg who objected to being addressed as 'lad'. Noting his displeasure she attempted a diversion -

"Vicar's wife's a stuck up bitch." Kelly nudged Sara. *"She sez ta me 'Don't you feel just a bit ashamed, Kelly?' So a sez back, well, a did a bit, but, oo, - a sez to 'er, when Wayne talks dirty, a can't 'elp meself! 'E sez ta me - 'Sprag thee legs, lass!'. Ooo it did turn me on! An is a big lad 'e is. An it were rate grand. Ooo when 'e shoved it oop me, ee it were grand! Ooo, an when 'e spunked in me - ee, it were rate loovely, it were!"*

At this, the two girls shrieked and screamed with raucous laughter and uncontrollable giggles. Gary smiled at her outrageous performance. Simeon, gob-smacked and disapproving but still attempting to be sociable, tried hard (but not hard enough) to resist assuming an air of his old Mr Hogg. With dead-pan face and his best Sunday accent he said -

"I suppose you are the product of what the progressives call 'free expression', Kelly."

"Ay?"

"It's just as well you don't live back in the medieval period when there was a special punishment for girls like you, girls of easy virtue."

"Wot were that?" said Sara, now curious.

"Oh, nothing dreadful, nothing too visceral. This was purely to humiliate the victim." He addressed Gary and Sara. *"Kelly would be tied to a hurdle, a sort of sledge in a sitting position and dragged through the village with a sign around her neck."*

"Wot's it say?" inquired Kelly.

"Oh no! Don't ask me - too cruel. I can't, I just can't tell you. It's just too awful!" replied Mr Hogg looking away in pain but also warming to his subject and getting exactly the response he wanted - an avalanche of protests, pleadings and demands to learn the appalling truth of how Kelly would be labelled before the entire jeering population of Horsley Woodhouse.

*"Well, if you **must** know, it said - 'Strumpet!'"*

"Oh no! Please don't say that. Say it's not true! Surely not

'strumpet'," joined Gary, on cue.

At this the girls were intrigued if not entirely convinced by the sincerity of this impromptu history lesson.

"Worse was to come," continued Mr Hogg. *"The villagers would follow the sledge and hurl vile abuse at the strumpet already suffering a bumpy ride."*

"D'ya mean they'd call 'er nasty names?" said Kelly with a big grin getting bigger by the moment.

"Indeed! They would shout 'scrubber', 'slag', 'cow', 'tart', 'dirty bitch' and - in very bad cases, perhaps even - 'whore'. In your case, Kelly, they may even go as far as - 'trollop'!"

As expected this precipitated a ribald and hilarious uproar of screaming laughter. Simeon left the scene with mixed feelings. A part of him had been amused at the tactics but the bigger part was outraged that he, a man old enough to be their grandfather, had been drawn into such an obscene exchange within an atmosphere of 'trendy teacher' bred familiarity. Sensing the root of this silence, now a brooding silence, Gary tried to put the episode into a more acceptable context.

"You'll never put the clock back, old friend, don't try. You've spent the last five years trying to put the genie back in the bottle - it's just not going to happen! Oh I know she'd never talk to Aunty Gertie like that, but then again, we're not Aunty Gertie. Be flattered that they see us as more modern and more 'with it'. Anyway - they probably 'picked us up'. They probably get 'life style' lessons in school.

Aw come on, Simeon! Don't go on the radio in this mood. It's what kids do, they push to the limit, they were testing. Don't sweat. Forget it."

But Simeon did sweat and he was never very good at 'forgetting it'. He stoked up to give vent to a controlled tantrum which started with a soft, almost whispered -

"What have they done to my world?"

"Pardon me?"

*"The world I once knew and loved. At her age we would never, ever, speak to an adult in that way - unless you wanted to get your face slapped - and slapped hard. They **know** what I do, for God's sake!"* Simeon reeled round and looked Gary directly in the eyes. *"I am entitled to the respect and dignity of my professional standing. How*

204

dare she! That foul mouthed lowly common slut ... "

*"**Whoa!** Hold up there! Do I see before me Mother Teresa? Or do I see the one time White Star of the Harlem Stud Baths? Who's had more meat - Kelly or Simeon? And who, yes, my friend, who would just **love** to get his paws on the ever horny Wayne Pickles?"*

In spite of himself, Simeon admired the way Gary could handle 'a situation'. It had happened so many times before: the skilful pricking at the bubble of pomposity. Gary Mackenzie had exactly the same knack as Brian Forrester, an ability to cool the heat of indignation by getting Simeon to see the funny side, to turn it around so he could laugh at himself. The schoolmaster could not deny the truth of these assertions. If unable to smile, he could hold up his head and say with measured precision -

*"At least I didn't boast to those girls and revile them with **my** sexual gymnastics. And I'm certain that Kelly, even in her short salacious life, has turned more tricks than I have, and - while we're on the subject of honesty, Gary Mackenzie, I'm certain that you've probably had more than both of us put together!"*

"Touché!" concluded Gary.

They separated. They had about a half hour to spare before it was time to leave for Derby so Gary decided to explore the other rows, the church and other interesting aspects of Horsley Woodhouse. Back in Aunty Joyce's back bedroom, Simeon's mobile rang with its familiar trill. A voice announced itself as John Winter, one time Detective Sergeant and former assistant to Detective Inspector Derek Russell.

"Many many thanks for your help in putting together that splendid document, Mr Winter."

"Call me John. It was an interesting challenge. We were quite taken up in it. Old men like us need a bit of stimulation now and again. I've just turned 81 and Derek will be 88 next month. Incredible bloke: he can still walk the legs off your average teenager and here's me looking more and more like Humpty Dumpty every day!"

"Now that's another sort of challenge; keeping trim after a busy stressful job," replied Simeon.

"Derek tells me you're still cycling, so you'll be OK. Now about the Forrester Mystery, Simeon. In Derek's letter, my contribution was to jog his memory and mainly stick to the facts. I know he penned a few suspicions, but if it's of any help, I can share

with you some personal ideas, ideas I wouldn't like to put in writing - if you know what I mean."

Simeon lay down on the bed and made himself comfortable.

"I'd be most grateful, John. I'm all ears."

"You know, of course, that we focused on that rich bloke, Algernon Hardman. Derek wasn't so sure, but I was keen - at first. I felt he was the type: a sort of recluse who'd taken refuge in a world of books. His life had just been devastated with the accident: a sudden loss, a shock which might have released the passion he'd been concealing. I was a young copper with lots of prejudices in those days."

"I'll bet!" thought Simeon. He also wondered if Winter or Russell had speculated about his own personal circumstances and if that might have coloured the information recently tendered. But no: these were unhealthy thoughts. As Gary would tell him, he must rise above these silly sensitivities. Detective Inspector Derek Russell and Detective Sergeant John Winter did not have to help him at all. It was kind of them to take the time and trouble. He was genuinely appreciative.

"Has the passage of time moderated your suspicions, John?"

"The passage of time has been very educating. Take the odd bods, the servants and the old man in Derby. I knew Simon Tonks when he worked for the Calder sisters at Belper. A nancy boy of the first order, but a nice one: church on Sunday and all that. No: not Simon, he wouldn't hurt a fly. Can't keep his hands off the men, but not a danger to boys."

"Little fat Dolly?" ventured Simeon. John Winter laughed.

"The dolly tub! No. It looked probable at the time, but again - too nice. Funny little bloke, quite enterprising and very entertaining. Just a hunch, but I'd strike them off as suspects. They're still there you know at Cressbrook Hall. Amazing isn't it. But a hunch is all I have. Not a scrap of evidence in all these years.

"The bicycle found at Belper?" added Simeon. John Winter responded with a bigger laugh.

"Oh! It brings it all back. What a horror! A revolting creature! I can still see those leering eyes undressing me. No. It was planted. I don't know who planted it, but I'm sure it was planted. Good move. Jasper was just the sort who would be a prime suspect in 1960. Incredible little man! His 'massage' business went from strength

206

to strength in the following years."

"I imagine he must have been good," spoke Simeon in a dry, slightly cynical note.

"He was very good with his 'extras'. Kept them hanging on for ages - if you know what I mean. One of our own became a regular visitor. Made a terrible stink down at the station when it all came out - I'll tell you! But nothing could be proved as far as youngsters were concerned. We looked into it a bit. His speciality seemed to be the rough type, road workers, labourers, that sort: perhaps a sprinkling of reps. Harmless type really. There was always a cup of tea and a nice piece of cake if you didn't rush off ... So they tell me."

"Did Guzzly Granddad make a nice cup of tea?"

"Do you know, those two blokes had a fair bit in common. Hated each other, but both had built up a clientele of casual callers. In Granddad's case there was a quicker turn over - well, it wouldn't take so long would it? You just walked in off the street ... so they tell me ... walked over to his chair, out came the old choppers ... well, I think the technical term is 'fellatio'. They joked at the station that it was all the semen which made him so gross: a vile man: sat there with his mouth open all day long. He was well named - a pig ignorant fat slob. Not exactly articulate, he just grunted at you."

"But you don't think he had anything to do with Brian vanishing?

"Again, no evidence. Over the following years, local boys were questioned as, and when they came to our attention. But not a sniff. Now Guzzly Granddad **did** *like young boys and by all accounts these street urchins liked Guzzly Granddad. He was quite a legend in the back alleys of Derby."*

"So where does that leave us?"

"It leaves us to consider 'opportunity' rather than 'motive'. Over the years we've had to re-think our perception of children after some appalling examples. Remember the Bulger case? I know we're speaking about your friends, Simeon, but in my experience many crimes are committed by the chap on the spot. Sometimes the decision to commit murder is taken in an instant of opportunity. They seize the moment. They take their chance."

"Go on."

"For some years now, I've focused on those minutes from the time that you five lads had arrived at the bottom of the hill, to the time when Scott and Rex went back to the top of the hill after their search.

Brian Forrester had not made it to the bottom. Logically you all thought he'd fallen off his bike somewhere between the top and the bottom of the hill. Scott took charge and sent Danny Forrester to the waterfall in Water-cum-Jolly Dale to make sure that Brian had not overtaken you. What happened next, Simeon?"

"Scott and Rex pedalled up both parts of the hill to look."

"Exactly. I've pored over that statement dozens of times. Scott took the shorter, more steep route, where he assumed an accident was most likely to occur. Rex took the longer, more gradual gradient with the hairpin bends, which met the other road near the top. Between them they satisfied themselves that Brian was not on any part of that hill. They assumed that he'd gone down the driveway to Cressbrook Hall."

"Where else could he have gone?"

"He could be injured at the side of the road - as was most probable."

"But they didn't see him!"

*"They **said** they didn't see him. It took about 20 minutes for both lads to reach the meeting place at the top of the hill. Scott was there first. That means that both lads were alone during those 20 minutes. Neither could corroborate the actions of the other. I don't think we will ever know what happened, or who was guilty - if indeed either Scott or Rex **were** guilty - but the opportunity was there."*

Simeon spoke his next words slowly and politely, but was unable to hold back a touch of derision -

"Motive? Means? And while you're at it, John, have you any idea of what they did with the body?"

"We underestimate kids. They can be very adept at disguising their true feelings. At the time, you felt it was a case of 'all pals happy together' - but are you so sure? You said it yourself - Brian Forrester was a joker, a teaser. He could have hit a raw nerve with either of 'the two leaders'. They were both proud, both powerful. Just suppose that Scott found Brian on the roadside, unconscious ... Well, you never know. He was strong. He could have throttled him, dragged his body quite a good way into the woods - by all accounts he was a weedy youth and there wasn't much of a body to drag. Our search really didn't get going properly until the next day. It would have been no problem for a youth as fast, strong and fit as Scott North to cycle back there in the middle of the night, drag the body even further away, drop

it down a shaft (plenty to choose from) or bury it in soft earth. Animals would do the rest. We didn't search everywhere. Rex had the same opportunity. It was less likely, but just possible that they acted together. Then they knock at Dr Hardman's door and say 'Can we have our friend back please'."

A sad sounding female voice meandered up the stairs -

Gary's 'ere. Yal av ta go ta Derby now if ya goin' on t' wireless at ten o' clock."

Chapter 27

An Appeal on BBC Radio Derby

In truth, neither Gary nor Simeon would confess to each other their low level of confidence for a successful conclusion to their quest. Gary believed in his own theory that Brian Forrester was dead somewhere in the vicinity of Cressbrook Hall and that the true details of his demise would go to the grave with those responsible. Simeon was less sure but equally pessimistic. He took the view that an investigation, however amateurish, would in itself be a therapeutic process and a token to the memory of his long lost friend. And there was always that small, slender hope that somewhere, within the range of the BBC Radio Derby transmitter, somebody would recognise a description of Brian Forrester or recognise any features of his personality: or, there was still the tiny outside chance that, somewhere out there, a man now aged 58 might just recognise himself.

Simeon was excited, it was his first ever radio broadcast. He had not given the experience much thought but was pleasantly surprised by the warmth of welcome and high level of cheerful courtesy. Gary was bubbling with excitement even though it was his third visit to a local radio studio. In San Francisco he was helping to promote 'Gay Rights' during the early 1970's and another time in New York he belonged to a militant group and went on the radio to denounce the gay equivalent of the black 'Uncle Tom'. Simeon harboured the distinct feeling that Gary was probably speaking about him!

After passing through several secure doors and being led through a labyrinth of passageways, they were finally shepherded into the inner-sanctum of the broadcasting studio. John Holmes was most pleasant. Surrounded by an intimidating futuristic galaxy of high-tech switches, buttons, knobs, levers and lights - he beamed a comfortable smile which put them immediately at ease and reassured Simeon (who was anxiously looking for the 'red light') that their current conversation was private between the three and not (at that moment) being shared by millions beyond. Incidental to the initial small talk, at a low volume, the music going out live could be heard. Simeon was delighted to discern familiar pizzicato strings and the strains of Adam Faith singing 'From Now Until Forever'. Very apt, but an unlikely coincidence as the following subject would be the William Howitt Secondary Modern School in the summer of 1960. The red light went on.

Simeon was intrigued by it all. He admired the smooth skills of the professional broadcaster, seen at first hand for the first time. The coaxing, rich, cultured voice welcomed -

" ... *Simeon Hogg and Gary Mackenzie, my guests this morning. They've travelled all the way from Detroit, Michigan in the hope of solving an old mystery which has baffled the police for the last 43 years. Now, Simeon, welcome to the programme, you were actually one of those six boys who ...* "

The interview tripped along nicely within the cosy confines of John Holmes's gentle probing questions, until he turned his attention to Gary ... Simeon was panic stricken! Until that moment he suddenly realised that they had completely failed to 'get their act together' with regard to procedure. Would Gary, manic as ever, now, with enthusiasm, take the public opportunity to vent his suspicions and launch into his attack on Algernon Hardman? He understood the dead could not be slandered but what about co-operation from the living? Detective Inspector Derek Russell, in his long letter, had stressed the importance of winning the trust and speaking to the local author Charles Hardman - who himself had been interviewed by Mr Holmes on BBC Radio Derby several times. Russell had always believed that Hardman's son, a twelve year old at the time, probably knew something but remained silent due to loyalty or fear of his father. And, God forbid, would Gary, even as much as imply that one of 'the six' might be somehow involved! The world might be listening this morning - and the world included Scott North, Rex Lloyd, Danny Forrester and Tom Day - and all their relatives! Simeon stared at the threatening red light listening to Gary's animated exotic Midwestern accent, racing along with no brakes, contrasted to the more controlled, calm, deeper tones of his host, the familiar re-assuring voice of the BBC.

The crisis passed. Gary Mackenzie had been the soul of sensitivity and diplomacy. He had spoken of the possibilities of a loss of memory. He mooted mine shafts. He paid tribute to the police, sympathised with their colossal job and the sheer impossibility of looking everywhere in that area of North Derbyshire. The dreaded words of 'paedophile' or 'rent boy' were never uttered, save for the fact that abduction or murder could not be ruled out. Nobody mentioned Cressbrook Hall until a woman from Bakewell telephoned the station -

" ... *so if you'll just put on your headphones, gentlemen, we have Anne Dean on the line. Good morning, Anne, what are your thoughts on this mystery?"*

"Could I ask Mr Mackenzie if he's a policeman or private investigator?" The voice was hard and suspicious.

"No way!" replied Gary *"Simeon and I are just a couple of old chums trying our hand at a little detection. As a school teacher he's more of the academic. I can poke around and bring a measure of Detroit street knowledge - and that can be pretty sharp! I may be able to see a different angle. We already have a few theories, but, like Poirot, we'll keep 'em to the last page."*

The hard unfriendly voice returned in sardonic tone -

"'Trying your hand at a little detection'! Do you realise that this game of yours, your so called 'detection', is turning lives upside-down?"

"What's your point, Anne?" asked John taking a hold of the situation.

"My point, Mr Holmes, is to put the case for my dear friends the Hardman family who are just as much victims in this business as the Forrester family. The late Algernon Hardman suffered a double blow in 1960. First he lost his wife in a tragic motor accident and immediately came under suspicion of kidnapping (or worse) when he returned home with his son Charles. As all your older listeners know, the press made a meal of it at that time. Algernon was hounded by reporters for months and the stigma of suspicion blighted the remaining years of his life. That cloud of notoriety which hovered over Cressbrook Hall, very slowly, eventually, dissipated with the passage of time and coming of new generations.

But what do we have now? We have Messrs Hogg and Mackenzie over here, uninvited, playing detectives to stir it all up again! Can't you leave that poor family in peace?"

The two 'detectives' wearing headphones sat rather forlorn looking like a couple of reprimanded little boys. Gary was sorely tempted to 'lay into the bitch' but, aware of the huge audience and his own frightful temper - restrained himself. John Holmes was about to take over when Simeon indicated his willingness to respond.

"You're quite right, Mrs Dean. It has been difficult for

*Algernon and Charles Hardman. I gather they were very close and sympathise with their situation, but I would like to answer your quite understandable concerns by making two points. Firstly, **you** are the one who has put Cressbrook Hall, once again under the spotlight. We have never mentioned the Hardman family. Secondly, just as you care for your friends, so I hold affection for my friend - Brian Forrester who might be out there somewhere."*

*"Mr Hogg! That impressive address will **not** get you off the hook. You know full well that the media will, once again, focus on Charles's poor father. You know full well all about the sordid and lascivious speculation which will, yet again, result from digging up the past. Charles and Helen were hoping that all this business had been laid to rest years ago. Must you throw more mud at them?"*

"On the contrary, I was hoping to speak to Mr Hardman. There's always a chance he may have seen something or perhaps remember something ... "

"Let me give you some good advice, Mr Hogg," interrupted the voice which was now distinctly threatening. *"Keep well away from Cressbrook Hall. You will **not** be welcome!"*

After this acrimonious exchange, to help soothe the sore atmosphere, the interviewer deftly made a light hearted reference to the detective duo -

"We've mentioned Agatha Christie ... I was just wondering ... which of you is Poirot and which one is Hastings?"

Gary bounced back with -

"I don't think it's quite as simple as that, John. But I think we could do with more help. How are you fixed for joining us? You could be our 'Holmes'."

"Now there's a thought! Gentlemen, do you have the courage to take another call? Jim Malpass is on the line. Go ahead, Jim."

"Hello, Simeon."

"Hello, Jim."

"I well remember the 'Peak Cycling Mystery' of 1960. Read everything I could get hold of at the time. Fascinating stuff. I think the last caller did the very opposite of what she intended and those friends may not have appreciated her comments, however well meant. It was sheer bad luck for old Hardman that his residence was the only one near the disappearance. But, did you know that there was a butler and

214

a gardener who also fell under suspicion?"

"That's right, Jim. We've done our homework and, as Gary said earlier, the folk at Cressbrook Hall may have no responsibility at all."

"Now I wonder, have you considered ... It **is** just possible that one of your mates could be guilty? Even you, Simeon!"

"Pardon?"

"Now don't take offence. You were all very young at the time and painful memories can get buried in the passage of time ..."

"Mr Malpass!" interjected Simeon, restrained but bristling "Have you considered the folly of your theory? Here's me, now, on the radio! Would I be likely to do that if ..."

"That is the very point of my theory, Simeon. If you have a guilty subconscious, a hidden memory, and I do stress **if**, then you **will** try to seek the truth - you can't leave it alone can you? A few minutes ago you said Brian has haunted you all these years. Well then, that points to a suppressed or possibly false memory. You may have a split-personality and this being a case of your good side returning to uncover the deeds of your bad side. I think you, and the other lads (men now) should submit to hypnotism. I'm only trying to be helpful, John."

"Thanks, Jim. We'll take that on board, but other callers are waiting." Simeon groaned whist John Holmes continued - "Kathy Syson has a suggestion. Good morning, Kathy."

"Don't panic, chaps! I'm not a hypnotist offering my services. I just wanted to tell you and everybody else that we have an annual school re-union in Heanor for former pupils of William Howitt Secondary Modern School in October. You'll be most welcome, Simeon, and, who knows - you may get the information you need."

"Great stuff, Kathy. You've put the smile back on Simeon's face. Mary Taylor, I gather you have a theory to offer?"

"Yes, John," spoke Mary in a rather thin and frail voice. "I was very young when this boy disappeared, but that's just it, he disappeared didn't he - into thin air? Well ... this is a bit far fetched, but, well ... He was one of twins wasn't he? Is it possible, just possible that some sort of conjuring trick was played on his friends? I mean, if Mr Hogg thinks back to the time, is he absolutely **sure** there **were** two twins in the first place?" At this stage all three men in the studio were wearing a pained look. "Is it possible, just possible, that the one brother somehow, in the first place, gave the impression to everybody that *there were two - and all the time, in fact, there was just the one! Then it would seem like one had gone missing - wouldn't it. I mean ... "*

"No, Mary." said Simeon, sharply, determined to end the embarrassing misery. *"Brian and Danny Forrester were two twins. They were not identical, in fact they were distinctly different in looks and personality."*

"Interesting stuff, Mary." said John hastily. *"Thank you for that contribution. We move on."*

"Aye oop, Dobba!"

Simeon froze. This was a familiar friendly cheerful voice, a voice he had not heard in 43 years. It was the first time in 43 years that anybody had called him Dobba. It was a special name, uttered only by a small select group of good people, bestowed upon him by a very special person. This name was magical. It had great power. It came with a change of life, it changed his life. He was reinvented by this name and Simeon Hogg, in the Radio Derby studio, became emotional during those seconds absorbing the full significance of this phone call. In a weak and unsteady response -

"Danny. Is that you ... Danny?"

"In person, Dobba! 'Ow are ya?"

"Fine ... "

"A just left me mobile noomber with the receptionist. Get in touch with us, won't ya, Dobba?"

"Yes ... "

"Hello, Danny," said John, coming to the rescue with cheery upbeat professionalism. *"Just confirm to us all that you really did have a brother."*

"A did an all! 'E were a grand lad, our Brian. We still miss 'im don't we, Dobba? We 'ad some good times, didn't we, Dobba?"

"We did, Danny, yes we did," was the shaky reply which very nearly broke.

After picking up this obvious intensity of affection which still existed between the two former pals, John Holmes encouraged Simeon to nostalge about his Howitt days which were described as open, sunny, kind, loving, leafy green and hopeful: this in sharp contrast to the days of Mundy Street Boys School which were described as claustrophobic, hateful, cruel, ugly, dark and despairing.

216

More calls came in with ever varied and exotic explanations for the sudden absence of Brian Forrester. One woman suggested that Brian, having fallen off his bike, wandered through the woods and came across the terrible Mandrake Tree which had a taste for adolescent flesh and left no trace of its victim. An authority on Druids and Satanism was certain that Brian, a concussed amnesiac unable to identify himself, was offered as a 'black rite' sacrifice at a nearby sacred grove in a ritual execution. One caller started with a plausible theory of Brian falling through a limestone hole (of which there are many in that area) but then pushed credibility beyond the limit with tales of his being taken prisoner by The Fairies of Caldon Low in their subterranean fairyland.

The last call was a welcome contrast.

"Now here's something exciting. We have Simon on the line who claims he knows exactly where Brian Forrester is. Good morning, Simon."

"Allo!"

'Another kook,' Gary Mackenzie silently mouthed to John Holmes, but for Simeon, here again was a familiar voice, a funny little voice, light high and camp.

"A just wanted ta tell ya, Simeon, that ya old friend is all right. Is 'appy an well. A get regular messages from 'im - is OK, don't ya worry."

"Simon! It's been a long time, but I seem to recognise your voice. I think we've met?"

"We 'ave met. A met you an ya mates in Water-cum-Jolly Dale in 1960. Am still lookin' after t' 'Ardmans at Cressbrook 'All."

"Are you the butler we've been hearing about, Simon?"

"I am, Mr 'Omes. Ave bin 'ere 51 years an seen Mr Charles grow up ta be a fine gentleman and a brilliant writer. 'E's inta mystery an folklore ya know."

"I know indeed, Simon. Charles Hardman has been my guest on several occasions. An interesting speaker, but do tell us, where is Simeon's long lost friend?"

"Is a long way off - in a different place, a very strange place, Mr 'Omes."

"Listeners may not know this .. " explained Simeon, *" .. but Simon Tonks is a clairvoyant and is able to communicate with the dead.*

217

Put us out of our misery, Simon, and tell us what happened to Brian Forrester on that infamous Sunday, July 24th in 1960."

"Yes, tell us, Simon," added Gary. *"This could save us all a whole lot of time and trouble!"*

Simon's initial chirpy exuberance was slightly tempered by a touch of sarcasm in his next offering -

"Do a detect a bit o' wot we call up 'ere, 'extraction of the urine'? Scepticism is not condoocive to arriving at the truth, gentlemen. Ooo said oat about 'im bein' dead? I do get messages from t' spirit world, but also, like anybody else, a get messages from the living - and Brian Forrester is living. In spite of ya attitude - 'ere it is. Your friend was abdooked by aliens from outer space! Flying saucers often coom to Derbyshire. Most of them are seen over Kinder Scout 'cus the attracted by ancient sites - the follow 'ley lines'."

At this point, Gary waved a circling finger at the side of his head and mouthed - *'Crazy! They're all kooky and crazy!'* Simon Tonks carried on -

"It'd be when 'e were goin' down t' big 'ill. 'E were taken. 'E dunt talk about it mooch, but is very 'appy an sez e wants ya ta leave 'im well alone an not disturb 'im, but sends ya all is good wishes. Is got a new life. Is 'appy - leave 'im be."

As John Holmes was thanking Simon and all the others who took part in the interview, Simeon was thoughtful, cogitating and mulling over the insistence and significance of Simon's last words -

'Leave well alone. Leave him be'?

Chapter 28

The Other Twin

It had been arranged that Danny Forrester would come to Bog Hole at three o'clock that Monday afternoon of April 28th 2003. Gary had remained in Derby checking out a few interesting spots. Simeon, taking advantage of the sunshine, was sitting outside with Aunty Joyce and a gaggle of relatives, happily soaking up all the fuss of a Hogg who, unusually had -

"Bin on t' wireless! Arr Simeon, on t' wireless! Now then!"

The chatter descended into myriad inanities such as Aggie Oaks's inflated prices, the cheeky youth in the next row, Mrs Grocock's shame and her dirty windows. Simeon tuned them out and began to think about the twin who did **not** disappear, the twin, soon to arrive in Horsley Woodhouse - his old friend Danny Forrester. Like himself, nearly half a century earlier, a once fifteen year old Danny was now approaching the age of 60. What would he be like? In voice and disposition, unchanged; it was the young Danny he heard through the headphones at Radio Derby. It was the same youthful Danny he remembered, cheerful, bouncy, open, candid, honest and sincere. Quite simply Danny Forrester was one of the best, the nicest person he had ever known.

And yet Simeon, the sensible mature man, knew, only too well, the basis of this idealised perception. Danny Forrester was seen through a window of time long past. Danny, essentially a good person, had been there for him at William Howitt Secondary Modern School, giving respect and friendship at a crucial moment of his life. What if that friendship had been tested by continuation beyond 1960? What if the friendship had been tested by the inevitable divergence of two different personal paths: divergence of temperament or sexuality? What if the friendship had been put to the test of a crisis - a friend in need? Simeon Hogg swept away these dark thoughts. He would rely on instinct. Danny Forrester had sounded just the same, he sounded fantastic ... A car drew up.

A car? Danny Forrester was getting out of a car! Not just any car. It was big and brand new. That was not right. Danny should have arrived on a rickety old push-bike. Until that moment, Simeon had been fearful of what he would see. Forty three years: Danny would be

58! How could Danny be 58? That was not right either. Danny would always be 15. He must stay in that time-warp - forever, just like in the treasured school photograph when he stood next to Miss McLening sporting his Double Diamond tray. Danny must stay frozen forever in that single moment of time just before Easter 1960. Simeon feared what he would see emerging from that car. Reality had forced itself into his mind. Danny Forrester might look old, he might be grey - like Simeon who, as Gary put it, regularly 'hit the ink bottle'. Danny Forrester might be bald and bent - but it was observed with sheer joy and relief that Danny Forrester was none of these things. Simeon recalled a scruffy, skinny Danny, ever wearing a big cheeky grin on his (if not handsome) pleasant and good-looking face. The man who alighted from that car wore the same big cheeky grin on a face which was hardly touched by the passage of time. The skinny frame had gone: gone, but it had not been replaced by fat or the disfiguring beer belly so typical of working class culture. The body which confidently walked tall towards the awe-struck man standing outside number four Bog Hole, was an improvement on the scrawny Danny of 1960. This was a fit man, well made and well proportioned.

They embraced. It was the first time that had ever happened. Heanor boys never embraced, it would have violated an unwritten and unspoken code. It was also within the perimeters of that same working class code that Danny would simply call out to the assembled Hoggs -

"Are ya all right then!"

He was acknowledged by a collective response of nods and smiles and a *"Huh!"* from Uncle Wilfred. Much to Simeon's relief, individual introductions were unnecessary. They walked towards the rec' away from the many curious eyes piercing their backs - not least the boring bullet eyes of Aunty Nelly.

They settled on a seat with a magnificent view of many miles out to a Derbyshire expanse of far hills and shades of green they both knew and loved as boys. And now they **were** boys. Danny Forrester and Simeon Hogg clung to their special place in that wonderful time-warp of 1960. They spoke of their mutual friends, the fun they had, the laughs, the time they were kicked out of the Belper Baths by the grouchy attendant for disobedience after warnings, incidents with Mrs Buxcey - lots of hilarious stories about Mrs Buxcey.

"We were so innocent."

"We were that, Dobba!"

220

Simeon suddenly felt contempt for the evil speculations and unwanted assumptions of Gary Mackenzie and Detective Sergeant John Winter.

The reminiscences continued. During these exchanges there was tacit agreement that the realities of 2003 should not intrude. On the one side there was marriage, children, much loved grandchildren and the successful career of a skilled plumber in constant demand. On the other side there was the unspoken significance of no marriage, no children and the mystery of decades in a distant foreign land many miles from the culture and compass of Horsley Woodhouse and Heanor.

The old repertoire of funnies were re-visited and re-rehearsed - Long John Silver, Omo washing powder and such juvenile bonding devices as -

"What's they know about rabbits?"

"Enough ta put they in a 'utch!"

Eventually the laughter and happy banter subsided and the conversation took a more serious turn.

"Did ya know we lost Titch, Dobba?"

"Dead!"

"Arr. It'd be ... what, 'bout ten year back."

"Rex?"

"Champion! A long distance lorry driver. Never changes. Still full of it. Barrel o' laughs. Grand chap. Good mate."

"Scott?"

"Done well, Dobba! Got 'is own buildin' business. Two great strappin' lads 'elpin' im. The all live in a big 'ouse."

Danny Forrester spoke of his own life style, a large part of which was the social round of public houses in Heanor. He enjoyed a drink - in fact he enjoyed several drinks and Simeon considered the early significance of the Double Diamond tray. As various amusing Heanorian anecdotes were trotted out, a comment from Gary was recalled to the effect that, perhaps it was really Simeon Hogg who was the real 'lost lad'. He had now moved on. He had moved so very far away from that Heanorian world of which he had once inhabited. It became clear that there were big differences between the two men who once shared a boyhood friendship. Notwithstanding, Simeon harboured a huge affection for the man at his side. Danny Forrester was so real and so genuine. Danny Forrester was such a total contrast to the artificial and affected parade of ponces he had stomached on and off over the past forty years.

Very gently, Simeon steered the conversation away from Danny's favourite pub to the conundrum of July 24th 1960.

"You must have entertained a few ideas of your own, Danny?"

"I expect we all thought it was that bloke 'Ardman, Dobba. Then there were t'other two. It didn't say much in t' papers but, well, there were plenty a gossip going round 'eana at that time."

"You mean the butler and the gardener?"

"A do, Dobba. A rate couple o' funny buggers! Well we met t' butler in that deep valley dint we? Talk about queer! Bloody 'ell!

"Not exactly the sort to be moving in your circles, Danny," laughed Simeon. *"But I'm inclined to think that type is fairly tame ... "*

"Ooo arr, Dobba. Ya right. They'd be gentle. The might 'av a go, but arr Brian ... well 'e'd see 'em off. 'E would ... "

Danny became pensive and stared out over to Crich. Simeon reminded him that he and Brian were twins -

" ... So did you have any special communication. Have you any instinctive feelings about what might have happened?"

"A know what ya mean, Dobba, but we were never able to read each other's mind or oat like that. No. But ... well ... "

"Go on."

"It's really joost a feelin'. Av always felt that ... What's 'is name, the son?"

"Charles Hardman."

"That's 'im! Writes them spooky books, ya can buy 'em at Shipley Park. Now 'e was about twelve at the time - joost lost 'is mam - well ya never know do ya? It might 'av turned 'im a bit funny. It might be imagination but ... sometimes it's as if arr Brian's tryin' ta tell me summat, Dobba."

"Possibly, but it could also be your own good sense putting together a theory. I really must try to speak to Charles Hardman - in spite of what that awful woman said. You remember Detective Inspector Derek Russell, the one who was so good to us, well, he tells me that old Hardman never let his son out of his sight for years. Took him out of a posh school and brought in private tutors until he went away to university."

"Could 'av bin protectin' im, Dobba!"

222

"From the law - possibly. I notice Tonks (the butler) joined the growing chorus of appeals for me to stop investigating. I must speak to him as well. Do you know, Danny, I'm starting to think we could get somewhere with this. We may yet get to the truth, old friend!"

"'Ope so, Dobba, but mind ya self. Be careful - ya never know."

Chapter 29

Ghosts

Gary Mackenzie makes friends very quickly. He made a new one in Derby who gave him a glowing report about a well known large gay sauna bath at Darlaston near Birmingham.

"It sounds just great! Swimming pool, jacuzzis, steam rooms, gym, cinema, restaurant ... How about spending the day there?"

But Simeon had already made his plans for this day, Tuesday, April 29th. From Danny Forrester he had discovered the location of Scott North's current building site, not far away, within an easy cycle ride. Seeing Gary's face fall, Simeon decided to be generous.

"Take the car, but make sure it's parked up safe."
"No problem, it has a 'secure car park' - guarded even!"
"It had better be."

Never once having been allowed to touch the precious vintage Cadillac, Gary was profuse with further assurances, giving many thanks and made a quick exit with the car keys whilst the going was good.

The high pressure persisted and warm comforting early afternoon sunshine encouraged the cyclist to push himself eastwards out of Horsley Woodhouse, through Smalley, along the Heanor road to a high point just past Holly Mount Farm where an expensive looking new house was under construction and not far short of completion. Simeon dismounted and approached with caution and some emotion. After 43 years he would, once again, behold the one and only - Scott North. At first he was galvanised by the sight of the two 'strapping lads' Danny had mentioned, both on ladders and both very busy. One of them noted the somewhat unusual arrival of a man on a bike. Responding to an enquiry, he told the visitor that he'd find 'the boss' within. Simeon wandered through a couple of empty rooms before finding the third man looking thoughtfully at a door which was giving trouble.

"Scott North?"

"That's me," was the slightly indifferent and uninterested reply. *"Can I help you?"* said the builder, still studying his awkward door but giving a split second to note a stranger standing in the hall wearing white shorts and a safety reflector band over his dark track-suit top. In

225

those initial seconds of reunion Simeon Hogg made a number of interested observations. He was looking at a man who was exactly his own size. In 1960 everybody looked up at Scott North the tallest lad at Howitt. Yet it was recalled that Dobba, Scott, Danny and Brian Forrester were all born within days of each other. The voice was a surprise. It still had its confidence, it was still rich, deep, with the same slight lilt of John Wayne, but, on the evidence of one word alone, appeared to have lost some of the local vernacular. Scott sounded the 'h' in 'help' which was as odd as seeing Danny get out of an expensive car. On arriving in the United States, the young Simeon Hogg with his thick Derbyshire accent found that he had to learn to sound his H's very quickly when listeners thought he was referring to his bottom, when in fact, he was speaking of his house - not his 'ass'.

Then there was the face. The face of 1960 had been beautiful, indeed, had been stunning. Here was the face of a stranger who could not be recognised. The Scott North of 2003 could have passed him in the street with hardly a first look, let alone the second. The effect was mutual. Mr North showed little interest in his visitor and no signs of recognition. Truth to be told, had Simeon not been expecting Danny at Bog Hole, would he have recognised Danny? But Danny was no Scott and a face which was once greatly alluring - has a long way to fall.

*"You **can** help me, Mr North. Just a few moments of your time? I'd appreciate it."*

Somewhat unwillingly, he left the problematic door and motioned that they be seated in the kitchen. Outside, the notice proclaimed that the property was 'For Sale' and Scott North had learned many years before never to despise any potential customer, even if they turned up on a push-bike. The Adonis had gone, but the firm body which swung around to be seated had been respected and well exercised by a lifetime of hard physical work. Any 58 year old would have been grateful for such a body. Even so, Simeon was doubtful that the former champion athlete would still be able to jump over the standing squat little history mistress, Mrs Buxcey, as was enthusiastically claimed by his supporters at that time.

Face to face, Simeon was now able to discern traces of the familiar countenance he had so admired four decades before. Again, it had to be said that any man pushing 60 would be happy with this face which any woman would have considered handsome, possibly very handsome.

226

"Like it?"

"Very impressive, Mr North. As it happens, I'm looking for such a house, but I was hoping to live up in The Peak - out in the wilds."

"You'll pay a pretty penny for that! Not that I can reduce the asking price on this one. Not the best time for buyers at the moment - it's a sellers market. Can I show you around?"

"Sorry, but I've not really come to buy ... Haven't we met before?"

Mr North was now becoming bored with the conversation and keen to return to work. A great deal of interest had been shown in this executive residence in a much sought after location with excellent views over to Shipley Park. It was a busy day. Many niggles had to be sorted out, not least the landscape gardener who was more than a week overdue. He rose, gave the cyclist a cursory glance -

"I don't think so. You'll have to excuse me ... "

"Do you know, I'm certain that we've met. My name is Dobba."

Scott North stood very still studying his visitor. Seconds passed. The serious business-like look gradually, very gradually softened to a half smile of wonderment.

"Dobba." It was a whisper - and then, falling into his native dialect with a familiar full beaming smile - *"Wot ya done we ya pimples?"*

They sat down and they laughed, they laughed until they nearly cried. The exchange took similar amusing twists and turns around their personal history and the geography of William Howitt Secondary Modern School as it did with Danny just 24 hours before. Scott demanded his favourite - a personal performance of Dobba's raving, boggle-eyed, half-mad hermit, who would leap out at them anywhere in the playground without warning -

"Repent! *Here me, ye vile lusting lascivious sinners!"*

As the anecdotes continued to fly, two large mugs of tea were brewed up. Jollity subsided into nostalgia and nostalgia subsided into sadness for a time and a world lost, a world they both knew and loved.

The conversation turned to the appalling standards of modern youth, contempt for authority, disrespect, vandalism and obscene language.   Scott was reminded about the time when Dobba had occasion to visit Mrs Cook in her room about half an hour after school. He was surprised to see a chastened and humbled Scott North emerge from her small stockroom holding a tray of jars containing paints and brushes -

"Where do I put these, Miss?"

Her face hardened before delivering a firm answer. Dobba's friend was clearly under punishment. A small incident in the annals of time, yet that image of a relatively tough lad, obedient and compliant in those few moments, came to have a great meaning in the light of future experiences in the teaching career of Mr Hogg. Even though Scott towered over the little old teacher, it would never had entered his head to refuse orders, be difficult, remonstrate or threaten to go home. Dobba's appearance did not trigger any silly or foolish behaviour. Having reason to impose the detention, Mrs Cook would not have hesitated to punish the mighty Scott North - possibly the most feared boy in the school. Mrs Cook was a teacher and in 1960, teachers were obeyed without question.

At a point in this retrospective binge, the recent conjectures of Gary Mackenzie came to mind and Simeon tried (and failed) to visualise the young Scott North as a pimp and co-conspirator to murder.   The gleaming new expensive BSA 'Golden Wings' 10 speed racer was mentioned, but Simeon felt unable to find a suitable form of words to suggest that a paper round alone could never have financed such a fine bicycle; consequently, the question remained unasked and unanswered.

Several times Simeon was severely distracted by one of the boys, tittilatingly attired in tight jeans and tee shirt, passing by conscientiously attending to his duty. Since Scott was seen to note his interest, Simeon felt obliged to make a suitable and, hopefully disarming comment -

"Your sons must be a great help in the family firm."
"Grandsons!"

That was a shock! How could he ever be a grandfather? The two terms 'grandfather' and 'Scott' seemed to Simeon to be totally incompatible. 'Grandfather' was more the image of Uncle Wilfred. 'Scott' had always been associated with 'young', 'modern and stylish'.   But then, what

228

could possibly be more modern, contemporary and bang up to date as 1959 with its bright colours and bold patterns? What could be more modern than the sleek image-conscious Scott North, the envy of Howitt who sported his new 'backsweep' or his 'bop' or, perhaps the next day - his 'bebop'?

A little later, one of the lads entered the kitchen, politely apologised to the men in deep conference and quickly removed a set of tools from a top cupboard. Again there was distraction. Simeon twisted his neck for a full view of this brief operation and ogled the hunk until he was completely out of the room. When those eyes had returned to the man opposite (who had been in full flow speaking of a memorable football match) they found that man silent, meditative and appraising. Scott asked a question -
"Did you ever get married, Dobba?"

Following a short moment of mutual reflection, curiosity on the one side and acute embarrassment on the other, both faces dissolved into, first smiles and then broke out into loud laughter. It was a comfortable laughter, the laughter of long past friends which is forgiving and eases tension. Scott North had a shrewd intelligence, but in this instance, he did not need to be all that shrewd - or intelligent. In the midst of such mirth born out of unspoken understanding, Simeon felt that the old chemistry had been re-activated, re-established between Scott and Dobba. At that instant questions flashed through his mind - was this then, the secret of Howitt? Was that particular chemistry, he had just felt, part of the magic, the secret of his past happiness? Was it something to do with the sheer humanity, common decency and tolerance of this man who was once the King of the School?

Inevitably, the subject came round to the very last time they saw each other and to the friend they never saw again. They exchanged ideas. Simeon outlined his suspicions about a possible paedophile ring -
"You mean somebody fancying Brian Forrester! You've got to be joking!"

The one time 'Cock of the School' was highly amused. They moved on to loss of memory. Many years before Scott did some research on the subject -
"There's something to be said for these new cycling helmets, if

Brian Forrester got clobbered with a severe head injury, he'd get what they call 'post-traumatic amnesia' causing 'a complete loss of identity', but even that rarely lasts more than a few weeks."

"I really must get a helmet - hate the thought of it though. 'A complete loss of identity' ... " mused Simeon.

"Apparently ... " continued Scott, *" ... there are other psychological angles. You can get folks with a hidden motive who (granted subconsciously) use an accident as an excuse to leave their past behind them, you know, making a fresh start."*

Scott, staring at his empty mug, was gently turning it with thumb and forefinger. Absently, Simeon was enjoying the distant view through the large patio windows. His eyes rested on a cluster of giant beech trees, green and brown, just breaking out into leaf, which surmounted an attractive green hill. This was the former site of the long demolished splendid Shipley Hall, home to the mighty Mundy family who once owned all of Heanor and most of the population. Scott was still speaking and took his guest by surprise -

"How well did you think you knew Brian Forrester, Dobba?"

"Oh! Well ... How well can any 15 year old know another one? He was a joker. Gentle chaffs and gibes: he'd wind me up a bit. No harm in him but, well ... not really like Danny."

"No. Not like Danny. Not many as good as Danny - completely frank and inoffensive. Good old Danny."

"Do you think Brian's dead, Scott?"

*"No, Dobba, I don't. Did you know that most people who vanish into thin air do so because they actually **want** to disappear?"*

"In that case he'll be the very Devil to find!"

"That's if he wants to be found. I shouldn't look too deeply into the past, Dobba, if I were you - it could be a dangerous past."

"Dangerous to who?"

"Dangerous to us all."

On that cryptic note, Scott North took the two empty mugs over to the sink and rinsed them. He turned to the man who was once known as Dobba, smiled, and spoke to him in his native tongue -

"It's bin a long time ant it, Dobba? But it's bin rate grand seein' ya again. Ad better get on."

They walked out of the house and along the drive to the bicycle. A sound of hammering caused Simeon to, yet again, observe the two young men precariously perched on top of their separate ladders doing something to barge-boards. Scott was amused -

"Should have introduced ya to me grandsons, Dobba."

"Just as well ya didn't," laughed Simeon. *"They're probably safer where they are. So long, old friend. Look after yourself."*

On the road there was indecision, but, on the spur of the moment Simeon, in nostalgic mood, made a decision. He continued north-east towards Heanor, down the hill, past the site of the old laundry, pushing himself up the final hill to descend into the rough old mining town. As in the days of Dobba, it was now a free ride. Gravity speeded him down still further into the nostalgic east gate of the one time William Howitt Secondary Modern School. There it was, unchanged for half a century, a lovely leafy glade enclosed by the mighty lime tree and an equally splendid copper beech. He wheeled his bike past the old canteen up to the hallowed location of Mrs Cook's prefabricated glassy classroom. An emotional moment for this man who stopped, stood silently and reverently gazed at the site of the happiest years of his life. It was late afternoon, the place was silent and deserted.

He approached and entered. For Simeon Hogg this classroom was a shrine. This classroom was all that was left of Mrs Cook. Now long dead, she existed only in the minds of those who remembered her. He felt the need to pay homage, to grieve for the Lady and the long lost time. He sat in the place where he used to sit and looked around at the approximate places of his friends. He looked over to Titch's place. Poor Titch. He would never see him as an adult and never be able to ask him about the lost lad. The room seemed smaller than he remembered, a room which was once filled with the powerful laugh and personality of Rex Lloyd. Simeon day-dreamed and indulged in dramatic reconstructions of jolly times. He heard the on-going circus, their lively voices, the endless censures of Mrs Cook and recalled the Ghost of Christmas Past telling Scrooge -

"These are but the shadows of things which have been. They cannot see us. They do not know we are here."

Simeon Hogg left that special place and spoke a silent 'goodbye' to his good friends and the Lady who had given him back his self respect and made it possible for him to become a teacher.

Chapter 30

The Thoughts of Simeon

It was now the last day of April. In spite of warnings and a horror of unpleasantness, Simeon Hogg, armed with his Sheet 19 1:50,000 Ordnance Survey map, was motoring north-bound on the A6 en-route to find the elusive and remote Cressbrook Hall and its even more remote and elusive master - Charles Hardman. A small part of his mind instinctively and mechanically attended to driving the car, the larger part was in a whirl of re-capitulation of facts, theories, opinions and prejudices.

He had his own memories which were based on his own knowledge of the five friends. Gary Mackenzie's thoughts had been abhorrent, yet Simeon was forced to own their logic. Scott **was** a magnificent specimen in 1960 and he may well have been approached and tempted by men with money, but that was more of a Detroit, rather than a Heanor view. Detective Inspector Derek Russell had laid before him an impartial narrative outline, a sequence of events which included consideration of his five principal suspects - Algernon Hardman, Simon Tonks, Adolphus Coggan, Jasper Wormall and Toby Piggs.

Hardman seemed to be the favourite. He was repressed, cold, remote and had just suffered a personal disaster. Simeon was far from convinced, but as a 'whodunit' enthusiast, he tried to curb his natural tendency to eliminate the most obvious candidate and, at the same time, tried to keep a grip on the simple fact that there was 'not a scrap of evidence' against Hardman.

The complete antidote to Dr Hardman was his funny little servant, Simon, a popular little queen who appeared to be exonerated by popular opinion. Yet it was Simon Tonks who said that Brian Forrester was alive and well, far away, happily enjoying his new life. He had said that just before Christmas, 1960, in the 'cycle seance' and also on Radio Derby just two days ago. Simon had a reputation for talking a lot of nonsense but at least he was consistent. Russell had warned that "Simon is no fool." Simple Simon or clever Simon?

There was no evidence against Dolly the gardener: funny little fat Dolly of the silken silver tongue. If paedophilia were afoot, then here was a reasonable probability: an enterprising rotundity who enjoyed delivering a service - but it was all speculation, no evidence.

Indeed, Dolly had offered practical suggestions: a disoriented Brian may have wandered into the woods ... he could have fallen down a hole ... the police cannot look everywhere. Simeon supposed that his friend's skeleton may well have lain for years in deep nettles and weeds.

Evidence. There **was** evidence, the only solid evidence in the whole business to link the alleged abduction of Brian Forrester with one suspect, a very likely suspect: the hideous little goblin who lived in a crooked cottage under a writhing blackness of cawing crows.

*"Perhaps in real life we should make the obvious connection between Jasper Wormall and the bicycle he was trying to hide. An ugly old queen: isn't he **exactly** the type to be a chicken hawk, the type who might try it on?"* continued the thoughts of Simeon, half noting a sign proclaiming Matlock Bath. He visualised a dazed and injured Brian Forrester, picking himself up, staggering into the woods, collapsing into unconsciousness and coming to with no memory. He mounts his bike and instinctively pedals off in the direction of Heanor, but somehow ends up in a little wooded nook of Belper - entirely possible. A kindly old man would promise to find out who he was and get him back home. There would be hospitality, tea and cakes, followed by a squeaky voice saying -

"Shall ya 'ave a rest on t' bed. Let me tek ya britches off. Ooo that's a nasty scrape! Let me joost ... "

At some point a reaction of sheer horror to the smile which had now become a leer and the kindly intentions which had become lewd and lascivious. Who knows what followed? Panic? Violence? Russell admitted that the Belper search had been intensive rather than extensive. Lots of woodland around Belper: Belper with its flowing river ...

"Hang it on the fags." is what Gary had said. Perhaps Simeon himself was falling into this homophobic trap. Detective Sergeant John Winter had said Brian's bicycle had been 'planted', but by whom? Guzzly Granddad was keen on young boys and they liked Guzzly Granddad. Perhaps they would do anything for him. Perhaps one of them would ride a bike from Derby to Belper and park it outside the cottage of Granddad's sworn enemy - entirely possible. These 'Granddad boys' were well treated. By all accounts there was a close camaraderie in

that version of 'Fagin's kitchen' where beer and fags were freely available to any boy who kept Granddad supplied with his 'daily mouth-full of vitamins'. Would such loyalty extend to covering up murder - if murder it was? Did Brian Forrester, once having been 'initiated', eventually find himself at some other sleazy residence and become a 'street boy' in some other city? Guzzly Granddad's boys have now all grown up into men. They could be anywhere.

Scott said that some people get lost because they want to be lost! Did Scott know something? Does Gary have a point? Has he hit on the truth? Has Simeon really been blinded by nostalgia and affection? Both Simon Tonks and Scott North believe Brian Forrester to be alive. Both said he did not want to be found. Both said to leave well alone. Scott said the past could be dangerous - 'dangerous to us all'. Like Algernon Hardman, Scott was now past middle age and a respectable father, grandfather and successful businessman with a lot to lose. He advised caution - or was it a veiled threat?

Simeon gave some attention to negotiating the main Bakewell roundabout and noticed a large book shop on the left. He parked up a side street and entered the rather quaint, well stocked bookstore, which was in keeping with the quality and tradition associated with the attractive town of Bakewell. An assistant directed him to the local section which was dominated by the work of Charles Hardman. The titles covered areas of high interest, legends, ghosts, UFOs, sacred groves, stone circles, ancient mounds, ley lines, witches and fairies. One book had a chapter about the Lost Lad and part of a poem by Richard Furness -

> Oft as the shepherds o'er the mountains went,
> Each cast a stone to mark the strange event;
> Till yonder cairn arose which marks the ground
> Where the lost lad beneath the rock was found.

On careful inspection, Simeon the serious historian was pleased to see detailed research and a tone of healthy scepticism woven into the text. In several places the author argued how people at different times needed to believe in the strange and the weird. This put Simeon in mind of Charles's close relationship and friendship with his old life-long servant, Simon Tonks. Charles Hardman and Simon Tonks - Simeon wondered ... Hardman's work was firmly rooted in reality. The reader would be entertained by fantasy and at the same time educated by reliable documented local history.

Having purchased three books, Simeon was once more motoring north on the A6 out of Bakewell and once more assessing his pool of information.

Detective Sergeant John Winter had put the emphasis on opportunity and taken the whole scenario away from a sexual angle - thus implicating Rex or Scott or Rex and Scott together. The 20 minutes: a lot can be done in 20 minutes. But, after all, John Winter was an outsider, clinically looking in at the little world of Dobba without the benefit of instinct, the instinct of friends who knew each other. Instinct?

Danny Forrester had instinct. He had his feet firmly on the ground and never claimed any telepathy with his twin brother. Yet he suggested a suspicion born of instinct, a suspicion he had nursed for 43 years, a gut feeling which steered him towards thoughts of that **other** boy who was there, on the scene, on the spot - Charles Hardman, the man Simeon was about to visit. Had the traumatised twelve year old murdered Brian Forrester? Russell had described him as nervous, very frightened, a boy who hardly spoke a word under the watchful eye of his stern authoritarian father. The detective said he felt sure there was 'something wrong'. If murder had really been committed, it was easy to imagine the strict instructions that child would have received from an unapproachable father who was determined not to lose a second loved one to the clutches of the law.

*"Charles. Look at me. Listen carefully to me, Charles. Very soon the police will come. They will ask questions. You saw nothing. You saw nobody. You **did** nothing. No matter how many times they ask - that is your position. I shall insist on being with you, but even if I am not allowed to be with you - do not tell them anything, and I will be able to protect you. Do you understand, Charles? What's done is done. We can't bring him back. Leave the matter entirely in my hands."*

Algernon Hardman did not let Charles out of his sight for the next five years. The son was completely dominated by the father, and yet ... everybody says that Charles adored his father! In his letter Derek Russell admitted bending to the strong will of the all powerful Dr Hardman and regretted that he did not find the means to interview that frightened child alone. Russell stressed the importance of Simeon

236

speaking to Charles Hardman - alone.

Simeon turned right into Ashford-in-the-Water and drove up the steep hill to Monsal Head. Briefly noting the grandeur and expanse of the Wye Valley, he descended down a precipitous narrow road into Upperdale, bright green in the spring sunshine, which led to Cressbrook Dale. The road started an abrupt climb up through dense woodland. Keeping to the left he avoided the less steep other road, the other longer road with the hair-pin bend he had descended with his friends, 'hell for leather', 43 years before.

Presently, there he was, at the entrance to the driveway which led to Cressbrook Hall.

Chapter 31

Nymphs, Naiads and Dryads

It was the first time for Simeon Hogg, he was about to do what Scott North and Rex Lloyd had done 43 years before. The large ornate wrought iron gates were still open and were still guarded by the two stone mythological beasts. Now, after the ravages of a further half century the monsters had eroded back into the womb of the original lumps of rock from whence they came. Slowly rolling down the drive, Simeon found the whole effect delightful, because, as a child, he was fascinated by the idea of Sleeping Beauty's palace. Here was a remote magical kingdom in the depths of Derbyshire, a special place caught in a time warp. He loved the natural effects of neglect and the resulting tangle of untamed growth over many years. There was moss and ivy a plenty. The yews, conifers and junipers seen by his pals on that fateful day long ago, were now even more lush, more stately and grand in scale.

And there it was, just as he remembered seeing it for the first time, a lifetime ago, as a stripling, from the depths of Water-cum-Jolly Dale. It could easily have been a fairy tale palace which had been sleeping for a hundred years: a riot of steep pitched roofs, ornate chimneys, lofty pinnacles and fascinating finials rising from the great trees. He knew he would not be welcome, but steeled himself to pull the bell at the side of the massive Tudor door which was wide open on this unusual warm afternoon for late April. After a decent interval he pulled at it again - no response. He put his head through the door and called out -

"Hello! Hello!" waited a minute but, again, no one came. Simeon became decisive.

"I'm going to be told off anyway" .. he thought .. *"so I may as well go in and get it over with."*

He walked slowly through an interesting dark entrance hall into another panelled room. The sound of music and laughing children came from a far door with the same Tudor motif. He knocked and a child's voice, like the tinkle of a silver bell, called out *"Come in."* The music stopped. The Jacobean gloom had disappeared. He was now in the brilliance of a large conservatory and welcomed by the sight of a group of smiling, small girls, who had been dancing in a circle. Little girls, but they could have been elementals dressed in floating cobwebs - fine, soft, sheer innocent little people who had no fear of this strange man who had simply walked into their home. He was totally enchanted by this unexpected array of nymphs, naiads and dryads, the spirits of water and trees. Rather more substantial was the small grinning boy in the centre, if anything, even younger than his gossamer playmates. Something stirred, some old memory struggled to emerge. It was the story once told by Simon Tonks of nine dancing maidens on Stanton Moor ... "

   "Can I help you!!"

It was this cultured, hard, hostile voice which broke the spell and turned fairies back into children. Simeon introduced himself, explained that there was no answer at the door and apologised for the intrusion -

   "I was rather hoping to have a brief word with Mr Charles Hardman. You see I ... "

   "I'm quite aware of your activities, Mr Hogg," interrupted the straight, tall, classic woman who had the bearing and air of Greek tragedy. *"I don't listen to the radio, or for that matter, read the local press but ... Children, off to tidy your playroom, as you promised earlier. Go on."*

As the last curious child unwillingly left the room, the visitor, keen to make himself agreeable, was about to say, in the old fashioned sense of the word - *'Charming'.* It was too late. She was too quick. She headed him off and turned on him in a tone of cool invectives.

   "My husband has nothing to say to you, Mr Hogg. With regard to that old business of the boy who went missing on the public road outside of this house; as far as we are concerned, that business was concluded when the police left here many many years ago. I can assure you he is not here."

   "Do you mean Brian Forrester or your husband?"

   "Whether or not Mr Hardman is in residence is hardly any of your business! I am not in the habit of receiving strangers who wander into my home. I must ask you to leave."

This was as far as Simeon dared push an unpleasant situation. Just for a moment they faced each other, she defiant and he uncertain, assessing his position. But his position was weak and in all scenes of a disagreeable nature, Simeon Hogg was disposed to maintain his dignity, counter with extreme courtesy and make a gracious withdrawal. Again he apologised profusely for the trespass and any distress caused. Helen Hardman stood mute, firm and regal like the 'Ice Queen', clearly a woman of 'good breeding' from a 'good family'. After wishing her a 'good afternoon' he left the house immediately.

This was practically the end of the road. Simeon took some satisfaction that he had tried, at least he had gone through the motions. Winding up that long beautiful drive, for the first time he pitched his thoughts beyond the search for Brian Forrester, he must find a place to live and he must find something to do ...

A fat man was standing outside the lodge, a small man with grey hair, a round body supporting a round head, a pleasant expression - looking at him. So this was Dolly the gardener, after all these years, still at The Lodge. Simeon rolled down the window.
> *"Hello."*
> *"Hello."*
> *"Am I addressing Mr Coggan?"*
> *"Am I addressing Mr Hogg?"*

There was something of a gentle comedy being played out here: that special touch of irony which comes from the amiable interchange of two men who immediately sense that they share a similar persuasion: that playful, easy and light banter, which leaves so much significance hanging in the air. The famous Dolly of Derbyshire with large dancing eyes was a past master of this clever and mischievous contrived comedy.

They spoke of the old mystery. As ever, Dolly's tone was benign and eminently reasonable. He was persuasive -
> *"I still think that sad event had absolutely nothing to do with Cressbrook Hall at all. If alive he could be anywhere couldn't he? And the boy you once knew, after all these years, would be so changed ... well, effectively, he'd be the same as dead. Hardly worth upsetting poor Mr Hardman is it? People do wander off you know, from time to time, especially young boys who get the urge!"*

Simeon was amused by this sibilant suggestiveness and subtle undercurrents of humour. He was intrigued by the mobile pappy face and could not take his eyes off those flowing succulent fat lips which moved so roundly, beautifully forming rich vowels delivered in such an unhurried manner. Dolly continued to make his case -

"I notice the police didn't examine the garden of Wellhead Farm. The Peirsons were equally as likely (or for that matter unlikely) to spirit away your friend as anybody here. You think of it: if he had an accident or went astray, where would he most likely go? Not here! He'd go back to base - the very same place you went to, wouldn't he? Stands to reason doesn't it? That's where you all felt safe."

"It's possible ... but they were such nice people."

"We're nice people too!" whispered Dolly in a deep seductive purr with his ball-like head cocked on one side and appealing wide orbicular eyes supporting the sound logic of his argument. Simeon cracked up finding the whole picture hilariously funny. Dolly smiled.

"I wonder if they'll remember me at Wormhill?" mused Simeon. *"There's nobody else left to talk to. I suppose I'm unlikely to find the old goblin at Belper still in residence."*

"Alas no," sighed Dolly. *"He lived to a very ripe old age. It was the protein you know, he always had a good regular supply from the postman."*

"Pardon?"

"Oh yes.." lisped Dolly, an octave deeper giving added significance and warming to the subject. *".. every day, except Sunday when there was no post, but that particular postman ... well, he came even when there were no letters at all for old Jasper!"*

"He came even when there were no letters?"

"Through the letter box."

Dolly looked at Simeon as one might look indulgently at a child struggling with a problem - blinked - twinkled and cocked his head on to the other side.

"Oh yes," he continued trailing off into a breathy whisper. *"It wasn't just a letter he pushed through Jasper's letter box! You must understand, Mr Hogg, Jasper was always at his best when nobody could actually see him. I gather his clients on the massage bed often requested a blindfold - very wise - much better."*

Simeon was shaking with mirth, but, at that instant, like a flash, he knew what he had to do with the rest of his life. If Charles Hardman had recorded for posterity the folklore of Derbyshire, so now, Simeon Hogg the historian would record the secret and hidden 'gaylore' of

242

Derbyshire. An untold history of such an unusual and interesting minority must be written down before it was too late. Not a bland history of the young and handsome, but a gritty colourful history of those hideous old-timers who had been warped and twisted by a repressive and homophobic society. He must interview Dolly and Simon Tonks, both men in their seventies, and hear their stories before it was too late. Simeon would call his book - 'Queens, Crones and Old Hags'.

"How old was Jasper he when he died?"

"Well, do you know, Mr Hogg ... nobody is really sure. Rumour has it he'd had several telegrams from the Queen! No. Dear old Jasper, gone but not forgotten. I do so miss that lovely click of his teeth when they came out, the prelude to pleasure, pleasure he gave to so many. Quite a traveller you know - oh yes, in the locality. You've heard of judges sitting, well, Jasper sat - for hours and hours in various cottages on 'his circuit'. All gone now. Who could ever forget those lewd leering eyes peering through holes. I expect he's sitting in that big cottage in the sky, sitting there, munching away on his cracker biscuits, chatting to Guzzly Granddad through the hole."

"I'm glad they've made it up," said Simeon with a twinkle. Dolly cocked his head on the other side, smiled and gently patted Simeon's hand.

"Anyway, you must promise Dolly to be a good boy. This is not a good time to trouble Mr Hardman. He's launching his new book this week. Very busy you know. He's got the readings tonight at St John's Chapel in Belper and tomorrow ... "

"I did see that advertised," said Simeon mendaciously interrupting and thinking quickly. *"Starts at 7.00pm doesn't it?"*

"Seven thirty," replied Dolly in beautiful English.

"It's been so nice talking to you, Mr Coggan."

*"Oh please, **do** call me Dolly."*

Simeon leaned a little further out of the car window, mischievously lowered his own voice and whispered -

"And you, my precious little dumpling, may call me - Dobba!"

Chapter 32

St John's Chapel in Belper

He was late. A bar meal at the New Bath Hotel had taken longer than expected. Simeon walked into St John's Chapel at Belper ten minutes after Charles Hardman had started to read extracts from his latest book. Now retired, the amateur historian had all the time in the world to visit such interesting and intriguing curiosities. Dating from the 13th century this, the town's oldest building is situated in the centre of ancient Belper, now a pleasant leafy fragment of the once great Royal Forest. It was cosy and comfortable inside where Simeon found just one empty seat on the back row.

Charles Hardman was not far away in this small hall which was filled to capacity. Simeon looked closely at the reader who was articulate, confident and very professional. He had no pre-conceived ideas of what a 'child killer' should look like, but was pretty sure that this man on the stage was not one of their number. The latecomer had given no thought to the appearance of this local author and yet, now, seen in the flesh, was pleasantly surprised to find him much younger and better looking than had been imagined.

"Why?" thought the onlooker. *"Why am I surprised? And why do I find him familiar?"*

As to the first part, he generally assumed that Charles Hardman would look, and be, a little like Detective Inspector Derek Russell's description of Algernon Hardman. The son was now older than his father had been in 1960, but had nothing of the father's 'dark leathery face, deeply wrinkled around a cruel mouth'. The man reading on the stage, if anything, looked younger than his 55 years, whereas Hardman senior, with his 'haggard and reproving glare', always looked older than his true age. So that explained the first part and the second had just popped into Simeon's head.

During the early 1970's, Simeon and Gary had been very keen on the photogenic and desirable pop singer, David Cassidy. Both would be glued to the television watching 'that cute little ass bounce around the stage' amid the frantic screams of teeny boppers. Just before they left the US, both watched a talk show in which David Cassidy was being interviewed - the David Cassidy of 2003! Both were braced to be shocked by the cruel ravages of 30 years on such a sexy chicken, but both were pleasantly surprised. Naturally the man over 50 was now more of a broiler, but as Gary put it -

"My God! Just look at him! He is still one sweet gorgeous doll. Who is going to turn that down? Who cares about age, just lead me to it!"

That was Charles Hardman. He looked just like the mature David Cassidy. A smiling handsome face, open and friendly, was occasionally looking up from the text, mischievously flashing stunning smiles and boyish grins, delighting an enthusiastic audience consisting mainly of women. He had enormous charm and generated great warmth.

Simeon had vaguely planned to approach the author after the readings and politely ask for his co-operation. Just a few questions, a few fragments of memory might be illuminating. He would suggest to Mr Hardman that he may be in possession of faint recollections, half forgotten shadows, whose value he did not himself appreciate. He would promise Hardman total discretion, assure him that it was a purely personal crusade for personal satisfaction alone and that there were was no intention of putting any findings into the public arena. Observing that good natured countenance, nicely tanned by a foreign sun, Simeon was hopeful. He could not have faced the frosty features of Helen Hardman again but felt that Charles Hardman ... he was a different matter: precious little hostility there.   After the Charles Hardman interview - that would be the end. The whole matter would be concluded.

Having extricated himself from these absorbing considerations, Simeon was now able to give some attention to the author's work which was his first novel. Inspired by Charles Hardman's original research about fake spiritualists in Victorian Derby, this was a story about several working class characters who had been 'taken in' by unscrupulous clairvoyants. As expected, Charles Hardman came across as smooth, cultured and well educated with an impressive upper class accent which, at least to Simeon, spoke of money, Oxford and a soft life. It was, therefore, yet another surprise to hear the reader cleverly affect a dramatic change of speech, from the 'Public School' standard to the 'Bog Hole' standard, when the authorial voice suddenly changed to the dialogue of locals. His characters came across as completely authentic: they were just the same as originals, typical of the area, a lack of H's, closed U's and numerous contractions.

It was a good book, an interesting book. Simeon enjoyed being entertained and yet ... and yet he found his concentration wandering. The audience was enraptured and so was Simeon, but for him, the sheer force of personality of the reader seemed to be greater than his subject matter. He continued to be mesmerised by those lovely eyes, twinkling teasing eyes, young eyes, sparkling eyes, sexy eyes ...

Intrusive thoughts intruded .. From a long way back he heard a choir of girls, strings ordinary and pizzicato .. fragments of words sung by a teenage boy -

"This love I have for you, will be my only love, my whole life through, it's strong and true, this love for you ... "

He was called back by an enthusiastic and loud applause which filled the hall. The author gave his thanks, stood up, spoke to a few fans, signed a few books whilst Simeon, pleasantly sedated, continued to sit at the back and ponder the odd nostalgic mood which had suddenly and inexplicably come upon him. People drifted out and finally the author walked down the aisle, towards the door, and out of St John's Chapel. This was the moment which the visitor had planned for. He had intended to approach Charles Hardman ... but Simeon remained in his seat on that back row. He was riveted by what he had seen. He had seen a ghost. Not the usual ghost, not the visual form of a figure, but an essence of movement invisibly traced in the air, a signature of movement, the signature of a familiar old friend - long lost - the lost lad.

Many times he had seen Brian Forrester move about and walk about. His mind went back to July 1960, that one last special sparkling sunny morning, the last morning in which he saw his friend. He was looking out of a bedroom window of Well Head Farm when he recognised Brian, at some considerable distance, just by the way he moved. Simeon identified Brian's distinctive gait, the individuality of his posture, bearing and carriage of head - the one thing which is most difficult to disguise - the way you move. Minutes before, Charles Hardman had stood on his feet, moved around his table to sign books, exchanged pleasantries with head nods and tilts. Finally he stepped off that low platform and walked out of the hall.

Minutes before! Simeon must pursue Charles Hardman - at once.

Chapter 33

Fantasy of Life

Simeon reasoned that the author would have likely parked in the same area as himself. The nearest convenient spot was just below, possibly in the Market Place or the Coppice. He rushed out into a shock of cold air under the darkening clear sky. Along The Butts, a row of quaint cottages on his right, down the steep High Pavement and he was just in time to see Charles Hardman about to get into a sleek golden Jaguar. Before the readings, that would have been fine, consistent with the image of a sophisticated and wealthy author. But this was after the readings and now it seemed as wrong as Danny Forrester getting out of his own expensive looking vehicle. Danny should have arrived on an old bicycle. This man too, should have been mounting an old bicycle.

Simeon Hogg approached the author who was still standing by the open car door. In silence both men looked at each other with blank expressions. In those moments time became warped and for both men it seemed more like minutes: minutes in which each party re-grouped, came to terms with, and took full account of the huge significance of that special moment: the moment of mutual recognition. Across the expressionless face of Charles Hardman there encroached a gathering softness born of inevitability, perhaps a softness born of sweet surrender. The softness melted into a warm smile, that familiar wide boyish grin Simeon knew only too well -
"'Allo, Dobba."

Two old friends were facing each other. They were sitting in the opulence and comfort of a beautiful new Jaguar. It was peaceful in that open market place of many pubs which had yet to come to life.
"I've so many questions," said Dobba. *"I don't really know where to start. Perhaps at the beginning?"*
*"Where **is** the beginning?"* replied the other. *"For me there was no definite end or beginning. I simply can't remember. It took me years to remember anything."*
"Years!"
"I only know what others have told me."
"But you remember me. You spoke my name."
Again that enchanting smile slowly broke across that handsome face as

he leaned forward and lowered his voice.

"I spoke your name first. I was never allowed to go to the cinema, so the cinema came to me. Father had it set up in our basement and one evening ... it was at the time of the Kennedy Assassination ... 1963 ... we were watching 'Treasure Island' ... how could we ever forget Long John Silver! I said one word - 'Dobba'. Of course it meant nothing to father, but it was my first glimmer, my first link with 'the past life'."

"When you say 'father', are you referring to Algernon Hardman?"

"Naturally! I'm referring to a grief stricken father who, right or wrong, took back a son."

"But your real parents ... "

"Are both long dead. Please try to understand. Even after seeing that film it took months for me to recall a cycling trip. Very vaguely I began to see a group of friends ... I couldn't see their faces ... but I knew one was called Dobba."

"Not even your twin brother?"

"In cases of severe amnesia the patient needs constant support and encouragement to regain his original identity. He needs people around, people of his own class who speak of family, friends and familiar places. If there is a conspiracy to withhold those familiar things, the process of recall takes even longer still. Memory loss varies from person to person and no two cases are ever the same. In my case a whole new life was substituted and I was groomed to receive a complete new identity. My little world was a handful of carefully selected tutors, Simon, Dolly and ... of course ... father. I hardly went anywhere until Oxford, when I was 18 - in fact I was actually 21.

"So you were a prisoner?" said Dobba, but Brian disarmed him again with another winning smile.

"Of course not! You got it all wrong, Dobba. I heard you on Radio Derby. Oh yes, I was listening - we all were. I heard the fear and dread in your voice, but let me promise you this my friend - nothing, absolutely nothing at all unpleasant or sexual ever happened to me. I was taken in, cared for and loved. It had nothing to do with lust - it had everything to do with love, love and grief."

"The accident in Albania," said Dobba, slowly and thoughtfully. He suddenly added - *"Grief for his wife ... "*

"And his son."

"His son? Charles Hardman? I don't understand? What did

250

they do with Charles Hardman? Where is he?"

"Buried somewhere in Albania with his mother where they were both killed in a motor accident on the Saturday of July 23rd 1960. My father went into a state of shock, he was like a zombie. The hotel manager was very kind, made all the arrangements, chartered a plane and got him back home as soon as possible. But home to what? He had lost everything ... and then he found me."

"He found the lost lad," meditated Dobba in a whisper. Two youths strolled past the car and disappeared into The Cross Keys, one of several public houses on the Market Place. It was getting darker by the minute.

*"Father never told me anything. He would never discuss the circumstances of my arrival. As far as he was concerned I was his son and heir Charles Hardman, born and raised at Cressbrook Hall. He treated me as one would treat a delicate invalid. He treated me as if I was the one who'd suffered the mental breakdown, struggling to come to terms with the trauma of an accident and the death of my mother. And that's how it really did feel. For years I believed I **was** indeed Charles Hardman. It was assumed the Albanian accident had taken my memory and identity, had robbed me of my past. Everybody called me Charles and recalled anecdotes of things I did as a kid. Simon kept talking about a dog I once had called Pilot. He showed me the toys I once played with - even a doll I called Jennifer! I'll tell you that got me worried!"*

They laughed. Brian sank back into the leather upholstery and idly watched three rowdy lads falling out of a pub.

"But eventually ... " encouraged Dobba.

"Eventually I started to ask questions. Not of father. It would hurt him. Yes, he was stern and could be very severe with the servants and strangers, but upon me, he heaped a massive amount of affection. He steered me through those years and gave me protection. He was an excellent teacher, inspired and encouraged me to write - he gave me everything. I came to love my father ... I wish you could have known him, Dobba, he was a wonderful man.

Eventually, yes, I was very curious. I asked Simon and Dolly questions. It was like trying to get blood out of a stone - but, gradually, little by little I wheedled out bits of information and started to piece them together. Simon found me. He and father took me in. I was unconscious for hours.

Dobba was absently admiring two young trees which had been planted outside The White Swan. Struggling with moral implications and unwilling to be confrontational, he was almost afraid to ask the next question.

*"Your real parents! What about **their** grief, Brian? What about your brother Danny? What about the pain and agony of waiting. Couldn't you have put them out of their misery? Did you not think about making contact?"*

"Many many times." Brian took a deep breath and looked directly into the eyes of his one time friend. *"Look, Dobba, forgive me old pal, but you really don't have a clue do you? You don't know, you can't possibly know what it was like to be me. Many times I talked to Simon and Dolly. I suggested to them that I should let mum, dad and our Danny ...*

*Our Danny! Sounds so funny to say that now. I proposed trying to get a message to Heanor, delivered secretly, just to say I was OK. But, you see, it was me against them. They were powerful and I was weak. A boy against the combined solid logic and wisdom of two persuasive adults. I was defeated by argument. Dolly said it would all end in disaster. He said that father would be arrested by the police and put into prison. He was right. Father would have been destroyed by that experience. And I could not let that happen to the man who was the centre of my universe. Look, this crisis of conscience occurred in 1964. By that time the world had assumed that I was dead ... and, Dobba, try to understand, it **was** like that for me. Brian Forrester was as good as dead. Of course ... every now and again he gets a jolt of conscience ... like on the radio the other day when I heard Danny say 'Hello, Dobba'. That wasn't easy for me. I was gutted.*

And ... I'll be honest with you old friend. Try to see it from my point of view. I had long talks with Simon. We both know what it's like to be poor. In my old life I had a loving family and I know they've suffered but ... what would you do? Would you, if you had the choice, say goodbye to Cressbrook Hall and a substantial income for life? Would you go back to Heanor, to the old life and become a brickie, or a plumber or for that matter - a teacher?"

"You certainly wouldn't be driving this car on a teacher's pay!" laughed Simeon. *"And you wouldn't have received the prestige and respect Mr Brentnall enjoyed from us!"*

"Exactly. Anyway, I wouldn't have got anywhere near a teachers college. Working class social pressure would have pushed me

towards a manual job and would have offered me a selection of girls from the next street. A girl like Helen with her 'county' background: my God, if she as much as suspected - I'd be treated as dirt under her feet!"

Simeon, who had taken an instant dislike to the haughty Helen Hardman (and was bitterly opposed to blood sports) resisted the temptation to put in a good word for Heanor girls. Brian continued to defend his position.

"Face it, Dobba, you went to America. You did the best for yourself. Algernon Hardman showed me a world I didn't know existed. He took me around Europe and showed me art, architecture, culture ...

Again he looked his old friend straight in the eyes -

"I have to admit it, Dobba, I rather like being the Master of Cressbrook Hall."

Brian exhaled a long held breath of stress, then flashed another boyish grin.

*"Simon was right. I mean his fantasy on the radio when I was supposed to be snatched up by aliens. That gave me a close call but fortunately nobody takes him very seriously, but, do you know, Dobba - he was quite right. Effectively I **was** abducted by aliens - two very odd queens and an erudite recluse!*

Simon and Dolly have always been there for me, always kind and loyal. They were servants to father, but for me ... they are family, just as much as Helen and the children."

"I met your children today at Cressbrook Hall. Utterly delightful, the girls and the small boy."

"Aren't they just. One correction, Dobba - grandchildren."

Another jolt, but Simeon had already been through that with Scott North. Suddenly an urgent thought intruded into domestic bliss.

"Brian! The police! I have all the details, they checked everything?"

"Of course they did. But you know, Dobba, sometimes they don't ask the right questions. They assumed that my father was with 'me' on the chartered plane. It never occurred to them to check the ticket which would have indicated a single person - not two people. They closely questioned the taxi driver who met father at Manchester

airport. They looked at the wrong thing. They were very keen and obsessed on checking times. They had no reason at all to ask the driver if a boy was also in the car. Why should they? They assumed Charles was with his father. Had a boy been mentioned to the driver, he would say 'What boy?'"

"Hang on a moment! I have a verbatim description of the official record from Detective Inspector Derek Russell himself - The Albanian authorities confirmed two fatalities in a head-on collision. Both cars were 'right-offs'. Did Algernon Hardman bribe the authorities?"

"Of course not! Again it was a question of natural assumptions. The English police assumed that the two people killed were my father's late wife Marjorie and the other fellow in the other car. Since I was at Cressbrook Hall, it was assumed that Charles Hardman survived - he didn't, it was the other driver who survived."

"And you were a young looking fifteen year old."

"Baby faced Brian! Oh yes, anyone would have taken me as a twelve year old."

Simeon conjured up a mental image of Brian, Danny, Scott, Rex and Dobba swaggering across Heanor Market Place having the time of their lives, shouting and generally larking around ... How different to his perception of this group of raucous boys who were now coming towards the car. After decades of permissive progressive education, Simeon felt threatened by this group, a group he regarded as yobs out of control. Brian appeared not to notice. He was speaking of his Uncle Jack and his Brownie 127 camera.

"That photograph was a joke. Nobody would have recognised me from that. Of course, you, Danny, Scott or Titch would have identified me immediately, but why should it be thought necessary for anyone to be brought to Cressbrook Hall to look at Charles Hardman? By the way, haven't you forgotten something?"

"What?"

"Fingerprints!

"My God, yes! Your fingerprints were identified because they were all over your house in Heanor - so why ... Oh! I think I see - gloves?"

"I wore them for months. Of course I've no memory of it."

"But in Russell's letter he said that they took copies of your prints, the prints of young Charles Hardman at Cressbrook Hall

254

together with Dr Hardman and Tonks. There would have been a match! The game would have been up!"

"But it wasn't and they didn't - let me explain. The forensic team on prints and dabs was just two junior officers. Simon had made it more difficult, or easy, which ever way you look at it. He was pretty handy with the duster and polish and there were fewer prints to find. Most of the prints in Marjorie Hardman's bedroom were, quite naturally, identified as belonging to her. The same thing applied to my father's room and to Simon in his room and the kitchen. Charles Hardman had the freedom of the attic, his play room. Plenty of his prints there - none of mine. The two police men believed that they had conclusive identification without having to steel themselves to approach my unapproachable father and ask him to get his fingers inky. Remember he was already hostile to the whole intrusion and barely tolerated the police in the house as it was. Algernon Hardman was a force to reckon with! He was like the Lord of the Manor, a friend of the Chief Constable and Lord Lieutenant. The two officers felt that they had made quite sure that Brian Forrester had never set foot inside of Cressbrook Hall.

It was a year before I was allowed into the attic to touch anything belonging to Charles and the gloves stayed on for a long time, just in case Detective Inspector Derek Russell had a brainwave and decided to return. Thank the Lord he never did."

Simeon sat silent for a moment to allow this intelligence to percolate into his head which was now swimming. Something was bothering him.

"The Lord of the Manor ... Brian, something's wrong here! You were questioned by Derek Russell himself. Charles Hardman went to a private school. He spoke with an upper-class accent. He was never allowed anywhere near the likes of us. Don't tell me this is a modern The Prince and the Pauper. We were as common, as rough a bunch of ragamuffins as they come! You'd be found out as soon as you opened your mouth ... "

*"I've absolutely no memory of opening my mouth at all. Simon told me that I was given strict instructions to say nothing but 'yes' or 'no' to the police. Of all people, **he** knows the importance of keeping his mouth shut at certain critical times! Anyway, father was with me all the time. If any other response were required, he would have intervened."*

This produced another silence as Simeon recalled being teased about his accent by his American friends in the early days. Suddenly - another thought -

"The bicycle!"

"Oh that bicycle!" guffawed Brian. He flung back his head, stuck out his sexy tongue and gave Simeon that mischievous sidelong look which transported him back so many years.

*"Well, let me put it this way, Simon is usually quite forgiving. He's a good natured fellow, always very patient but: after all: well ... that dreadful old man at Belper **did** try to get him sacked from his job which would have meant losing his home as well - and, Simon **can** cycle!*

"It was Simon Tonks!"

"I gather it was just after Scott and Rex left Cressbrook Hall. Simon was given orders to ride that bike as far away as possible and return in a taxi before the police would be alerted. His revenge nearly landed us all in queer street. He went much too far and got back with just minutes to spare before the law descended on Cressbrook Hall. Very naughty of him to park it at Belper outside the 'massage parlour' - but it was just too tempting. Simon will always be Simon - bless him."

They both sank back into the comfortable seats. Belper Market Place was gradually coming to life and Simeon was unconsciously enjoying the rich scent of 'new car' during this silence. An observer might consider this moment, a moment of danger. After all this was a moment where truth had been revealed. One party, armed with damaging information could be seen as a threat to the other party and both parties were quite aware of this. Yet, notwithstanding - it was a good silence, the comfortable silence born of affection between two old friends separated, but now united and glad to be united. It was Brian who spoke. His thoughts had been philosophical.

"So which of us is the lost lad? Is it you or me? We both revere and treasure the time of Howitt. It was good then, we were all innocent, we all had fun ... but somehow ... well ... we all got lost didn't we?"

Simeon was startled to have the whole situation summed up for him in this way, yet he had to acknowledge the soundness of Brian's reasoning. Gary had often told him - *'You can never go back'*, but

Simeon had grieved more than most for his lost youth. He was, and always would be, by temperament and disposition, nostalgic. In these few seconds there were thoughts on both sides. Both men held the unspoken thought that Simeon Hogg now had a choice before him and both men held a childlike faith that Simeon Hogg would make the right choice - the only logical choice - the only kind and considerate choice. As if to anticipate that decision Brian said -

"You'll forgive me if I don't invite you to dinner, Dobba. It could get complicated."

Dobba smiled. Again, a great deal of unspoken understanding was hanging in the air. Dobba had no choice at all. He could not discredit the memory of Algernon Hardman because that memory was precious to his adopted son. He could not destroy the life of his long lost friend. He could not destroy the lives of the children and grandchildren of Charles Hardman and so he decided to address Charles Hardman in a cheerful brisk manner -

"Well, time marches on. Thank you for your time, Charles. I've found our chat illuminating and most interesting, yes ... most interesting. I've come to the end of the road. One hates to admit defeat ... but ... we can't always win ... can we?"

Brian's eyes were sparkling more than ever, but these were the sparkles of emotion, not actual tears, but very near. He offered out his hand which was taken by his boyhood friend who found it warm and grateful.

Two friends sat looking at each other in a comfortable silence. Far from being defeated, Simeon was feeling triumphant and free. He was free from his hated progressive school of the far left and free to live in the wilds of Derbyshire where ghostly owls would be the soothing sounds of the night instead of the infuriating electronic thumps of the hard yob culture which had just started to bang out from one of the nearby pubs.

Simeon Hogg was optimistic. He would research and write his book about curious quirky characters and was looking forward to the challenge. Simeon Hogg was thinking about the future.

Simeon Hogg was thinking about life.

Cameo Roles

The author would like to thank the following for agreeing to appear as themselves -

Freda Cirillo nee Brentnall, John Holmes of BBC Radio Nottingham, Lord Ralph Kerr of Melbourne Hall and His Honour Judge Keith Matthewman QC. Yvonne and Barry Peirson of Wellhead Farm in Wormhill are still offering an excellent standard of accommodation. Carol Robinson nee Bestwick, Kathy Syson of the William Howitt Secondary Modern School Annual Reunion and Percy Wilson of Canal Cottage on the Cromford Canal.

Special thanks to Mrs B. Hull-Bailey for the use of Cressbrook Hall, still there today, a period family home offering elegant guest accommodation in a magnificent setting overlooking Water-cum-Jolly Dale.

The ever popular Exmouth View Hotel in Babbacombe appeared by kind permission from David and Milka Browne.

I am grateful to the artist Lesley Robinson of Shipley Park for her first class work in designing and painting the front cover.

Finally a big 'thank you' to John Holmes of BBC Radio Nottingham for, once again, allowing his good name to appear in front of my work. His generous encouragement and support over the last six years has been invaluable.

About the Author

Narvel Annable's first book "Miss Calder's Children" (1997) described his early post war schooldays in Belper, a quaint Derbyshire mill town. His second book "Heanor Schooldays" (1998) was also autobiographic, covering his unhappiness in a grim, gas-lit, Dickensian, Church of England junior school from 1955 to 1958. Adolescence and the move to William Howitt Secondary Modern School, *"A culture of kindness"*, in September 1958 was a dramatic improvement, graphically retold in the second half of the social history.

In 1963 he emigrated to the United States and arrived in Detroit on the day before the assassination of President Kennedy. The next seven years saw him in a variety of jobs which included labourer, lathe-hand, bank messenger and camera salesman. In 1975 he graduated from Eastern Michigan University (magna cum laude) and taught history for a year at St Bridget High School in Detroit.

In 1976 he returned to Derbyshire to help organise and launch 'Heritage Education Year 1977' at Sudbury Hall. From 1978 to 1995 he taught history at a large comprehensive school which gradually became more progressive. Mr Annable criticises these changes in some detail in his first two books. Seizing retirement at the earliest opportunity, he started to write historical and educational articles for the local press and has been interviewed several times on BBC Radio Derby and BBC Radio Nottingham. "Death on the Derwent" - A Murder Mystery set in Belper 1949, his third book and first novel was published in 1999. His fourth book, "A Judge Too Far" - A Biography of His Honour Judge Keith Matthewman QC of the Nottingham Crown Court, was published in 2001.

Inspired by 'Heanor Schooldays', Mr Annable's second 'whodunit' novel and fifth book "Lost Lad" A Mystery set in Derbyshire in 1960 ISBN 0 9530419 6 4 - was published in 2003. He is currently working on his sixth book "Scruffy Chicken" A Derbyshire Mystery set in 1965.

By the same author ...

A Judge Too Far

A Biography of His Honour Judge Keith Matthewman QC
of the Nottingham Crown Court

ISBN 0 9530419 9 9

A tough judge with a tough reputation, he is more concerned for the victim than the criminal; a judge whose sentences are often reduced by the Court of Appeal, but a judge who is regularly applauded for his outspoken radical views by the press and the public.

Narvel Annable explores the fascinating story of his former teacher who has spanned the social divide from a Yorkshire coal mining background to being listed in 'Who's Who' and 'Debrett's People of Today and is now described as legendary in the local press. This is an extraordinary lifetime in which praise is matched with criticism, as we follow the twists and turns of the last six decades to see Keith Matthewman, the student, the scout, the memorable and creative schoolmaster, the enthusiastic left-wing politician, the film maker, the articulate barrister and the stern judge who -

" ... had to deal with the raw end of life, the mad, bad and desperate - a parade of failed humanity ... rapes, incest, violence, dangerous driving, arson ... "

Judge Matthewman went on to become a broadcaster, a controversial television personality, strident critic of the Criminal Justice System and latterly the President of the Friends of the Galleries of Justice Museum in Nottingham.

In 1992 he featured in Central TV's award winning documentary 'Caution - Our Hands Are Tied' and a year later he was the first British judge to have a regular slot on 'Crime Stalker'.

Readers will also find, imaginatively interwoven in this life-span, an enjoyable and informative history, brought to life by photographs, documents and newspaper extracts which will re-kindle local memories.

This book takes you through the years of the Second World War in Chilwell, the 1950's in Long Eaton Grammar School and then on to University College London. The 1960's will see shop-keeping at Aldercar, school-teaching and politics in Heanor, leading on to Rolls Royce in Derby and ending up with many examples from the riveting daily drama of lives in crisis in the Nottingham law courts. This work of 271 pages is supported by forewords from -

The Rt. Hon. Geoffrey Hoon MP the Secretary of State for Defence
and Lord Bach of Lutterworth.

261

"I found it an entertaining read. If I am looking for an outspoken judge in future, I shall certainly know whom to contact."

Joshua Rozenberg, Legal Editor, The Daily Telegraph 02.05.02

" ... a career which is interesting in itself, but is also a glowing example of the strengths of our social and education system as it was before it was finally dumbed down in the name of equality of opportunity.

In general this book is enjoyable, instructive and refreshing. Narvel Annable has researched well and interviewed widely. For my money Judge Matthewman ought now to be Lord Chief Justice rather than a retired Crown Court Judge."

Maxwell Craven, The Derby Evening Telegraph 18.01.02

"Personal tales add to the character of the story ... a must read for former pupils of the Long Eaton Grammar School. This intriguing and amusing biography is thoroughly enjoyable."

Karen Payne, The Long Eaton Advertiser 20.12.01

"Narvel has painstakingly researched the full background of Keith's life. Controversial and imaginative."

Pauline Oldrini, The Belper News 12.12.01 and the Ripley and Heanor News 13.12.01

"An extraordinary life and an informative social history."

Derbyshire Life and Countryside Magazine, February 2002

"Congratulations to Narvel Annable ... so many interesting stories in this biography about (as he is dubbed by the press) 'the hanging judge'."

John Holmes, BBC Radio Derby 06.12.01

"Narvel's made a very good job of this book."

Brian Tansley, BBC Radio Nottingham 07.12.01

"Eagerly anticipated and twice read to date! I was full of admiration for the way in which Narvel Annable has successfully translated such obviously painstaking research into such a fascinating insight into the life and times of a colourful character.

I feel very proud to be associated with this publication which brought memories flooding back and felt quite a few pangs of nostalgia."

Judy Cullimore, former Crown Court Reporter of the Nottingham Evening Post 19.03.02

"A fascinating story with photographs, documents and newspaper extracts which stir local memories. As many criminals have found to their cost, Judge Keith Matthewman is indeed a tough judge with a tough reputation."

Mike Astill, Nottinghamshire Today, April 2002

"A pity that it had to end - I had to make myself put it down during the read in order to give time to reflect and consider what had just been read to see how it fitted into the 'big picture' of Mr Annable's subject - a man with such outstanding and distinguished features and qualities. A big 'thank you' to Narvel Annable for giving readers the opportunity to have his biography to read and enjoy. I particularly appreciated his unique style which demonstrated that biography is not linear but a complex mesh of happenings and features. It was simply superb. I am left in wonder as to the author's skills to compile, collate and style such a portrait and insight of, and about, such a wonderful person."

Philip Judge, Lambley, Nottingham 28.12.01

"An excellent book providing fascinating social and historical insights."

Nick Seaton, The Campaign for Real Education 30.12.02

"Mr Annable, an author with unusual disciplined powers of concentration and single mindedness, has done enough meticulous painstaking research to have earned two doctorates in this work which is interesting and highly educational. I am envious of his creative drive. The few create; the many enjoy.

Alex Hart, Highland Park, Michigan USA 04.04.02

"A Judge Too Far" can be obtained directly from the author by sending a cheque for £11.95 to -
44 Dovedale Crescent, Belper, Derbyshire DE56 1HJ.

Death on the Derwent

A Murder Mystery set in Belper 1949

ISBN 0 9530419 2 1

Join the formidable schoolmistress Miss Florence Calder and her small cantankerous hunchbacked sister Miss Madge, as they detect and attempt to unmask a clever murderer in the leafy, ivy-clad, quaint and quieter Belper of 1949.

This entertaining blend of fact and fiction, set against the skilfully described background of spectacular Derbyshire scenery, is both an intriguing 'whodunit' and also a local history. Atmospheric narrative will take you around the nooks and crannies of the old mill town, in both bright sunshine and also in menacing thick fog.

It is complete with a body in a boat, psychic phenomena in the candle lit haunted halls of the rambling old Bridge House School, a seance, a conjuring trick and all ending in a surprise.

Some hilarious, colourful and quirky characters spanning the social divide from the past poverty of Cowhill, to the opulence of Bridge Hill, combine with suspense and dramatic tension to produce a thoroughly enjoyable thriller. 204 pages.

"So who has done it? Well Narvel has, but he'll keep you guessing right up to the final breath."

John Holmes, BBC Radio Derby.

"A remarkable murder mystery novel ... gives a new twist to the whodunit genre ... a skilful mixture of fact and fiction ... strong historical interest ... complications and twists, red herrings and false trails. Mr Annable has got himself a real-life, ready made character in Miss Florence Calder. This could be - should be - the start of a series of Miss Calder novels."

Geoff Hammerton, The Derby Evening Telegraph 17.12.99

"Peopled with distinctive characters ... meritorious for the descriptive detail. A well produced book. Worth reading a second time or more to fully appreciate the construction of this ingenious novel."

Margaret Beardsley, The Belper News 23.02.00

"Great characters!" **Bob Attewell, The Belper Express 13.01.00**

"I loved the rich and qualitative language, the machinations, twists and turns of the plot. I was empathetic with the characters as they desperately tried to unravel the mystery Mr Annable has so brilliantly created."

Terry Ladlow, 'Terivision Productions', Wetwang, Driffield, East Yorkshire 22.03.00

"Simon Tonks is the village fool who ends up as a servant to the Calders, Claud Hoadley is the pompous Belper man-turned-snob who teaches elocution so that the townspeople can 'better themselves' and Aubrey Pod is a pushy 'Mr Toad' character always full of himself."

Paul Imrie, 'Talk of the Town', The Derby Evening Telegraph 23.11.99

"Interesting and amusing." **Marla Addison, Peak Times 10.12.99**

"Death on the Derwent" can be obtained from **Derbyshire County Library.**

Heanor Schooldays
A Social History

ISBN 0 9530419 1 3

This book deals with the last hundred years but majors on the author's personal experience of the 1950's and 1960's in which he recreates the optimistic social atmosphere of teenagers enjoying the popular culture of the day. You will also gain insights into the gritty, unpretentious, honest character of Heanor folk.

It is a graphic colourful and emotional journey from the depths of despair to the heights of happiness. Along the way, Narvel Annable honours the memory of teachers, headmasters and headmistresses who have shaped the lives of countless Heanorians. Disquiet is expressed as discredited modern teaching methods are contrasted to the successful tried and trusted methods of past years.

Forty-five photographs and fifteen documents will rekindle memories. The work is supported by a foreword from His Honour Judge Keith Matthewman QC and contains first hand accounts from many contributors including the one time local lad, The Rt. Hon. Kenneth Clarke QC, MP, the former Chancellor of the Exchequer from 1993 to 1997. 205 pages.

"I was enthralled. A cracking collection of tales."

John Holmes, BBC Radio Derby.

Vivid and detailed memories of a 1950's childhood. Sensitively written, Narvel explores the vagaries of the educational system which helped to develop his character and prepare him for adulthood. This is an important snapshot of social history, and the author brings it to life with recollections of strict discipline, bullying and extreme forms of punishment. A roller-coaster of emotions."

Pauline Oldrini, the Ripley and Heanor News and the Belper News 05.11.98

"Mr Annable mixes anecdote with comment to provide an important record of changes made in education as seen from the sides of both pupil and teacher."

Geoff Hammerton, The Derby Evening Telegraph 04.12.98

"This autobiographic book charts a gritty history and weaves a graphic tapestry of Derbyshire school life 40 years ago. It is littered with colourful characters, interesting facts and first-hand accounts."

David Mark, The Nottingham Evening Post 27.10.98

"Heanor Schooldays" was on the 1998 list of 'Recommended Publications' by the Campaign for Real Education at 18 Westlands Grove, Stockton Lane, York YO3 0EF.

"Narvel Annable has managed to do what most authors never could; that is, to make a book about his schooldays a thoroughly enjoyable read.
        In his unique style he gives us a history of people and institutions. He gives us his views on education, past and present, and we are treated to a fascinating glimpse of a school-life in the fifties and sixties, complete with all its sorrows and joys. You do not have to remember those days to enjoy this book: you do not have to be an educationalist to enjoy this book: but if you are in either group, or both, you will enjoy it all the more - and so will your children."

His Honour Judge Keith Matthewman QC, November 1998

*"Thoroughly enjoyable and a privilege to read. He writes in such an enthusiastic way and keeps one enthralled to the very end of the book. Indeed, I wish it would have **not** ended!"*

David Tye, Oban Divers Caravan Park, Laggan, Glenshellach, Argyle, Scotland PA34 4QJ 12.05.02

Heanor Schooldays can be obtained directly from the author by sending a cheque for £8.95 to -
        44 Dovedale Crescent, Belper, Derbyshire DE56 1HJ.

Look out for Narvel Annable's next whodunit novel -

Scruffy Chicken

A Mystery set in Derbyshire 1965

Outside it is a dull, wet, cold Wednesday afternoon. Inside the steam room of the Derby Turkish Baths - it is a hissing haze of hot gurgling boiling anger, a chamber of pea-soup where visibility is down to an arm's length. Dimly seen, a man is resting in the corner, head leaning back, eyes closed, pleasantly soaking up the heat. He looks very comfortable.

Various bathers come into the steam room. Bathers enter and bathers leave. They are all regulars and they all know this ugly effeminate man, head gently lolling, who frequently secludes himself in his usual corner. They all know the outrageous, the common Becksitch Betty, the local drag act, the acid queen who has inflamed so many passions in the nervous closeted gay communities of Derby and Nottingham in those dark homophobic years of the mid 20th century.

Nobody wants to bother this odious individual who remains undisturbed, left to doze in the swirls of vapour, left to doze in a miasma of his twisted hate and jealousy. Nobody wants to speak to the execrable entertainer who remains quiet, continuing to be caressed by swirls of hot fog: the infamous bitch who stays very very still. Leaning against the hard white tiles of that old Edwardian steam room, that was the very last time the hated old hag was ever seen. Nobody saw him dress and nobody saw him leaving the building which had no other exit but the main entrance: a small foyer well guarded by two watchful kiosk women who knew all the regular bathers.

Becksitch Betty never returned to his mean little cottage in Belper and was never, ever, heard of again ... until ...

On July 12th in the year 2005 Simeon Hogg is celebrating his 60th birthday. By a freak chance he stumbles upon the truth and solves the old mystery of the disappearance of the infamous, the long past Becksitch Betty. That same ugly old queen Simeon once knew when he was a scruffy chicken forty years before.

Narvel Annable delivers yet another cracking autobiographic whodunit which begins in Detroit on the day before the assassination of President Kennedy and eventually takes us through the bitchy underworld of crones, queens and social climbing snobs of the mid 1960's. Follow the candid young Simeon on his Derbyshire cycling trip through a labyrinth of the high and the low, the pretentious and the pompous, the scented and the sneering, the common and the crude.